"Sofron!" Bey shouted. "Everybody wake up!"

She turned to see a line of White Killers rising as silently as mist from the Deep. Wearra shook Sofron off like a dry leaf and vanished.

Suddenly they were surrounded by a deafening noise. Everyone in camp was awake and shouting. Then the human voices were swallowed up by the uncanny whistling that seemed to come from every direction, confusing perception of other sounds. There was a shriek as some kind of projectile hurtled across the campfire and found a target in human flesh . . .

By Toni Anzetti
Published by The Ballantine Publishing Group:

TYPHON'S CHILDREN
RIDERS OF LEVIATHAN

Books published by The Ballantine Publishing Group
are available at quantity discounts on bulk purchases
for premium, educational, fund-raising, and special
sales use. For details, please call 1-800-733-3000.

RIDERS OF LEVIATHAN

Toni Anzetti

A Del Rey Book®
THE BALLANTINE PUBLISHING GROUP • NEW YORK

A Del Rey® Book
Published by The Ballantine Publishing Group
Copyright © 2001 by Toni Anzetti

Del Rey is a registered trademark and the Del Rey colophon is a trademark of Random House, Inc.

www.randomhouse.com/delrey/

Library of Congress Catalog Card Number: 00-109921

ISBN 0-345-41872-7

Manufactured in the United States of America

First Edition: February 2001

10   9   8   7   6   5   4   3   2   1

From low orbit, the world called Typhon looked like a paradise. Sunlight gleamed on the globe-spanning oceans, blue or green or gold where drifts of living organisms caught the light. From that height, the clouds above the ocean looked as white and soft as wings, showing no hint of the dark ferocity of the storms they wreaked in their shadow. Land areas were small and few. Pale sand and green forest showed like jewels displayed on a vast expanse of blue silk.

The surface shone in the sun. And the surface hid the life that warred and rioted in the depths below. Typhon's children lived there, in the underworld of storm and fire and reef. The blue surface hid their secrets.

Sofron stood on the shore. A part of her mind noticed the sunset light gleaming on the breakers, but the greater part stayed alert to every splash that might mark the location of a predator. From the corner of her eye, she kept track of each of the children who scavenged at the waterline. The White One from the Deep often came at twilight. She watched for him, too.

"I call Wearra 'him,'" she mused out loud. "I have no idea, really. He could be female. Or his people could use entirely different methods. After all this time, I still don't know him well enough to ask about his sex life."

Little Ling, busily digging a mollusc out of the tidal flats, glanced up at her and murmured "sex life" to herself with apparent satisfaction.

"Sex life, sex life," she repeated. "Funny sound. What is it, sex?"

"I'll explain it later," Sofron said. "It has to do with reproduction."

"Does the Bone Thing have babies?" Ling asked.

"I don't know," Sofron said. "Maybe they come from eggs. But call him 'Wearra,' not 'Bone Thing.' I don't know if he would like that."

"Don't make Bone Thing mad," Ling said thoughtfully. "It has lots of teeth."

"Yes, he has lots of teeth."

The glowing edge of the sun touched the horizon, and long fingers of fire reached out across the water. The other edge of the world dipped slowly into shadow.

"He isn't coming tonight, anyway," Sofron said. "Call the others. We'll go home."

Ling picked up her handful of knife-shaped shells and hurried down to the water to wash them, calling and beckoning to the other children as she went. She did not run. Her legs were short and bowed, badly shaped. She hurried with a waddling motion, but she could not run. It had been a victory when she learned to walk. Some of the other children still could not.

Sofron heard Ling calling the others above the rising sound of the surf. The wind was strengthening as the sun sank. The children came toward her slowly, with their bits and scraps of scavenging tied up in nets or bird-skin bags. The stragglers rolled or hitched themselves along laboriously. Chilsong, who could not walk at all, paused often to swipe at his lips and eyes with his most functional hand. To roll himself forward, he had to lower his head into the sand.

Sofron still had to fight the urge to hurry to him and try to help. But she had determined when they first landed on this shore never to do for the children what they might soon enough have to do for themselves. True help meant helping them learn to survive. She wanted to wipe the sand from his eyelids before the grit got into his eyes and made him cry, but she turned away.

"Jaya, wipe your brother's eyes," she ordered. "Carefully!" She had to teach them to take care of each other. They might not have anyone else.

They made their way up the shore to their one place of relative safety. A line of flat-topped rocks stood between low tide and the actual shore. When the tide came in, the rocks were cut off from the shoreline by a stretch of water that was evidently wide enough to discourage most of the marsh dwellers who lived on the brackish margins of the land. Sofron had built a night shelter on the biggest, flattest stub of rock.

The agile children swarmed up the rope ladder to the shelter. Jaya, whose arms and legs were longest, pushed and shoved to be first up the ladder. But at the last minute, Ling beat him by climbing over his back and using his head as a stepping rung.

Sofron had rigged a platform with ropes and pulleys so the nonwalkers could use their arm strength to haul themselves up to safety. This arrangement was one of Sofron's multitude of worries. She had done her best to explain the workings of the block and tackle to the children, but she wasn't sure they would be able to keep it in repair without her. Chilsong, the oldest, was only seven, and Ling had just turned five.

Chilsong rolled onto the platform and pulled himself and Ven toward the top of the rock. His arms were strong, Sofron thought, but he had trouble keeping a grip. Maybe she could attach loops so he could push his wrists through them rather than trying to close webbed fingers around the rope. But that would mean reweaving the rope. Maybe she could put some of the nonwalkers to work on it after they finished the latest round of net repairs. Sofron sighed and pushed the sun-bleached, salt-sticky hair back from her face. There was always more to do. Their toehold on this shoreline was precarious.

The children adjusted the sides of the shelter to block the freshening breeze. It really wasn't even a house. The walls were movable panels made by weaving tough leaves on a frame of sticks and lashing the finished panel to saplings driven into cracks in the rock and anchored with more stones. It worked well in the good weather. In storm season, the surge washed completely over the rocks, and the wind carried away the flimsy structure. Then Sofron had to seek shelter for them on the shore, where all the land predators vied for a hiding place from the flaying winds. That was where they had lost Dilshad last year. Sofron vowed for the hundredth time that she would never let that happen again. But so far she had not thought of a way to prevent it.

The children huddled in a circle, eager to pool their finds before the last of the light went. Ling shared out the clams. Sofron accepted her portion and chewed it raw, salty and gritty. Chilsong had picked up and cleaned some weed pods. They were bitter but crunchy, and Sofron made sure everyone had a bite.

"There are invisible things called vitamins in green food," she said. "If you don't eat enough, you get sick. Your teeth might fall out. You get mangy, like those fish we saw with the scale rot."

"Fish don't eat bitter pods," Ling said rebelliously.

"No, I guess not, but their bodies are different from ours."

Jaya had caught a fish in the surf, with his hands. It was a plump silver shillik, a rare treat since shilliks usually stayed out beyond the reef. Sofron examined it suspiciously to make sure it hadn't been slowed down by illness, but it seemed healthy.

"I don't need a net," Jaya boasted. "I can catch them bare-handed."

"One shillik doesn't make a school," Sofron reminded him. "Tomorrow or the next day you'll need the net again."

Jaya was the most functional of the children, but he had little patience with tedious lessons on net-knotting and the building of traps and seines.

"We don't need all these lessons, Teacher Sofron," he had complained. "Look at the fish. They swim naked, and they're all right."

"We're not fish; we're human," Sofron had replied. "We need to know things that keep us safe." But she had seen that he was not convinced.

Now they divided his fine fish, a mouthful for everyone. Sofron sucked the bits of flesh from the backbone.

"I found some not-food," Ven said shyly. "Want to see?"

Jaya and one or two others laughed scornfully.

"Not-food is easy to find," Piersall said. "I find that all the time."

From the scuffling in the shadows, Sofron guessed that some rudeness had been committed.

"I want to see," she said firmly. "There's more to life than what we can eat!"

Ven held out his find. Sofron expected a shell, or maybe an unusual seed pod blown into the surf from somewhere on shore. But the thing in Ven's hand seemed to have no particular shape. She didn't recognize it in the twilight.

She picked it up and brought it closer to her eyes. The feel of it was familiar. Suddenly she knew what it was. She was holding a fragment of kemplex, in the familiar orange color of emergency equipment. It might have been a piece of a boat's hull, or a fragment from the float-packing for medical instruments. An eyebolt for attaching lines was still glued to the edge of the fragment. Whatever it was, it had been shattered somehow, and the edges were still jagged, not yet smoothed by water and sand.

The children saw her excitement and drew closer.

"What is it?" Ven asked. The malformations of his face and mouth made his speech unclear sometimes, especially when he was excited, but despite the slurring, Sofron understood. "Is it from the Old Ones? Like the things we find for the Bone Thing?"

"No," Sofron said. "Better. It's from us, from our own people."

They looked again, even more eagerly, but after a moment their expressions showed disappointment. The bit of kemplex meant nothing to them.

"I forgot about our own people," Ling said. "I can't see a picture of them. Are they still alive?"

"We have to hope so," Sofron said, clutching the orange shard. "We hope so very much. Because we need them to come and find us. This piece of orange kemplex that Ven found, it could mean they are alive. It comes from something of theirs, and the edges aren't worn down yet. It seems fresh and new. Maybe they lost it when they were near our shore. Maybe they were looking for us. It could be."

She ran her thumb over the still-sharp edge of the shard.

"But it's broken," Jaya said practically. "If it came from their boat, the boat is broken. So maybe they're *not* alive."

"Lots of things got broken when the big fire came, but we're still alive," Sofron said. She found she wanted to shout at Jaya, browbeat him for even offering the suggestion that the others were dead. But she bit back the words and put encouragement into her voice instead. "Our people are tough. Even if the boat is broken, they could still be alive."

It was getting too dark to see colors anymore. Sofron placed the shard in her special box for safekeeping. She added a careful handful of sticks to the fire. The children curled up on their mats to sleep. Their coverings were meager, pieced together from small skins cut in strips and woven together. The nights were fairly warm, but the children tangled themselves together in a heap for comfort.

Sofron slept at the outer edge, ready to build up the fire and to defend their nest against night robbers. Her nights were wakeful.

"Tell the story," Ling urged sleepily. Sofron had repeated it every night for the two years they had been castaways on this shore, hoping they would remember it if anything happened to her, hoping they wouldn't lose all traces of their identity. There was a long version and a short version. Tonight she was in a turmoil of hope and fear, and she had no heart for more than the shortest snatch of story.

"Once there was a cold world called Skandia," she began. "There the water froze and the sky froze, and the people wrapped themselves in thick, thick skins to keep out the cold. The Deep was small, and the Dry was big. You could walk from sunup to sundown without seeing water. But the people there led happy lives. They had houses and lots of food. They lived together in a peaceful way.

"But they made eyes out of glass and called them telescopes, and with their eyes of glass they saw a long, long way off to a blue world called Typhon. No people lived on Typhon, and the people from Skandia thought they would like to try a warm world of sun and water.

"Between the two worlds there was a big Dark, like the Deep beyond the reef, cold and silent. The Skandians built a boat that would keep out the Dark, and they sailed to the shores of Typhon. Those were our people.

"I was one of those people who crossed from the cold world to this one. Those people were my friends, and were your mothers and fathers. But blue Typhon has many dangers. There is fire at the heart of this world, under the blue water. The fire down below broke up through the island where the people were living, and the mountain burst apart in fire.

"When that happened, some of the people died, and some got into boats and sailed away. The water boiled and churned, and some of the boats were lost, but not all. Up on the mountain there was a big house called the children's house, and all of you were staying there. You were little then, just babies, and you weren't able to get away by yourselves. Some of the mothers and fathers tried to save you. But the fire was coming very close, and we all had to go different ways. I took you on a small emergency raft and sailed down the side of the mountain on a river, and so into the Deep and away from the burning mountain—the volcano, we call it.

"Along with the fire that split the mountain came big waves that churned up the Deep, and our raft was carried far away from the others. When the clouds and smoke were gone, we were far away from our people. We landed on this shore after many days, after all our water was gone. Someday when you are grown, we'll build a boat and go to look for our people, but until then we have to stay here and take care of each other. We have to remember our people on the other island, and hope that someday they will find us.

"Remember the names of your parents, so you will know them when they come. Remember especially the names of Lesper Rogier and Koreng Lee, who helped to save you. And remember the name of Per Langstaff. If anyone can find us, Per surely will.

"And remember—"

Sofron broke off. Lesper and Koreng were almost surely dead. She had seen the wall of fire sweeping toward them, faster than a man could run. She spoke their names as a memorial, not from any real hope. Tonight she felt very tired. She didn't think she could stumble through the list of names, thinking of the people she would probably never see again.

"Try to say the names in your mind," she finished unsteadily. "See how many you know.

"We'll sleep now."

Most of the children were asleep already, but Sofron was far from sleep. She remembered very well—too well. She remembered Per: stubborn, lonely Per who never gave an inch, who never compromised and never surrendered. She believed her own words: if Per was alive, he would try to find them. But there were other words, ones that she left unspoken and wished she could have left unthought: *He hasn't found us. So maybe he is not alive.*

There were other things she wished she could forget: there had been a moment's space when they could have left the children. There had been time for them to run, Sofron and Lesper and Koreng. They could all have escaped if they had left the children behind. Sometimes she couldn't help but wonder what would have happened. She saw herself with Per and her friends, well and happy on some other island.

And the children? Well, truth to tell—and truth to leave ever unspoken—no one had wanted them that much. Not their parents, who had left them in the children's house, in the care of others, because they were so imperfect. Not the rest of the colony, who had argued constantly about what to do with their malformed lives. Many would have breathed a sigh of relief at being so luckily released from the unwanted burden of Typhon's ill-formed offspring. No one would have blamed Sofron for saving her own life and letting theirs go.

But I would have known, she thought. *If they were at the bottom of the ocean, I would be remembering that now, and even if I were lying with Per on a perfect island in a sea like blue silk, I wouldn't be sleeping. And I would have no hope of ever sleeping in peace again.*

As it is, I still have hope. It's only a shard of hope, but I hold to it.

"Per," she whispered under her breath, "don't let me down. Come and find us."

It seemed as though she had just closed her eyes when something snapped her upright and awake. The fire seemed colorless, black coals and white ashes in the pale moonlight. Greatmoon and lessermoon held to separate quarters of the sky, casting separate tracks of brightness on the waves and tagging each solid object with conflicting shadows. It was impossible to pick out any suspicious detail in that flickering, unstable vista.

Sound was as unreliable as sight. Waves chuckled and sighed, pebbles rattled, tubewood ticked along the surf-washed shore. No single sound stood out.

She almost cried out when suddenly there was a tremendous splash just below the rock. A black bulk that gleamed in the moonlight surged from the water and subsided again with an echoing smack. Again it rose and smacked the water. This time she caught sight of a rolling eye the size of her fist, a mouth that opened in a gleaming line of teeth. Instinctively, she spread her arms in front of the children, as if she could hold off this monster with her bare hands. Would it leap? Could it hurt them? Did it even know they were there?

She recognized the intruder: it was a keto. In the early days with the colony, she had seldom seen them. They preferred deep water. But she had seen the marks of their teeth on boards and boats that had accidentally ventured into their territory. Though no one had ever seen a keto directly attack a human, they were reckoned one of the most dangerous of the large predators, on the same list with tangleweed and boogers.

She wondered what brought this one so close to shore. Could it be sick? If it had come to shallow water in search of easy prey, it might be a threat. She held very still, hoping the small glow of the fire would be enough to blind the keto to her presence in the shadows.

It moved on down the shore. She saw its black bulk arching from the water as it nosed among the rocks. She felt a chill along her spine. The keto looked as if it was searching for something, and she couldn't shake the feeling that it was searching. Maybe ketos were more intelligent than humans had thought. But even so, she told herself, such an idea was surely impossible.

Then the creature was gone, and the night noises whispered and hushed as before. Sofron's head drooped as she sat by the fire.

Abruptly, she found herself wide awake again. This time, the sounds were unmistakable: splashing, thrashing, and a chorus of unearthly whistles. A struggle of some sort was going on. Terrified, she crawled out on a ledge and peered down the line of rocks. She could see the white of disturbed water rising and falling. The black shape of the keto showed for a moment against the foam, with something white clinging to it—not foam, but a solid form.

There was more than one. They swarmed over the keto. She heard a series of shrieks. They were on the edge of human hearing, but even to human ears they carried the sound of extreme distress. The thrashing rose to a frenzy, and then subsided. The water gleamed in the moonlight, undisturbed.

There was no reason to think the keto's appearance and sudden departure had anything to do with her, but Sofron found herself smothering the fire with damp seaweed. *What are you doing?* she cried inwardly. *It took so long to build that fire, so long to nurture and tend it. Now you're putting it out in a panic?* But her hands still moved in frantic haste. The fire must be covered. It must not reveal their presence.

The smoke! she thought. There would still be a smell of smoke. She piled on more weed. She could only hope that the wet, green scent would help cover the biting traces of burning. The wind was from the sea. That might save them.

Another sound made her gasp. There was a splash, then a footstep on the rock. Moonslight gleamed on pale, thin limbs, on taloned feet against black stone. It gleamed on eyes like pebbles of opal and lips that parted over goblin teeth. The Bone Thing was here.

"Wearra," it said in its harsh, hissing voice. She breathed again. At least it was the one she knew. It started every conversation with the statement of its name.

"Sofron," she whispered.

It looked toward the wet remnants of the fire and made a clasping motion with its hands, as if sweeping minnows into its grasp. This was the sign Sofron believed meant "good."

Then it pointed to her, the whole hand with its long pale fingers extended vertically, and swept the hand in a circle, to include the sleeping children.

"You go," it signed. "Go, go."

She tried to indicate confusion, bewilderment. The Bone Thing ignored her and pressed on, signing urgently.

It slapped its chest and then pointed to the water, pointed again and again. She thought it meant the others like itself. She knew there were others, though she had seldom seen them.

A double row of short, sharp spikes ran from its forehead to the nape of its neck and spread out to the shoulders. It made the spikes rise and showed its teeth, then clawed air with the taloned fingers. "Anger." Maybe "killing." The others would be angry? The others might kill?

Again it pointed to the water. *"Bad, bad,"* it signed. It pointed to the shore. "You go."

Sofron looked around, palms raised, lips drawn back in a grimace that she hoped might mimic the face the Bone Thing made when it failed to understand her. "Where? Why?" she tried to sign.

The Bone Thing tilted its head from side to side, focusing one eye at a time on her, triangulating her face. She found this gesture disconcerting. It made her feel as though Wearra was judging the distance for a spring. But it turned to the water, and its forearm made a leaping curve. "Up, down; over, under." The keto, leaping, she thought. Wearra pointed its long hand at her again. The back of her neck went cold. It seemed to think the keto had come for her, as well. What was going on? All she could do was to shake her hand in the air, the sign she thought meant *No*.

The Bone Thing looked at her. Its expression was absolutely impenetrable to her. She wondered if it could understand her any better.

"Give box," it signed abruptly. When it came to collect the results of their foragings, it made that sign. Obviously, it expected to take their latest gleanings before it chased her away. Sofron was still fumbling for signs to tell it there was nothing when it stooped with a quick, reptilian movement and seized the box.

Its fingers closed over the bit of kemplex. It dropped the box and gave a sharp hiss of shock or satisfaction—she could not tell which. With the other hand, it felt around its torso, and from some hidden fold of skin, produced another, larger shard of matching color and material. It held the two bits out, side by side, and stared at her. Finally it made both pieces vanish again. "You," it signed. "Yours." Pointless to deny it, Sofron thought. She could seldom read the Bone Thing's body language, either, but this time every inch of its fishy skin expressed conviction. It knew.

It pointed again toward her, and again out toward the water, repeatedly. "You, and more and more of you—out there."

She held still, neither confirming nor denying.

It slapped itself again. "Me, and more and more of me."

The killing gesture.

"The people like me will kill the people like you."

It pointed once again, with finality. "You go."

It turned, ready to slip from the ledge. Sofron knew she should leave well enough alone, but she couldn't let it go so easily. She caught its arm. It was cold and slippery. Wearra turned on her with a gleam of teeth and eyes and another, louder, hiss.

Sofron summoned righteous indignation. No fear! If she started showing it fear, she was done for.

"Mine," she signed forcefully. "Give me!"

She wanted her piece of kemplex back; she wanted that little eggshell fragment of hope.

The Bone Thing groped at its waist and stretched its hand out, grasping a long sliver of white with a gleaming edge. For a moment, Sofron was afraid she had gone too far. But it extended the object to her and allowed her to take it. It had misunderstood her, perhaps deliberately. She had asked for the return of her find; it had assumed she wanted payment. Just as it had always brought fish and other useful items in return for the artifacts she and the children scavenged, it was now giving her what it considered a fair trade.

As she looked at the object in her hand, Wearra twisted around and disappeared into the sea without a splash. The object it had left with her was a knife.

The blade was a foot long; it was razor sharp, hafted with tightly shrunk layers of a rough, leathery substance that might have been some kind of skin. The blade was pale and smooth like bone, but too dense to be any common kind of bone. It was a formidable weapon. Perhaps Wearra thought she would be needing it.

She hoped not. All the distaste of her Skandian training rose in her as she turned the knife in the moonlight and watched the flicker of light along its lethal edge. This was no tool, like a fish spear or gaffing hook. It had no excuse for existence save the wish to harm other beings. Yet it was beautiful. She looped a quick twist of net twine and hung the knife from her belt.

"Wake up," she whispered to the children. "We have to go."

Ling was one of the first to sit up.

"Go where?" she demanded. Then, as the scene registered, she said accusingly, "The fire's out!"

"Yes, I put it out. Wearra came to warn us that more Bone Things are coming. We have to leave this place."

"Where can we go?" Ling said again. Sofron continued packing their few possessions, by moonlight and touch. She knew where they could go. There was a place.

They had a raft stashed onshore above high tide. They used it to reach the river mouth where they did their scavenging, and sometimes they used it to sail to deeper water and fish. But to reach the raft, at night—

"Help me take down the shelter," she ordered. "Come on, let's wreck it!" She tried to make it sound like fun, and the bigger children joined in enthusiastically. She reassembled the supports and walls into a square that was flimsy, but large enough to carry them and their possessions across the calm shallows. The children helped her to lash the corners together.

They pushed it into the water, risking the splash, and Jaya scrambled down to it, holding to the rope so it could not float away. Sofron stayed atop the now-bare rock, and lowered them all down for the last time. She glanced around to make sure they hadn't forgotten anything important. The next storm would obliterate every trace of their existence. She let herself down and began to paddle.

After a few minutes of paddling, she stopped. She could feel that the waves were carrying them toward shore anyway. Many creatures in the water beneath were acutely sensitive to rhythmic sounds and the pale shine of splashing water. It was best to go silently and try to look like a piece of debris.

When they ran aground, they were still some distance from the river mouth. Sofron distributed the bark bags and nets that held their possessions, and she had Jaya carry Ven on his shoulders. This one time, she picked up Chilsong. She felt a rueful twinge of happiness at the weight of him. He was growing bigger. He was getting enough to eat. It was another little victory. There was no one to carry Piersall, but she had developed her own way of getting along, moving doggedly backward on wrists and elbows, with a pad to cushion her dragging body. They stayed on the hard sand, where the waves would erase their tracks.

Sofron could see the children looking nervously around. They seldom came out at night. The brilliant golden beach they knew by day looked different now, all the color and warmth leeched away by the passing of the sun. The tricky black-and-white patterns of shadow and sand were hard to read. A rustle on the ground might be a dried frond blowing in the breeze, or a beach eel with needle-sharp teeth ready to bite.

Ordinarily, Sofron would have tried to take their minds off the fear with songs and jokes. Tonight she wanted to keep them silent. But then Ven started to cry, tears tracking silver down his cheeks in the moonlight. It was catching. Piersall's face twisted woefully as she struggled along. Ling sniffled, too, and Ven began to whimper out loud.

"I'm afraid of Bone Things," he sobbed. "I don't like the dark. I want my bed." His thin crying sounded like the bleat of some small, helpless animal—just the thing to call the hungries out of the night, Sofron thought.

"Why . . . are we doing . . . this?" Piersall panted. "You let it . . . tell you what to do!"

"I took Wearra's advice," Sofron said in a slow, quiet voice. Maybe she could make it sound like the wind. She had to stop Ven's crying. "It was good that he warned us. He thought there might be danger for us on the rock. So we'll just go up-river for a few days. It'll be nice. We'll eat river fish for a change, instead of ocean fish. Maybe we'll find a chewyfruit tree. It'll be like a vacation."

"What's that—a vacation?" Ling asked.

Sofron laughed. "Well, it's something we used to have on Skandia. After people worked hard for a long time, they got to spend a week or two having fun."

She tried to remember her own vacations on Skandia. She had been a poor student from a small living group, and her group had not approved her choice of studies. So the vacations had been minimal. They seemed very quaint and far away now.

"One place I used to go was up in the mountains. You know, like a high island that goes way, way up. They built some wooden houses there, bigger than ours. Built them out of logs from the thickest trees. It was very cold. The whole mountain was covered with snow. Snow is white like sand, but it's cold. It's made of water, and it sparkles like starlight, but if you hold it in your hand, it turns back into water again, and there you are with a cold, wet, empty hand."

They stared at her, enthralled. The remnants of Ven's tears ran into his gaping mouth, but he had stopped crying.

"Vacation has snow?" Ling said, trying to puzzle it out.

"No, not for us. You know, if those people from the snowy world could see us, they'd think we were on vacation all the time. Swimming and fishing, and living on the beach—that's what they all wanted to do. But only the really lucky ones ever had a chance."

They found the raft where they had left it, in a dense clump of giling trees a little way up the beach. Giling had already started to sprout up around the raft, and it took some tugging to get the raft free. Sofron let it sit on the sand for a few minutes, where the waves could break over it. She had found that this was useful for chasing away populations of lizards and stinging bugs that came to live on the raft when the humans weren't using it.

Then they all piled on, and she poled the raft through shallow water to the river's mouth. High tide carried them part of the way up the channel, to a stretch of beach where they usually stopped to search for artifacts. But Sofron was determined to go farther. They were still too close to the Deep, where the Bone Things might be waiting.

Going on upstream would be hard work. Raising the sail was no use. There was a light breeze on the face of the sea, but this far inland, it had died away. Sofron passed out paddles to Jaya and Piersall. Without strong legs, it was hard for Piersall to brace herself, but Sofron ordered Ven to sit back-to-back with her, to provide support. She put Ling in the stern with the steering paddle. She herself took the last paddle and set the rhythm, trying to correct their wobbling course as the varying strengths of the others sent the raft wavering through the water.

They made slow progress. It would have been faster to tow or push the raft, but Sofron wasn't about to invite the dwellers in the shallows to nibble her legs. She had seen many hungry creatures on daytime forays upriver. She doubted that they would be less hungry by night.

The broad inlet where the river met the sea was dappled

white with moonslight, and the crescent of beach shone silver. But as the raft crept upstream, it moved into the shadow of taller trees. The water there was dark, so dark it seemed the raft was floating through horizonless night. The children stared anxiously into the whispering shadow of the banks, but saw nothing. The air began to smell of river instead of sea; a damp, sweet-sour, heavily green smell.

The paddlers were almost exhausted when the raft rounded a tight curve and emerged into moonslight again. The river spread out into a shallow lake whose edges blended with the edge of the forest. As Sofron steered toward the center of the lake, they moved out of the current. Finally they were able to sit and rest while Sofron kept the raft steady with occasional strokes of the steering paddle.

The children gazed around, openmouthed. They had been here before, but not often, and the place looked very different at night. Moonslight made a bright, blind mirror of the expanse of water. At the edges, spindly trees stood knee-deep or neck-deep in the river. Skeins of tanglewood hung between the trees like drying nets. In the center of the mirror, dark stubs like reaching fingers extended from the water. Sofron steered toward them.

When she had first seen them, she had assumed they were the stumps of drowned trees. But when she had come close enough to touch them, the apparent roughness of water-logged bark and the seeming tracks of worm and beetle had resolved into black rock, veined with white. She had thought then, without looking closely, that the rock was weathered in a curiously regular pattern. But everything in Typhon was strange, and that had been the least-pressing strangeness.

Afterward—on the second or third trip upriver—she had come close enough to recognize that the weathered striations were rows of carved glyphs, clearly created by some being that once had tools capable of cutting igneous rock. The symbols were worn nearly smooth in most places. The tool user had lived a long time ago.

Sofron had found no clue to tell her if the glyphs meant anything or if they were merely decoration. But even though she could not read them, they had given her one very important message. They had allowed her to guess where the fragments and odd artifacts they picked up in the surf had come from. They had come from the toolmaker's dwelling place, now—perhaps—lying beneath the river's waters.

She thought that surely the Bone Things must have seen the shaped stone and had similar thoughts. But some mystery kept the Bone Things away from the land. Wearra might know of the carved stones, but he never spoke of them, any more than he spoke of the bits and pieces the humans scavenged for him. Sofron kept her secret, and Wearra kept his. She was certain he had not told his own kind that she and the children lived on the edges of the Bone Things' domain. By not telling, he allowed them to survive. And by continuing to find things for him, they bought his continued silence. They had never developed a vocabulary to communicate this agreement in words, but Sofron believed it was true.

She looped their bark rope around one of the stubs and tied a knot that could be quickly cast off.

"A good night's work, children," she said softly. "Now we can all go back to sleep. Who has the blankets?"

As she watched them curl up in the center of the raft, she resolved to sleep lightly. Once, she would have resolved not to sleep at all. But soon she had learned ruefully that hypervigilance only made her groggy in the long run. Now she trusted her senses to wake her if anything went wrong. Someday she might be an instant too late. She lived with that risk. She went to sleep sitting up, with her back against the mast socket.

2

Something cold tickled her hand. *Always water running somewhere,* she thought, drowsily trying to move away from it. Was she ever going to find a dry place again?

Suddenly she was on her feet, eyes wide open in the shocked instant between sleep and action. The cold tickle now flowed over her bare foot. It was something like a wiggly rug, stealthily spreading itself over the corner of the raft. It had almost reached Piersall's sleeping head. The edge of the rug lifted itself up and wavered to and fro, the wiggling bits underneath reaching out as if in search of something.

"Hey!" With a loud, forceful shout, Sofron lifted her free foot and slammed the heel down onto the rug. Instantly, the flat part curled around her ankle and tugged. She crashed backward onto the deck and was just able to wrap her arms around the mast socket before being dragged off the raft. The children were awake and screaming now. They retreated behind Sofron, making the raft tip.

"Stay away from the water!" Sofron shouted. She didn't know where the main body of the creature was, or how much of it there was. She tried to kick her leg free but could barely move. She could feel herself slipping. In another minute, the thing would yank her into the water.

There was a splash and a ripping sound, like sticky-zips being pulled apart, and a tube as thick as her leg shot up out of the water next to the raft. A mouth slit flexed open and shut. The tube bent and strained toward her, and the rug part kept edging up her leg.

"Shit!" she yelled.

19

At that moment she remembered Wearra's gift. It was still hanging from her belt. If she let go of the mast to reach it, she would have about half a second to use it before she was pulled off the raft and swallowed.

She screamed and grabbed for the knife.

She shot forward toward the mouth and didn't have time to do anything but grip the knife in both hands and hold it in front of her. As the creature pulled her close, the knife sank into its tubular body. Sofron twisted to avoid the mouth that was groping for her, and jerked the knife sideways. The wound didn't seem to slow the creature down at all.

She pulled the knife out and jabbed wildly at everything within reach, hoping to find a place that would hurt it. The tubular stalk stretched higher, bringing the mouth within reach of her head. She forced the knife into the open mouth, past some kind of sharp grinders. The rug convulsed, losing its grip on her leg. She clung to the knife as the tubular part thrashed about.

Then the resistance weakened. There was no longer anything pushing against her. The tube seemed to unravel before her eyes. It came apart into a dozen separate strands that writhed weakly. Sofron kept slashing until the strands fell to the deck, severed. The flat, ruglike part slid off the raft and disappeared.

Sofron sat there, panting. Her arms were wet to the elbows with slime, mingled with her own blood oozing from scratches where the teeth had cut her. She still clutched the gleaming alien weapon.

"That was disgusting beyond all measure," she said weakly.

The children, some of them still sobbing, edged toward her.

"You were *great*," Jaya said. "You *killed* it!"

He reached for the weapon, which she quickly moved out of his reach.

"What is that? Can I have it?"

"Certainly not," she said.

"You said 'shit,' " Ling said. "You said '*shiiiiit*!' "

"Yeah, well, what I may have said and what you get to say

are two different things. Now don't touch me till I wash off this repulsive goo."

"Repulsive goo," Ling said happily.

Sofron washed the Bone Thing's knife, too. It was razor sharp. She would have to make a sheath for it if she intended to carry it with her.

The children were investigating the creature's tendrils that were left on the deck, yanking them playfully back and forth.

"Is it food?" Ling asked.

Sofron grimaced. Her mouth tasted sour.

"I don't know."

She sliced off the end of one tendril. The segment looked like a tough ring of muscle, smooth and hollow on the inside. Ven was already chewing on the end of another tendril.

"It's good," he said.

"Don't put strange things in your mouth," Sofron scolded. "Not until you know it's safe."

"It's all right," Ven insisted.

With an effort, Sofron put the segment in her own mouth. Privately, she thought that Ven probably was right. The children seemed to have a better sense of what was edible than she did. She wondered if that came from being born here. There were some things they found savory that she detested—some kinds of fish livers, certain roots, some varieties of mussel. And several times she had been about to eat something that seemed harmless, only to have one of the children firmly refuse it. She remembered a bunch of succulent blue berries that had been so tempting she had eaten them anyway, and she had been sick all night.

At least the berries had tasted good going down; that was more than she could say for this gamy lump, she thought. She chewed it doggedly. It was slick and rubbery, with a sweetish taste. Her teeth seemed to make no impression, and she was wondering if she should spit it out or swallow it whole when it suddenly yielded and came apart in her mouth into a wad of fibers. She swallowed, and waited; her stomach didn't reject the mouthful.

The same thing had apparently happened to Ven.

"That's fun to eat!" he slurred. "Give me some more!"

She sliced the rest of the tendrils into pieces and let the children consume them. At the end of each tendril was a section that was lined with rows of hard, sharp-edged, toothlike scales. Sofron set those aside. A picture formed in her mind of somehow wrapping that skin around a stick. If it dried tight to the stick, then the sharp parts would make an edge.

She chewed harder at the resistant flesh of the thing that had tried to eat her. What made it suddenly dissolve like that? Perhaps some enzyme in human saliva. She thought again of Per. That was the kind of detail that would have intrigued him. He would have found a way to follow it up, to turn it to an advantage.

At least I can give the children those toothed sticks, she said to the shadow of Per in her mind. *They won't be as sharp as the Bone Thing's knife, but they might be useful. What would you have thought of that?*

About time, the shadow answered. *Hell, you should have found weapons long ago and armed every one of them. What took you so long?*

She didn't need the memory of Per to tell her the answer. It was the old fear and suspicion of *weapons* that all Skandians learned. The programming against any sort of violence. Even on Typhon, few colony members had become avid fishers. Fishing required spears and harpoon bolts. It was killing. The Skandians who did fish preferred to do it with nets and traps, where the fish could die quietly, without cutting and stabbing.

Yes, die quietly, Sofron thought. *Just as we'll die if we don't grow some teeth.*

Greatmoon had set, and lessermoon, now a lumpy crescent, was fading as the sky paled. A cool morning breeze wafted toward them out of the trees, and the surface of the water came alive with diurnal something-or-others that went *pop* across the surface, pursued by skittering ripples from below. Sofron thought they were insects, but she had also seen brightly colored froglike amphibians that were small enough to skate on the surface tension with their footpads splayed. Thanks to the attack of the rug thing, she didn't feel very secure at their mooring. So she cast off and paddled slowly upstream, weaving in and out of the trees that stood out into the margins of the river.

There, where the water was shallow, she could see down to the bottom, past the drifting weeds. In some places it was dark and muddy; in others it was bright with sand that reflected the sunlight. In places it was smooth rock, marked by lines where it joined together, like a brick path. The rock was some kind of continuation of the worked stone of the place where they had moored for the night. She followed the rock idly, zigzagging from spot to spot where it was visible.

"I'm looking for an open area," she said. "So we can tie up with a clear space around us, where enemies would be visible."

She tried to talk out loud, even when she was talking to herself. Back in the colony, the children would have had ambient noise to learn from—the constant conversation of adults to which all kids half listen, picking up knowledge without knowing it. Here, they had only her. So she tried to give them as much speech as possible, even when she was only muttering to herself. Someday their lives might depend on a fact she had forgotten to teach them, but had mentioned in passing.

"It would be nice to find somewhere dry, raised above the water. That way the water predators couldn't get to us so easily, the way they did last night. But that's not too likely."

She paddled cautiously past a screen of young tubewood, netted with tanglewood. The tanglewood stretched out a few curious tendrils, questing after their scent, but they weren't close enough to arouse its full hunger. The line of sprouts stopped abruptly at another patch of the worked stone, its joins still tight enough to have resisted the incursion of roots.

Sofron kept paddling as if she knew where to go. In fact, this inland landscape terrified her. It was full of entirely new predators. She had learned what to watch for on the beach, but the river forest was strange to her. She was afraid she might plunge them all into some unrecognized danger at any minute. She had to find some place of relative safety where they could sleep, but she didn't know where to look. She followed the stone paving in a half-formed hope that it would lead to an area that might be less overgrown.

The water flowed faster, and it became harder to keep the raft going upstream. She called to Jaya and Piersall to paddle with her. The worked stones still showed in quick blinks through the swiftly moving current. They were no longer in the broad main stream of the river. They seemed to be following a tributary. The banks were stone now, not mud, rising gradually until they were over Sofron's head. No more trees or weeds grew in the shallows. Sofron could hear the rush of water echoing from the stone walls. She wondered if it was wise to continue, but she liked the feeling of height and motion. She dug her paddle harder into the water.

"Look, Sofi!" Ven called. Just ahead, the walls closed in, and they were overhung with intensely green tongues of what looked like a flat-leafed, fuzzy fern. Even in the middle of the stream, they could not pass without brushing the leaves. The bushy growth might hide venomous insects or snakes, or the leaves themselves could be poisonous. But if so, all they would have to do was stop paddling, and they would shoot back down, away from the danger. Sofron scooted forward so she would be the first to touch the ferns.

"Keep going!" she shouted.

They entered the dark shade of the leaves. Cool drops tingled on her skin. But it was only dew cooled by condensation in the shadow. There was no pain. The flat, furry fronds brushed past her, and then they were out of the narrows into a wide space, with nothing touching them. But they were in darkness.

"Hey!" The children yelled in surprise, and the sound echoed. The rush of water made it impossible to tell exactly where the echoes came from. The raft spun and dipped, caught in an invisible current. Again they were slapped by wet leaves, a smothery, clinging feeling. Sofron fought to keep paddling, against the weight of the leaves.

Suddenly they emerged from the ferns' embrace, into sunlight. An eddy took them sideways, bumping against stone.

Sofron caught hold of the rock, to hold them steady while she tried to figure out where they were.

The water still flowed between stone banks, but the banks no longer looked like natural rock. They were flat like docks, and were only a couple of feet above the water's surface. At the edge of the flat area was a raised coping with holes in it at regular intervals, as if for tying up boats.

"What is this place? How did you know it was here?" Jaya asked. From the look in his eyes, Sofron thought she could have told him she had found it while flying like a bird and he would have believed her.

"I don't know what it is, and I didn't know it was here," she said. "It may be just as dangerous as the river. But we have to find out."

She took a good look around. The dense vegetation that normally overhung the water had pulled back, restrained by stone banks. The river itself had been diverted into stone pools and basins that formed an intricate pattern of spirals and circles.

The stone that formed the basins was clearly not natural. The background stone was a close-grained gray rock, probably native limestone, but it had been polished smooth in places and carved in others, and it was closely set with a rainbow of different textures and colors of rock, from a lumpy red like jasper to a polished black that shone like silk or glass.

"Are there p-people here?" Chilsong said, forcing the words out in an excited stammer.

"I don't know," Sofron said. She could hardly believe her own eyes.

"B-but you said only people made b-beauty. It's pretty, this. F-fish don't make pretty things."

"None of our kind of people made this," Sofron said. "It's old. We haven't been here that long."

Possibilities raced through her mind. Could one of the vanished earlier attempts to colonize Typhon have done this? But the work must have taken years. History said that none of the colonies had lasted that long. Could Wearra's kind have done it? She was sure the White One was intelligent—but he was naked and his only tool was a bone knife. And besides, if his people had built this, why did he avoid coming inland?

The final alternative she could fashion was the most likely, and perhaps the most frightening. It was possible that someone completely different had made this, someone she had not yet encountered. It might have been the makers of the artifacts Wearra collected. The stonework was so cracked and worn; perhaps the makers no longer existed. But she couldn't be sure of that.

They were drifting slowly backward as she stared. She dug her paddle into the water and steered out of the main current. She chose a flat stone terrace near the bank as the best landing place. The terrace rose from a series of shallow basins where the water was clear and it would be easy to see any potential trouble coming from below. There was some danger that a predator could leap the gap between the terrace and the bank, but it was impossible to escape danger completely.

The terrace wasn't actually dry. An inch or two of water sheeted constantly across its surface, creating a dazzle of color as the sun reflected from changing ripples over the colored rocks. But the water was warm, and the rock was warmed by the sun, and pleasant to sit on. So she sat, watching the patterned shadows on the water. This place had been shaped by beings clever enough to smooth the stones and guide the stream—but more than that, by beings with eyes that saw the sinuous ripples as beauty, and ears that heard the music of falling water. Sofron felt the water like a fleeting brush of fingertips, like the whisper of a distant voice. This place communicated intelligence.

The heat of the sun and its hypnotic sparkle on the water made Sofron feel dizzy with the need to sleep. They had to rest sometime. The raft had not proved safe. This wasn't an ideal spot, either, but at least it was clear of vegetation. She made her decision.

"We'll stop here and rest."

"I'm hungry," Jaya said, and the others echoed him.

"Take a big drink of water. We'll look for food later. Right now we're too tired to be alert. And we need to be alert in a strange place. Remember that."

They curled up on the flat stone terrace, behind a jumble of broken rocks a couple of yards from the water's edge. Sofron thumped and thwacked the pile first to make sure there were no lurkers. The children grumbled at the hard surface, but fell asleep in minutes, their heads pillowed on each other and on carry sacks and mats unloaded from the raft.

3

A chittering cry woke her up. She found herself staring directly into the goggling eyes of a semicircle of dog-sized animals that looked like lizards. Their mouths hung slightly open, emitting a scent of fish and salt. Narrow tongues protruded, flicking slightly, tasting the air. She couldn't see any teeth, but the bony ridge that rimmed the mouth looked sharp. Like turtles, she thought. Turtles can bite your finger off. She saw all that in one groggy moment, then leapt to her feet with a shout.

They scuttled away in comic alarm, stumbling over themselves. Their legs bent out at the elbow so that they dragged themselves with bellies low to the earth, like salamanders. Their feet were flat and webby, ill suited for speed on land. They looked as if they would be more at home in the water, yet they were clearly comfortable in the dry. The moist skin of their flanks quivered. She wondered if they were really panting, or if they breathed by some other, invisible process.

Again they called, a kind of barking chirp. Their rounded skulls rose sharply behind their snouts. If that was their braincase, Sofron thought, it held plenty of room for intelligence. Stepping out in front of the children, who had been roused by the commotion, she picked up a chunk of stone and hurled it, not to strike the creatures, but to shoo them away. There was brief consternation among the lizards, an explosion of slithers. Then they were back, regrouped and lurking, only a little farther away.

She was inclined to fear them simply because there were so many of them, but so far they hadn't done anything threat-

28

ening. She approached them slowly, and they didn't flee. She stretched out a hand, and the foremost of the group took a tentative step toward her. She touched its head, and it did not try to bite. She rubbed the wrinkled skin behind the complicated neck folds. The skin was cool and smooth like a frog's, not rough and scaly like a lizard's. The round eyes half closed as the creature stretched its neck forward and emitted a low whirring sound. Immediately the others scrambled forward and mobbed Sofron, pushing damp snouts against her hands and her thighs.

"Hey!" she yelled, and they retreated again, but not as far as the last time. If they had wanted to bite, she thought, they'd had plenty of chances. Perhaps she didn't smell right to them. It would certainly be a wonder if there were *one* species on Typhon to whom humans did not smell like prey.

She heard one of the children laugh, and turned around. They were all awake now, and watching.

"I want to touch him," Jaya said, and the others followed, agreeing, scrambling toward her like the lizards.

"Well, you can't," she said. "Not yet. We have to watch them for a while, see if they're really harmless. Maybe they're just not hungry right now."

"What are they called?" Ling asked.

"I don't know—I guess we'll have to make something up," Sofron said. "Do you remember those animals I told you about that are called dogs? These guys run around and hang their tongues out like dogs, but they're wet and don't have any fur. What if we call them water dogs?"

"I want to pet the water dogs," Ling said instantly.

"I thought you were hungry," Sofron said. "Don't you want to look for food first?"

The children's first thought was to return to the sea and find fish, but Sofron preferred to stay away from the sea for at least a few days.

"We're on vacation, remember? So let's look around here and see if we can find some new kind of food."

They returned to the raft, and she paddled upstream far enough to get away from the water dogs. The traces of worked stone continued along the banks. The stony bottom didn't seem to attract many fish. Sofron pulled ashore and ordered the children to stay put while she waded cautiously upstream.

She came to a zigzag bed of fleshy plants with dark green leaves. The bed was an odd, sharp-edged shape, in the middle of the river, not touching the banks on either side. Plants didn't usually grow that way. Approaching it, she saw that the bed was bounded by low walls of rock, as if it had been planted and confined there deliberately.

Sofron touched the closest leaves, jerking her hand back quickly. The plant did not sting, numb, or stick to her. It didn't even move. She plucked one of the leaves and looked at it suspiciously. It remained an inert green leaf. On Typhon, that seemed unusual. She pulled off a fragment and put it to her lips. It tasted like spinach, with a sweetish tang but no other flavor. After a few minutes, she was pleased to discover her mouth had not gone numb. She did not prickle or itch, or feel sick or short of breath. She took a larger bite and let the crumpled remnant float away. In an hour or two, if nothing more happened, the children might risk eating this.

Beyond the weed beds, the river was deeper and narrower. Sofron waded in until she was chest-deep and starting to get nervous. The river bottom was no longer smooth stone. It felt soft and furry underfoot, tufted with more weeds. The stone walls continued in serpentines that formed another set of barriers.

Sofron bent, her face inches from the surface, and looked down into the nearest pool. "Jackpot!" she exclaimed. It was full of fat, whiskery river fish. As she watched, one of the largest made a leap just under her nose and splashed down on the far side of the wall. But there were plenty left inside. She was about to hurry back for a net and start catching lunch, but she wondered suddenly why this enclosure was full of fish. How *could* it be, hundreds of years after its makers had vanished?

Upstream there was another such pool, and another beyond that, and each was full of fish. Sofron put her head underwater and investigated. Bright fish swam past her nose, peering back at her. In the back wall of the first pool, there were three or four holes, too small for the fat fish to swim through. Sofron was beginning to understand.

The holes were fish gates. The pools were self-sustaining fish traps. Small fish swam into the pool, and most of them stayed there, growing too fat to swim back out. Since the builders were no longer there to harvest them, the biggest fish probably escaped by jumping over the ledge and swimming on downstream. But that still left plenty of fish in the pool. Sofron smiled at the simple ingenuity of it. This was the first safe and pleasant discovery she had made in a long, long time.

She turned around to tell the children she had found their lunch, and froze in horror when she saw what they were doing. They were waist-deep in the water, surrounded by creatures so brightly colored that Sofron could see even from a distance what they were—swarms of tiny snakes.

"No!" she screamed, and launched herself downstream. She swam so fast that she arrived in a swirl of foam. There were pencil-slim, wriggling reptiles all around her. She had no plan. She clutched the nearest child and tried to heave him out of the water, away from danger. It was Ven.

"Stop, Sofi!" he said petulantly, kicking at her. To her horror she saw that he was clutching one of the snakes. She could see the tiny bright eyes, the tail lashing about. Maybe it wasn't too late. Maybe he had not yet been stung.

"I *like* them. They're nice!" Ven protested. "They tickle." He tried to hold his prize away from her, but she gripped his wrist so tightly that he had to let go.

"You're hurting me!" He burst into tears. The little snake tumbled onto Sofron's shoulder. Immediately it wrapped its tail around her arm and slithered downward toward her wrist. Its scales were intensely scarlet and shone like enamel.

Sofron had to drop Ven to keep the snake away from him, but more darted toward him as soon as he reentered the water. Then the little serpent curved its head back and struck at Sofron's wrist.

It felt like a pinprick. She could not even see teeth. She felt the blood draining from her face as she waited for the effects. The snake poised motionless, as if it, too, were waiting.

Nothing happened. The snake slid from her wrist, back to the river, leaving behind a single pinpoint of blood that dropped from her skin into the water and vanished. Her racing heart slowed gradually, and she realized that her dizziness was only fear, not poisoning.

Time came back into focus as she looked around. Ven had already forgotten his pinched wrist as he watched in fascination the new, bright blue snake that circled it. All the children were laughing and happy, and all had tiny snakes in rainbow colors circling their wrists or ankles.

Ling paddled up to Sofron and looked up at her anxiously.

"What's the matter, Sofi?" she said. "You look scared."

"It's all right," Sofron said. "I thought the snakes were poisonous."

"Oh, no, they're friendly," Ling said. "And they're pretty, too." She looked at Sofron's bare wrist. "Why don't they like you?"

Sofron could only shake her head. "I don't know." She sank down on the stone terrace to rest for a minute.

But there was still the question of lunch. She took a deep breath.

"I found some good fish," she said. "Jaya, bring the net and come with me—it's a little deep for the rest of you."

Ten minutes later, they were all sitting on the ledge eating juicy chunks of raw fish. There was no sufficiently dry place to build a fire, but they were used to eating their food un- cooked when storms damped down the fire in their shelter.

Sofron used the finger-length cutter she had salvaged from her emergency kit to chop up the fish. She felt squeamish about using Wearra's knife on flesh, though it did come in handy for knocking down a cluster of giling pods. Sour-sweet giling juice made raw fish firmer and tastier, almost as if it had been cooked. She laid the bone knife down beside her, because it got in her way when it dangled from her belt.

As she ate, Sofron thought about the fact that the "cutter" really was a knife, too. On Skandia, it was considered more polite to use a colorless, functional word, rather than one freighted with violent implications. But the cutter *was* a weapon, as well as a tool. Perhaps on Typhon things should be called by all their names.

Her attention had drifted for only a few minutes when she heard a shriek from the direction of the bank. She jumped to her feet, reaching for the knife. It wasn't there.

Jaya was twenty feet away, on the bank, halfway up the nearest giling tree. He hung from a branch by his hands. A tanglewood frond had coiled around his foot and was tugging him toward the heart of the tangle. The bone knife lay at the foot of the tree, where he had dropped it.

Ling and Ven were already wading toward the bank, too. Sofron caught up with them and pushed them roughly back.

"Stay here!" she ordered, splashing through the shallow water. She grabbed the knife from the forest litter, clenched the handle between her teeth, and began to swarm up the tree.

More fronds of tanglewood were already seeking out the tree, their white tendrils like deadly fingers. They seemed fumbling, but once attuned to the scent of their prey, they would cling and coil with deadly accuracy. In her haste, Sofron scraped her shins and arms against the tree's rough bark, releasing the smell of her own blood to further arouse the tanglewood. Jaya could not hold on much longer; by the time she reached him, his legs would be fully enmeshed in the hungry fronds.

She was almost within arm's reach of the tanglewood now, but she couldn't climb and strike at the same time. A bright streak of red moved down Jaya's leg. For a moment, she thought that the tanglewood had slashed him as it sought for a hold, and he was already bleeding.

But it was one of the snakes. It had uncoiled from his wrist and moved rapidly down his body to the place where the tanglewood gripped him. It struck in a blur of motion. The white frond recoiled, lashing about as if stung to frenzy. It struck against Sofron's shoulder and clung. She could feel the bite and the numbness spreading out to disable her. She was shifting the knife from her teeth to her good hand to strike at the tanglewood when she lost her grip on the tree and crashed to the ground. Jaya fell almost on top of her.

The deep forest litter of dry leaves and fern tufts absorbed some of the force of their fall. Jaya jumped up and retrieved the knife, but Sofron was stunned. It took her a few painful moments to pull herself upright and verify that nothing was broken. Her nose was bleeding, and her left arm dangled uselessly, temporarily numbed by the tanglewood toxin.

The tanglewood thrashed about, perhaps still smelling their blood, but it at last withdrew into its nest deeper in the trees. It dragged several limp fronds that looked useless. Sofron wondered if the snake had actually done something to harm the tangle. It must have been a potent dose, considering their relative sizes.

Jaya faced defiantly toward the woods, clutching the knife as if guarding Sofron. But his eyes flicked guiltily toward her.

"Give me that knife, Jaya," she said. He handed it over, and as he did, his lips quivered, as if the knife had been a protection that was now removed. He hurled himself against her, his wiry little arms clinging to her waist, and burst into tears.

"I'm sorry, Sofi, I'm sorry," he wailed. "I just wanted to get more giling, and I thought I could do it like you. I didn't mean to—you weren't using the knife—and then the tangle came out—" Speech failed him.

Sofron walked him back to the river and bathed his face gently with the tepid river water until he stopped hiccuping.

"Jaya, are you ready to listen now?" she said. "You know what your mistake was, right?"

"I took the knife without asking," he said reluctantly.

"Yes, and what else?"

"Acted without thinking?" It was a phrase he had repeated often.

"Yup, that's right. It was a good plan, except for one thing—you forgot the tanglewood. So I got hurt, and you scared everyone else half to death. If you had checked with me, I could have told you there was tanglewood. I saw it before. So what are you going to do next time?"

"Double-check the plan and ask—ask for information from others."

"That's right. And *think* before you act. If you let your

stomach lead you around, you'll soon become food for something else."

There was much more she felt like saying, but Jaya could take in only a few statements at a time. If she lectured him anymore, he would only forget everything.

"Well, there's no harm done," she said, smiling to cheer up the others. "My arm will be fine again in a couple of hours."

"Your face is bleeding," Ling said reproachfully.

"Oh, that's just my nose. Noses bleed over every little bump. It's not dangerous."

She set Jaya down on the flat rock and waded downstream a little way to wash her face.

"See this? Always wash blood downstream of you, so if anything hungry smells the blood, it won't come all the way up to where you are."

The children still stood around solemnly, looking worried. The little snakes had not gone away. They coiled around wrists and ankles, one or two or three to a child, as if they planned to stay permanently.

"Have you thought of a name for those yet?" Sofron said.

"Brightsnakes," Ling said promptly, and the others nodded.

"They're pretty," Chilsong said.

"Don't feel bad," Sofron said to Jaya, stroking his hair. "We did learn something important from your action."

"What?" He brightened up.

"We found out the snakes will bite tanglewood. That's very interesting. The brightsnakes can do something tanglewood doesn't like, and it almost looked as if they were protecting you. That could be a very good thing. We'll have to think more about it.

"All right, now, the next thing . . ." She glanced at the sun. It had already moved past the point of noon. "The next thing is to find a safe place to stay tonight. Let's go look back where we landed. There was no tanglewood there."

4

Deep in the waters of Typhon, Dilani danced with the ribbons of light that streamed down from the surface. She loved the warmer layers where the sun still shone, and the light was easy for her new, gleaming eyes to gather. Sometimes a memory of old times, before her gills had grown, would catch at her throat and make her feel for a moment that she must be choking. She would thrust for the surface, finned heels and long-fingered, webby hands churning in panic, before she remembered that she no longer needed air. Then she would allow herself to drift back down again, savoring the sweet and salt of Typhon's ocean waters as they flowed across her tongue and gill slits. Sometimes she stayed in the water for days at a time, until one of the others came searching for her anxiously.

Usually whoever came looking for her was one of the oldgens—the adults who had grown up on the other world called Skandia. Both the oldgens and the newgens, who had been born here, had recently been transformed. But Dilani thought the oldgens still seemed little different in their minds. Their bodies had changed, but their thinking stayed the same.

Sushan Melicar, the colony doctor, seemed worried that Dilani felt so little attachment to the land. Sushan kept trying to lure her to return to the shore, for no reason she could see, as if walking in the air were necessary to her well-being.

There was one group of oldgens who never walked onshore. Their transformation had not yet been completed. Dilani wove her way through drifting tendrils of harmless weed to check them once again. They slept in the shadow of the reef, deep down, where the light was dim and blue, and cool currents whispered through the warm lagoon. Each curled form was enclosed in a tough translucent membrane, like a bubble or a transparent egg.

Dilani peered into the bubbles. Once those faces had been well known to her. As the transformation continued, they had become harder to recognize. The eyelids lay closed over eyes that grew bigger and more lucent, like ripening berries. Skin stretched smooth over changing bones, and colors glowed where skin had once been monochrome tan or brown. Plain human necks, ankles, and wrists flowered into frills and convolutions of membranes and spines: a ruff around each neck, and fins for wrist and ankle. Lips pulled tight over teeth that had changed from mere nubbins to keen ivory weaponry.

Dilani ran her narrow, mobile tongue along the inside of her own teeth. She found them very satisfactory. Sometimes she missed her old face. Sometimes she dreamed she still had long hair and felt it blowing in the wind of the Dry up above. But then she dove again and felt the strong currents of the Deep caress her, and she left the old life on the shore, like a shiny pebble whose colors would fade as it dried.

She remembered what the transformation had cost her: days of agony as her old body was wracked and stretched into its new shape. Staring at their motionless faces, she wondered if those others truly slept, or if they writhed and screamed inside in fever dreams of their own. She wondered if they would ever wake up. She didn't much care. They hadn't been kind to her when they'd walked on land and had the power to rule her life. If they woke only to scold and punish her again . . . She turned in a swirl of bubbles and left them. As she cupped water with her webbed hands and swam, she flexed her fingers and admired the strong, sharp nails, almost like talons. If the sleepers woke, they would find her well able to defend herself.

A shadow trailed its crooked fingers across the rocks below her. She looked up and saw Subtle. The godbits that had transformed him had modeled his features on the only human they had analyzed in detail—Per Langstaff. But that face, as usual, had no expression. It just sat there, like a tool he had never bothered to learn how to use. Yet something in the twist of his body as he swam conveyed to Dilani that he was not happy. That wasn't unusual. Subtle had perhaps lost more than the rest of them when he was transformed.

"How do you feel?" Dilani signed to him. "What are you thinking?"

Subtle shrugged. He had learned the gesture from Dilani, but it looked different on him. The shrug rippled his whole torso, not just his shoulders. Even now, the muscles in his trunk weren't quite right, not quite like those of a human being. Unlike the Skandians, he had not changed from one humanoid form to another. He had come from the Round Folk, and had traded twelve tentacles for a pair of legs and a pair of arms. Only two of his cherished tentacles had survived the metamorphosis.

"Bad," he signed morosely.

"Bad how?" Dilani insisted.

"Sign is no good," Subtle signed. "Talking is no good. Can't tell my feelings. Bad."

He turned over and dove below the cluster of bubble-wrapped humans, coming up on the other side. Dilani caught up with him and grabbed hold of his shoulder. He was a faster, stronger swimmer than any of the humans, and she couldn't keep up with him if he really wanted to escape her, but she could make him tow her.

He darted toward the open sea beyond the reef but slowed at a flash of sleek, silver-striped black fin. The ketos were still swimming their endless patrol, guarding the humans from any harm that might come out of the Deep. The ketos were big and wild; they shot through the sea like black-and-silver thunderbolts. Their teeth were like knives. Their songs were full of laughter and death. Dilani could not catch much of their meaning, even with the newfound sea-senses that let her hear their part of the Deepsong.

Ketos humored the humans and held off from them, as if under orders from powers that Dilani did not fully understand. They had been ordered to guard those who were changing, and they did so. But they were not friendly. They were even less friendly to Subtle.

Dilani liked the ketos, but it seemed strange to her that Subtle liked them, too, in spite of their attitude. Or perhaps liking wasn't the right word. He watched them and followed them. Even when they had roughly butted him aside and sped away without him, Dilani had seen him turn and swim after them. Though he wore a human form now, he showed no such affinity for the humans. He shunned most of them as the ketos shunned him.

Dilani couldn't talk to him as long as he was swimming, but she was so close to him that she could feel the skin language confirming what he had said. Indeed, he was uncomfortable and anxious, even fearful. She didn't know how she knew these things. Something in the water, invisible as thought, told her how Subtle felt when she swam nearby. It was one of the changes that had come with her new body. Sushan, the doctor, said it was a "kemmy-kal" and called it a "feromone," but there was no sign for the words, and the mere sound of them meant nothing to Dilani.

Dilani could also see that Subtle's skin was changing colors around her fingers, where she gripped his shoulder. When she had first seen him, his body had been round and fringed with twelve powerful tentacles. When they had learned to exchange signs with him, he had named himself Subtle, in his own language, for the complex, ever-changing color patterns in his skin. Now that Subtle and the humans were more alike, it was easier to share in the skin language.

Just now, Subtle's skin patterns registered unease and irritation. But Dilani noticed that where her fingers touched his skin, the patterns pulsed calmly, showing warm yellow against the prevailing somber hues. She smiled. Subtle's skin communicated in spite of him. As solitary and silent as he appeared, he was still her friend.

Subtle stopped swimming and drifted, staring after the rapidly disappearing ketos. His extra limbs, the two strong tentacles left after the others had fused to arms and legs, curled around his torso and uncurled again. His colors shifted restlessly.

A low whistle vibrated through the water behind them. Dilani turned and saw Bey Sayid. He somersaulted in the water and came up facing them.

"Today you checked the eggs?" he signed.

Dilani nodded briefly, bored.

"Soon they'll hatch," Bey signed.

Dilani shrugged, a large gesture that caused her to drift away from the others. "Do I care?" she signed. She continued to rotate until she was upside down from Bey's viewpoint.

Patiently, he turned to match her.

"Yes, you care. Because what happens when they hatch? Remember how we felt when we changed? We were scared. You didn't know who I was. Subtle couldn't talk or swim. They'll be scared, too, and some of them won't be happy that we did this to them."

"We didn't do it."

"You know what I mean," Bey insisted. "We put them in the water so the change viruses could work, so the godbits could help them change."

"Without us they would have died," Dilani signed.

"Maybe some of them don't believe that. And maybe some of them would rather have died."

"That's stupid," Dilani signed automatically. But she thought about it as she revolved slowly.

She knew that Bey was thinking of his father, Whitman Sayid. Whitman had been the colony leader. Dilani remembered how Whitman had screamed when they put him in the water, how he had called Bey "monster." She wondered how Whitman would like his new face, and if he would still be the colony leader now that they were all monsters.

But while she was still wondering, the ketos came back with a rush that spun her in the water.

"What the hell?" she signed, righting herself.

Subtle signed with arms and tentacles. "Broken, open, out!" Then he plunged after the ketos before Dilani could grab him for a tow.

Finally she understood the edgy flavor of change that had caused Subtle's agitation. It must be the oldgens. They were hatching!

She swam after Subtle into a swirling mix of fear, triumph, and astonishment. As she dove toward the bubbles, she bumped face-to-face into a goggle-eyed, newly changed being, mouth wide in distress. Dilani couldn't tell at first who it was. The oldgen pushed past her, frantically stroking for the surface. Whoever it was still felt the human drive to the air and had not noticed that she was already breathing underwater.

Dozens of oldgens surged toward the surface, surrounded by twinkling clouds of godbits, like bubbles that did not pop. Another newborn bumped Dilani, trailing ragged skeins of gauze, ripping at them in panic. For a moment Dilani thought the trailing rags were torn skin and was repulsed, but then she realized it was just leftover bubble membrane. She tugged at it and let it shred away into the water, freeing the new one to flee for the surface. This time Dilani thought she knew the face, transformed as it was. That was Torker Fensila, once boss of the fishing labor roster. His body was thick and powerful in spite of all the changes, and somehow his expression had stayed the same—though his flat nose now pinched shut underwater and his heavy brows were hairless and freckled with cobalt and maroon.

It seemed they were all hatching out at once; Dilani flipped over and followed them up. Their splashing churned up the surface. The doctor had joined Bey and Subtle, and all three tried to talk to the newly transformed, to calm them. But most of them were shouting and gasping so loudly that words went unheard.

A few of them had the sense to locate the shore, and they began swimming for it desperately. Bey and Subtle rudely shoved the rest in the right direction, and soon the whole group was floundering toward the beach like a school of confused and awkward fish.

When Dilani came ashore, the other humans no longer looked like fish. They huddled like a flock of bedraggled birds. Some of them she couldn't recognize at first. Others, like Torker, had kept a more obvious resemblance to their original form.

She knew Whitman Sayid right away—partly because Bey hovered near him, but partly because he was on his feet and talking, the center of attention as usual. In the past, Whitman had always used his voice and manner to soothe the colonists and guide them in the direction he wanted. But what he was saying now was not helping the humans feel better.

"This is a nightmare," Whitman cried. "A nightmare!" He kept repeating that single phrase, his voice rasping on the rough edge of hysteria. He turned around and around as he tried to see clearly the fringed spines that were now attached to his neck.

The crest stood out stiff and bright-colored with alarm. To Dilani, it seemed handsome: the skin new and fresh, the colors intriguing. Whitman had been a self-possessed man who kept his clothes neat and his hair short and well combed. Dilani would never have expected such an explosion of crimsoned and purpled emotion from him. Perhaps those colors had been inside him, she thought, waiting to burst out just as he had waited to burst from the clear membrane of his hatching.

Whitman could not see the colors he displayed. He clawed at the spines with his long, webbed hands, as if he could force them down and away.

"It can't be, can't be," he groaned. "A nightmare!"

It looked as if he would hurt himself.

Subtle stepped toward him.

"You is being calm, is being smoothing, good colors," he tried to explain. Subtle kept his extra limbs tucked around his torso to avoid further alarming the distraught human. But Whitman backed away from the strange face and harsh, toneless voice.

Dilani couldn't understand Whitman's horrified expression until he spoke.

"A blue troll with Per's face," he said. "Get away from me!"

The other adults, for the most part, stood speechless, staring at their changed hands. Some crouched by the river inlet, bright-crested heads turning from side to side as they tried to grasp their own unsteady images in the shifting mirrors of the water.

One of the oldgens—Dilani thought it was Phun Skanderup, but she was not completely sure—was worse off than Whitman. She whirled and staggered across the beach, as if she could run away from the changes. She slashed at her unfamiliar flesh, drawing blood with her sharp nails. She uttered sharp, whistling cries of pain and fear, and the inhuman sound of her own voice drove her further into terror.

Dilani shook the doctor's arm.

"Do something!" she signed. "You have to help them! They're going crazy!"

In the stress of the moment, she had used the language that was most familiar. Then she remembered that she could use the mouth language now.

"You help!" she shouted. "You need help!" No, that wasn't quite right. She tried again.

"You got help! You must help!"

Melicar broke away from her grip. "I hear you, Dilani," she said, looking closely into Dilani's face so her mouth shapes were clear. "I hear you, but there is nothing I can do. I need sedatives—I need sleep-medicine—but I don't have it."

"Tangleweed!" Dilani said. It took a minute for the doctor to understand her version of the word. Then Melicar shook her head.

"No. You can't drink not-cooked tangleweed juice. It poisons your stomach. And we have no juice that is cooked and prepared." She signed rapidly, not confident Dilani could understand that much speech.

Frustrated and angry, Dilani watched as Melicar moved toward the hysterical woman. Dilani no longer wanted to touch the doctor. Even in air, she could taste the tangy, anxious fear/guilt on the doctor's skin.

Melicar was a kind, gentle person. Dilani knew that. But she could see the doctor's spines rising ominously as Melicar moved closer to Phun.

We are making more fear and anger, Dilani thought. *It goes from skin to skin. We must be calm. Smooth. Like Subtle says.*

She thought of deep, blue, peaceful water, before the oldgens had hatched out to create more trouble. She thought of them sleeping peacefully inside their glassy eggs. She found herself baring her teeth in distaste. She did not like them. They were always angry, always making the loud sounds. They didn't belong to Typhon.

But she forced her lips to close smoothly over those new, sharp teeth. She made an exaggerated, nice face, smiling skyward, spreading her neck spines pleasantly downward, exposing them to the warmth of the sun. The anger was still there, burning defiantly inside, but she rolled it tighter and smaller so the flames couldn't reach out and change her skin. Nice. Smooth.

She approached the doctor and touched her arm again. This time she saw the colors change to calm ones, spreading from her fingertips. She smiled again, really pleased this time. Her trick was working.

"You give nice," she suggested. "Make them smooth."

Melicar frowned at her, and Dilani felt herself getting irritated again, thinking that no matter how she tried, she could never use their words correctly. But she thought quickly of the pleasant sunny colors and smoothed away the dark ones for another time.

"You are doctor," she said. "Smooth yourself."

Phun had collapsed on the sand, sobbing. Her blood seeped into the shallow pools that had been left by retreating waves. Dilani could see bubbles coming from the damp sand where hungry little beings already worked their way toward the scent of food. Melicar continued trying to reach out to her, but whenever she approached, Phun scrambled away.

Subtle gave up on Whitman and approached the bleeding woman. He circled behind her and wrapped his arms around her before she could escape. He unwrapped his spare limbs and delicately curled them around her gills, careful not to cut off her air. She screamed again in fear at the touch of his tentacles, but the shrieks gradually died away into muted whimpering. She stopped struggling.

Subtle cautiously released her, and she sat still, gazing at her slashed arms with dawning comprehension.

"What happened?" she said. She looked around at the transformed humans, searching for some familiar face. "I'm hurt."

Now Melicar bent over her, hands outspread in a peace gesture.

"Let me look, please. It's me—the doctor."

Her face had changed, but her voice carried the same calm assurance she had always given to her patients.

"Doctor?" the woman said. Since her expression was no longer distorted by fear, she was beginning to look more like Phun. *"Sushan?"*

"Yes, it's me." Melicar showed teeth in a brief, down-turned grin.

"But how did this *happen*? I remember being in the—in that shelter you built after the storm. I remember the storm. We were sick. I was thirsty, and you wouldn't let me go to the water. But then—what *happened*?"

"We'd like to tell you that if you would all calm down."

The transformed humans gathered around Phun as the doctor checked her cuts.

"Need godbits?" Dilani signed.

"They're shallow," Melicar said. "They'll heal by themselves. Look—that gel stuff is already forming over the cuts. That's what I call a really useful mutation. If only I knew what was in it."

Instinctively, the humans huddled together, but as they did so, their anxiety levels started to rise again. As they jostled each other, spines rose and once-peaceable Skandians showed claws and hissed at each other.

"Please back off," Melicar said calmly. "Give me some room here."

She turned to the watching newgens, who stood nearby. "Get in between them," she said.

Dilani moved to obey her, pleased that Melicar was finally understanding. *Smooth, nice,* Dilani thought. *Be calm, be calm.* Bey moved from person to person, touching wrists and shoulders, leaving his calming skin motes. He avoided only Whitman. But Subtle was now standing at Whitman's side, and the colony leader was visibly calming. Dilani observed that touch was a good technique, but she was not prepared to use it. Standing near the oldgens was as close as she wanted to get.

Whitman got himself under control, though the nervous blinking of the translucent extra membranes over his eyes made it clear that he was still agitated.

"Melicar, will you please explain in as few words as possible what in hell's name is going on here?" he asked.

The last time Dilani had seen him, he had been crazed in the grip of the changing sickness, screaming curses at his son as Bey dragged him into the water. From the look on the doctor's face, Dilani thought she might have similar memories.

"Do you remember what happened after the storm?" the doctor said.

"Of course I remember the storm," Whitman said. "And I remember circumstances afterward. I remember that some colony members were behaving . . . irrationally. You reported your belief that many of us were seriously ill. Beyond that—nothing really specific. Is there something I'm *supposed* to remember?"

Melicar shrugged. Perhaps Whitman was lying in self-defense. Perhaps the transformation process really had wiped out his traumatic memories. She couldn't blame him if he preferred to forget.

"We *were* sick," she said. "I would like to emphasize that, in my professional opinion, we were dying. Every single one of us. There was nothing I could have done to save any of our lives. Most of you were unconscious or delirious when it happened."

"When *what* happened?"

Melicar gestured around their little circle with one hand. The hand itself was as eloquent as the gesture. The frilled wrist fin spread automatically as she extended her webbed fingers.

"This. This transformation. Bey and Dilani tell me it is

caused by a virus in the water. The same kind of virus caused the genetic defects in the newgens, and made the adults gradually sicken. The original virus was trying to change us, and failing. The new one finished the job. Like it or not, we have now been assimilated into Typhon. We were aliens here. We now incorporate genetic material native to Typhon. Now we can survive.

"That's the good news. The bad news is that we now find ourselves in this somewhat unconventional form. It will take some getting used to. But I urge you to have patience and be calm. We can live with this."

Whitman stared at her as if he was trying to assimilate the information. When he spoke, however, it was clear that he was far from it.

"Viruses? Where did you get these ridiculous ideas?" he said scornfully. "Who has been feeding you this absurd nonsense?"

"Per Langstaff always believed an infectious agent might be responsible," Melicar said. "It seems he was right. Bey and Dilani tell me that during the storm, they traveled to a place where Per made contact with an organism that actually produced these viruses. Per was not able to stop their effects, but he was able to redirect them so they changed our form rather than killing us."

"I might have known Langstaff would be involved in this," Whitman said. "And where is he now?"

He raised his voice and looked around dramatically as if the culprit might be hiding under a fallen tree.

"Where is Per Langstaff? I demand that he answer for himself."

Melicar hesitated. Her information was all secondhand. But Bey could no longer keep silent.

"Per Langstaff isn't here!" he shouted. "He *can't* answer for himself! He had to let this . . . this creature assimilate him so it could learn about humans. You can't blame him for what happened to us. You'd all be grateful to him if you'd seen what he did, if you'd spend five minutes trying to understand it. The doctor is telling the truth."

"Are you saying that Per is dead?" Whitman said. "I thought you maintained that he was still alive."

"He is alive. His mind is still alive. It's just his body that is lost."

"Then where is this disembodied mind?"

"I . . . I don't know. But I know we can find him again. The ketos know."

"The ketos know," Whitman repeated. He paused, allowing his spiny ruff to spread majestically as he contemplated his son.

"The one thing I'm sure of is that Per is not here," he said finally. "You may be right. This may not be his fault. I respect your feelings of loyalty, but I think the kindest hypothesis may be that you all experienced some kind of hallucination. It wouldn't be surprising, if you were in underwater isolation for a long period.

"If Per is alive, and if he is responsible for this tragic alteration, then I guarantee that we will confront him and demand that he reverse the process. But this isn't the time to discuss it. We need time to recover and adjust to this situation. I request volunteers to construct shelters and build a fire. Meanwhile, Sushan may continue her examinations. Please check the injured first, and report all findings when you have completed your rounds."

He turned and walked away inland.

Bey stepped forward to respond, but Melicar laid a restraining hand on his arm.

"Let him go," she said softly. "There's no point in arguing with him now. Give him time to recover his face."

"But he's using us," Bey said. "He used everything I said to make it look as if we were liars, or crazy. And he's using Per—making him the enemy so the oldgens will have someone to blame. I can't let him get away with this."

"You don't have much choice," Melicar said. "Their minds aren't open to what you're telling them. They are not able to imagine what happened to you and Per. Their bodies have changed, but the minds inside haven't caught up. By giving them someone to blame, Whitman is helping them put their situation back into a framework they can understand. Otherwise *they'd* be the ones to go crazy.

"You weren't raised on Skandia. You don't know how important it was to be normal, to look like others, *not* to be altered. Suddenly, overnight, they have turned into monsters. Whitman has offered them some hope: if Per caused this, they can make Per change them back. Meanwhile, the only way they can cope is by acting a little bit crazy. Let them be. Don't focus their anger against you. You may not like his methods, but in his own way, Whitman was trying to protect you. He doesn't want them to see you and Dilani as Per's accomplices."

"You're right. I don't like it," Bey said. "He's not protecting me. He's protecting himself. Like always."

"Stay calm if you want to outthink him," Melicar said. "And remember, you have the advantage now. You're used to this world. He is still a stranger here. You can afford to take time. Now I have to look after the rest of these people."

She moved up the dunes, into the debris of fallen trees and flotsam where the volunteer teams were struggling to light a fire.

Bey moved closer to Dilani and Subtle, who were left behind, like him, on the shore.

"They don't need that fire," he said. "It's a lot of work for nothing." The evening breeze felt warm against his cheeks. If he stayed out of water long enough, the air would dry and irritate his skin, but he never felt cold.

"Stupid," Dilani agreed.

Subtle moved closer, fascinated as always by the sight and smell of fire. He had learned to use the human word for it, but his hands shaped the signs that meant "painful beauty."

"Fire is power," he said. "Is showing humans still has memory. Sky is making dark, humans is making brightness anyway. Like Great Ones in the long-time, humans is showing power. Not so stupid."

《5》》》》》》》

The fire had died down to white ashes over red coals that glowed and faded under the breath of the wind. Most of the oldgens were slumped in exhausted sleep. Bey leaned against a roll of salvaged matting, but he couldn't sleep. His skin was drying out, and he felt itchy and irritable. Even the tendrils of smoke that remained stung his sensitive gills.

A shape came out of the shadows and crouched down by his side. It was Whitman.

"Bey, I appreciate that you did what you thought had to be done," Whitman said softly. His large eyes gleamed in the dark. "I may not agree with you, but I admire that. It shows character." He thought for a moment, or gave the appearance of thinking. Bey suspected he had worked out every detail of this speech in advance.

"I don't clearly remember everything that happened in those last few days, after the storm," he said. "I'm afraid that I wasn't clear in my mind. If I did anything that offended you, I'm sorry. I hope you'll overlook whatever may have happened."

Bey remained silent. He remembered very clearly how the dart from his father's gun had sounded and felt as it tore through his arm. Whitman had tried to kill him, and had nearly succeeded. He remembered his father's voice screaming "Monster! You were never my son!" But his father had been a Skandian, with tanned skin, dark hair, and stubby-fingered, human hands, not this webbed, finned creature.

Bey remembered, too, how he had dragged his father to the water and pushed him in. He had done it to save his life. But maybe he hadn't been completely sorry to see Whitman become a monster, too. Under the circumstances, he could neither excuse nor blame. So he said nothing.

"I had to interrupt you out there," Whitman continued. "Talking to these people about viruses is a mistake. In the old days of war, viruses were used to transfer engineered DNA into human cells. If I'm understanding you correctly, you're saying that's what has been done to us. Telling these people they've been gene-bombed could drive them right over the edge. Melicar should have known better."

"But it's the truth," Bey said.

Whitman's spines rose irritably. "I blame myself," he said. In Bey's experience, this phrase usually preceded a scolding. "You haven't had the education they'd have given you on Skandia. You would have learned what the wars were like, why our foreparents fled to an isolated system like this one just to get away from them."

"Per told us about it," Bey said. Next minute he wanted to bite his tongue. Had he betrayed a secret that would get Per in trouble? But Per was far away now, beyond human reach.

"Whatever he told you obviously wasn't enough," Whitman responded. "On Skandia, as a public servant, I had access to restricted historical records. Whole nations were poisoned by drones that popped in and out of the atmosphere and seeded the air with weaponized diseases. Gene-bomb cancers, flesh eaters, brain bugs and blinders, or just a targeted self-killer that made sure they'd never have children and wiped out the planet in one generation—those were the common, ordinary things."

"He told us about the monsters," Bey whispered. "But he said there was beauty, too. There is beauty in the Deep, Papan. There's freedom. When you go there, you'll feel it. We are alive. Does it matter so much that we live in a different form?"

Whitman tried to keep his colors smooth and restrained, but Bey noticed the freckles deepening on his skin. They were dark in the dim light; Bey wasn't sure what the color meant. Whitman briefly laid a hand on his arm, and Bey tasted a tang of unease—or was it covert excitement? Whatever it was, Bey sensed that Whitman was not displeased with him, and that in itself was strange.

"We'll discuss it later," Whitman said. He wandered off again through the camp, bestowing a word here and there on those who were still awake.

Bey rubbed his itching back against the matting. The conversation with his father had done nothing to soothe him. Stretching himself into a more comfortable position, he luxuriated in the sight and feeling of long, powerful legs. If he was to be considered a monster now, he had been thought a cripple before, and he knew which he preferred. To be whole and agile, as tall and swift as anyone, was worth almost any price, he thought. He couldn't see or feel his genes. He didn't care what happened to them; it was the result that counted.

He waited until the oldgens were asleep and then went back into the water. He could no longer sleep on land.

The oldgens had been hooting and waving their arms for some time on the beach before Bey rose to the surface and took notice of them.

He couldn't make out what they were saying, but then a small figure that must be the doctor signed in broad, shout-sized gestures, "Father wants you. Come!"

He returned to shore reluctantly.

"You shouldn't be out there," Whitman said as soon as he was within talking distance.

" 'Out there' is my home, Papan," Bey said. "More than this island."

Whitman scratched irritably under his ribs.

"It's dangerous out there."

"Maybe," Bey said. "But we need the water now—or hadn't you noticed? You'd be a lot less cranky if you took a swim yourself. You'll have to get used to it sometime. All of them will. It would look better if you could lead the way. Help them adjust."

Whitman kept rubbing at the dry skin, but more thoughtfully.

"You could be right," he said at last. "Your point is well

taken. In fact, I'm glad you raised this question because it goes right to the subject I need to talk to you about."

He placed a hand on Bey's shoulder and steered him toward one of the few shady spots left on shore. Bey's neck frill flared nervously at the unaccustomed contact. He was astonished. Normally when he goaded his father, he could expect a stinging lecture on the nature of respect and duty, and on the total irrelevance of his foolish statement. Now Whitman was treating him like a valued adviser. He wondered what his father could possibly hope to gain from this tactic.

Whitman made himself comfortable in the hollow of a sand dune. Bey's skin prickled at contact with the dry sand, but he sat obediently at his father's side.

"I haven't always appreciated you in the past," Whitman said, without his usual smooth preamble. "I underestimated your abilities. I'm sorry for that. I've been thinking this over, and I can see that you have learned much about this world, much that we all need to know."

"But?" Bey said, when Whitman fell silent.

"No buts. I will need your help in guiding this colony. You have grown up a great deal, as well. You are a young man now, not an irresponsible boy."

Bey's spines rose angrily.

When was I ever permitted to be irresponsible, Papan? he thought. But he said nothing, and Whitman didn't notice his bristling neck frill.

"However, you must understand that not all of the adults can realize this. To them, you are still a young one, and they will not willingly take your comments and advice. I want— and need— your input. But I think that for them, it will work better if direction comes from me. It's what they're used to."

"You mean you want me to come to you first, not just express my opinion to everyone?"

"Exactly!" Whitman pressed his shoulder warmly. "You see—I knew you were mature enough to understand."

Bey opened his mouth to protest, but Whitman continued. "You're right; this island is no longer our home. We stayed here before because we had no incentive or means to move elsewhere. To head out into the ocean without navigational gear or maintenance equipment or adequate water supplies would have been suicide. But now we don't have to worry about supplies. We can live in the sea. You can help us learn how.

"As well, you and Dilani and the alien have some familiarity with the area to the east of us. You can help guide us to a better home."

"Well, we didn't actually *see* any other islands. Just some underwater seamounts. Maybe Subtle knows if there's land farther east."

"Southeast. We had charts in the medical computer, up until the last storm destroyed the clinic. But no matter. I remember much of the information on those charts."

He leaned closer to Bey, his eyes alight with excitement.

"Southeast of here, there's a chain of small islands that culminates in a larger land area that's almost big enough to be called a continent. Actual dry land! A stable foothold! We could survive there."

Bey finally broke in.

"You still don't get it," he said. "It's true we don't need the island now. We don't need *any* island anymore. We can survive anywhere."

Whitman shook his head, putting his hand up for silence in the gesture that meant there was another lecture coming.

"That's where you're wrong. That's where your inexperience with human beings shows. We *are* still human beings, in spite of these—temporary, I hope—physical changes. Inside, we have the same needs. We need a permanent home. Yes, we can survive in the ocean, physically; but we can't survive as a human culture without memory, without a plan for the future. We can't just drift in the sea."

The words sounded so convincing that Bey found he could not argue. He looked down at his hands and saw how the colors of his new skin deepened with misgiving. Whitman could not read the colors yet. The Deep would have to teach him its language.

"Why didn't Skandia drop the original colony on the continent, if it's so much better there?" he said.

"I argued in favor of it, but others were against me. The last colony before us tried to settle the continent and failed. So, instead of going back and trying to build on their foundation, the Board of Colonization Review decided to try a different location and hope for a more favorable outcome there."

"There were other humans there before us? How long ago?" Bey was suddenly curious. To see other humans, people he hadn't known all his life, would be exciting.

"They fell out of contact thirty years ago, shortly after they landed. The BCR listed them all as dead.

"But this is the important thing: it's possible we might find equipment or supplies we could use. There's no reason to think they experienced the same kind of catastrophe we did. The people may be dead, but whatever they took with them could still be functional. We might be able to reestablish contact with Skandia. Or, at the very least, to maintain our society at a greater level of technology. Not be reduced to the level of savages."

"Subtle isn't a savage," Bey said. But Whitman didn't seem to hear him.

"So you'll do it? You'll help me convince them to leave the island?"

"Sure, I guess so. If you need any help."

"And if you have any more good ideas, you'll come to me with them?"

"Sure."

"As a matter of fact, there's a favor you could do me right now. I think we should build a couple of rafts, to carry what's left of our equipment. We have plenty of downed timber going to waste here. Maybe you could get some of your friends to make a little preliminary survey of the possibilities. Then, after I present the idea to the forum, we can get a jump start."

By the next day, Whitman had persuaded the remaining oldgens to leave the island. He pointed out that each night they burned a significant fraction of the available scrap wood on the island. It wouldn't be long before they were completely out of fuel, and then they would no longer be able to build rafts. The typhoon had left the island denuded of live vegetation; it would be years before the trees could return.

Whitman painted a picture of heavily forested shores on the big island, a place rich with potential resources. He let the colonists think about it for a while, then suggested that anyone who preferred the familiarity of their current home was free to stay behind. Most of the colonists were eager to leave a place so full of grievous memories. The diehards looked sideways and counted each other. In a few hours, all of them were resigned to the move, and they set out to build two rafts.

They used most of their remaining fabric to create a small sail. There was some debate about whether they should first provide themselves with better garments. Few of them had more than a scrap of waist cloth left, and many were completely nude. But those who wanted to fashion new coverings lost the argument. Clothing was not really comfortable anymore. It rasped against their sensitive, always damp skins. The new bodies showed no need for it. So the sail was made and rigged.

There was only enough cloth for one; a second sail would have to be improvised from woven giling fronds. Constructing it took them a few more days, and the added time gave the oldgens a little longer to recuperate from the shock of their metamorphosis. It amused Dilani to watch them. Soon they seemed almost to forget that they had changed. They argued and bickered like the humans she remembered so well, and only noticed their new forms when sand got in their gills or they tripped over their own fins.

At this season, there was a brisk breeze from the west. They all set out at ebb tide on the day the sails were finished, and by late afternoon, the island was a smudge on the horizon, the reef invisible far behind.

Bey arranged to have ropes trailing from the stern of each raft. Most of the newgens were in and out of the water all day, frolicking astern and then swimming hard to catch up, or taking a tow on the ropes. The oldgens huddled on the rafts with their remaining possessions. When their skins became uncomfortably dry, they dipped up a shell full of water and doused themselves.

The newgens grazed on fish as they swam, but the adults were still reluctant to enter the Deep. Some of them ate the remains of their preserved food. Others accepted gifts of fish from the swimmers. Phillips Roon, cranky as always, had insisted on building a small sandbox on the raft, where he and some of the others nursed a tiny fire of wood chips and seared the fish. He claimed that it was necessary in case the fish contained parasites.

The ketos swam with them until the island was out of sight. Then they disappeared. Bey thought they had gone to hunt and would come back soon. He didn't start to worry until the sun was low on the horizon. He swam around below the rafts until he found Subtle, who had refused to come out of the water for any reason.

"Where are the ketos?" he asked.

"Gone," Subtle signed with a laconic flick of his tentacles. With his arms he kept swimming doggedly.

"When are they coming back?"

Subtle's skin flickered with surprise. "I don't think they are coming back," he signed.

He stopped swimming to communicate more fully.

"They argued. The one the god calls Slow Lightning said the

god ordered protection for humans of his pod. The others said the god ordered protection for humans of the Dry place. Humans are not on the Dry place now. So the ketos can go. They are tired. So they go. Slow Lightning goes with them, but his flavor is bad and he is showing teeth."

Bey moved away, grabbed one of the trailing ropes, and hoisted himself onto the raft. He plunked himself down next to Dilani.

Since she had gained hearing, Dilani had been experimenting with the properties of sound. Human speech struck her as stupid and irritating. She sometimes got lost in watching people's mouths move, and forgot to pay attention to the words. But pure sounds fascinated her.

She was mesmerized by surf, by rain, by running water. On the island, she had spent hours rubbing and banging together sticks and rocks in complex combinations of rhythm and texture. Bey had sometimes found her alone, facing the sea, crooning three notes over and over, or singing out one sustained tone until her breath ran out.

One day Henner Vik, the meteorologist, had given her a whistle cut from a dry reed. Dilani had soon figured out how to cut her own reeds and notch them to make different notes. She was playing a set of reeds when Bey slumped on the raft beside her. In theory, she could have been playing music. In fact, she seemed to be deliberately seeking out combinations of raucous squeaks and discordant burbles.

"For heaven's sake, will you stop making that awful noise!" Bey said.

"Hear, hear," Roon called from the far side of the raft.

Dilani favored him with a sullen look. She had just discovered a particularly earsplitting chord, and she blew it vigorously several more times before taking the pipes from her lips.

"Did you know about this?" Bey said. "You've been spending a lot of time with the Bright Teeth. Did you know they were just leaving?"

"Not leaving," Dilani signed. When she was in a bad mood, she didn't like to speak out loud. "Not leaving! Slowbolt will come back for me. Per made me drink the fish milk. Now I smell of his pod. He'll come back."

She picked up the pipes and began to play again at top volume. An angry groan sounded from Roon's side of the raft. He threw a pair of sandals at her, but she ducked. The sandals went into the water and Roon was forced to go in after them, quenching his ire. Dilani kept playing.

Bey gritted his teeth. But after he had forced himself to listen for a while, he started to hear a kind of pattern that was satisfying in an odd way.

"It's kind of pretty," he signed. "Not so bad."

He thought that would please her, but she glared at him again.

"It's not for pretty!" she signed. "I'm learning to talk like ketos. They make more sense than you."

She turned her back to him and went on playing.

7

Sofron liked the feel of the terraced area where they had first landed. It was rocky and clear of vegetation, and they had seen no wildlife except for the water dogs. She led the children downstream a little way, to see what happened there.

The stream fell in a series of little waterfalls that looked as if they might have been deliberately installed. The stream's path cut deeply between rocky walls that soon rose above Sofron's head. Then, surprisingly, it simply ended in a third wall of stone. The water swirled away into a dark hole in the hillside. Ling hurried over to investigate.

"Don't go in there," Sofron called.

Ling went as close to the hole as she could without actually disobeying, and stuck her head inside.

"It roars inside," she said. "Listen!"

Sofron, about to pull her away, paused by the opening and heard a rhythmic booming, deep inside.

"That sounds like waves," she said. "Maybe there's a cave that connects to the ocean, somewhere inside there."

She decided they had better have a look at the cave while it was still daylight. If it did connect to the sea, it might be too dangerous to stay here. Wearra had never explained just where the others like him lived, or how she could avoid meeting them, but she knew he wanted her to stay away from the shore. On the other hand, if the cave was safe, if it turned out to be small enough and bare enough, it might be a good place to hide for the night.

Carrying a stick she had picked up by the river's edge, Sofron peered through the dark opening and thought she saw an unsteady light within. They squeezed through, wading cautiously at first. Then the current swept them off their feet and carried them back through a moment of darkness, and on into a silver-gray dimness. Again they climbed out onto flat, worked stones.

It was obvious that the stonework had been made by the same people—Sofron could only think of them as "people" now—who had decorated the riverbanks. It showed the same pattern of closely fitted stones, in patterns playing rough against smooth, and color against sober gray or black.

She was focusing on what was closest to her eyes when she heard the children shout, "Look! A man!" By the time she looked up, they were hanging on to her arms, jumping up and down and shouting, "What is it, Sofi? What is it?"

But she was speechless.

She rose slowly to her feet. They stood on a flat stone floor inlaid with spiraling symbols. The smoothed stones enclosed a pool that must have been twenty meters long, opening at its far end from the tunnel they had come through. The water of the pool was glassy-clear, but it moved uneasily with the motion of the sea, communicated faintly from some distant place. There was a constant rhythmic mutter at the low end of their hearing, like drums; it was the sound of the waves outside. High above them, openings in the rock roof let in drifts of sunlight that softened to a dim, silky texture by the time they reached the water.

The rock of the end wall, above the tunnel's mouth, had been smoothed. It was inlaid with a mosaic of stones and, on top of that, carved in bas-relief with a fantastic figure that must have been ten meters tall. It had two legs and two arms; but the feet and the raised hands were long, thin, and webbed, and they ended in nails like talons. The face had eyes and a mouth and something that passed for a nose, though it was flattened against the face. But the mouth was long and narrow lipped, and the eyes were carved with pupils that were slits like those of a lizard or a snake. It was hairless, but around the neck rose a delicate, spiny pattern that seemed to be attached to the skull and skin. The stones that formed the body were inlaid with tiny flecks that gleamed with pearly or metallic glints. The sunlight, filtering down from high above, touched them and made them flash with sudden random sparks.

"What is it?" the children asked again. Their voices echoed in the stone chamber, sounding as small and shrill as frogs chirping, compared to the towering carved figure.

Sofron found her voice finally.

"I don't know. It could be one of the people who made all this."

"They were giants," Jaya said in awed tones.

"No, they probably weren't that big really. They exaggerated. Humans do the same, on Skandia. In the parks and public buildings they have really big statues of famous people. They're big so you can see them more easily and they look more awesome."

"It looks like the Bone Thing," Ling said. "A giant Bone Thing!"

It was true; the figure resembled Wearra. Sofron hadn't planned to mention that; a ten-meter-tall Bone Thing would not be a comfortable roommate for the night.

"It's a little like him," she said cautiously. "But Wearra only has a few short spines around his neck, not all that in the picture. And his face is a little different. Also, they've made this one with all those different colors in the rocks and those sparkles all over his body. It's not pale, like Wearra."

"Did the Bone Things make it?"

"I don't think they would know how. It must have been someone else, someone who could come up on land and use tools. Maybe they didn't even look like this. I've seen pictures of places on Sol-Terra and other worlds where they made statues of gods. This might be one of those places, a religious place. They make the gods look bigger than humans, fiercer. Sometimes they have things that humans don't have— like that frilly thing around its neck. Probably it does look kind of like them, though."

"Are they still here?" Chilsong asked, looking fearfully around the empty space.

"I don't think so," Sofron said. "I think this place was important to them. If they were still here, they wouldn't have left it all alone like this. It's ours now."

The figure grasped a long, thin object in each hand and stood on a rounded surface of some kind, in a commanding position. To human eyes, the way it overlooked the pool made it look like a guardian, as if the pool were important in some way. But there was no way for Sofron to guess what meaning the makers had truly intended.

She leaned over and looked into the pool. It was deep, and without a direct light she could not see the bottom. But the water was very clear. The only sign of life within was a fringe of growth like fat ferns, all around the edge about a foot down.

Hefting the long stick from the river's edge, Sofron went to the far edge of the flat area and walked all the boundaries. She rattled the stick in every shadow. The chamber seemed to be sealed at the edges. She found no openings in the walls. There might be cracks higher up, where she could not reach. But there were no droppings, bones, or other traces of midnight snacks having been eaten here. Danger could only enter from the water.

She was turning back toward the pool to taste the water when there was a splash that echoed around the walls, and the children started to squeal and exclaim again. All of them scooted back toward her and seized her legs, her hands, any part of her they could reach.

For the second time in three days, Sofron watched in amazement as the black-and-silver bulk of a keto rose from the sea and looked her in the eye. The keto had found its way through the submerged entry and into the pool. Somehow she was certain that it was the same one.

Her first thought was that this answered her question about the cave. If a keto could find its way in, the place was certainly too close for comfort to other things that might lurk in the Deep.

After the first splash as it rose to the surface, the keto moved with surprising gentleness. It heaved its massive body to the edge of the pool and let its jaw slide along the stones. It whistled softly, a sound that to human ears was plaintive.

"Aww, look, Sofi, it's hurt," Ling said. "It sounds as if it's crying."

Ling let go of Sofron's leg and leaned out over the pool, trying to reach the keto's upraised flipper.

"Come back here!" Impeded by the other children, Sofron made an unsuccessful grab for Ling. "For all we know, that noise means 'Hello, lunch!' Get away from the water!"

Ling wriggled to get away from her, looked back over her shoulder, and fell into the pool.

Sofron pushed the others out of the way and made a flying leap into the pool. She landed almost on top of the keto, scraping one arm against its rough hide on the way down. She seized Ling and boosted her out of the pool. Then she turned to face the monster.

The keto opened its mouth. She could see every tooth distinctly, each wet, razor-sharp edge. She could almost count them all. The keto had her pinned against the edge so she could hardly keep afloat; she could neither escape nor fight. She wondered if the keto would bite her head off or merely snap her in half.

It took her arm between its teeth and shook its head.

It doesn't hurt, she thought. *I must be in shock from the fear.* At a great distance, she could hear the children screaming.

Slowly, the keto opened its mouth again and let her go. Numbly, she looked at her arm, expecting to see a bloody ruin. One or two points of blood showed where a needle-sharp tooth had broken the skin, but there was no other damage. The keto closed its mouth with a snap. She could hear the teeth clash together.

The keto turned its head so the huge dark eye looked directly into Sofron's face. "Well?" it seemed to be saying. It had demonstrated that it could hurt her, but it had left her unharmed.

She felt for the edge of the pool, to pull herself out, but the keto turned quickly and nudged her away from the side. The message was clear. "I won't hurt you, but you can't get out."

"It's all right," she called shakily to the children. "It's not going to hurt me. I guess . . . I guess maybe it wants help."

She tried to see how badly the keto was hurt. If this was the same one that had been swarmed by Wearra's people, she was surprised that it had lived. She could see tears in the flipper nearest to her, and in the tall back fin, but they weren't bleeding. They seemed to have been closed by patches of a kind of gel. In fact, the gel coated large areas of unharmed skin as well. It looked slightly bubbly, like frog spawn. She wondered if the gel itself might be the problem. Maybe it was some kind of parasite that had infested the wounds. She let herself float a little closer to examine it.

As she watched, the gel began to ravel out into the water. It looked as if it was separating into tiny bubbles. She was still staring, wondering if it might be a skin secretion, after all, when she realized that some of the bits were drifting from the keto's skin and attaching to her arm. She scrubbed at them with her other hand, but they stuck tight. Then she felt a sharp sting.

Allfather, they must be some new kind of jelly, and they're venomous. I'm stung! She tried to call out a warning, but a swift numbness, more deadly than tanglewood, spread through her before she could form words. A mere croak came from her lips. Dazed, she felt herself sinking. There was a confused noise of alarm in her ears. She knew it was the children. She tried to shout to them to stay away, but it was too late. The cool waterline crept upward over her face. She felt the water rocking as they jumped in to save her. Her last thought as she went under was that finally, she had failed them.

8

Per Langstaff floated, wide awake, thirty meters down. A faint light still penetrated from the sky edge, even at this depth. Per had a memory of sunlight, but since he no longer had eyes, the lack of it did not bother him. The undersea crater where he floated was illuminated by a cool blue glow produced by the bioluminescent organisms that lined the cracks and crannies of the long-cooled lava flow.

Per's perception seemed to him like sight, but he was fairly sure that it was mostly hearing, brought to him by a system of sensitive membranes that perceived changes in pressure and vibration in the Deep around him. It gave him total clarity in every detail, in a sphere extending for quite some distance in all directions. And he perceived specific sound messages from even farther away.

The one thing Per could not see, nor clearly perceive, was his own body. He had seen the god from outside, as it came to assimilate him. It had looked like a room-sized, globular jelly, translucent except for veins and bubbles colored with cells that looked like glowing blue and red beads. In spite of its seeming simplicity, the god was a creature of vast complexity, host to a storehouse of organisms, viruses, and bacteria, and, as well, to a multifaceted consciousness that now included all that was left of Per Langstaff.

Per wasn't sure how long he had been the god. All the normal rhythms that told him of time passing were hidden by his new body. He thought it had been some weeks, but it was hard to guess.

He had a partner in this body: Kitkitdildil, the alien who had been absorbed into the god hundreds of years before. But their communication was still difficult, and Kitkit was unwilling or unable to explain some of the things that Per wanted to know.

Per wasn't sure he could maintain his sanity under these conditions. But then again, he wasn't sure what it meant to be sane, now that he was a jellyfish in an extinct volcano thirty meters underwater. He had allowed this to happen to him. He had chosen this existence over true death because he believed he might be able to help the other humans to survive where he could not. And until he helped them, or until he learned for certain that they were beyond his help, he had to maintain the identity of Per Langstaff—a human, if only in theory.

If he spent too long focusing on his true surroundings, he got dizzy. It was like an unending solo free fall. He turned and turned in the unchanging blue light, weightless and flooded by the inescapable brilliance of 360-degree awareness, all the time. It was falling and never touching down. It was dreaming and never being able to close his eyes. He was an eyeball in the Deep, mirroring the Deep's blue gaze. He was the self-awareness of Typhon's sea, and his own self faded in that light like a scrap of overexposed film.

Kitkit had shown him a place to go when full consciousness became overwhelming. When he narrowed his focus, the memory felt as intense as a direct touch when he'd still had his body. He was in the room where Kitkit's mind lived. He was waist-deep in the warm waters of Kitkit's bathing pool. The blue world of the Deep still surrounded him, in reality. But the picture of the stone walls of this room, rich with ferns and blooming mosses, partially closed it out of his awareness.

Per had seen Kitkit—or at least, the memory image Kitkit still held of himself and was able to share. Kitkitdildil meant "Flower of Rushes," in the language of the long-gone inhabitants of Typhon who had called themselves the Great People—*Kalko'uli* in the language they had once used. Kitkit was tall, even taller than Per, and instead of hair, his head was crested with a line of spines that lay flat when he was calm and rose like a cockscomb when he was alarmed or angry. A ruff of similar spines circled his neck, protecting the delicate gill slits.

Kitkit's fingers were long and webbed, and ended in pointed talons. His wrists and ankles were adorned with swimming fins that folded neatly when he emerged into the air. His skin was smooth and hairless, and marbled with rainbow colors that changed with every mood. His eyes were bigger than a human's, more luminous, with a slit pupil like a lizard's and with transparent membranes that slid over the eye to protect it without closing off sight. His people had once lived in the shallows, in reefed atolls and shore margins. For Kitkit, a shallow pool like this would have been the heart of his home, as the hearth fire would have been for a Skandian.

This was Kitkit's refuge, but it was not Per's. He wondered what place he *would* call home. His shack on the shores of the atoll where he had lived before the storm drove him out into the Deep to meet the god? That had been the equivalent of a refugee's plastic tent. It had never been a place he meant to stay. He thought briefly of the hut he and Sofron had built together on the island where the Skandians had originally landed. Yes, that tiny, sandy room had welcomed him, but it hadn't been the place that mattered. It had been Sofron; her presence had been home to him, and that could never be re-created.

Suddenly it occurred to him that he might be wrong. Maybe he could take refuge in a memory of her that would seem as real as a finger's touch against rough clay.

He could have a virtual Sofron. He could have a simulation that would make him forget the absence of the real person. The pain this thought caused him had no location. He had no heart to be torn apart; he had no eyes to fill with burning tears. The pain had nowhere to exist, but it was unbearable. His self-image smashed its phantom hands against the tiled pool; it ran full-length against the stone walls, but he felt nothing. He needed physical pain to drive away the anguish of his mind, and there was no way to summon it.

In another instant, his need would show him the path to Sofron's image, and his godhood would weave her shape and call it into this room. And then he would never be able to let her go. They would be two shadows in Hades. He would be satisfied in his prison, and he would never get out.

He raged around the peaceful, empty room, grasping for some trigger for an escape. *Kitkit!* he howled. *Where are you?* But there was no answer. As soon as Per stopped thrashing, the water in the pool was completely serene, as if it had never been disturbed. Something about this place was familiar to him; that was why he could find his way to it so easily, though it had been created by an alien.

Any puzzle, no matter how trivial, provided a distraction. Per sat down on the edge of the pool to think. Although he had hurled himself around the room, his simulacrum was not breathing heavily. It did not stink of sweat and rage. He was serene, like the water of the pool.

Water. A pool formed in his mind. It was smaller than this one, too small to sit in. He was looking down into it. But it wasn't at his feet; it was waist-high. That didn't seem right. He looked down at himself. His hands and feet were smaller, paler. His body was stick-straight and thin. The pool lay cupped between green peaks, only as high as his head. As in Kitkit's room, there was a green scent of growing plants, and the air was heavy with moisture.

The tiny trees! All his life he had been haunted by a memory of perfect trees so small he could hold them in his hands. His grief and fear were gone now, lost in wonder. The trees grew here, on the miniature mountainsides. Within his line of vision, he saw full-sized hands, carefully cupping another perfect tree—turning it, tending it. There was the sound of an adult-deep voice murmuring in his ears. The voice frightened him; it was associated with something terrible. Yet he was drawn to it, too; he felt he had been hearing it all his life.

He was no longer in Kitkit's room. He was in another garden, in another time. The miniature landscape spread out around him, but only a few feet away there were other kinds of trees and vines, taller than his head, and beyond them, rows of green leaves sprouting from containers. He looked up. There was no sky, only a blazing streak of light so bright he could not see past it. This was not Typhon, and it was nowhere on Skandia. It was another world, a skyless world, where the walls were metal and there was no sun.

"My name is Rameau," the voice said.

"I know," said the other voice, the small, youthfully pitched one—his own?

"But do you know what it means? It means 'wing' in one of the old Pre-Flight languages. With a name like that, I should be able to fly away. But here, in this ship, my wings have been clipped, just as I clip the branches of this tree."

The voice seemed to find that funny, and it laughed. And Per had a curious doubled sensation. In the memory, he had not known what the laugh meant. Now he was, or had been, a grown man, and he knew why a man might laugh like that at his own predicament.

He allowed the voice to bring back the face that went with it. In the memory, the child-self he had conjured up raised his eyes and saw Rameau.

It was a shock. The face was so familiar, he must have seen this man every day. Yet his conscious mind, in the now, had no recollection of it. This face was all angles. It was a fox face, a cunning face, a face full of secrets. The nose was long and pointed, and so was the chin. The eyes were narrow over high, narrow cheeks, and the eyebrows slanted off the edges like cryptic marks in the margins of a manuscript. The skin was pale, as Per's had been.

Now, in this vision, Rameau held up the tiny tree so it obscured his face. The child saw occasional glimpses of his sharp eyes through the foliage. Rameau's long, skillful hands were in the foreground, pinching a leaf here, bending a branch there, and then twisting flexible, dull wire to hold the branch in its new position.

"Are you hurting the tree?" the high, anxious child voice asked.

Rameau set the tree down. Then he nurtured it, pouring precise sips of purified water and a sprinkle of nutrients. He turned it, assessing the gloss of the leaves.

"No, little Per, I am evoking certain potentials. You see, in a wild place, on some world, for instance, the tree would be subject to constraints: cold, wind, nutrient-poor soil, and so forth. The tree's response to those constraints is a creative one. It finds a way around each obstacle, and in overcoming them, shapes itself into something we perceive as beautiful.

"Here, aboard the *Langstaff*, a stable environment is provided. The tree has all it needs. But then, each tree would be alike, symmetrical, the same. So I must help the tree to achieve its individuality by providing artificial limitations."

"It would be more beautiful if you left it alone," the child said. "You're making it twisted."

"That is one theory," Rameau said absently. He was already occupied with another tree. "We can discuss aesthetics when you're older."

The child watched.

"Why am I here?" he said suddenly.

Rameau put down the tree and turned his full attention to the boy, his eyebrows crooked in wry appreciation.

"That's a large question," he said.

"I mean here, in this room. Why am I with you, not doing station drill with the cohort? Why do I not have a cohort? Why am I a singleton? Are you going to put wires on me?"

"And those are many questions." Rameau walked through the mountains, waist-high on him as if he were a giant, to reach the boy's side. His hand brushed the boy's short-shaved hair, and the boy shivered. He would have liked to duck away, but he could not.

"You are perceptive," Rameau said. "You were designed that way. Others were designed for other purposes. Their fate is not yours."

In the watching mind of the adult Per, ghosts rose. He had seen the others who inhabited this ship. The Original Man cohorts wore the human form. The transhumans who served them had been built upon that scaffolding but had become far other. They had walked his nightmares as monstrous shapes whose origins he was not permitted to remember. The nightmare potential lived within him, too. He did not want to call it out, with wires or any other method.

Rameau sank to one knee so he could look into the boy's face.

"I shall continue to evoke your potentials," he said. "But I will not hurt you. There will be no wires. And remember this:

you are not like the trees. My work with you is for your survival, not for my amusement."

But there was hurt. There were wires, Per screamed. The figures in his vision could not hear him. They wavered and disappeared.

He was in another sunless room, but the walls this time were painted a precisely chosen shade of pink to calm the mind, and the light was soft and sunlight-proportional. It was a room designed to make him calm, but he was screaming. There were delicate wires netting his head. They evoked memories; he saw things he didn't want to see, and when he saw, the treacherous wires, delicate and venomous as a swarm of insects, stung his mind until he howled with pain. He wanted to brush them violently away, but he was immobilized.

"This discomfort is very temporary," the other voice said. It was not Rameau's voice. This was not Rameau's world. "As soon as the installation is complete, it will cease to exist. Please try not to resist the installation. We are sorry to cause you discomfort, but it is for your own protection and well-being. The discomfort will cease. The disturbing memories will cease. And by tomorrow none of this will have happened."

The voice assuaged its own discomfort, but Per still screamed. The pain was always with him.

But when he returned to the present, the pain was gone. He looked around, and he was back in Kitkit's room. The water was calm and serene. There was no pain. He thought deliberately of Rameau's face. He said his own name. Langstaff. The Langstaff. *There was a ship, a jumpship, called the* Langstaff. *I journeyed on it. I knew a man named Rameau. He worked for the Original Man jumpfighters, the destroyers of worlds. And someone installed this pain in my mind so I could never have these thoughts again.*

But the pain had gone. He had lost the body that recognized those commands. He was not Per Langstaff anymore, but he was free at last to remember that he had been that boy. He looked up.

Kitkitdildil was there.

9

Per had wanted him before, and now he did *not* want him. But there was no way to banish him.

"Where were you?" he said.

"I thought of other things," Kitkit said. "Now intense activity at this site recalls my attention."

He lowered himself into the pool. In Per's perception, the temperature rose several degrees.

"Ah. Comfort," Kitkit said. Kitkit's envisioned body, here, expressed thought in alien sounds—the sounds a lizard's mouth might make—and in changing skin colors, and in perfumes of mood infiltrated into the water. In reality, neurons exchanged chemicals in the god's ganglia. But Per had learned to let the perceptions come to him as a language he could recognize.

"It took you long enough," Per said.

Kitkit allowed his colors to express surprise. "Your perception is distorted, possibly. Duration is not the same within our shared consciousness. I am always here, as you are. How could I be absent for a long time? But memory is confusing. It gives an experience of false duration. Were you involved in a disturbing memory?"

"A memory I never knew I had," Per said.

Kitkit nodded, allowing the tall spines of his ruff to move gently.

"I spent a long time of subjective duration ordering my memories. The first period of my godhood was difficult. I had no one to explain these things to me. All that was in my mind still lived in the mind of god. As myself, as Kitkitdildil of the

73

Kalko'uli, the Great People, I was not free of my mind. Only some parts came to my call. I do not know how it is for your kind."

"The same for us," Per said. "No one has complete access to all memories. Most of our students of the mind think it is not possible. It would madden us."

He had hesitated for a split second on the word "mad." There was not always a word in the language of the Kalko'uli that matched what he wanted to say. But the word had been uttered, so it must be a concept Kitkit could understand.

"Yes. But here, in the mind of the god, all is accessible and may be triggered with the appropriate key. At first I constantly was washed away by knowledge that, as you say, I did not know I had. All thought would cease as memory waves swept past me. But one learns to sort and to store, so that memory comes when willed to come. You will have times of loss, when you feel subjectively that you have gone elsewhere, when you do not perceive yourself as the god. But soon you will be first elder in your own mind and rule it in good order. Then we truly can be partners."

"I don't want to be here that long," Per said.

Kitkit registered surprise. "We have no choice," he said. "I thought you understood that."

"No, I don't understand that. And I don't see how you can think it. Look, if you have the information on the human body downloaded and stored to the point where you can manipulate human genes, why can't you reverse-engineer it—build it backward? Oh, you know what I mean—and make a new body? I admit it could be a challenge, but we've got nothing but time. I'm surprised that you haven't tried it before, in all the years you've been here."

Kitkit's colors darkened, and the inner lids slid shut over his eyes.

"I was taken into the god to serve my people. I never tried to shape another form because I could not have served in that form. I would have been mortal and limited. I could not have controlled the god from a mortal form."

Per sensed something that he could not quite grasp. He

tried to trigger a clear opening to the data, but he was inexperienced and could not make the god's consciousness open that pathway. Kitkit withdrew in some subtle fashion. Yet Per felt certain that Kitkit could have answered his question if he had wanted to.

"There is a possibility," Kitkit admitted. Because of the swiftness of communication within the god, Per saw it happening at the same time.

He saw the god spinning out a globe of its substance. The globe doubled within itself like a blastocyst so that it contained an inner and outer surface. Multihued cells poured into it from the parent body. Slowly, it detached until it held its own form, connected to the god's body only by a thin strand of clear jelly through which the red and blue sparklets danced.

"Bekkila," Kitkit said—or that was how Per heard him. "It's for translation and recording. For translation, it holds a language. For recording, just cells ready for patterning. We used to make them for the Round People, to talk, or for the Bright Teeth to carry."

The little globe spun and expanded, like a blob of molten glass on the end of the glassblower's rod, and thrust out a fringe of tentacles. It danced, and translucent colors showed on its surface, like an oil slick.

"When it is full of memories, we allow it to rejoin," Kitkit said.

Abruptly, the globe fell inward on itself like a popped bubble, and was sucked back into the parent body.

"With this you can exchange thoughts with the others," Kitkit said.

"I don't want to exchange thoughts," Per said. "I want out. I want to return to the human world."

A mild irony pervaded the water, stinging yet soothing, like astringent balm poured on a cut.

"This is not a human world," Kitkit said. "It was the world of the Kalko'uli . . . for a time. And it was our world only because we fought for it and made great sacrifices. Now your humans have bodies that can live here, but that is only the beginning. Many dangers will not let them live. If you rejoined them in a mortal body, you would die with them. It is brave, but stupid. If you stay here, your fight will have purpose."

"My fight? Who am I supposed to be fighting? I am a scientist, not a warrior."

The water laughed around him, rippling before it regained its calm.

"I was reverse side," Kitkit said. "Warrior, not scientist. That was in the long-ago. When I was Clan of Fire."

Kitkit reached out, and the pool spiraled around Per. He was carried with it, as with a tide.

Clan of Fire. He was sharing Kitkit's vision now. He was walking through the fire. No, he was not; but tall fires burned head-high on either side. His skin prickled with heat. Everyone who entered the gate of the Clan of Fire had to pass between the fires that burned night and day in a reckless, wasteful show of power. The new-changed who tended the fires suffered in the heat; their tender skins blistered and toughened. Fire was the source of the clan's pride and wealth. No other clan could master it as they had.

Within the gate, one passed through the sprawling, boastful quarters of the warriors of the clan. Their luxury and extent showed the world that the Clan of Fire could sustain many sleek, bold fighters who had no need to labor or to instruct their young. Beyond the warrior quarters lay protective and beautiful gardens, and beyond that the bustling compounds of the sustaining families who worked and nurtured hatchlings in pleasant, ordinary comfort. Within the City of Fire, at its very core, stood the enclosed towers of the scholars, with their deep wells opening to the sea, with their secret passages piercing to the hidden fire.

"City of Fire, house of my ancestors, glory of the world." Per felt his lips moving in speech, and was startled. Then he realized that he shared the body of Kitkitdildil's memory, and it was the Kalko'ul who spoke.

Per wanted to go toward the towers. He could almost taste their scent of fire and hot metal. But Kitkit's decision ruled. Per found himself outside the city again. Broad marshlands stretched all around them, moonslight glittering in broken patterns where open water showed amid reed, thickets, and sedgy islands. Far off, at the edge of the marsh, Per could see the dark line of the sea, rising and falling against the star-hazed sky. They stood on a stone causeway, smoothed to feel good against sensitive bare feet, and continually wetted by the rippling marsh waters.

Far to the southeast, Per's eye was caught by twinkling lights that moved in the sky, descending slowly in sweeping arcs. As they neared the ground, his view was obstructed, and he could no longer see them.

"What's that?" he said. His voice sounded strange. The words were full of hisses and clicks. They were not his words, not a human language, yet he understood them. He put his fingers to his lips; they were not his fingers. They were the long, webbed, madder-and-saffron fingers of the Great People. He took a step and felt his crest sway with the motion.

"This is my memory," Kitkit said. "I have no memory for an alien in the City of Towers. You must wear the form of the Clan of Fire here."

Per grimaced, trying to get used to the feel of his strange face.

"What are the lights in the sky over there?" he repeated.

"Skyfins," Kitkit said. "The young scholars build them for the warrior children. They ride the air as the waveslips ride the waves. They are toys, but the clan chiefs use them to send messages and to gather weather news. They built a smooth field there, beyond the towers and gardens, for them to land on."

Per felt a surge of excitement. These people were on the verge of crossing from a Pre-Flight culture into the explosive growth phase of the Flight Era.

Pre-Flight, Flight Era, Planetary, Total Solar, Pre-Jump Migratory, and finally the transformative stage of Jump itself—those were the stages of civilization as he had learned them on Skandia. The Great People stood at the very beginning. He envied them the thrilling discoveries that lay ahead for them to seize. Then he remembered. In real time, this race had ended. All they had left behind were the broken toys of a people that had died in childhood.

"Are they powered?" he asked. He could not hear engines, but the wind was against him.

"That is a question for the scholars," Kitkit said. The words had the pat ring of a phrase that had been repeated often. "The Clan of Fire does not discuss scholars' business with outsiders."

He stopped abruptly and made a chittering sound, accompanied by rapid alternation of colors in his head and neck. Per realized that Kitkit was laughing.

Just as suddenly, Kitkit's colors became somber again.

"Regret mistake," he said—a pro forma apology. "When I visit memories, I sometimes forget that the Clan of Fire is no more, and all this city fallen. To keep from madness, I must think as if they still live and the city yet holds my vows."

"These vows," Per said. "What were they exactly?"

Kitkit's crest rose ominously. Per had given offense again.

"We of the Clan of Fire do not discuss—" he began.

"Stop, stop," Per said. "I'm not interested in the secret words or whatever. That isn't what I meant to ask. I meant, what were the duties you performed for the Clan of Fire? What was your job? I was a marine biologist for the Skandian commonality on Typhon; that was my job. What was yours?"

Per noticed in passing that the words had come out meaning something more like "I was a scholar of great-life-in-the-Deep, for the Clan of Skandia on Typhon."

Kitkit's spines flattened down on his neck. "Regret mistake," he said again. "My task was one of danger and opportunity. I was the hand outstretched between Tower and Gate. Half scholar, half warrior, as the Great People live half in Deep and half in Dry."

Security liaison for the Department of Research, Per translated to himself. Now he understood what kind of person he might be dealing with. Such a liaison had to be aggressive, tough, even ruthless perhaps; yet wily, a politician, too. And he would be smart enough to have at least an overview of the scientists' concerns, and the possible implications of their work. Kitkit could be a dominating ally, a formidable opponent. Yet, the hand outstretched would be always at the periphery. It was doubtful that he would have the expertise or the subtlety of mind to fully understand the precise nature of the science he protected. That might be Per's only advantage.

"You study the greatlife," Kitkit said. "I will show you how our life began."

Instantly, Per found himself knee-deep in the distant marshes. It was still night, but greatmoon blazed high in the sky, like a pale silver sun, and lessermoon moved swiftly, low on the horizon, so the shadows changed with it. Wild spring scents of churned silt and flowering rushes filled the air. Other, more intoxicating scents breathed from the skins of his clan members as they danced in ever-widening spirals. They splashed and shouted as they moved into deepening water, and the music grew wilder and more ragged.

Per was caught in the spell of those remembered motes. He longed to dance, to spin, to stamp, to inhale damp air thick with enticing scents. He would dance until the water reached his flanks, until he could plunge in and slide along, belly pressed to the cool delicious mud. He would churn out his own dancing circle in the marsh, and trill his song there until they came to him, his clan members with their slick skins burning with loveliness.

Then all his limbs would be stretched out in the mock battle, the sleek struggle, to drag them to his own circle or be overcome and pulled to their strongholds, victory or defeat equally desirable. Oh, the whirl of skin motes, the dance of light on water . . .

He realized that he was swaying with knees half bent, his gills engorged, his neck frills raised in full display mode.

"You are not of our clan," Kitkit muttered.

The scene changed again. Summer had dried the marshes, and he stood high and dry on crumbling sandy soil. The mature, wiry reeds rattled together, head-high.

Per was stunned by the shock of being snatched from the spring scene so abruptly. He felt foolish and embarrassed.

Evidently Kitkit had decided not to involve him in the complete mating rituals of the Great People.

Ahead of him, the deepest part of the pool still held water, and something shimmered and moved there. A sand-walled nest held a cache of gelatinous globes about the size of his own head. The silver lances of moonslight woke a golden shimmer in them. The water was not rocking them; they moved of their own accord. They were eggs, he realized, and they were hatching. These must be the result of the joyous dancing in the marshes.

The eggs rocked more vigorously, and then the glimmering surface of the first one tore, releasing a lizard-shaped creature whose wet skin seemed made of opal. Per was puzzled; he had assumed the hatchling would be a baby Kalko'ul, but this had no relation to the biped adults he had seen.

He wanted to turn and ask Kitkit, but something interrupted their contact. He felt a brushing, a tingling of sensation, like wire against his skin. He thought he caught a wisp of keto song, on the very edge of its range, audible only because of its extreme distress. He stretched all his senses toward it and found himself back in the quiet room of ferns and water so suddenly that it gave him vertigo. There was still a ringing in his head. What was it?

"Voices of the Bright Teeth." Kitkit answered the unspoken question. "Your messenger is in distress!"

Per focused. Somewhere, membranes tightened, sensitive to every vibration. Chemical messages sent to useful fish species in the area triggered them to amplify their own perceptions and repeat them to the god. From all sides, the keto song was received and synchronized.

He perceived bright pinpoints and darker blurs. They swam together, assembling an image in his mind, as a reflection re-forms in trembling water. He saw Sofron's face. Her eyes closed, and her face faded into shadow as if it sank deeper into the water.

The blessing/The twisting
She receives/It seizes her

She sleeps in peace/She dreams in pain
Awaits what waking . . . what waking?
As the god ordered
I have obeyed.

The keto's song held multiple layers of meaning. The darker counterpoint horrified Per.

"What have you done to her? Why didn't you stay with her and guard her?"

The time delay would have seemed long even if he had been using a radio. To a god, with his swift altered perception, it seemed a long age of anguish.

"The Bright Teeth are swift but not reliable," Kitkit said. "They like you because you swam with them and your other body bore their scent, so they try to help you. In the old days, the scholars made instruments to imitate their song. Some few warriors whose music pleased them were allowed to swim with them. But their understanding is not like ours. They get bored and swim away. It's all play to them. Even death is only part of the game."

Kitkit sounded wistful, but in his agitation, Per could hardly listen. He wanted Kitkit to be still so he could focus all his perception on the first hint of response from the messenger.

The keto's song was scornful when it came.

Go/Come
Guard/Report
Protect from all Typhon/Overpower all through Typhon's god
Slashed by White Ones I am/Wounded in mind by god's anger
The god has two heads
I have but one
O god, decide which song you order sung.

"What is he saying?" Per said. " 'Overpower all . . .'" He struggled briefly; then he knew what Kitkit knew. "I sent the keto to find her. You sent godbits with the keto. To change her. And now . . . 'She dreams' . . . In hell's name, she has the changing sickness! Oh Allfather, and she's alone. What have you done?"

Rage at the alien tore through him like the jagged fire of a lightning bolt. It was himself he was tearing apart. The room disintegrated around him. The water boiled. Black-and-red lumps of molten fire engulfed him. Kitkit filled all his senses with howling, but he would not listen. The pain in his mind was worse than anything the Skandians had ever made him feel.

When consciousness came back, he remembered the moment when everything had gone dark. He was immobilized by something soft and yielding. The pool rocked him gently.

"We cannot hate each other," Kitkit whispered. "It destroys us. Tell us our mistake but hate us not unless you want to die. Please."

Per felt sore everywhere, as if he had been beaten. But when he looked at his own simulated body and Kitkit's, they were both untouched.

"The female is of your clan," Kitkit said. "An elder? Of so great importance?"

"She was my . . . mate," Per said. Kitkit only looked puzzled, and Per knew why. He could see the flowering marshes in the alien's mind. There were so many mates, every spring. How could one have such importance?

Then Kitkit's eyes glowed with fresh color. "She was your ally. Now I understand."

"You understand, but I don't."

"Among one's cohort, there are always some who have greater affinity," Kitkit said. "One treasures these bonds, for they have influence through life. Sometimes there is one with whom the bond is greatest. One pledges support, nurturing for each other's hatchlings. There is friendship, confidence. Alliances change with shifting interests, but the life-ally never changes. Sometimes that brings great tragedy, but still we envy those who find the ally."

The water darkened around them as if Kitkit called to mind

such tragedy, but Per was distracted before he could pursue that feeling.

The keto sent back a final verse, or a parting shot.

Deserted by gods and humans/
The not-now-human dreams.
Only the White One
Is faithful (a mother swimming by her young)
Is patient (a hunter watching the prey's hiding place)
Who will suckle?
White nourishment/milk
Red nourishment/blood.

Kitkit felt the turbulence building in Per again and communicated hastily.

"I don't know what he means! Yes, he says before there is a White One swimming alone. But they never go alone; they cannot. It must be sick or dying. There can be no threat. He says this to play with us because I chide his leaving.

"Listen. I see my mistake now. I thought her your clan only, or I would never have added to your order without full assurance you agreed. Now I have changed your ally, and this causes much turbulence within; I know. But seek calm; you wished to save her, and we have saved her. This was the only way. Unchanged in her body, she would die like the others. How could we bring her here to us, unchanged? Not possible! You think, you search our mind, and you will see."

Kitkit was silent then, allowing Per to think. The simulated cocoon that held Per's remembered body gradually loosened, supporting but no longer immobilizing him. The water was soft and fragrant. Kitkit let a succession of musical tones wander across the pool like a cool breeze.

He's trying to butter me up. He's hiding something, Per thought. Then he wondered how much of his thought was transparent to Kitkit. The Kalko'ul had every advantage over him in this form. Kitkit had lived in the god for so long and was entrenched in all its systems.

But that does not distress me, Per thought. *I find myself very calm. I shall just go to my special place for a minute to think about my ally in peace.*

He was back in the garden with metal walls. Rameau wasn't there. Now that it was quiet, Per could hear a deep, constant sound in the walls, like an immense heartbeat. The garden was inside something.

It's inside the Langstaff. *It's a garden in a ship, in the Deep, in my mind, in the god, in another Deep. Always a world within a world, and all worlds within a great darkness through which we fall.*

And in all those worlds, Sofron's body and Per's will never touch again.

The thought came stealing back again. *You could touch. You could remake her, here, and she would be just as alive as you are now. You are only a ghost anyway. Why not accept the ghost of love?*

No! His rejection swelled to fill the walls of this metal world. *The Skandians tried to transform my mind, and I refused. My fellow humans couldn't do it to me, and I'm not going to take it from a jellyfish. They can change my body, but they can't change me. Sofron and I will walk again in a real garden beneath a real sky.*

It was an impossible goal. Once he had vowed himself to reach it, he felt truly calm, and for the first time in the god's body, he felt truly alive.

He thought about the moment when he had blacked out. Kitkit had told him that the god never slept.

He said that we had everything in common. But he has some way to hide things from my mind. That means that I can hide from him, too. The first step is to find out how.

He pressed that thought very small and curled it among the branches of the smallest tree. Perhaps Kitkit would not think of looking there. Then he returned to Kitkit's pool.

"Thank you; I am calmer now. I regret the disturbance, and I see that we have done what must be. Let us find news of the other humans."

Kitkit led him to that information eagerly.

"The Bright Teeth say the humans are no longer in the Dry.

They are on the Deep yet not of the Deep. Therefore the Bright Teeth swim with them no longer."

He spread his hands apologetically. "I told you the Bright Teeth could not always be counted on. They are twisters of words."

Per examined the fragmentary images that had come in from the ketos by the island.

"I think they are on a raft. They must be carrying possessions they don't want to lose. The Teeth would not understand that."

He extrapolated their course.

"They are coming to the Big Dry, the place where Sofron was seen. Send to the Bright Teeth that they must follow. It is not right for a lone White Killer to dance more faithfully than all the Teeth together. The Teeth must herd the humans back into one pod."

The song went out into the Deep; it was flavored with grace and daring, with the joy of the impossible, and the Bright Teeth leapt high from the water and turned to follow it.

White nourishment (milk)
Red nourishment (blood)
Bright nourishment (song) heals all.

❧❧10❧❧❧❧❧

The water closed over Sofron's head. She felt the splashes, saw the silver bubbles rise as the children jumped in, too. She couldn't move a hand to save herself or them. The venom had paralyzed her.

A cloud of bubbles moved slowly across her face, but the bubbles were substantial, clinging. They covered her mouth and nose. She knew she was drowning. But she felt a strange euphoria; freedom from pain, freedom from action. Deep inside there was a great sadness and rebellion, but it was drowned too deep to rise. More jelly bubbles gathered around her and covered her with their soft, clinging touch.

The water rocked a little now, but the children floated quietly, arms and legs dangling, faces staring calmly down, their floating hair and eyelashes beaded with silver. Bubbles gathered around their faces, at first obscuring them, then smoothing out into a glimmering halo that enclosed their heads, that crept downward over their bodies.

How can I still be seeing this? Sofron thought. She couldn't even close her eyes.

The pool darkened around her. She could hear a deep sound, like a massive heartbeat, sweeping rhythmically through the water. She couldn't remember where she was. She thought of the pine trees on the mountains around Whiteford on Skandia, and the sound of the wind sweeping through them. Something massive and mountain-dark rose slowly beneath her, singing. The round silver moons with children's faces bobbed gently in its wake, carried down, down until they vanished and the darkness was complete.

* * *

For some reason, she thought she had been sick for a long time. There had been pain and burning, a bad taste in her mouth, and bright flashes behind her eyes, the kind that only come with the worst kind of fever. But she felt luxuriously comfortable now. For the first time in ages, everything was all right.

She thought there had been many faces looking at her. She remembered that there had been something frightening about them. They had been so pale. She felt the first twinges of anxiety as she tried to move, and found she couldn't. Something confined her. And it was dark. *Of course,* she thought vaguely. *I must be tangled up in the sheets.* She struggled, and her arms came free. There was a tearing sensation as if she had ripped cloth away. She opened her eyes, but it was still dark. She opened her eyes again. *I'm dreaming I have two sets of eyelids.*

But her eyes were open, and it was still dark. Just above her head there was a line of irregularly shaped glowing objects. She thrust out a hand toward it, lost her equilibrium and thought she would fall. But she was floating. She grabbed for the light and shot upward.

I'm in the water! Where are the children? Panic gripped her throat. She tried to scream, and nothing came out but a choking gurgle. Her head broke the surface, and she was gasping and shouting in a place that echoed. One flailing hand struck something solid. She dragged herself out of the water, scraping herself painfully on a rocky surface.

The sense of well-being vanished.

She called their names, but there was no answer. Her voice sounded hoarse and alien as it reverberated in the stone chamber. Was this even the same place? Or had she drifted while she was unconscious and surfaced elsewhere? She was completely disoriented.

Suddenly it occurred to her that if she had survived her immersion, the children might have lived through it, as well. She threw herself back into the water and groped frantically around the edges of the pool. Once she thought she touched a cold hand, but it was only a finger of the luminescent fronds that edged the pool. Repeatedly she rose for air and dove again, working her way around the pool and finding nothing. She had not yet searched the bottom, in the center. She hung on the pool's edge, panting, trying to fill her lungs deeply. Then she dove, sweeping her arms before her to find the bottom.

Nothing met her groping fingertips. She forced herself deeper, fighting off the need to breathe. Suddenly her air hunger was overwhelming. She kicked for the surface, expecting her head to burst through at any moment. But there was no surface. She didn't know which way was up. She saw a faint glow ahead of her and stroked toward it. There must be a way out. Her lungs were bursting. The need for air twisted wildly within her.

Her flailing arms crashed painfully against something hard. Then the water, too, was tossing and churning, tumbling her about like a stick. She could no longer see the faint glow of light. Sparks burst behind her eyes. She could no longer control the urge to breathe. The last of her air burst out in a cloud of bubbles, and she gasped, knowing this was death.

As if in a dream, the water she inhaled was cool and pleasant. There was a momentary spasm, a stinging sensation in her lungs. Then welcome oxygen flooded into her blood. Her eyes opened. She was underwater, but she could see. A dim blue glow illuminated the black bulk of rocks all around her. She could feel the turbulence that threatened to fling her against them. Now that she was back in control, she evaded the obstacles with an agility that surprised her. She was out in open water again, with nothing to see but pale shafts of light filtering through the twilit water. She knew where up was— toward the light. After that first breath, she had not taken another. Yet she felt alert and calm.

Am I dead? But she could feel her heart pounding. *Funny kind of death, that stops your breath but lets your heart go on beating.*

Besides, her arm and side hurt where they had been bashed against the rocks. *Once the body is dead, it stops hurting, right?*

Panic threatened to overwhelm her again. She had to get

out of this shifting, shadowy realm and find firm ground somewhere. She followed the light upward. Finally her head broke through the glimmering surface. She was in the ocean, tossed gently up and down by the swell beyond the breakers. Now, for the first time since inhaling water, she choked and coughed, and water ran down her chin. She was breathing air again. But she didn't want to stop and think about that now. She swam hard for the beach, and at last felt firm sand under her feet and staggered up onto dry land.

As far as she could tell, it was the same familiar beach. She thought she could see the curve where the river emerged, and even the line of rocks where she and the children had once built their shelter. It seemed like a lifetime in the past. She raised her hand to wipe the streaming water off her face, to see better.

It wasn't her hand. She heard her own cry of shock—a strange, whistling yelp. It took her a minute to realize that it was her voice, and not some animal. She held the hand in front of her and looked again. It was connected to an arm, and the arm connected to the body that was connected to her face. But none of these parts were anything she had ever seen before.

The hand was longer and thinner than her own hand, and the fingers were tipped with short, sharp talons. Between the fingers, webs tightened when she spread them. The skin was pale and moist, and bruiselike blotches patterned it. They seemed to be moving under the skin's surface, but she put that down to the vagaries of moonlight.

The same kind of blotches covered all her skin. Maybe they were bruises. Maybe she had hurt herself on the rocks. But when she touched them, there was no pain. There was a clear distinction between the odd, colored spots and the obvious scrapes where she had hit the rocks.

She pressed her hand to her throat to make sure her heart was really beating. Her throat wasn't smooth; there were rubbery, closed slits beneath her ears on each side. Poking a finger into them hurt, like a too-harsh probe of human mouth or nose.

Gills, she classified them automatically.

There was no hair on her head, but there was a mobile, cartilaginous crest of spiny growths. She could see it moving around the head of her shadow.

She could see everything very clearly. Lessermoon had set, but greatmoon still stood high in the sky. And it was full. It had only been in half phase when she and the children had entered the river. That meant that—somehow—two weeks had passed, and she had no memory of anything that might have filled them.

She called the children's names once more, but without hope. Her voice cracked. It didn't even sound like her voice. At that moment she almost despaired.

She thought of Per, his face the talisman she had clung to for so long. But in her mind, his expression wasn't pitying or horrified or even sad. He seemed more pleased with her than anything else.

Interesting! he said, as she had heard him say so many times as they worked together.

Oh, sure, she thought. *And I thought things couldn't get worse.*

But she felt better. She still lived, after all, and she still had a purpose: find the children. She had the same tools she'd always had: her mind, her fingers, the world around her. She had to keep going.

She took a deep breath. A whole array of scents sprang into her awareness. The world had more flavors when perceived through her new senses—and not all of them were pleasant. She turned toward the dark, familiar smell that demanded her attention.

It took her a minute to see the pale figure crouched amid shadowed rocks. A White One was watching her. The breeze carried his bitter, frightening scent her way.

Then he spoke to her.

"Wearra," he whispered.

Before, that had always meant that he wanted to open a conversation. She did not know what it meant now. It could be a different White One entirely—maybe they all looked the same and maybe this wasn't a name, but just a noise they made. Sofron desperately wanted to talk to him. Cautiously, she moved toward him, trying not to trip over her own webbed feet.

The White One tensed and hissed as she approached. Suddenly she realized that he could not tell who she was, either. Nothing about her was the same. She wondered what had happened to Wearra's gift, the bone knife. She searched about her waist and found it still secured by its cord. The handmade bark string was matted and sticky, but still in place.

Carefully, trying to avoid any hostile-seeming moves, she loosened the knife from its loop and held it out on flat palms.

"Sofron," she said. "See? It's the same one you gave me."

She winced at the sound of her own voice. That might have been a mistake, she thought. There was no way the White One could recognize her speech now. Something had happened to her vocal cords, and the words came out with a harsh, whistling overtone. In fact, she sounded like the White One.

The White One looked at the knife. His dark eye slits widened briefly, then narrowed, and Sofron could not tell what that meant. Then, hesitantly, he gestured. Sofron recognized the signs. They were the same ones she had often used to Wearra when her scavenging expeditions had come up empty. "Regret I have nothing to exchange."

"No, no." Sofron hastily signed a negative. "Not exchange objects." She hesitated. They had no shared sign for "information"—or for most other abstractions.

"Exchange talk," she signed. Wearra might have been watching what had happened to her. He might have seen the children.

The White One shuffled closer, without rising from his crouched position. Sofron held her ground, but warily. The White One did not appear to be armed, but she wondered if even the long knife would be a match for his teeth and claws.

He stretched out one hand toward her, and she clenched one hand on the haft of the knife. But he stopped short of touching. Instead, he began to sign again. He rolled an invisible ball, marble-sized, between thumb and forefinger. Then he squeezed it down. *"Tiny, tiny."* He placed many of them in the air around his head. Then his fingers made swimming motions. The tiny invisible balls swam toward his face, and he mimed something spreading over and around him, an envelope that covered head and torso.

Then he returned to signs that Sofron recognized from her last conversation with Wearra.

"Tiny balls kill the people like me," he signed. "Kill, kill."

It must be Wearra, Sofron thought. He's using the same signs. He must have seen the little jelly bubbles.

But something had changed about him, if it was Wearra. Sofron had always had the impression before that the White One considered himself far superior. He had intimidated her, intruded himself into her space. Now he remained in a crouched position, and he seemed almost afraid to come too close.

"You—not," he signed. "Not kill. I saw."

Again he stretched out an arm. The fingers of his other hand mimed dots on his own pale skin. Then, very slowly— Sofron felt convinced he was afraid, she could almost taste the fear—he brushed his taloned fingers against the colors of her skin.

Haaaaah. A long breath of relief, of awe perhaps, exhaled from his parted lips. His flat nostrils worked as if he plucked some message from the air.

His fingers felt cold and leathery against her wrist. She could smell the sour, mingled chemical and organic scent that always signaled his presence, but now it seemed to get inside her and coat her mouth and throat, as if his touch were translated into taste and smell.

He said a clicking, rasping word. Then he briefly withdrew his touch to sign again.

"You make good—" he signed, as he had sometimes when Sofron and the children found a particularly fine artifact to trade. Fingers dabbed at his thin lips, a new sign: "—taste."

You taste good, she translated.

"Huh!" She jumped back. But he wasn't trying to eat her. By "taste," he seemed to mean something other than chewing and swallowing. He simply shuffled forward until he was close enough to touch her skin again.

She allowed it. Anything to put him in a good humor.

"You saw the bubbles come to me?" she signed.

He assented silently. He signed something very big and fierce going through the water.

"Big, toothy swimmers brought them."

"Big-toothy" must mean the ketos, she thought.

"Children," she signed. If this was Wearra, she knew that he would understand that sign. "Where?" She looked all around, miming her quest, making sure he would understand.

"Bubbles," he signed, again moving his hands across his face, showing someone enclosed by an envelope.

"Yes, bubbles," she responded. "But *where*?"

Sofron felt the spines around her neck rising. That must be a reaction to fear or threat, she thought. She certainly was fearful. What had the ketos done with those fragile, sleeping bubbles? She could see the teeth piercing, the wicked glee as the ketos bit this tender fruit to the red rind. Her hands trembled as she signed. "Ketos eat?"

The White One's spines rattled briefly; Sofron thought he looked startled.

"No. Ketos eat me. Ketos not eat bubble children."

Sofron dared to clutch at the White One's wrist in her urgency.

Releasing him, she signed, "Then, where did bubble children go? You take me there!"

Wearra's eye slits narrowed to thread size, and he pulled his hand away. He hissed faintly as he signed.

"No. I not go there. I die there."

Sofron had a new idea. If he would not help her, maybe there were others of his kind who could.

"Take me to see people like you," she demanded.

Wearra moved back even farther, shaking his spines. His mouth stretched until she could see his teeth. He signed the same thing he had when he warned her away from their sheltering rock.

"No. No. People like me will kill the people like you."

He was saying the same thing—almost. The first time, on the rock, he had pointed to the children all around when he signed "people like you." This time his hand reached high, to show full-sized beings. Sofron had to get clarification.

"Kill children?" she signed.

"Not—kill—bubble—children," Wearra signed slowly, as if he thought she was pretty dim. "Kill like you!" He was still crouching, but his long, lean arm reached up, clearly designating a height that matched her own.

" 'People like me'? Where?" Sofron signed urgently.

Wearra stretched up to his full, imposing height again, and looked out to sea. Through parting clouds, greatmoon poured a wash of dazzling silver over the waves. Wearra hissed in dislike.

"I go," he signed. Before she could stop him, he had crossed the beach and vanished into the water. She ran to the water's edge, intending to follow, but by the time she got there, every trace of his passing had vanished.

She trembled with exhaustion and fear. Where was the place where Wearra could not go, the place where the children had been taken? Had Wearra seen the people like her? Were they somewhere out there, on the ocean? She had not thought to ask him if he meant people who were like her as she had been, or people who were like her *now*. If they looked as she did now, they could not be human. It made no sense. She had to have more information, but she had no idea how to find Wearra again. She could only hope that whatever had lured him to her would bring him back.

"I'll begin looking in the morning," she whispered, as if the children could still hear her. "When it gets light. Don't worry; I'll find you." Her legs failed her, and she collapsed hard on the wet sand. It wasn't a very safe place to rest, she knew. But she didn't know anymore where safety might be found.

In the morning, she found herself parched, starving, irritable, with small sand crabs already nibbling at her extremities. Her situation did not seem more hopeful by daylight. It seemed worse. The Deep looked as flat and empty as a mirror; the Dry seemed busy with mindless life-forms filling their bellies.

Entering the water, she discovered that she could feed her hunger with living fish. She was startled by how easy they were to catch, thanks to her new body. She learned that the Deep would assuage her thirst. But as far as she hunted, as deep as she dared to dive, she found no signs of her missing children. Not a taste, not a fragment to mark their passage.

Despair would be realistic at this point, she thought, looking out over the immensity of the Deep.

But she didn't give up. Instead, she turned inland. She cut reed bundles and made a small, unsteady raft that allowed her to paddle laboriously upstream until she regained the area with the stone banks where she had last seen the children. She was unhappy, but not surprised, to find that her original raft had disappeared. She reentered the cavern of the pool. The huge carved figure still stared arrogantly down with its glittering eyes. There was no trace of the children, no hint of intruders in the pool.

Every day, she hunted along the reef, then scouted a new area of the coastline. She accumulated cuts and scratches, as well as a collection of brightsnakes. They had rejected her in her human form, but now found her acceptable. They seemed to protect her against the worst of the insects, and they eased the sting of envenomed plants. She wasn't sure how they lived, but she suspected that they somehow fed on the slick exudate that helped keep her skin moist.

Every night, she returned to the beach, hoping that Wearra might come back. That was really her only hope. She searched the night for him feverishly. He knew where the children had gone. He knew they were still alive. Their lives now depended on her finding the White One again.

To the bone knife dangling at her belt, she added a peeled stick on which she notched the days and the moon phases. She no longer trusted herself to remember them without help. Eight days from her reawakening, by that count, there came a day when she heard voices in the forest.

≪11≫≫≫≫

Each day, Dilani played her rough music to the blank face of the Deep, but the ketos did not show themselves. She would have stayed up all night, still trying to lure them with her pipes, but the other colonists had made it clear to her that if she tried to play while they were sleeping, the pipes would be sunk into the depths.

The older generation seemed relieved that the ketos had gone. Ketos were fierce predators, big enough to smash the raft with a few well-placed blows. No one knew or trusted their intentions. To have them constantly following had been a source of constant tension for the adults. They had not wanted Dilani to succeed.

Stubbornly, Dilani sat up late anyway, forced to be silent, but trailing her feet in the water and staring into the darkness for any hint of a fin breaking the black waves. Sometimes she brought the miniature tree that was all that was left of Per's garden, and cradled its pot on her lap, as if to give the tree a look at where they were going. It was a reminder of him; usually she left it securely stowed in the center of the raft, but sometimes she liked to have it near her.

Bey joined her sometimes. Even the newgens were afraid of the dark and did not like to dive at night, but Subtle had retained more acute night vision than the humans, and he often sported and hunted behind the raft at night. Sometimes he would hang on the edge of the raft and join in their conversation.

They had been traveling for more than two weeks, carried mostly by the current, with some assistance from the prevailing winds. In that time they had seen no further sign of ketos. The oldgens were beginning to get nervous and to wonder if they had come too far from known land, if they might drift forever. Whitman remained confident, or at least it seemed so.

"We're passing through a gap in the island chain," he had said. "All we have to do is stay in this current, and we can't miss the big island or some of its outliers."

Bey was thinking about that statement as he and Dilani watched tiny night-glowing creatures phosphoresce in the raft's wake.

"Do you think Whitman is right?" Bey signed to Subtle the next time Subtle's head broke the surface.

Subtle writhed his shoulders in a shrug.

"Yes, we will find the Dry," he signed with his hands, wrapping a spare tentacle over the gunwale to keep himself above water.

"When?" Bey signed.

"Sometime." Subtle seemed indifferent to questions of time. "I never traveled this Deep-way, in this fashion. How long? Don't know. It matters?"

"To humans, time always matters," Bey signed. But he let his hands fall quiet as he thought about that. Time mattered a lot, on dry land. There was always something that needed doing right away—food plants to tend and harvest, structures to repair against times of storm. Actions were measured against the season, or against the span of life left to live.

Maybe it was different in the water. Seasons came and went, but there were always some fish around to eat. If one dove deep enough, the storms vanished. And how long would they live, in this new form? No one could say. Time had changed form, as the humans had. But the oldgens were still gripped in the habit of impatience.

Dilani seized his arm. "Look!" she said out loud. Bey was startled. He knew that she must be greatly excited to speak aloud.

"What is it?" he said. He peered in the direction she was pointing, but he saw nothing.

"I saw," Dilani insisted loudly. One of the sleeping adults

behind them turned over and grumbled. Bey still saw nothing.

"What kind of thing?" he signed.

"A splash. A white thing. In the water."

Subtle let go of the raft and dove. He came up a few minutes later, shaking the water from his face.

"This-I is seeing nothing," he said. "But is tasting something—motes—" He grimaced, then shook his head again. "Motes is too few to name."

He did not go back into the water, but perched on the stern and brooded. Bey woke occasionally during the night and saw him still watching.

The next night, the three of them were watching the stars in the brief dark time when neither moon was in the sky. Stars were still a wonder to Subtle—one of the few sights his new eyes saw more clearly. It had taken him a while to realize that they kept fixed positions relative to each other; he had expected the sky to have currents like the Deep.

This time it was Bey who saw a flash of white in their wake. It was on the periphery of his vision, and it vanished as soon as he looked in that direction. A few minutes later he thought he glimpsed it again, from the corner of his eye. But when he called to the others to look, they saw nothing.

"Probably just a fish," he said.

But Subtle slipped back into the water, carefully and soundlessly this time. He was gone for a long time—long enough for Bey to begin counting seconds nervously on his fingers.

When he returned, he lunged back onto the raft in a single motion, as if he did not wish to stay in the water longer than necessary.

"What was it?" Bey said. "Did you see something?"

"Not seeing," Subtle said. "Motes." He curled one tentacle around Bey's neck and one around Dilani's, sliding the wet flesh against their gills. It was a shocking sensation, like strong-scented cloth suddenly shoved against the nostrils. Dilani gagged and pushed the coiled limb away indignantly.

Bey's throat was full of an oily, musty taste. It was familiar;

his heart jumped with fear before he could consciously identify it.

"White Killers!" he exclaimed.

"Is not seeing," Subtle said. "But is finding strong trailing motes in water."

"Are they following us?" Bey said.

"This-I is not knowing these waters," Subtle said gloomily. "Is could being they follow, is could being we-I is coming to places White Ones is living."

The next morning they told Whitman of their fears. By then the scent of the Killers had long faded, and Whitman wasn't inclined to put much faith in something smelled by an alien or briefly glimpsed by sleepy newgens. He wouldn't even agree to ask for a volunteer night watch.

"There's enough free-floating anxiety here already, thinking of the dangers we already know. No one but you three has seen these bogeymen at all. There's not enough evidence to warrant alarming everyone. Of course, if you want to keep a lookout, you can. Tell me if you get some concrete evidence that there's something out there."

Bey took to napping in the daytime so he could spend more time awake at night. Dilani slept at night, but played her pipes all day, with renewed determination that sometimes kept Bey awake, too. She remained convinced that the ketos would come back to protect them.

Several more nights passed without any further alarm. Bey was tired of watching and had fallen deeply asleep. He never knew what had awakened him, but suddenly he found himself wide-eyed and fully alert. He lay with his face toward the Deep. He cautiously scanned all within his range of vision.

Then he was bolt upright and shouting.

"Look out! There it is!" he cried.

The raft rocked as the sleepers all around him jumped up. There was a burst of incoherent noise as they, too, cried out. By the time they were truly awake, the thing that had jolted Bey out of his dreams was long gone.

"Let us sleep, can't you?" Adil, one of the geologists, grumbled.

"Yes, it's hard enough with these scratchy logs and Adil's snoring," Henner Vik, the meteorologist, said.

"Newgens—nothing but trouble," Phillips Roon snorted.

"What is this all about?" Melicar said. "Bey, are you all right?"

Bey wasn't sure. His spines were rattling around his head, and he couldn't make them lie down again.

"I saw one of them—the White Killers," he said.

"What did it look like, this thing you saw?" Melicar said patiently.

"Just like I told you before," Bey said. "It was one of those things that attacked us when we were with Per, like the ones that took the lifeskip. It looks sort of like a human—I mean, like what we look like now. Only it's white all over. Even the eyes are pale colored. Its head looks kind of like a skull. All bony. And with sharp teeth and claws. I know what I saw! You can't mistake it for anything else."

He shivered.

Whitman had come to see what the shouting was about.

"I thought I told you to keep your bad dreams to yourself," he said in a low, angry whisper.

"I wasn't dreaming," Bey said.

Melicar touched her wrist to Bey's neck.

"He's pretty upset," she said to Whitman. "Maybe he did see something."

"This-I is tasting bad motes in the water," Subtle asserted. Whitman ignored him.

"Could we just drop this and go back to sleep?" Adil said.

Whitman stared out over the water. Again, it was the time when both moons were down. The only light was dim starlight and the faint phosphorescence of occasional wave crests. Nothing could be seen.

"There's nothing out there," Whitman said finally. "Let's all just relax and forget about it. Bey, calm down and get some sleep."

But Bey could not sleep. He watched the water long after the others had dozed off. At last the moon rose, but it was only lessermoon, and the waters were still dark and impenetrable.

He gave up trying to sleep and swam over to the other raft, where Torker Fensila sat silently brooding.

"Teacher Fensila—" Bey began automatically with the old term of respect, and then stopped in confusion. "I mean, well . . ."

"You can say Torker," the former fish boss said. "One good thing about turning to fish—we can drop all this Skandian slop. 'Teacher this, teacher that, respectfully express disagreement'—Huh! What do *you* want?"

"I want to know how many harpoon bolts you have left," Bey said. "Those white things are coming back, but my father doesn't believe it. If we have any weapons left, keep them close to you. Whatever Whitman thinks, I'm not going to just huddle up and wait to die."

"Huh." Torker stared at Bey for a few seconds. Crouching next to him, Bey could sense his skin motes shifting from neutral to a slightly favorable mode. "Good for you," he said, and gave Bey a slap on the arm that nearly knocked him off the raft. "I'll get Miko and unpack what we've got. But it's not much."

Dilani had stopped playing her pipes and slept, facedown with one arm trailing in the water. Whitman and most of the other adults were asleep, too; faint snores were audible across the quiet swells. With everyone on board, the rafts were covered by sleeping bodies, and rode so low in the water that an occasional wave washed gently over them. Bey hoped that Whitman was right, that nothing would break this calm, but it made him feel better to see Torker's dark bulk still upright against the moonlight, with Miko Narayan and a few others next to him.

There was a sudden splash and a thrashing of arms and legs right next to the raft. Bey sprawled backward, choking off a cry. He must have been asleep. At first he could not see who was coming.

"Its-they is here," hissed a familiar voice. "White Killers."

It was Subtle, surging out of the water with uncharacteristic haste. The long, thin, scholar's knife he had carried through all his travels hissed, too, as he drew it from its fish-bone sheath.

The night pressed in on them, hiding the enemy. Then Bey realized that he *could* see. His new eyes perceived the pale heads of the White Killers bobbing in the waves. The Killers' skin seemed phosphorescent in the faint moonlight.

"Wake up!" Bey shouted. "Everybody wake up! The White Ones are here!"

At that, the shapes ducked back under the surface, and total confusion broke out. The raft rocked, water sloshing over it, as most of the colonists tried to push inward toward the mast, as far from the Deep as they could get.

"Bey, for heaven's sake!" Whitman shouted. "When is this going to stop?" He had completely lost his patience.

For a long moment, nothing happened.

"They is here," Subtle repeated.

"I hear them," Dilani said, almost at the same time, and a moment later, everyone heard the faint, high whistle. It swelled and grew until it was deafening, coming from all directions equally so they could not hear any other sounds of their enemy approaching.

Then they saw them—pale faces rose from the water again. This time encircling the rafts. Suddenly the heads disappeared, and the eerie whistling no longer sounded all around them, but rose, muted, only from the dark water.

"Join up with the other raft," Torker shouted from across the water. "Paddle!"

Hastily, they maneuvered the two rafts together and lashed them in place. Bey wondered if that was the best plan. Two separate rafts would have split the White Ones' forces in half. But this way reduced their perimeter and concentrated the few weapons they had.

They all crouched, panting, staring out into the night. A few clutched knives. Torker, Uli, and Bader held the remaining harpoons. A few more pointed fish spears and gaffs at the dark waters. Most had no weapons at all and grasped any heavy object that had come to hand in the darkness.

"The hand lights," Bey said. "Someone get the hand lights

from the emergency kit and pass them out. We might be able to blind them temporarily."

Subtle's teeth were bared. Bey realized that his own face was set in the same fierce grimace. Everyone's neck spines bristled at their fullest extension, and the colonists were packed so tightly that turning one's head too swiftly risked raking spines across a neighbor.

Then, surging up together like a foam-tipped wave, the White Ones appeared. Their long-fingered hands splayed out on the rafts, seeking a purchase. The Skandians' first impulse was to scream and pull back from the scrabbling talons.

"Do something!" the doctor shouted. "Knock them off the rafts!" She held a cooking pot by its handle and rained blows on the White Ones crawling up her side of the raft. She blocked their advance, but the pot wasn't heavy enough to inflict serious damage. The others caught the idea and began smashing the invaders with whatever they could lay hands on.

They were bashing and screaming like a collection of demented cooks who had seen a bug in the kitchen. Bey was terrified, but it was funny, too, in a ghastly kind of way. The adults who were too frightened to do anything else huddled against the mast and shone their hand lights into the attackers' eyes.

The White Ones only paused for a moment. Then they dragged themselves inch by inch across the rafts. The edges began to tip under their weight, and water sloshed across the surface. There was a grinning, skull-like head almost at Bey's knees, and the talons reached out for him. He gripped the gaff he held in both hands and brought it down on the White One's undefended skull. The impact stung his hands. There was a horribly audible crunch. The White One slumped, but the gaff was stuck. Bey screamed. He kicked and shoved until the gaff came free and the White One slid slowly from the raft and back into the ocean. But Bey kept screaming and slamming the gaff right and left into every White One within arm's reach.

All around him there was a fury of screaming and stabbing. He could feel the rage like a thick red perfume that dizzied him with every breath. They were winning. They were hurting the enemy. The White Ones were withdrawing.

Then the raft rocked rhythmically, with increasing violence.

"Trim the boat!" Uli shouted. But the humans were not the ones creating the imbalance. Those near the edge had to drop their weapons to hang on. The White Ones were back in the water, clinging just to the edges of the logs and rocking them.

Bey saw it all in a flash—the rafts tipping, the humans helpless as hatchlings in the Deep. A brief thrashing, a drifting downward into the Abyss, and a silent forever. Per sending out godbits in vain . . . No answer.

Ashes of the chip fire Roon had kindled hissed as droplets splashed into the sand of the firebox. Bey pushed his gaff into the hands of an astounded elder and crawled toward the firebox. The can of precious cooking oil was still in the storage basket. Bey scrabbled in the storage boxes until he felt the familiar handle of the fire starter.

"Move back! Move back!" he yelled hoarsely. No one could hear him, and he gave up; they would move back soon enough. He sloshed the oil along the edge of the raft. He had always heard that oil would float on water and still burn. He hoped that it was true. He poured an extra splash of oil over the pale hands that clung to the logs nearest him, pressed the fire starter against the wet flesh, and pushed the button.

There was a *foomp* and a sizzle. The oil fizzed and sputtered on the wet wood and then caught and blazed up. For a nightmare moment, the oil-doused White One surged straight up out of the water, his hands like branches on fire. Then he plunged into the Deep, leaving a shriek behind him.

The humans were all screaming, too, and crushing each other as they pushed away from the flames. Some of them started to climb the mast to get away. But the raft stopped rocking as the scorched White Ones dropped off. The raft drifted onward with a skirt of golden fire, leaving behind fragments of debris that flared and then went under.

The wood was so wet that little beyond the logs' edges burned. The screaming died as the colonists realized they weren't going to go up in flames. The fire burned quietly for a little longer, and then its companionable muttering faded. Again it was dark, and only reflected stars flickered on the face of the Deep. The humans still clutched their weapons, almost holding their breath, waiting to see if the White Ones would come back. But the surface remained calm.

"We'd better save this," Bey said, carefully tightening the cap on the bottle of oil, and he could hear himself speak. Gradually the humans relaxed their death grip on the mast, the raft, and each other. Their neck frills drooped. They shivered, and their colors were low and muted. The doctor moved around among them, checking for injuries. When the fire died, Bey dipped his hands in the cooling water. Somehow he had scorched them, though he didn't remember doing it.

"You did good," Torker said to him. "I thought we were dead when I saw the fire go up, but that was a good idea." Torker plunged his own hands into the water. Bey saw dark stains on them and looked away.

Bey had a funny taste in his throat, as if he had swallowed too much of that mist of rage.

"Probably just smoke," he muttered.

Dilani crawled over to him. Her eyes were still large and lucent with excitement, her colors agitated. She dragged a fish spear with her, as if her fist were welded to its shaft. She started to sign, realized she was holding it, and laid it down reluctantly.

"I killed them," she signed. "I killed them and killed them. Many, many of them. I killed like the Bright Teeth. I will sing to them when they come back." She thought about it for a minute. "The Bright Teeth eat their enemies. Do they eat White Ones?"

Bey could only shake his head. He didn't know and didn't want to know.

Subtle came to them, making room for himself by squeezing others out of the way.

"Be still, Disquieting One," he signed. He wrapped Dilani's wrist with his hand, twining their wrist fins together. He rocked her back and forth, and her colors stopped swirling and smoothed out a little. Her eye slits relaxed and expanded to a normal width.

"Bey is needing calming, is needing soft water. Otherwise is might catching fire. *Sssszzk!*" He gave a good imitation of the fire starter going off. Bey jumped and then laughed weakly. Subtle's motes were powerful. Bey felt his own skin relaxing, the colors deepening. The bad taste in his throat diminished. Suddenly he was so thirsty he thought he would die. He longed to jump into the water, but he knew it still was not safe.

Subtle picked up a pot someone had dropped and dipped up water; he poured it over Bey's neck so it ran deliciously down his gill ridges. Bey grabbed the pot and greedily drank what was left in it. He remembered when salt water had choked and burned his human throat, but now it seemed fresh and delicious. The salt only gave it flavor.

They shared the pot among the three of them, drinking and drenching their parched skins in healing water. Around them, the others poured water over themselves and gradually recovered. Soon there was exhausted silence on the raft. Even the doctor slept. Only Torker and Whitman remained propped up against the mast, eyes open and watching. They kept watch together, but they did not talk. Each, perhaps, had his own thoughts.

Bey woke up to the sound of oldgens arguing—a familiar sound, even though the raised voices were punctuated now by loud hisses and the occasional whistle of irritation.

"Something terrible is happening to us," Phun Skanderup wailed. She had wrapped her arms around her knees and was rocking back and forth. The doctor sat next to her, looking tired and cross, her eye slits narrowed.

"Oh, what I wouldn't give for a cup of coffee," Sushan said. "You're so right, something terrible is happening. We're being chased across miles of ocean by all kinds of things that want to eat us. *That's* terrible. Surviving an attack by predators that want to rip us apart for no reason—that's not so terrible."

"Phun's right," Whitman said. "We're Skandians. We've learned since childhood to solve problems in peaceful ways. But here we are, meeting violence with violence."

"Remember what happened before the storm?" Melicar said. "You were willing to use force on Per because he stood up to you."

"That was completely different!" Whitman protested. Bey had seldom heard him raise his voice like that. "I never threatened him. I merely took precautions. And it was a reasoned decision. Not this . . . this meaningless frenzy."

He pressed his hands to his face, and Bey saw the cuts and bruises on them. Whitman had engaged in the frenzy like all the rest.

Melicar took a deep breath. "All right, Whitman," she said. "You're right about one thing. We're experiencing a non-human phenomenon. Of course it's disturbing, because we aren't used to it. It's something that goes with these bodies we're in. It's some kind of group reinforcement phenomenon. When we have strong emotions and are jammed close together, the emotion is intensified. Dilani noticed it first, on the beach. I guess you weren't in a condition to be aware of it then. But last night—did you get that funny taste in your mouth, when we were hammering the White Ones?"

"I did. It was awful!" Phun grimaced.

Whitman nodded with difficulty, as if someone were pushing his head up and down. "Yes, I noticed it," he said in a low voice.

"Group rage. Look, Whitman, it's nobody's fault. It goes with the bodies. We have to be able to admit it and think about it."

"No," Whitman said. "We are humans. We have control over our emotions. We are not animals."

Melicar shrugged. "Go ahead and control yourself, then. I wish you luck."

"But what happens when they come *back*?" Phun said.

Bey joined the group.

"I don't think they'll come back in the daylight," he said.

"When they attacked Per and us before, it was in the dark, too. They don't like the light."

Everyone on the raft crowded in to hear Bey's words. He was embarrassed. He wasn't used to receiving so much attention.

"We're fortunate that you and Dilani had some experience with them before," Whitman said. "I see now that part of your story was true. Now tell us all as much as you can about these white things. What are they? And why would they attack us?"

Bey shivered and felt himself shrinking back into childhood at the mention of the White Ones. He wanted to go back to the time when it would have been the oldgens' job to protect him. But he knew that that was no longer possible.

"I don't know why, Papan. We saw them first when we were with Per. I think they stole the lifeskip while we were diving. *Someone* took it—someone with a tool sharp enough to cut the line.

"Later, they attacked us in a group, and they came after us when Subtle took us to the god—that jelly thing we told you about. Subtle tried to tell us something about them. He kept saying they would 'kill god.' "

Without thinking about it, his arms shaped the signs Subtle had made, as well as he could with only two inflexible limbs.

"Have we done something to alarm them?" Whitman asked. "Are we encroaching on their living space?"

"I don't think so," Bey said. "From what we saw, and from what Subtle said, I think they live in the Deep. They can't stand the light and the air for long."

"They have tools," Whitman said. "They must have some intelligence. Maybe we could learn to communicate with them. Negotiate."

Bey shook his head slowly. "I don't think so. There's something missing. It's like . . . like they have minds, but there's room for only one thought. They're not like us. You saw."

As always, thinking about the White Ones made his skin crawl. There was something *wrong* about them, something that made them seem far more dangerous and alien than any of the other predators. Perhaps it was because they had the humanoid shape yet seemed so utterly inhuman. He could not put his unease into any words that would make sense to Whitman.

"Per knows more than I do, if we could get to him. Subtle knows something about them, too. Subtle knows more about Typhon than any of us; it's his home. You should learn to talk to him. His human speech doesn't always sound as if it makes sense, but once you understand him, he's very smart."

"You would probably communicate with him better than I," Whitman said smoothly. "Perhaps you could let me know what you find out."

Sitting this close to Whitman, Bey could taste the skin motes in the air. Whitman was afraid of Subtle, and repulsed by him. It might be a long time before the elder Sayid could treat an ex-cephalopod as an equal.

"Meanwhile, what are we going to do?" Melicar said practically.

"We must stand watches," Whitman said, "and keep our . . . uh . . . defensive equipment close to hand."

There was no need to assign people to guard duty. Half the colony stayed awake in fear each night, only dozing when the sun was high in the sky. But Bey had been right; the Killers did not come back by day. Luckily, the next few nights were bright ones, with greatermoon nearly full and in the sky for most of the night. Though there were a dozen false alarms, no White Killers approached the rafts again. The humans began to hope they would make landfall before their assailants came back.

Subtle scouted as far from the raft as he dared, and came back in muted, gloomy colors. The motes that he brought back were faint, but still recognizable as the scent of White Killers.

"They follow us?" Dilani signed to him.

He shrugged, his colors fluttering.

"Maybe they-I is following. For sure they-I is living in these waters. We-I is swimming through danger."

The newgens knew that land was coming long before Whitman and the other elders sighted the telltale clouds on the horizon. Subtle had taught them the feel of the currents moving landward, and the changing taste of the water.

"There's freshwater," Torker Fensila said. "I can smell it."

"You're right," the doctor said, surprised. "It must be a river. Interesting that we can tell from this far away. The sense of smell is much more acute."

The sun was just setting as they approached the beach. The newgens had never seen land bigger than the atoll where the colony lived. The oldgens remembered land but had never seen anything like this on Typhon. White breakers foaming against the solid shore filled all the space once occupied by a blue and distant horizon. The coastline curved out of sight only far to the north. The roar of the surf filled their ears. Both generations of humans watched in awe.

12

The smell of the land made Subtle's skin quiver with excitement. It was rich, thrilling, overwhelming. Stories were danced, among the Round Folk, of scholars who had approached the Big Dry on their quests for metal for their scholars' knives. But Subtle had found his metal in the Deep, among the fallen cities. The Dry he had experienced had been the small Dry, the little islands where the humans lived. He had never known anything like this.

Subtle breathed deeply of that unfamiliar scent that allured and alarmed him. It was the smell of water without the tang of the Deep. He wondered why they called it "fresh." It was not a clean, clear scent. It was heavily laden with organic motes, with the sour richness of many beings living and dying. In another minute he saw it—the smooth dark green current curling into the blue Deep.

Subtle helped them pull the raft ashore. As the surf swirled and crashed around his legs, he felt that keen mixture of wonder and regret that assailed him so often. He was reminded again that he had been twisted and changed. His round, graceful body was lost; he had become a lurching monstrosity. Yet, on those stiff, awkward legs, he stood high above the surface of the water that had once been the limit of his world. He could stride boldly out into the Big Dry of the Great People, into the world of legend.

On land, he also experienced the great strength that had been granted to him in the change. His limbs and torso, built from the material of his long, powerful tentacles, made him stronger than any of the humans, even the one they called

Torker. He hauled on the rope and felt the raft slide through the sand. It was a good feeling, to be strong. He wondered if this was how the females of the Round Folk felt, with their boastful hunting games.

In the twilight, the trees at the edge of the sand loomed forbiddingly, like a dark wall.

"We'll explore inland when the sun comes up," Whitman said. "Pull the rafts up above the tide mark and set up a temporary camp for tonight. We should build a good fire and keep it going."

He gave the newgens a meaningful look.

"And I must strongly request that *everyone* stay out of the water for tonight. We don't know what's in there."

It was extremely unpleasant to lie in the sand, Subtle thought. He had never slept out of water, even on the raft. There might be unknown dangers in this weak water—what they called "fresh"—coming from the channel they called a "river." But he thought his senses would warn him in time. So he slipped off into the sea as soon as he could.

Dilani, after scuffling irritably in the sand for a few minutes, followed him. She pretended not to hear Whitman's orders to come back. Since no one wanted to go after her in the dark, she got her way, and Subtle had to accept her presence.

Bey knew that Whitman would not let him get away so easily. He didn't think the comfort of the water would be worth the struggle he would have to get there. He sighed and settled himself as best he could in the gritty discomfort of the Dry.

But he did not sleep soundly. He had fallen into a doze when he was startled awake, as he had been on the raft. He sat up with the same sense of mysterious terror he had experienced then, the same hammering heart and rattling spines.

For a moment he looked straight into another pair of eyes, alien eyes, reflecting the dead silver of moonlight. The pale, skeletal shape of their owner poised for a moment, printed on the dark, and then vanished, leaving Bey's startled cry as the only mark of its presence.

"What is it?" "What is it?" the others asked, in varied tones of sleepy alarm.

"I don't know." Bewildered, Bey sank back into the sand. He couldn't be sure he had seen anything at all. The air brought him no motes, and Subtle was nowhere at hand to investigate. "It might have been a dream. Probably nothing."

But instead of the expected mockery and grumbling, there was a strained pause as those who had awakened peered into the dark.

There was no sound, no movement.

"Bey's seeing things again," Adil said finally.

"Still, we should have posted guards," Phun said. "Tomorrow we'd better have some guards."

It was nearly dawn by then, and no guard was needed because Bey couldn't go back to sleep anyway. As soon as there was enough light, he searched for tracks along the edge of the water. There were plenty of taloned footprints, and all of them could have been made by a human as easily as by a White Killer. The tide had erased those that had been closest to the water. Bey had to give up.

They had to go back into the sea to hunt for their breakfast. The offshore waters were rich with schools of plump fish, and they feasted on better food than any of them had tasted since the storms. No trace of White Killers was found in these shallow waters, and Subtle said that he had rested all night without incident.

"Bey is maybe dreaming," Subtle said. "In long memory, Round Folk is never hearing about White Killers in the Dry. Never is they coming in Dry."

"Even if Bey was dreaming, perhaps we should take that as a warning," Whitman said as the oldgens finished their breakfast on shore. "I say we should explore inland, up the river, and look for a place that's farther from the water, safer."

The oldgens, still afraid of the Deep, were enthusiastic about this idea, and the newgens were willing to try it just for the novelty.

They packed the rafts again and paddled hard through the choppy surf where the breaking waves met the river pouring out. Soon they were gliding upstream, digging their paddles against the current. Tall forest trees, thickly interwoven with lesser growth, crowded the banks and even stood knee-deep in the stream.

Subtle found it harder to breathe. The air had suddenly turned still and damp, and he felt suffocated. Nothing in the Deep had closed him in like this. There were weed forests off the coasts of some low islands, but the Round Folk did not go there. He could tell by the anxious motes lingering in the heavy air that some of the young humans felt the same. Dilani crouched near him, glowering at the green shadows. Bey thrust harder with his paddle, as if they could get out of the forest by going faster. But they only penetrated deeper into its grip.

Whitman sat cross-legged at the front of the first raft, eyes on a measuring device whose cord he had looped around his neck to ensure its safety. The device tasted motes in some artificial way, and it also sent out a call that was answered when metal was present nearby. Subtle was very curious to find out how it worked, but Whitman had not yet explained it to him.

Although the device hadn't signaled the presence of any metal, Whitman waved them to ground the rafts. There was a break in the trees, and through it they could see a wide, brilliantly green field.

"What is it?" Subtle signed to Dilani. She only shrugged. But the older humans seemed excited.

"A meadow!" Phun exclaimed. "Oh, how pretty. How long it's been since I've seen a field of grass like that."

"It probably isn't grass," the doctor said. "Not as you and I understand the word."

"Well, it looks like it, anyway," Phun said. "I can enjoy looking, can't I?"

The humans formed a line for walking across the green expanse. Subtle tested it curiously with his feet. The apparently flat greenness was composed of myriads of tiny hairlike spikes, holding cool, dewy moisture. They brushed against Subtle's skin as his feet sank into their softness. At first the sensation was delightful. Then he felt an unpleasant tingling that grew more insistent until it burned and stung. He hopped from one foot to another but found no relief. Was this a common feature of walking in a "meadow"? But all the humans were hopping, too, and exclaiming in pain and alarm. Looking down, Subtle saw a bumpy red irritation sweeping over his feet.

He turned to hurry back to the river. But the humans were pointing in another direction. There was a cleared area ahead, a place where no "grass" grew. From a distance, it looked like a flat gray rock where they could take refuge.

When Subtle caught up, the humans were already crowding together onto the smooth surface. It didn't feel like rock, though. It had a resilient, leathery texture, more like—

"Skin!" one of the humans shouted, just as the surface wriggled unmistakably beneath their feet. "Look out! It's alive!"

They leaped off the flat gray that was now shuddering and heaving in waves. The woman named Henner tripped and fell, and she did not get up. She thrashed on the ground. Something had wrapped itself around her leg. The gray thing was slithering back and forth across the grass in an uncanny rippling motion. Some of the humans were running back toward the river, making the ear-piercing noises that signaled human alarm. A few of them danced to and fro at the edge of the gray thing, stabbing at it with their sharp tools. Some lucky hit must have loosened its grasp on Henner Vik, and her friends tugged her loose and ran.

The humans who had run for the river were coming back, making louder noises than before. At first Subtle only saw a disturbance of the ground behind them. Then a long tube rose wavering, waist high, and split open to reveal sharp grinders within. It lashed back and forth, trying to get close enough to seize the fleeing prey. Behind it came more of the gray things; in fact, it was connected at its base to the leathery gray pelt. The gray thing Subtle had stepped on rolled to one side, and a similar tube with a maw that gaped struck out at him.

The humans ran screaming across the green field, the minor irritation of their feet forgotten as the ground rose up in rippling gray waves to pursue them. Subtle clutched his knife in one tentacle and struggled to keep up. His legs were as strong as theirs, but he was unused to leaping, one foot after the other, to produce locomotion. It tired him, and he stumbled often. He was falling behind, into the last rank.

Ahead of them the green wall where the jungle resumed was drawing nearer. Draped between trees was a pale net that registered unpleasantly on Subtle's senses. As they came closer, he smelled the same motes that in the water meant the White Arms, what the humans called tangleweed. This must be a form that could survive in the Dry, he realized. If they ran to escape the hungry gray skins, they would be snared by the deadly pale fronds.

The humans knew dry-land tangleweed. They turned and tried to drive back the gray things with the bobbing maws. But all their stabbing and prodding seemed to have no effect. Subtle, too, sliced at the edges of the hungry pursuers, but the leathery gray pelts closed up seamlessly after every cut. They could not find a lethal spot. The gray carpet flowed on, and they were pushed ever farther back, toward the jungle.

Subtle wanted to spin himself quickly and grasp the whole situation, as he could have when he was round, but instead he had to turn his whole clumsy body. As he looked behind, he spotted a bright-skinned figure running toward them, parallel to the jungle's edge. It wasn't screaming like the others. The newcomer uttered short cries, as if to get their attention. Was it a belated member of their group? He didn't recall seeing those colors before. Bright circles wrapped its arms and legs. From a distance he could not tell if they were ornaments or an integral part of its body that would make it different from the bipeds around him.

It waved toward the dry-land tangleweed. That was not new information. Subtle was aware of that threat already. It pointed more insistently and shouted. The sounds meant nothing to Subtle, but the rhythm and intonation reminded him of human speech.

Finally the humans had noticed the running figure. But by that time the creature seemed to have given up on attracting their attention. It hurled itself into the dry-land tangleweed. But instead of snaring it, the tangled fronds recoiled from it. Bright marks appeared on the pale fronds. Subtle thought he was seeing things. Tangleweed did not bleed. Nonetheless, the edge of the dry-land tangleweed curled and receded defensively, leaving a three-cornered gap between the fronds and the thicket they infested. The new creature had not died or gone limp. It kept shouting.

"Go! Go!" Subtle urged the humans around him. Whatever the reason, they had one last chance to escape. Humans making hoarse sounds of breath exhaustion, their skins rank with fear, crowded through the gap, inches from the deadly fringes of the dry-land tangleweed. Subtle and one or two of the larger humans lingered to the last, jabbing with sharp tools and knives to discourage the gray pursuers.

As they retreated through the narrowing gap, gray pelts poured after them. The dry-land tangleweed, revived, lashed out with its whiplike branches, snaring the gray pelts. The fronds tightened until they cut into the gray things. The long tubelike necks thrashed and the maws fastened to the dry-land tangleweed, but in moments they hung limp. The humans burst through the remaining undergrowth, onto the riverbank, and ran downstream toward the place where they had left the rafts.

Only one of the pursuers made it through the gap, but it continued to pour along the forest floor after the humans, in mindless, undaunted greed. The biped stranger continued to shout, but most of the humans were hysterical and no one could hear it. Subtle glimpsed its gestures as it danced wildly around the gray thing. With a stiffened finger, it jabbed at its own mouth.

"The mouth!" Subtle shouted, but no one was listening to him either. He found himself directly in the gray thing's path. He feinted with one tentacle to draw the eyeless maw-tube toward him. In the other limb, he grasped his scholar's knife. He thrust it directly into the bobbing maw. He felt the gnawing grinders scrape his skin in passing. If he had mistaken the meaning, his flesh would be ground to a pulp. The edge of the gray pelt quested along his arm like a thousand tiny fingers. Still he stabbed fiercely.

In the very act of seizing him, the gray thing faltered. The maw-tube slid away. Before his eyes, the long tube disintegrated into a bundle of stringy fibers, like a bundle of fleshy roots. The flat, peltlike part fell apart, too, revealing a tough skin layer undergirded with thousands of tiny fingerlike stubs on which it had flowed along the ground.

He was left panting like a human, standing face-to-face with the new stranger. Its gill slits trembled as it tried to suck in air. It seemed winded by its exertions. It stretched a hand toward his face.

"Gods of the old worlds," it said. "A blue Per. With tentacles."

ᦉ13᧠

The stranger took a step toward Subtle, stumbled, and fell to its knees.

"Not Per." Subtle forced out the words in a hoarse hiss. He felt himself as astonished as the stranger. He was almost sure he knew who this must be.

He lifted the stranger and dragged it with him to the rafts. The other humans had piled on board already. As soon as Subtle caught up with them, they pushed out into midstream and paddled furiously. Subtle looked back and saw nothing following. After a few minutes, the humans also realized there was no pursuit. They stowed the paddles and sat, catching their breath.

Only then did they see what Subtle had brought aboard. They crowded closer to get a look at this stranger who had helped them. Then someone shouted, "Look out! Snakes!" They all jumped back again.

Subtle would have pulled away, too, if the creature had not been clutching his wrist. The bright-colored bands on the creature's arms and legs, which he had taken for body parts or personal ornament, were tiny live serpents, twined around its limbs.

"Don't . . . They're harmless . . ." the creature said faintly. It seemed close to losing consciousness.

"It talks," Uli Haddad exclaimed.

Subtle supported its shoulders. He could taste its motes on his skin. They were fearful, sad, excited—but unmistakably like a human's.

"You-I be helping this-I," he appealed to the others. "Is like you, is being human."

The doctor pushed forward to help Subtle.

"You speak our language?" Melicar said. "Are you all right?"

"*Your* language?" the creature said. "Are you human? *Skandian?* I'm from Skandia. I'm Sofron Nordby."

For a minute, it looked as if the doctor would fall off the raft in shock. She seized the stranger's arms.

"Sofron," she said. "We thought you were dead."

" 'We'? Who are you?"

"It's me; it's Sushan!" the doctor said.

"Sushan?" the stranger repeated, as if she could not quite believe it. "And is this . . . everybody else?"

"This is everyone who's left," Sushan said. "Well—and the ones on the other raft. You'll see them when we land."

She pointed to the others, urged them to say their names. Sofron's eyes roved over the rest of the humans, obviously seeking faces that weren't there, but she did not question the absences. She seemed stunned, like a fish stung with tangle-weed venom.

Melicar shook her as if to awaken her.

"Sofi! Come on, you know me—it's Sushan! And I'm so glad to see you!"

She embraced the stranger, and Sofron clung to her.

Subtle watched their colors swirl and blend, the matching patterns spreading back from the fingertips—skin harmony. Finally Sofron looked up. Her eyes had recovered their brightness.

"For a while there, I thought I was dead, too. If so, I'm having a very weird afterlife," she said. She shook her head. A moment later she continued.

"I'm sorry. I just can't get used to this. In all the times I pictured you showing up to get me, I never imagined anything like this."

"You would have had a worse surprise if you'd seen me before these changes," Sushan said. "I got burned in the eruption. My face, my arm, my leg. It healed, sort of. I limped. Not a pretty sight. Believe me, I look more like myself now than I did then."

That seemed to draw Sofron's attention back from her own thoughts.

"You got hurt . . . I'm sorry. What about Lesper? Koreng?"

"They didn't make it. They died on the mountain. We thought you had died, too."

Sofron didn't respond for a long time.

"I've been saying their names every night," she said finally. "For two years. I kept telling the kids so they'd remember, in case you ever came. So now you're here . . . and they're not." Her eyes went back to their ceaseless roving of the forest.

"Sofron? What kids? What are you talking about? How did you get here?"

"I put the children on the emergency raft and went down the river. Not the big one—that cascade on the east face." She spoke as if she were in a trance.

"The main channel of the eruption was flowing on the south, into the harbor. We got slammed around; I thought we were done for a few times. Then we got out into the lagoon. I tried to paddle over to the rest of the boats, but there were stretches of boiling water in between and I didn't know if the raft could get through. I tried to go the long way, and then . . . the lid blew off the island and this huge, dirty gray wave . . . Full of ashes, I guess. It was hot. It pushed us out over the reef.

"Then there was a huge boom, like the sky coming apart. I looked back, and there was a cloud that went all the way up to the jet stream. The underside was all lit up with fire. The Deep just . . . *lifted* under us like the world turning over.

"I don't know where it took us. I didn't try to go back because I wasn't sure there was anything there. I knew there were islands to the east, and the current was taking us there anyway. We came ashore just after we ran out of water. And here we've been. Until now, I thought we might be the only ones."

"What children?" the doctor asked again.

"I just grabbed everyone who was on the veranda at the children's house: Ling, Piersall, Chilsong, Jaya, Ven. And

Dilshad, but I'm sorry, we lost him last year. I'm sorry. I couldn't get them all. Lesper went in to get the babies who were still in cribs, but I don't think he ever came out. There were rocks the size of your head falling all over the place. I'm sorry about Lesper."

"I've missed him."

"Me, too. He was a good friend. I think he probably . . . wasn't with us anymore by the time the fire got there. This was a good thing."

"I know."

They were silent for a minute. Then Sofron looked up.

"Sushan, have you noticed that you can't cry in these bodies? They'll exude a tear or two, but they won't really weep. I was disappointed. For two years I wanted to cry and couldn't allow myself to do so. Not in front of the children. I thought I'd cry like a baby when you all finally came to get me. But now this body won't allow it."

She clung to the doctor as if the flavor of her skin were the only certain reality.

"Sofron—where are the children now?" Melicar asked. She was afraid of the answer.

"We were in the cave, by the water—" Sofron suddenly wriggled around to peer backward, upstream. "Oh, damn, we're going the wrong way. It's back there. We'll just have to turn around when we—Hey, where are we going anyway?"

"Just back to the beach," Sushan said. "We've only been here one day. We don't have a home."

"I must have been up there in the cave when you landed," Sofron said. "I was there with the children."

"Last night?" Sushan said.

"No. I've been like this for—" She checked the stick dangling at her belt. "—eight—no, nine days. We were next to the pool. A keto came. The cave had an outlet to the ocean, though I didn't find that out until later. I thought the keto was hurt. Then Ling fell into the water . . . and I went in after her . . . And what I thought was a scar on the keto started to weep these tiny bubblelike things . . . and they . . . *swallowed* us.

"The other kids jumped in after me, and the bubbles engulfed them, too. There were just more and more of them. They enveloped us. I lost consciousness. Then I woke up. I was underwater, it was dark, I was like *this*, and the children were nowhere. I've been looking for them ever since."

Her colors darkened like clouds when the sun sinks.

"I know this sounds crazy, but it's the truth," she said desperately. "*Look at me!* There's no way this could have happened to me under normal circumstances. Something completely unheard of is going on here."

"Tell me about it," the doctor said. "I guess you've noticed we aren't exactly normal, either. This happened to us right before we left the atoll—the one where we've been hiding out since the eruption. It's a long story. I'll tell you later.

"We were sick. Per was right; there was an indigenous virus at work, but it was even worse than he thought. It caused the deformities in the children, and it was killing the rest of us.

"The same thing happened to me that happened to you. The bubbles, the transformation. Those bubble things are highly sophisticated little messengers. They injected us with a transformative virus. It fixed our other problems, but we ended up—like *this*."

"Per," Sofron said, as if she had been trying to spit out the word for some time, as if it were the only word of Sushan's speech that she had heard.

"This is so complicated. It will take days to catch you up."

"He's not here," Sofron said. "I can see that."

"No one can say he's dead, Sofron. But they can't seem to say that he isn't, exactly. He was fine until the last big storm, just a few weeks ago.

"Losing you—that hurt him. He wasn't the same after. I knew Lesper was gone. I got used to it. But I don't think Per could ever quite believe that you were dead. After we landed on the atoll, northwest of here, Per wanted to look for you, but Whitman wouldn't let him have any of the boats."

"Whitman!"

Her crest spines rattled as she showed her teeth.

"You don't know the half of it," Sushan said. "But don't

hate him to nine nines, because he did save Per's life once. Per was going to jump into the water to go after you, when the island blew. He would have killed himself. Whitman didn't let him go."

"Then where is he?"

"The kids say—" She stopped and cleared her throat. "Dilani Ru and Bey Sayid say that they saw him . . . well . . . assimilated by a native organism. Their friend Subtle—with the tentacles—took them to find this, this god. He says a part of Per is still alive in the body of the organism. But according to them, he isn't alive in his own body anymore.

"I can't figure out if this is reality or some kind of dream or religious thing with Subtle. He's an indigenous creature, by the way. The kids say he started out as a cephalopod, but he got caught up in the changes, too. The kids insist that Per is the one who caused us to be transformed. The way they explained it to me—"

Subtle interrupted.

"Per is living in the mind of god," he said solemnly. "Per-god is giving this-I this body. Is giving-sharing face and language so this-I is not losing thinking. Per-god is giving humans new body so they-I is not dying. Per-god is saving all we-I."

"Per-god," Sofron repeated faintly. "I see. So he's a god now! And I'm a fish. And an alien is wearing his face."

She started to laugh helplessly, choking and snorting.

"I didn't know I could still do that," she said when she finally recovered her breath.

Subtle tasted her motes. The flavor was unique, disturbing yet pleasing. He almost wished that he, too, could experience this disruption in functioning.

"I believe you," the stranger said to Subtle. She touched his tentacle, and he tasted her skin vividly. "If anyone could have caused this, it would have been him. And he put his face on you. It's like initialing the project."

"You-I is having smooth thinking," Subtle said. He was startled by her perception. Her mind had a powerful flavor.

Most of the newgens had been on the other raft. As soon as

the two rafts grounded on the beach, they mobbed Sofron. They had figured out what was going on and couldn't wait any longer to greet her.

"Remember Dilani?" the doctor said, pulling the newgen in front of the rest.

"You've changed," Sofron signed. "Grown taller."

As soon as she saw her sign Dilani accepted that this was Per's Sofron. Her sign had the style she remembered; only the shape of the face and fingers had changed.

"I can speak now," Dilani said proudly. "But sign is still better," she added with her hands.

"And Bey," the doctor said.

"Your curly hair—your brown eyes—gone," the stranger said. "So different. But your legs!"

"I was glad to make the trade," Bey said. "Are you really Sofron?"

The stranger smiled.

"Sometimes I wonder," she said. "But I remember when each of you was born, so I guess I still know you, anyway."

"Why do you have snakes on your arms?" Othman Jayawardene said. "Are you sure they're safe?"

"I'm sorry; I forgot," she said. "I was scared, too, the first time I saw them. But if you're like me, they won't hurt you. They're symbiotic, I think. They eat my skin slime, and their venom discourages tanglewood. That's how I tore a hole for you, through the tanglewood curtain. They're some kind of protection, I think, left by the people who were here before."

Whitman joined the joyful round of greetings in time to hear that last statement. His spines stuck out belligerently.

"You claim to be Sofron Nordby. Well, don't you recognize me?"

"Huh. You didn't recognize *me*." Her voice was unsteady. "It's been a long time, Whitman. Why didn't you come before? Why didn't you look for us? What the *hell* happened?"

Whitman waved a hand as if to brush aside her questions.

"That's all in the past. We can discuss it later."

He spoke in his usual smooth, soothing manner. He was

beginning to get control of the strange vocal cords, so that his voice was becoming calming again, even in his new form.

Subtle wondered if calming motes were spewing from the leader's pores. It was too bad Whitman didn't like to go in the water. In the Deep, his motes could be tested to see if they were dominant over the others.

"We'll convene a forum as soon as camp is set up," Whitman continued.

Sofron's teeth were showing.

"You didn't even try to find us," she said accusingly. "I guess you had your reasons. But if you want to make amends, you can forget about convening a forum and help me now. My children are missing, and I need someone to help me search."

She turned to the rest of the Skandians, who stood watching the confrontation.

"*My* children? They're *your* children. Hey! Askil Aigner! Piersall is alive! Hamam Karttila, Chilsong lived! Where is Kosi Chetil, and Ting-she and Lif Nansen? Jaya and Ling were both fine, when I last saw them. They fought to stay alive, and I'm not giving up on them now until I've taken this place apart pebble by pebble. Help me look for them!"

Whitman got between her and the others and grasped her hand.

"Ting-she, Lif, and Kosi are no longer with us," he said. "You couldn't have known that, of course." His voice reproached her nevertheless. "I wanted to talk this over in an orderly way, but if you're going to insist on it, I have to warn you that you don't know what you're doing to this community.

"The disaster was a terrible thing. But we've come to terms with our losses. At least we were secure in knowing that the children were no longer suffering. Now you're insisting that they're alive, but lost, in this very place where we just happen to have landed. And how likely is that? You're just creating anxiety and suffering.

"You've been living in isolation for a long time. Please, give yourself time to reorient yourself before you make any more rash assertions. And please, give us all time to exchange information and discuss all the potential courses of action. You've learned all kinds of things that we need to know."

This time it seemed to Subtle that the leader's motes weren't overcoming those of the stranger. She pulled away from him and called out to one of the other females.

"Hamam, please, don't let Whitman mislead you. I have truly seen the children. Chilsong is a fine person. He still can't walk, but he contributes to the rest of us every single day. I told him you'd come and find him one day. Don't make me a liar."

The one she addressed bloomed with colors of deep, angry red, and her hands rose in a gesture of reflex threat.

"As far as I'm concerned, Whitman is right," she hissed. "Chilsong was like a baby. He couldn't even roll over in bed. There's no way he survived in a place like this. He died on the mountain. Isn't that bad enough? I don't even know who you are. How can I believe you're really Sofron? Just leave me alone!"

Sofron turned back to Whitman. "You're trying to make them think I made this up." She shot her hands skyward, as if appealing to the blank blue for mercy. Perhaps on a human it would have been a harmless gesture, but her strong talons made it look threatening.

"Oh, glorious rescue." She looked disgusted. "*That's* when I was living in a fantasy world, Whitman—when I imagined you would actually help me. You're so busy protecting yourselves from the past that you're losing your future."

Subtle was amazed by the difficulties of this social species. The impatient female questioned the wisdom of the leading elder. That was typical. But instead of going apart to ponder until each reached a decision, they herded closer, wreaking strong emotion on each other.

The newgens, by contrast, with no more communication than a glance, moved together as one, surrounding Sofron and cutting Whitman out of the group.

"We'll help you, Sofron," Bader said. "Newgens don't leave newgens, right, Bey?"

Sofron's colors softened. "I'm sorry. I'm not sure I know who you are. Everybody's so different."

"I'm Bader Puntherong. You taught me sign when I was little."

Sofron touched his face, as if the smooth skin might prove to be an illusion. He had grown tall. When she had last seen him, his cleft palate and malformed lips and chin had made his appearance grotesque and his speech almost incomprehensible.

"The changes were good for some of us. I got my face. Bey got his legs. Dilani can hear."

"I'm glad for you, Bader."

The stranger's colors trembled with extreme agitation.

"Seeing what you've become—now I know there's a chance the other children could be healed like you, could have good lives. I just can't lose them now! Now, when there's finally some hope! I've got to find them. Everything else has to wait."

"Yeah, well . . . you always treated us like people. So if you need help now, the newgens are going to help you. The rest of them can do what they want."

Meanwhile, Whitman had given up on controlling the entire group and had drawn Melicar aside to speak to her in a voice that was low, but not so low that it couldn't be overheard by some of the other adults.

"Now what?" Melicar demanded.

"Look, Sushan, I'm sorry, because I know that you and Sofron were friends . . ."

"But?"

"But we don't have any proof that this *is* Sofron! A lifeform appears and gives a name, and you assume that it's one of us. Yes, it could be Sofron. Or it could be a creature who has extracted information from her, and is somehow impersonating her for purposes still unknown. In the absence of genetic testing, there really is no way to be sure."

"Oh, come on, Whitman! This is absurd. I suppose you think that I, and the rest of us, are also just impersonators. It would make as much sense."

"It *would* make sense for all of us to exercise a little caution," Whitman said grimly. "And even if this is Sofron, please consider the thought that what she's been through has been more than enough to make her delusional. She has been completely alone for more than two years. Guilt and stress could have kept those children very much alive in her own mind. You're the doctor. Exercise some professional judgment."

"In my professional judgment," Sushan said, "I can learn more from talking to Sofron than from listening to you and your paranoid speculations. And you should consider that if you're wrong, there's a very real risk that children from this community are out there in danger, while we argue. Children who could provide a valuable addition to our tiny gene pool, I remind you."

While they were debating, the sun began to dip close to the horizon. Though Sofron obviously chafed at any additional delay, she wasn't willing to take the newgens into the forest at night, even to continue her search for the missing children. There was still time for some last-minute feeding forays into the water before dark. The more watchful members of the group quickly gathered driftwood, dried fronds, and brush from the forest margin to provide fire materials. Torker laid and lit a small fire, leaving the remaining stack of brush as a reserve supply.

"This way, we won't attract too much attention, but if they come back, we can light a big fire quickly."

"If *they* come back?" Sofron asked.

"Things that attacked us on the raft, on our way here. They're pale. Bony. Big staring goblin eyes. Claws. The kids call them 'White Killers.' Have you seen them?"

Sofron felt a chill of fear.

"Not 'them'—just one of them. We called him the Bone Thing. The one we knew acted differently from those you saw. He was always alone. He stayed away from them. He used to trade with us. We brought him things we found, and he gave us food. Before we got . . . bubbled, changed . . . he came one night and warned us to move from our shelter spot. I guess it was true, what he said."

"White Killer *spoke* you—I?" Subtle's eye slits opened

wide. His amazement knew no bounds. The Round Folk had thought the Killers incapable of language. They signaled each other with whistles and snarls, but that was all.

"What did he say?" Torker asked.

"He didn't say, actually. We used sign. He signed, 'The people like me will kill the people like you.'"

That gave Subtle much to think about. This scholar-human had brought him news such as the Round Folk had never known. A Killer who used language, and who conferred a benefit on another species. Never, in his knowledge, had the Killers brought anything but death. He could hardly believe it.

"I never saw any others like him, though," Sofron continued. "My impression was that he wanted contact with us, for some reason of his own, but he also wanted to keep us a secret from the rest of them. He had a name, I think. He called himself 'Wearra.'

"After I woke up from being bubbled, I saw him on the beach, near here, at night. He indicated that the children had been taken somewhere; I got the impression that the Killers took them. He said they wouldn't hurt the children. But I don't know. Are you sure they were trying to harm you?"

"Totally." Torker poked his little fire to a greater blaze. "They would have torn us apart. Bey figured out that they don't like fire. That drove them off. Otherwise they would have killed us."

"But you haven't seen them on land," Sofron said.

"Not yet."

"I wonder if they would attack here, on the beach," Sofron said. "Wearra wouldn't venture onto land, except for short visits right next to the water. As far as I could tell—which I admit wasn't very far—he seemed to have some kind of fear of the land. Almost like a superstitious reverence, if you can say that about a fish on legs. I thought that was why he wanted to deal with us, so we could go on land to get things for him."

"But if this White Killer you saw was on the beach here, the others could come here," Phun said fearfully.

"What do you think, Subtle?" Sofron said.

Subtle was surprised. The human sought his opinion!

"This-I is not self-seeing White Ones on land. Is only seeing dancing of oldest scholars. Always they is dancing great fear of White Ones for places of Great People. Great fear and great desire. Is dancing that god was forbidding White Ones in those places. They is fearing, is never going. But if White Ones is going now in Dry, this-I is thinking, maybe all is changing now. Maybe White Ones is seeking places of Great People, too. This is time of great changing. Here, everywhere."

Whitman listened, showing little patience.

"We'll be ready for them if they come," he said. He had assigned some of the group to serve as sentries, in rotation, and had passed out their few weapons.

"You can't be ready for what you don't know," Sofron muttered. She trembled with hope at the news that the other humans had actually seen Wearra's people in this area. She might be able to find them, follow them; at least it would give her something to aim for in the trackless Deep. But equally she feared terribly for the children; Wearra had said that the others would not kill them, but if they would kill adults, why not the unconscious children?

Finally back with her own kind, she felt herself grow weak with shock and the accumulated burden of long days alone. She knew she had to sleep, and surrounded by the others, it would be safe to do so.

For at least one night, she could rest.

14

Bey thought he was awake until Subtle hissed in his ear and he realized he had been dozing. Subtle crouched next to him with tentacles writhing, poised to strike at some unseen enemy.

"White Killer," Subtle hissed. "This-I sees him at the wet edge, walking with feet. White Killers is coming in the Dry."

As stress sharpened his senses, Bey smelled the alien presence. It was a bitter, oily, iodine smell with a tang of musty rot; it was a cold smell from waters without sun.

"White Killers," Subtle said. "In the Dry. Never is this happening."

Bey sprang to his feet to raise the alarm, only to find a hand over his mouth and another voice at his ear, whispering "quiet!"

It was Sofron. If it had been anyone else, he would have shaken off the interfering arms.

"But they're coming," he protested in a low voice when she took away her hand.

"If it's only one," she said, "it might be Wearra. I have to speak to him. I don't want him killed."

Bey and Subtle moved cautiously, crouching, until they were beyond the small circle of firelight. Out of the light, they saw better; the moons were down, but their night-sensitive eyes could see far along the beach once they were away from the glare of fire. Bey glimpsed the pale shape of the White One for the first time, half concealed among rocks a hundred feet away. Sofron walked toward him slowly but without fear, holding the bone knife from her belt out before her on flat hands. Subtle's motes were so strong that Bey could taste them—fear, with a tinge of awe. To Bey, the White Killers were a threat, like any predator. To Subtle, they were legendary monsters from another time.

"Sofron," she whispered as she approached the White One.

Her heart leapt at the sound of his harsh voice answering "Wearra."

"Where are the children?" she signed.

She knew he understood; but he refused to answer. With one hand, he wiped out what she had said. Then he pointed out toward the Deep.

"Kill you!" he signed. "You go! You go, go!"

"Where are the children?" she insisted.

"Not go there," he signed. His eyes flashed opaque white as he turned suddenly and looked out to sea. He showed his teeth and hissed; she saw that he was about to flee as he had before. He looked as if he had heard a signal of some sort that was still inaudible to her.

"No," she cried, and seized his bony wrist.

"Sofron!" Bey shouted. "Everybody wake up!"

She turned to see a line of White Killers rising silently as mist from the Deep. Wearra shook Sofron off like a dry leaf and vanished.

Suddenly they were surrounded by deafening noise. Everyone in camp was awake and shouting. Then the human voices were swallowed up by the uncanny whistling that seemed to come from every direction, confusing the perception of other sounds. There was a thump and a shriek as some kind of projectile hurtled across the campfire and found a target in human flesh.

Whitman came leaping toward Bey and Subtle, stumbling on webbed feet he had not yet learned to manage.

"What do we do?" he shouted. "How the hell do we—*ow!*" He flung himself headlong as a dart shot past him. It gleamed for a moment as it passed over the remains of the fire and disappeared again.

"Make brightness!" Subtle said.

Torker was already piling twigs and brush on the fire. The coals smoked and hissed as he flung on half-dried handfuls of leaves. Then flames began to lick from beneath the fronds to catch the larger sticks.

"Everyone stay low," he shouted. "Pile on firewood!"

As the fire flared up, Bey could see the scared and startled faces of the other humans huddled, clutching at each other. A flicker of light showed one of the white figures coming up from the shore, caught in the glare for one frozen moment. Darkness swallowed it again. But Bey knew that the White Killers were not frozen. They would move in as close as they dared, and if the threat of the fire held them back, it would not hold back their weapons. Darts and spears flew toward the firelight, striking at random among the crouching humans.

A pale figure loomed toward Bey, raising a bowlike apparatus armed with a pointed bolt. Bey ducked, but too late. He shrank from the tearing impact he knew would come—but the bolt slid harmlessly past him. He had seen the deadly accuracy of the White Killers in the Deep. How could this one have missed? Even as the thought passed through his mind, he grabbed the dart that had almost struck his father and hurled it back toward his attacker. The White One dodged in turn, but Bey's missile scraped along its flank, drawing pale blood. The White Killer danced back out of the light, its lips drawn back in a grimace of pain. Its great eyes were hooded by their inner membrane, the pupils compressed to slits.

A few other humans followed his example and seized spent weapons from the sand to menace the unseen Killers.

"Get down!" Bey shouted. Dancing against the now-roaring blaze, the humans made perfect targets. Bey was frantic. They didn't know their danger. They knew nothing of weapons, but the Killers could use theirs with deadly skill.

The other humans did not hear, or did not obey. Yet time after time, the darts and spears just missed. Their victims seemed to be mostly those who clung to each other, motionless.

Suddenly Bey understood the advantage they held. He

grabbed Whitman by the shoulders, trying to shake him out of his fear.

"They've never fired in air! Papan! Their aim is off! Don't you see?"

Whitman didn't comprehend at first, but Subtle did. With a guttural noise of approval, he charged to the fire, seized a dart in each tentacle and a flaming stick in one hand, and attacked the wavering line of White Killers. The weapons danced in his hands as he eluded shot after shot from the White Ones.

"Go after them!" Bey shouted. "Get burning sticks! The light will blind them! Keep moving! They can only hit you if you hold still."

A few of the newgens followed him—a pitiful few.

"Torker! Sushan!" Bey appealed to the adults he thought might help. They picked up burning sticks and joined the circle facing outward. Bey hoped the flames behind them were bright enough to blind the Killers. There were barely enough humans standing to make a complete circle. They moved cautiously outward, jabbing at the attackers and driving them back.

If only the others can pull themselves together enough to keep the fire going, Bey thought desperately. *If they let it go out, we've had it.*

Then he was face-to-face with one of the White Killers. It gripped a barbed spear and suddenly stabbed at his face. He jumped sideways; the point missed his eyes and scraped past his shoulder. It was only a small wound, but the pain seemed agonizing. Bey's heart beat so hard that he felt as if it would burst. Terror threatened to paralyze him. But somewhere deep within him was a refusal to let that jagged point come close to him again.

His arms moved without his conscious wish but with startling force as he swung the smoldering branch he held. The glowing end smashed into the White Killer's chest. The White One's damp skin sizzled. That sound, and the stench of scorching flesh, seemed to fill Bey's world. The White One voiced a whistling shriek.

Bey jabbed the stick again, into the sensitive folds of its

gills, and it staggered backward toward the shadows. He leapt after it. His neck spines stuck straight up, protecting delicate tissues. All his teeth were bared in a fierce grimace.

Then came a smashing blow against the back of his head that dropped him to his knees and left him stunned. He lost hold of the stick. When someone grabbed him from behind, he tried to turn and face them but fell backward instead.

"Stupid!" It was Dilani; he knew her more by the familiar motes diffusing from her tight grip than from the face he could barely see. Bright sparks of pain danced behind his eyes. She pulled him upright and pushed the stick back into his hand. A White Killer lay at her feet. Tufts of marsh grass around the body flared and crackled briefly where they had been ignited by the embers of Bey's fallen weapon, but the White One did not stir.

"Stay close to the fire," Dilani signed. "Or else they sneak up behind you and bop you on the head." Her hands demonstrated what Bey's skull still felt. He understood what he had done wrong. He had moved too far out of the circle, and one of the Killers had cut in behind him. Apparently it had already fired its own weapons, or he would have been pierced by a dart instead of merely clubbed. He had been lucky.

Bey saw Torker Fensila dragging Uli Haddad across the sand. The other humans backed slowly toward the fire, their smoldering sticks still at the ready. The White Killers had expended their darts. Surely, Bey thought, they would give up now and go away.

It was the last coherent thought he had for some time. The Killers rushed in on them with teeth and claws and jabbing spears, and with that skull-piercing, unvarying whistle that was terrifying in its inhumanity. Bey was pushed back and back, blindly warding off blows with his stick, giving way until there was suddenly a searing pain in his foot and he realized he had stepped on the coals at the edge of the fire. He could hear despairing, frightened screams all around him and did not know which of his friends might be hurt or dying.

Then something turned over in Bey's chest. Suddenly he was no longer frightened, striving just to stay alive. Now he wanted to kill his enemy. He was glad when a White Killer thrust its face close to his. That made it easier to strike. The red scent of fury was smoking through his veins again. Rage seemed to burn on his skin like a flame without ash.

He pushed forward again, step by step, and the pain in his foot was forgotten. He snarled and snapped as fiercely as any of the White Ones.

When he came back to himself, breath was sobbing painfully through his chest, and he hurt all over, but it was from exhaustion, not from injuries. Others were weeping in pain; he could hear them again. White Killers lay tumbled in the sand, six or seven of them. They lay still. Gradually he realized that they were dead, and that there were no others. They had given up.

Bey limped over to the first White One Dilani had knocked down. He reached out a foot and jostled it, but there was no movement. He bent to examine it more closely. The back of its head looked dented and oozed a pale moisture. When he poked it with his stick, it gave sickeningly under pressure, like a cracked egg.

"Could have been you," Dilani signed. "You should be more careful." The fire was dying down again.

"Get wood," Bey called. His voice cracked. He was hoarse, as if he had been shouting, but he had no memory of it. They dragged in all the fallen branches and reasonably dry leaves they could find within reach of the light and piled them on the roaring blaze. Only then did they feel safe enough to stop.

Bey's head throbbed with every movement, and his skin felt ready to crack with dryness. His own weight seemed to pin him to the earth. He longed for the buoyant, soothing water, but he dared not go there. The White Ones were there.

"Who's crying?" he said thickly.

Kusma, one of the other newgens, was near him. She was clutching a gashed arm, wincing with pain.

"It's Madan," she whispered. "He's badly hurt."

Melicar still had a precious handful of painkillers. Eventually she gave some to Madan, and the noise stopped.

Bey crouched in the sand until the doctor came around to

examine his skull. Her cool, expert fingers diffused some comfort, even though she had no medicine to offer. She brought him water, which he gulped thirstily, and washed and soothed the cut on his shoulder, which he had almost forgotten.

"Who else was hurt?" he asked. "Is Madan going to be all right?"

She grimaced. "Madan is cut from here to here." She pointed to neck and belly. "Looks like claw marks. Those talons make a nasty cut. It's not really so bad, or shouldn't be. It's a pretty shallow slash. But he seems to be in a lot of pain. Maybe it's just shock. He should be better when he comes out of it.

"Other than that, Uli's probably the worst. He was shot with one of those darts and lost a lot of blood, but it scored along his ribs and didn't penetrate deeply. Phun was shot in the leg, or speared, or something, and the leg is quite torn up. Then there are six or seven people who got clawed or bitten, but most of those wounds are superficial, if only we can keep them from getting infected. No one has been killed so far. We must consider ourselves lucky."

"Luck, nothing," Torker said. "Some of these slackers would be fish bait if Bey hadn't figured out why the Killers kept missing."

"I saw how good their aim was in the Deep," Bey said, "when I was there with Dilani and Subtle, and Per. If they could shoot that well in air, we'd all be fish bait."

"We'd be fish bait if Wearra hadn't come to warn us," Sofron said. "That was him. He must have known the others were planning a sneak attack. I don't know why he helped us, but if he hadn't, we would have been killed in our sleep."

Bey sat with his head hanging. Now he understood why *war* was an obscenity in the Skandian language. Now it didn't seem so bad, all the endless discussion and the consensus groups and the little lectures on avoiding polarization, and the other behaviors that the oldgens in the forum engaged in so earnestly. He found he yearned for the old days, when an argument with his father was the worst conflict he could imagine. Anything was better than having your flesh sliced open for reasons you couldn't even understand.

He curled up in the sand and fell into a dead sleep.

Most of the community seemed to have followed his example. When he woke up, feeling gritty and dry, he saw that most of the others were just getting up, too. The fire was down to white ash and a few flickers. A few people were already trying to clean up the camp.

He heard his father shouting much more loudly than usual.

"Stop that!" Whitman ordered. Bey turned to see what he was doing.

Hamam and Adil had gathered up the spent darts that still lay in the sand, and had been about to pile them on the dying fire. They looked up, incredulous at Whitman's angry tone.

"We were afraid someone might hurt themselves on these," Hamam said.

"Don't burn them," Whitman said. "We can modify them to use with the harpoons. We need anything that could be used for defense."

"Darts and burning sticks won't do it if they come back and their aim is better," Torker said.

Whitman turned to Sofron.

"You said there was a place upstream where you had seen remnants of earlier inhabitants," he said.

"Yes, but I didn't see any artifacts. No tools or anything like that. If there were people there, it was a long, long time ago."

"As everyone knows but you, Sofron, one of the reasons I urged moving here after our . . . uh . . . metamorphosis was the hope that on a larger landmass we'd find more resources. Possibly even some items of technology that might have been left behind by an earlier expedition. We have a metal detector, but the dense forest makes such a search impractical right now. And if there were indigenous people who lived near the sea, it might still be possible to find something we could use."

Bey couldn't believe that Whitman was still making speeches in his usual, domineering way after so many of them had nearly been killed. But the rest of the colony seemed almost to welcome it. He supposed it was because they were used to it. It gave them something to focus on besides their fears.

Not everyone welcomed it, though.

"That's not a bad idea, Whitman, if we had time to think about it," Sofron said. "Right now we should be thinking about five children lost in the Deep, or in that forest, with Killers like that on the loose. I have no other priorities. If you can't help me, I can't help you. I'll just go my way, and you can find those sites you're so interested in on your own."

"You're blackmailing me," Whitman said. His taloned fingers worked at his side. "Blackmailing all of us! You're still putting five lives—*theoretical* lives, since they're all probably dead already—against the welfare of the whole community."

Sofron's teeth began to show, but her voice was still low and even.

"Certainly not. Mutual benefit, and harmony through cooperation. Weren't you taught those things in social-ethical class?"

Bader Puntherong spoke unexpectedly.

"Mutual benefit," he said. "The newgens volunteer to go with Sofron to where she saw the children last. On the way we scout for useful things. Agreement?"

Sofron agreed reluctantly. But once the decision had been made, she was obviously in a hurry to get going.

"We search for clues before we search for weapons," she said. "That way it won't be a complete waste of my time."

She turned to Whitman while the others who wanted to go with her began packing up.

"Whitman, since you seem destined to spend your time facilitating everything, this warning is for you: Anything you see can grow a mouth, and it *will* eat you. Can you understand that? Don't go in the woods. I've learned some things about what to avoid. And the brightsnakes protect me from some things, too. But I won't be here to advise you."

She turned to the rest of the group.

"Make him understand that you have to stay here. If he takes you out bushwhacking, you'll get yourselves killed."

Whitman balked at sending out essential equipment and able-bodied citizens without official supervision. Finally Torker volunteered to accompany them, and Whitman reluctantly let him take the metal detector. They were about to push the raft out into the water when the doctor stopped them.

"There's one question that must be answered before anyone goes anywhere," she said. "As your medical officer, I insist. How are we going to dispose of the bodies?"

"Can't we just drag them into the Deep?" Hamam said.

"No." Half a dozen people, mostly newgens, spoke simultaneously. Bey shuddered. The thought of those pale corpses rotting in their swimming space, their source of life, made them sick.

"Uh . . . bury them?" Miko suggested.

"It's hard to bury things deep enough, on a beach," Adil said. "I, for one, do not want to see any part of them coming back up."

"Well then, can we just get some wood and burn them?" Torker said.

"It's actually not that easy to get bodies to burn without an accelerant," Melicar said. "I don't think anyone here really wants to do that."

Torker looked exasperated.

"What's your idea, then? I say they're dead; let's get rid of them. I don't care how."

"Put them on the raft," Sofron said. "We can take care of them on our way upriver."

"You're not going to dump them in the river?" Engku said, her voice quivering a little. "I don't like to think of them . . . coming back down."

"No, I'm not going to dump them in the river," Sofron said. "I'm going to dispose of them elsewhere. I know a place. Don't worry; you won't see them again."

She refused to have anything more to do with the bodies, however; she left it to others to lay tough leaves on the raft and sling the bodies on top of them. Then, finally, they set out.

They went upstream a little way, cut into the jungle before they came to the tanglewood grove, and hacked their way through to the edge of the green stingmoss meadow. Sofron made disposable bark sandals for all of them. When they came ashore, they lashed together a makeshift skid out of fallen branches and pulled the bodies out into the meadow. They rolled the bodies off the skid onto the smooth green surface.

The hair-thin tendrils of moss were instantly alive, clinging to the tough skin of the dead White Ones, trying to get through to the meal within.

"The stingmoss will make them disappear in a few days," Sofron said. "I figure this is good. If we can get one enemy to eat the other, they deserve each other."

Dilani signed fiercely to Bey. She would not deign to use speech on this occasion.

"If I die here, put me in the water. I will go and find my parents. If something eats me, it should be something fierce. I won't be eaten by a plant!"

"Where are we going?" Torker asked as the raft swung out into the current again. They all felt more cheerful now that the bodies were gone and they were away from their injured companions. It was easier not to think about it.

"Upstream. Past the point where you all disembarked. There's a part of the river where it's been channelized and you can still see the stones. It seems to be pretty safe. Whoever made it used a variety of techniques to discourage the natural predators."

" 'Whoever'? You really think someone lived here before?"

"I don't know who they were, but I can show you a picture later on. I haven't seen any signs of life here, though, and it all looks very old. There's what looks like lava flows, rockfalls, other damage that looks as if it was done ages ago, and hasn't been repaired. So I think whatever kind of people did this have been gone for a long time. When I first saw you, I thought you might be the owners coming back. But it was only you . . ."

They passed the point of their encounter with the tube-mouths the day before.

"My feet still hurt," Dilani said. She turned up her feet and examined the tender soles. The skin was still puffy and reddened.

"That's left over from getting into the stingmoss yesterday," Sofron said. "It penetrates the skin and extracts blood and fluids. Each filament only absorbs a few blood cells, so it's not really dangerous to large prey, unless you fall unconscious. Then it will suck you dry.

"I've seen small prey head across a stingmoss field. They get groggy and dehydrated before they know what hit them. Then they fall down, and the field gradually finishes them off.

"But for once, there's no venom involved, so when you get over the skin irritation, you'll be fine."

With several powerful paddlers and a well-constructed raft, they reached the upper reaches of the river faster than Sofron expected. They passed through the shadowed channel and into the shaped branch of the river, then paddled on through shallow water, clear and warm, with a sandy bottom that showed occasional patches of vegetation or multicolored pebbles.

It would have been a pleasant journey if Sofron hadn't been in such a hurry. Her thoughts and worries were interrupted by an exclamation from Torker.

"Hey! Whitman's little widget actually works! I'm getting a reading that there's metal in this area. Iron, nickel . . . Hell, that looks like a reading for aluminum. That can't be right. Maybe it's not working after all."

He knelt on the raft, turning slowly and watching the device in his hand.

"It's over there, in that rocky area."

The land rose steeply, seeming to bar their way. The rocky slopes were broken and tumbled, and were covered over with the black masses that looked like the cooled lava flows in the Deep. If there had been stonework here, it had been demolished long ago.

"The sea's on the other side of that headland," Sofron said. "The lava pretty much covers the area and extends out into the water on the other side. If there's something buried beneath it, Whitman will have a hard time finding it."

"Maybe it's reading ores in the rock. I'm not an expert with this thing. But I think I should be getting a different spectrum if the metals were mixed with impurities. This looks like metal in a pure form."

"Pure aluminum in a lava flow? I don't think so."

Torker shrugged and let the device fall from his hand and dangle from its cord.

"Fine, Whitman can hike up here and check it out himself."

He looked around. The banks had risen around them until they were almost in a canyon. The sound of running water echoed loudly from the rocky shores.

"What now? Do we have to turn around?"

"No! We've just started. The last place I saw the children was in there." Sofron pointed to the massive ridge that barred their way. The water disappeared into a dark cleft in the rock.

"We can tie the rafts up here," she said. "There are some stubs carved in the rock that look as if they were put there on purpose for mooring."

She didn't say anything about the emergency raft that had disappeared from this very spot.

"It's all right to jump in the water. It's pretty safe here—as safe as anywhere."

They were already waist-deep when Sofron saw a brightness in the water and remembered the tiny snakes.

"This is where I got the brightsnakes," she said hurriedly. "Don't be afraid! They won't hurt you. They just want to sample you. Let them come—it's a good thing."

There were a few nervous shrieks and giggles as the snakes surrounded them in a ticklish swarm. Sofron was tired of listening to the Skandians' outcries at every novelty or danger, but she was pleased that most of the newgens accepted the snakes with more curiosity than fear. She knew Torker was afraid, because she was standing next to him and could feel his motes diffusing toward her, but he remained stoic. When a grass-green snake had attached itself around his arm, he held it closer to his face and looked at it. Then, to her surprise, he grinned.

"Pretty," he commented.

*   *   *

Subtle sat on the bank and watched. The snakes did not like his taste, it seemed; there must be a residual flavor of the Round Folk about him. Like the humans who had traveled with Subtle before, these humans balked at entering narrow spaces. Humans feared the close confinement where Round Folk found security. But after urging from Sofron, they splashed into the shadows of the cleft and disappeared. What was left of Subtle's original nervous system urged him to pull his limbs together, compress himself, and slide through the opening. But his new body would not compress. He scraped himself on the edges and cursed the awkwardness. Then he was safely into deeper water that held a welcome taste of the Deep.

As he rose to the surface, he could hear the humans' voices echoing, loud and excited. Even before he had time to look around, he could tell by the sound that they had entered a space that was wide but still enclosed. When he saw what the humans were looking at, he forgot everything else.

The giant carving on the wall sparkled fitfully in the shifting light that entered from far above. Subtle felt its ancient eyes on him, piercing him to the core. He spun himself in the water, trying to shape the "god" sign of awe with his stiff, dangling limbs.

The voices of the humans came to him faintly now.

"Look at Subtle! He's turning white."

He felt their hands on him, dragging him from the water's embrace. Didn't they know he needed their motes to recover? The empty air struck harshly at his flinching skin.

"What's wrong with him? What is it?" the stranger female said.

"Is being Great People," he said. "Is great oldest elder of beings coming from the Deep. Is standing feet on back of Guardian, showing-wishing Guardian is protecting Great People, and Great People is ruling Deep. Is boasting-wishing both together."

The stranger female knelt down beside him.

"What do you mean, Great People?"

He liked the fact that she addressed him directly. Most of

the humans still spoke to Bey if they wanted information about Subtle.

"They-all is making this place. Long in the long-time is making god. Is changing all, is changing selves. Long in the long-time is going far away. This-I is seeing in eldest's dancing, is never seeing in self-eyes."

The frustration of not being able to dance freely the memories that spun in his mind nearly choked him. How did they bear it—the constant confinement by their hard bones?

He slapped the hateful, flipperish limbs against his torso for emphasis.

"The god they-all is making, it is making-changing this-I. Is making this-I like to Great People, giving-sharing shape of great eldest changers."

That was the amazement that had taken his senses and colors from his skin: this hated shape he wore now was the legendary shape of the Great Ones. He hated the shape of the Great Ones. Oh blasphemy! He was honored with the shape of the Great Ones. Oh glorious surprise! He had sacrificed his old life to attain this metamorphosis, and now he was not satisfied. Oh folly! What an unforgettable dance this would have been. The Round Folk would have passed it on for many lifetimes. And now they would never witness it. Oh sorrow!

He felt a heart-shaking tremor passing through his whole being. It shook him from side to side and burst from his mouth in weird barking sounds.

"He's going into convulsions," the big Torker said.

"I think not." Sofron laid her hand on Torker to stop him from lifting Subtle from the stones. "He's laughing."

Color released again into Subtle's skin in a dizzying flood. The barking stopped, and he lay panting. His gills quivered.

"Is calling this laughing?" he said weakly. "Purpose what?"

"We've never determined that," Sofron said. "It comes when there is great contradiction within, great surprise—but with some cleverness, some joy. It makes us feel better."

Subtle was not sure if he felt better or not. There was an empty place inside him where the laughter had been, but he could not call it back.

"These Great People—they made all this? What is this place for?"

"Is you-I not reading walls?" Subtle said. "Is they not telling?"

The female's eye slits widened. "The carvings have meaning? You know what they say?"

"Maybe." Subtle shrugged. "Round Folk is learning memory walls from Great People. Is maybe same. Possible to try."

"Please!" the female said. "It's very important to me," she added. "This is where I changed, and where the children disappeared. If I set something in motion, something left by the makers, I need to know."

Subtle started with the lower rows of glyphs, where he could rub his sensitive limb-tips over the carvings.

"Is mostly boasting-praying," he said after a time. "Great People tell how great they are, to many generations. Is hoping greatness continues, into more generations."

Then his fingers encountered a symbol that sent a shock through him. It was oval and smooth, and in the center was a circle divided into four.

"This is 'life,' " he whispered. "Or . . . could be 'egg.' Or 'hatching.' " It was like touching the life source of the Great Ones themselves. He was awed.

The symbol-phrase continued. "Place of life," he translated. "Or place of hatching." Subtle felt it was sacrilege to go on, to reveal the secrets of the long dead to these interlopers. But he reminded himself that he was a scholar and all knowledge was, respectfully, his province. The Great People had looked favorably on the long minds of the Round Folk and their capacity to remember. He did no harm.

"This is praising for Guardians. Is asking they come always to this sacred place and show favoring of Great Ones by taking eggs and protecting. Or—no . . ."

He could feel his colors shimmer through uncertainties and back into confidence.

"Not eggs, but hatchlings who is changing. Eggs is lying in nests, in moving water, then is hatchlings coming out and swimming to the Deep. When hatchlings is growing big and strong, is coming home to city that was, long past before this city is fallen. Hatchlings is curling up small, small. Is looking almost like egg. Is sleeping-changing into Great People. Carvings is saying sometimes in long past, Guardians is taking hatchlings and protecting. Is making hatchlings wise, is swimming with Guardians before they is coming back. This wall is hoping-asking Guardians come always to this place, bringing protection, making wise."

The female placed her hands on his limbs as if to catch more meaning from his skin.

"Subtle, what are the Guardians?"

Subtle could only point to the symbol on the wall. "This-I is seeing twice only, on journey to god. And is not seeing with self-eyes; in Deep is not light enough for all of Guardians—they is being very big, very mighty. Is hearing song of Guardians. Greatsong, Deepsong. Old old Round Folk is dancing, every song is coming from Guardian song in the long past. This-I is not knowing."

Subtle could feel the female trembling.

"But the Guardians come no more," she said. "Isn't that right? They don't come here."

"Is true," Subtle acknowledged. "Is being long since any news of Guardians is dancing in this-I's sensing. This-I is feeling much surprise when Guardians is coming to help god, that time when we-I is with Per. Since Great People is passing from this place, Guardians is leaving all alone."

"But I heard some kind of music in the Deep," Sofron said. "As I was waking up. It seemed as if something huge was turning over in the dark. Yet when I woke up, I was alone."

She looked around wildly, her skin trembling with spiral patterns of alarm.

"I'm remembering things that don't make any sense. What if I'm still in the water, drowning?" She clutched her head and gave a high-pitched whistle of frustration and rage. "Who is playing with my mind?"

"What's wrong with her?" Torker said. "Is this changing thing going to make us all crazy?"

"You-I come in the water," Subtle said. "This you-and-I is understanding better in water. Be trusting my skin."

He tugged at Sofron, and Torker reluctantly let him slide the female into the pool with him.

The tremors of Sofron's skin had deepened into a trembling of all her limbs. Her inner eyelids had closed. As they entered the water, a cloud of skin motes bloomed around them. Subtle took control of the mix and turned it toward calming and soothing. He was beginning to get tired of those particular motes, but there seemed to be a great demand for them.

Demanding memories surged through Sofron's mind. She saw children's faces cradled in egg-shaped membranes luminous with moonslight, lit by a glow of cool blue sparks. The water was pitch black, but with senses beyond sight, she knew that giant forms rose beneath her and turned away again. The giants were singing in the Deep.

The taste of calm was in the water around her. She surfaced, and Subtle spoke to her as smoothly as he could in the awkward human language.

"I know your confusion. This is happening to me, too. Be not afraid. Soon you understand better. Godbits came to you, yes?"

She moved her head up and down, the way humans indicated agreement.

"The seeds of change are carried inside the godbits. They grow in your body and change it. This happened to all the humans. But it's not so bad because you is two legs, two arms, eyes in front, and is still so. Only with different breathing and some other things."

Her motes showed high anxiety, but she was still in control. She was listening.

She turned on Subtle with her neck spines quivering. "You . . . you're the one! You took him there. But why have you changed shape?"

"This-I is different. Is starting out Round." In his new shape, he could not even form the sign for "Round Folk." It was a small but constant grief to him that he could not even name himself. Instead, he had to make the human sign for a cephalopod and then sign for twelve limbs. But the human scholar signaled understanding.

"This-I is having Round sight, Round hearing, Round limbs all around. Now is two sides, eyes front. The mind is finding no place with this body, is losing thinking. You understand?"

"That makes sense. Your mind was wired up for a multi-lateral body. It wasn't enough to just change you to a biped if your brain couldn't run that body."

"Godbits is bringing little changes to mind, too, not just body. Is changing memories. Per-god is sharing mind with this-I. Per mind-bits and this-I mind is linking together, making one thing, so this-I can remember body that is never having.

"Same for you, this-I is thinking. Per-god is sending god mind-bits for you, to share mind with you. Now you-I is awake, but new memories is feeling like dreams. Confusing. You-I must let confusion in, let dreams come. You-I mind and mind-bits ties new net."

Sofron's colors cleared. "I understand," she said after a minute. "Those bubble things—you called them godbits? They can create memory transfer? Interesting."

She was truly a scholar, Subtle thought. Understanding turned back her fear. She looked more like herself. Then he realized that the familiarity of her face came not from his own memories, but from those ghosts of the god's mind that haunted his new body. Nevertheless, he felt that he knew her.

She is my friend. I will protect her.

Had the seeds of those feelings come from Per-god? It no longer mattered to him. He wanted her as his own friend.

"Takes time to knot this net," he said. "Not all comes clear in one seeing."

Sofron floated calmly now, thinking. She tugged at the edges of her own memory. There was something hidden there, something that had been covered up by the additions. After the dark forms, there had been one more thing—something that had frightened her before she fell asleep.

Suddenly she clawed at the edge of the pool and scrambled out of the water.

❧15❧❧❧❧❧

"They were there. The Bone Things. The White Things. They were looking at us. Wearra was right. That was no dream!"

"White Killers here, too?" Torker said. "I thought you said they were afraid of the places that belonged to the old people."

"This pool is very deep," Sofron said. "It goes out to the Deep, beyond the rocks. Maybe, after all this time, if they found the way in, they would dare to try it."

"But why? What are they looking for? Why do they keep following us?" Torker said.

Sofron frowned. "I don't know. Things from the old people—that's what Wearra wanted."

"What happened to the keto?" Dilani demanded.

"I don't know that, either. I don't remember a keto anywhere around, when I woke up."

Dilani whistled angrily. "Evil! They kill my pod mates!" she hissed.

Sofron was looking down into the pool, trying to see past the faintly glowing fronds around the edge.

"We could go through the passage into the sea, and search all the way down to the true Deep," she suggested. "I've been as far as the edge of the island slope, but I didn't dare go all the way down, alone."

Torker held out Whitman's sensing device, which hung from its cord around his neck.

"I need to finish checking with this first," he said. "It's not just for Whitman. If we go searching in the Deep, we're going to need some kind of protection. Anything we could find would help, even if it was just a metal stick to hit things with."

"All right," Sofron said. The demanding memories were fading, allowing her to focus on the present again.

She stuck her head back in the pool and took a long suck of water, savoring its brackish flavor. Then she followed Torker in his search.

The readings led them directly to the foot of the wall that held the giant carving.

"Well, if it's embedded in here, it's not going to do us much good," Torker said. "Maybe we're getting readings from little nodules in this decorative stuff."

He swept the device back and forth in front of the wall.

"It still reads like solid, concentrated lumps, though. Wish I had a scanner instead of this thing."

Sofron stared at the foot of the bas-relief. Cautiously, almost reverently, she stepped closer and touched the carving.

"It's still so clear, the shapes so perfect, after such a long time," she said. "As if they'd just gone away for a little while. I feel as if I'm trespassing here. On the other hand—"

She rubbed her palm over the rough surface of the carved Guardian carapace that bulged from the plane of the carving into the room, like the prow of a ship.

"On the other hand, this world has assimilated us, whether we like it or not. So we're at home here, I guess.

"Come here, Tork. Didn't you ever have a hiding place around your group home? A loose brick or a hollowed stone?"

He looked at her without comprehension.

"Oh, well, probably not. Your living space was probably in much better repair than mine. There were plenty of loose bricks around Whiteford, believe me."

She felt her way around the stone. "Ah, there it is! I said come here, Tork. This might need two."

Subtle followed them, entranced, in time to see them slip their hands into curved notches on either side of the stone, depressions that had been hidden by the pattern of the carving. The porous texture of the rock made it easy to get a purchase even when the hands were wet and slippery.

They gave a tug, and the stone opened like a shell before his eyes. Inside were treasures no one had seen since the Great People went away. Subtle's colors trembled like morning light behind clouds.

"So what the hell is this?" Torker said.

Pulling out a bundle of silver-colored sticks wrapped in a sling net, he aimed Whitman's measuring device at the bundle.

"This registers as aluminum," he said. "Hard to believe, but there it is." He pulled out one of the sticks and tossed it in one big hand.

"Not much of a weapon for Whitman. I suppose you could use it like a baton, but it wouldn't last long. Forget it if you hit someone's hard skull with this."

Subtle quivered with indignation. One of his limbs strayed to the scholar's knife at his belt. For that precious bit of metal, he had quested for more than a year and had risked his life innumerable times. The human held wealth for which the Round Folk would have given many lives, and he set it down with a shrug, like something without value. There were two more bundles like it. Subtle picked them up and slung them to his own belt, hastily, lest the humans decide they were not worth keeping.

Even more of a puzzle were the three remaining objects. They hung from mesh straps of some tough material that had survived however many years the objects had been waiting. Sofron lifted one from its hanger, and Dilani, curious, darted in and seized the next.

The objects were roughly boxlike, but they were put together from a random-seeming piecework of differently colored metals, as well as something slick yet hard. Subtle did not know what to call it in human terms; Sofron said that it could have been ceramic or enamel. Each object had the same general shape, but the coloring and patterns were different. Each surface was interrupted by protrusions and depressions.

Sofron tilted hers carefully, but nothing emerged from the nozzlelike protrusions.

Dilani turned her box over in her hands, seeking the most comfortable way to hold it. She pressed down on inserts that looked like buttons or keys, but nothing happened. Nevertheless, she hung it around her neck by the cord, with the same kind of instinctive greed that had prompted Subtle.

"Is that it, then?" Torker said. "Whitman will be ticked. This doesn't amount to much."

Sofron reached inside and searched the squared-off cavity inside the rock.

"If you want to get all your New Year's gifts, you have to make sure to shake the box," she admonished. "There is something else in here, in the corners."

She pulled out three tubes about a foot long. The sides were a dull, sandy color, like the inside of the rock, but one end was polished and clear. One side of each tube was marked with a long, straight groove that held a smooth glass bead. Sofron flicked her thumb across the bead and discovered that it slid along the groove. And as it slid, something within the tube began to glow. The light had a green tint. It was a soft, diffuse glow at first, but it brightened to a greenish white beam too bright to stare at directly.

"Now these will be useful," she said. "To scare off White Ones, if nothing else."

She looked longingly at the dark waters of the pool.

"We could go down and make a quick check around," she said. "With the lights—maybe we could find some clues."

Torker looked upward to check the position of the sun. Already the light coming through the high window was less bright, as the sun sank. He nodded, but made Sofron promise to return in half an hour.

Subtle and some of the others submerged with her. They confirmed what she already believed—that the pool opened to the Deep. But the tide had come and gone often enough to erase any possible traces of those who had followed that pathway.

Even after Sofron reluctantly surfaced, she still lingered on the edge of the pool, her gaze following the beam of light as far as it would reach into the depths, and farther. What drew her away was a familiar sound—a chittering and squeaking—followed by startled exclamations from the humans.

She came out of the cave just in time to prevent Torker from whacking the excited water dogs with a stout stick.

"Stop! They won't hurt you!" she shouted.

"Do you say that about *everything*?" Torker said, but he put the stick down. The water dogs continued to bump and sniff him until Sofron came into view. Then they abandoned him and whisked over to examine her, with enthusiastic exclamations.

"We called these guys the water dogs," Sofron said. "You can see why. They're awfully friendly, for lizards, or salamanders, or newts, or whatever they are. They seem awfully smart, too; look at those skulls. Assuming they have brains in them, that is. They got really friendly with me and the kids, but I haven't seen them since we changed."

The water dogs rubbed their necks happily against the humans' wrists and ankles, all the places where the skin was most sensitive and motes were easiest to detect.

"I suppose it's like dogs sniffing each others' butts," Torker muttered. "But why do they want to sniff us?"

Sofron shrugged. "I don't know why, but their colors get brighter. You can see if you watch for a while. It seems as if our motes are good for them."

She felt a little foolish because she was so happy to see the water dogs again. She supposed it was because things, and people, vanished so fast on Typhon. If anything you liked came back to you, it was a remarkable event. She hoped it was a good omen.

When they got back on the raft, the water dogs milled around on shore, squealing pitifully. Then, apparently possessed by the same good idea, they swarmed the raft.

"Hey!" Torker was about to start throwing them off, but the newgens protested.

"We want everybody else to see this," they said. "They're fun."

"And there are damn few things on Typhon that are fun," Bader added.

So the water dogs accompanied them, sliding on and off the raft. Sofron noticed that by the time they reached the shore, Torker was actually smiling.

They arrived back in camp just before sunset. Whitman and those who remained in camp had gathered fire materials and piled them in heaps that formed a defensive perimeter. They had already started a small fire with long sticks laid ready to serve as torches.

Sofron noticed some of the adults hacking at the ends of long sticks with their utility cutters. She assumed it was something to do with the fire, but then saw that they were deliberately making sharp points on the ends. They avoided her eyes in shame when they saw her looking curiously at them. Skandians were making weapons. It went against every principle they had ever been taught.

Sofron watched the slow creep of shamed colors roll over Whitman's face and chest.

"Yes, we're making weapons," he said, a little too loudly. "There's nothing in the social covenant that says we have to let ourselves be eaten by wild animals."

"These are wild animals that can learn sign," Sofron said. "At least one of them could. Let's not deceive ourselves about what we're doing. We seem to be preparing ourselves for our own little war."

The word "war" crashed violently into their Skandian ears.

Whitman's spines flared. He hissed at her, a startling, reptilian sound, and stalked away from her to examine their booty.

Meanwhile, the newgens gathered around to play with the water dogs, who slithered happily around the group, checking everyone's motes, and pairing up with selected humans by ones and twos. Sofron noticed that they seemed to prefer newgens, though they also liked some of the adults. They markedly avoided Whitman, as well as the sick people, but the mood in camp lightened at their coming.

"What is the meaning of this invasion?" Whitman exploded

when the water dogs came frolicking down to the beach. "The last thing we need is more creatures. Lizards, snakes—can't we have one corner of the beach that isn't infested?"

He completed his inspection and turned on Torker.

"Is this all?" he said. "We need tools, weapons—yes, *weapons*—something useful. This is junk."

"I appreciate you, too," Torker muttered. He was playing with the metal tubes. The separate sections seemed to fit together, making two long poles about the height of a human. They were pointed at one end and had grips at about the right height for a tall person to grasp while standing upright. Torker put his hands on the grips and flailed the poles around, but they seemed awkward as weapons.

"Hey!" Bey jumped out of the way as the silver pole whipped past him. "That could really hurt."

"I suppose. But it would be hard to kill anything with one of these. They're way too fragile."

He stuck the poles into the ground, where they nodded gently in the wind, like saplings.

Whitman had regained some of his equanimity.

"I'm sorry, Torker; we all appreciate your efforts, and those of the others on the team. I had hoped for more. But this does show there may be more artifacts available. Tomorrow we'll plan a systematic exploration. If we can do this well in one day, we should be able to find something really helpful eventually."

"*Tomorrow* we are beginning a search pattern in the Deep, to find our missing citizens," Sofron said. Whitman chose to ignore that for the time being.

Dilani kept working at the box hung around her neck. She was hoping the box might unfold and reveal something more interesting within. Two of the six sides were marked by deep, smooth grooves. Remembering how Sofron had opened the box made of rock, she tried slipping her hands into the grooves, and found that they fit perfectly. Suddenly the box felt comfortable in her hands. Her fingers explored within the grooves. Then she felt a click as her talons slid into invisible notches. She pressed tentatively.

A blast of sound reverberated. All the humans pressed their hands to their ears, and some of them shrieked. Dilani dropped the box, tripped, and fell to the ground. Water dogs scattered in all directions. Dilani sat and stared at the box for a minute. Then she seized it and enthusiastically repeated her actions, with the same result.

"Stop!" most of the adults cried simultaneously.

Sofron was laughing. "I think you've found a musical instrument," she said. "Unless it's a warning siren. But maybe you should postpone further practice until you're on the open sea. It's kind of loud in a close group."

Nevertheless, Dilani and the other newgens experimented persistently with the boxes, endlessly trying the patience of the adults. Bey and several of the others soon succeeded in producing musical tones, and even something that sounded vaguely tuneful, but Dilani seemed intent on creating discordant combinations, overlaid with trills and whistles.

"Dilani, put that thing down or it's going into the sea with the fishes, bye-bye," Torker said irritably. "It's ten times worse than those pipes Henner made."

Dilani stopped playing, but strolled down to the shore and splashed noisily in the surf, just to show she wasn't intimidated. Knowing that sounds could seriously annoy other people made hearing marginally more attractive, in her estimation.

Sofron hadn't seen her friend the doctor when the others had come to greet the exploration team. So she sought Sushan out and found her rigging a shade for the injured to sleep under.

Sofron looked curiously at the people who had been hurt: Madan, one of the engineers; Engku, a teacher; Wayan and Kusma, both newgens; a couple of others. Sushan had made a pallet of soft new giling leaves for Phun Skanderup, whose torn-up leg looked messy and painful, and for Madan, who was still semiconscious. Uli Haddad had taken himself off the sick list as soon as his lacerated ribs had scabbed over.

Sushan strolled down the beach with Sofron, as if casually, but her skin showed anxiety.

"It's tough being a doctor when your feelings are tattooed

on your face," Sushan said. "They say 'How am I doing?' and I say 'Oh, you're going to be just fine,' and they say 'Liar!' "

"What are you so worried about?" Sofron said. "They look like a bunch of slackers to me. Those little scratches and things are nothing. That gel stuff our skins make now seals up cuts like magic."

"Well, that's the funny thing," Sushan said. She looked around to make sure no one was close enough to hear.

"I would have thought the same as you. Except for Madan, their cuts in themselves are nothing. But their general condition is worse than the injuries seem to warrant. They act as if they've had some kind of systemic shock. Some of those with the cuts and bites are worse off than Phun, who got her leg cut open. Makes me wonder if there's some venom or even just a foreign substance that's causing an allergic reaction."

She lowered her voice even further.

"Tell you what really worries me—have you noticed the way Whitman's been acting?"

"Sushan, I haven't been around Whitman or any of you in a long time. I don't know what's normal for him. He was always self-important and devious, and that hasn't changed."

"His colors aren't good," Sushan said. "And he gets angry. He always had control. Now he's slipping."

"But he didn't even get hurt last night," Sofron said. "He spent most of his time on the ground with his hands over his head."

"Not last night," Sushan said. "But he did get clawed the first time we were attacked. On the raft. His hands were scratched up. The cuts are healing, but have you noticed? There are white patches, like a skin disease or something, spreading up his arms."

"I've always considered Whitman as an annoying rash anyway."

"Very funny," Sushan said, but she didn't look amused. "We've already lived through the genetic damage done to the newgens by a virus we picked up from the water. I'll be ecstatic if this is nothing more than a skin rash. I don't want to get my patients worried about it unless something more alarming develops. But I did want to tell you so you can double-check me. You have the most objective eye of any of us, just because you've been outside the group for a while."

Sofron felt uncomfortable.

"I'll be glad to help out if I can. But I don't want you to count on me and then be let down. My first and only concern is finding those children. The rest of the colony can take care of itself. You're all grown-ups—even the newgens. If the colony will help me, they'll have my full devotion. But if they don't, I'm going to do whatever it takes, alone if necessary."

"Fair warning." Sushan sighed. "I wish I could go with you. But my job is here, with the sick. As always. I'm not as sure as you are that they can take care of themselves."

༄16༄ ༄ ༄ ༄

Through all his life as a human, Per had wanted his memories back. He had arrived on Skandia at some point in early adolescence. The physicians who had studied him and turned him over to the care workers in the living group at Stonefield had assigned him an age of fourteen, Skandian. The truth remained a mystery.

He had brief, fractured glimpses of life before Skandia, like reflections from a shattered mirror. He had been told that he'd been rescued from a derelict ship, that he'd been in cold stasis for a long time, and that the memory loss was probably damage from that time. After all, he had been the only survivor found on board. He was lucky to have the remainder of his life, they had told him; let go of the fragments, they said.

Later on, he had found that he *couldn't* remember. Any attempt had cost him unbearable pain. As he grew up, as he studied biology and the functions of the human body and learned how those functions could be affected by targeted intervention, he had realized that his pain was not the inevitable result of stasis damage. Someone had intentionally denied him his past. They had never meant to give him a choice.

Now, the death of the body they had tinkered with had set him free from their restrictions. At first he had exulted in the freedom to search for his memories. But he still had no framework to fit the new knowledge into. He was battered and confused by a past he still could not understand. He had been set adrift in a sea of demanding images. Kitkit hadn't really given him a choice, either.

He was tired of drifting. And he was beginning to suspect

161

that Kitkit wanted him to wander around his own head, distracted from the here and now. He did have a choice, though, and he was determined to use it. He wouldn't give in to the ebb and flow of another's wishes—even if that other called itself a god.

He pulled away from the seductive memories and forced himself back to the disconcerting reality of his new existence. He was swimming in a sea of raw data. He started trying to sort it out.

The first layer was the water itself—temperature, depth, currents and waves, and all the different subtle flavors caused by varying salinity, mineral content, and body traces of the inhabitants.

Layered over that were the stable features that echoed back sound and water waves. He could sense the configuration of the sea floor and the seamounts around him, all the crenellations of coral, and the different textures of rock, sand, mud, or shell.

The movements of individuals within this soundscape were the most exciting and the hardest to track. Like an orchestra with a thousand instruments, they sang to Per with interwoven voices. He struggled to tease out of them the one song he wanted to hear—reports of human travels.

He was surprised and puzzled to find no human form echoing anywhere in keto song, or even in the mindless mirrors that were the eyes of the schooling fish. Finally he locked onto a strange keto who was complaining of a foul flavor, one that was familiar to Per—the taste of something burnt. He zoomed in on the data stream that ketos constantly broadcast to each other and came face-to-face with a dead White Killer.

The body had caught on a stub of rock halfway down a submerged seamount; otherwise it would have fallen all the way to the floor of the Abyss, where ketos do not go. It had been partially eaten by scavengers already, but the blackened arms and hands were still visible.

Suddenly, Per was aware of Kitkit's consciousness sharing this perception with him.

"You've examined them in detail, right?" Per said.

"Oh, yes." The Great Person's tone sounded grim, though

Per knew it was only in his mind. "I have had hundreds of years to know them."

"How could you get a specimen?" Per said. "Did you get the ketos to bring you dead ones?"

"Yes . . ." Kitkit's tone was vague. "It is almost impossible to find the White Ones dead. They have little buoyancy. They sink to the Abyss as soon as their vitality fades. At times their fellows eat them. The flesh of the Killers is tough, and bitter with unpleasing motes. But to the White Ones, meat is meat."

A ribbonfish drifted into the keto's field of view. It fastened needlelike teeth in the dead flesh and tugged off shreds.

The keto whistled disgust at base creatures who would eat dead flesh. With a flick of the tail, he was elsewhere, and the scene presented through his soundsense shifted away. The White Killer vanished.

Per's mind plunged through the scene before him, as if his step had shattered a thin pane of ice and plunged him into the depths below.

He fell back into his own memories.

Again in the steel-bounded garden, he held a plastic scoop with which he shoveled a damp, black, fibrous substance from a conduit to the trays and beds where the plants grew. The fox-faced man named Rameau followed him, spreading the black stuff around the roots and spraying it with liquid from a fat hose.

"Be careful with that; don't spill," Rameau said to him. "These are the cast-off bodies of your cohorts. Treat them with some reverence."

At that, the young Per in the memory jerked the scoop back, scattering a whole load of black stuff across the kemplex floor and startling the Per who watched and had forgotten that he had no control over this scene.

"Don't act so surprised," Rameau chided. "Surely you knew that everything we eat, breathe, and drink has been recycled thousands of times. We are a fertile island in a dark sea. We have no access to resources beyond this steel sky."

"The dead cohorts go into total conversion!" the boy shouted. "They are 't-*transfigured* in the purity of fire.' It's what they say in the parting ceremony. They don't bury them in the garden."

He knelt and sullenly scraped the spilled material together. "You're just playing with my mind again," he said.

"It's not a game," Rameau said. "I'm trying to get you to *use* your mind. Of course they tell you the bodies go into total conversion. It sounds better. But you don't seriously think we could waste such a valuable nitrogen source, not to mention all the other elements that are so scarce here. We scavenge everything. Including each other. Your dead cohorts' blood turns up in your tomato juice next week."

"I don't believe you. That's horrible," the boy said.

The man aimed the hose and sprayed the last fragments of compost across the floor and into a nearby drain.

"Emotional reactions cause waste," he said. "There's a lesson for you to remember."

"We're not cannibals," the boy said.

"Oh, but we are. That's one of the nasty things the planet-bound say about us: that we consume one another's flesh to preserve our unnatural existence. And it's true."

The boy stared at the dark, moist heap with distaste. Then, with a resolute movement, he thrust his hand into the pile and brought out a fistful. He bent and smelled it.

"It smells good," he said. "It's just dirt. Like what's already here. It doesn't smell like dead things."

"It is, though. Dead flesh and waste and spoiled food—everything we think of as ugly because it's out of place. Put it together a different way, it's tomato juice. Or blood. Or black earth waiting for the seeds. The world's a puzzle with a billion pieces. You can put them together all kinds of different ways."

The boy had a sudden thought. "How do the planet-bound get their dirt?" he asked.

"Same way as us, little Per." Rameau patted the boy's head as if he were a trained cat. "Exactly the same. Now you're thinking. Don't forget to shovel while you think."

Per found himself back in Kitkit's pool.

"Where did you go?" Kitkit said.

"It was one of those uncontrolled memories," Per said. "Something you said triggered it, I guess. What does that look like, from your point of view?"

"Your image remained. But it ceased to move and speak. It was only for a moment, as if you had been distracted."

"So, you don't see my memories just because I'm seeing them?"

"No," Kitkit said. "They are physically stored in a different part of the god's body. Your connections to that place are more complete than mine. In the same way, you do not perceive all of my memories. The synaptic pathways to them have not formed for you. Over time, we might become equally linked to the whole body of the god. For now, I must provide a link for you before you can share my memories."

With a movement of his hand, he opened a door in the seeming air above the seeming pool, and through the door's arch all was shadow and silver. Per could feel the night breeze blowing through the door, ruffling the surface of the pool, and his skin quivered with pleasure. He had been so long in the womb of ocean, closed away from the free air.

But Per resisted returning to the remembered city.

"Why don't the ketos bring me news?" he demanded. "What happened to that White Killer? It was burned. Where did the fire come from? I thought you were going to explain that to me, not talk about eggs."

He sent out the questions to the wandering keto as he spoke. His communication was not as smooth as Kitkit's, but it was powerful.

Sun descending to the water/Fire bursts upward from the waves
Hands of whiteness/hands of fire/hands of human color
Water burns
Bone screams

The keto sang out in a single burst of sound. The rest of his pod commented antiphonally on their own invisibility:

following the humans unseen, yet with human fire brightening their eyes.

"Wait," Per said to Kitkit. "They knew where the humans were? But they didn't help them? Humans were fighting White Killers on the Deep, and you didn't tell me? What is going on?"

In the back of his mind he could feel the ketos springing out of water in injured innocence.

The god directs/the god questions
Two-headed god swims in circles

They complained.

"I did not order the ketos to leave them," Kitkit said. "The Bright Teeth misinterpret! They thought humans were safe out of water! So they only watched."

"But when the Killers attacked them, when they made the fire, why didn't the ketos go to help them?"

"No one was killed," Kitkit said. "Your friends are all right."

The ketos helpfully informed Per that they had seen many White Killers approaching the Big Dry, but all had fled to the Deep again—they thought. Ketos took a casual approach to strict numerical accuracy. There was much laughter at the dilapidated state of the returning White Ones.

Tiny-teeth humans—big bite

The ketos chortled approvingly.

"Show me the humans," Per cried out to the ketos. The crude force of his call made ketos within a radius of many miles leap and shake their heads. "They are my pod!" he shrieked. "Find them or I show big teeth!"

The ketos protested that the humans were all in the Dry where they could not be seen.

Per turned his rage on Kitkit. "Make them save the humans," he said, "or I will never help you. Whatever you want from me, you'll have to get without my cooperation—if you can. I will stir up madness within us until you have to kill me. You *must* help the humans."

"You fool!" Kitkit's anger scalded Per. "You are like the Bright Teeth—no horizon to your sight, gobbling the moment, seeing nothing more! I try to help your kin, and in thanks you threaten me! You must understand that we are all in danger. See this! See it!"

Without permission or courtesy, he was thrust back into the City of Towers. The sun sank and it was dark. The night scents blew from the marsh—sweetness of night-blooming flowers, mouth-watering spiciness of spotted frogs and other prey. But with the good scents came something dangerous, something wrong. It smelled of deep airless water, of old iron, of oil and rot.

They came up from the marshes, not through the fire-guarded gates. They were pale and lean, like ghastly shadows of the Kalko'uli. They seized the hatchlings and the newly changed, and rent and tore them. Screams of agony and whistled alarms filled the air. Bold, gleaming warriors attacked them and killed many. But not all. And not all the warriors attacked; some refused, held back by a fear Per could not translate.

Again and again they attacked, and each time Per saw fewer of the warriors answering. In the last scene Kitkit let him see, the White Ones grasped a struggling hatchling and carried it with them, still alive. Its eyes begged dumbly for help even as it disappeared with its captors into the dark water. Kitkit felt a sickness and revulsion that swept Per, as well, though he didn't know why.

The air was thick with smoke that stung the throat. Every breath burned with unescapable motes of rot, of burning, of death, of evil. Kitkit knelt not on the smooth ceramic rim of a still pool, but on the torn and muddied ground of the City of Towers. Before him, a pile of livid corpses smoldered, half consumed. Clan members poured a harsh-smelling liquid over the heap, and the fire roared up anew. Similar heaps were everywhere. In the distance warriors ran to and fro, and shrieks sounded from the distant battlefield.

Then it wasn't so distant. The enemies had come within the

gates of the city, and clan members ran mad with terror in every street.

Abruptly, the scholars' towers went dark. Frogs still sang in the marshes, but the voices of the Kalko'uli had fallen silent.

"The White Killers came," Kitkit said in a harsh whisper. "They came, and we were destroyed. They will come for your people, too. Help me kill them. Help me drive them from the Deep. Then you can return to mortal form, and my ancestors will at last sleep quietly."

Per was still angry, but with understanding came a cold anger tinged with fear.

"This was your plan all along, wasn't it?" he said. "You didn't take me in and break down and remake my people out of some vague helpful impulse, or because you were lonely, or any of that other pap you've been feeding me. You needed cannon fodder to fight off the White Killers, didn't you? *That* is the role you intended us to play.

"You told me you were sending the ketos to find the other humans—and maybe you did, but you told them just to watch, not help. You called off your pet ketos so we'd have to face the Killers by ourselves. You baited the trap, and stupid Whitman has doubtless walked right into it. The humans have confronted the Killers and begun the war. We have no choice but to play out the game."

"You made the choice to come here," Kitkit said. "You desired to be one with my world—to replace my people. How have I wronged you? I give you a chance to live. Take it or not—there is your choice."

Per still faced up to him.

"Send the ketos to them. Bring them here and let me speak to them. You don't understand them—they were never trained to fight, and they've had no enemies for generations. If you try to make them fight the White Ones, they'll die."

"They will be supplied with tools," Kitkit said. "The transformation has already given them the ability to fight, if they will use it. I *will* bring them here, and you will see for yourself that what I do is necessary. You are a scholar. You could fight for them with the god's weapons—find a way to kill the enemy from within. Then your people would be safe. They could live a long time in the Deep. Maybe as long as the Great People.

"Now leave me. I mourn for my city."

Per fled the darkening room. He spent a long day coaxing the ketos. He found Slowbolt and sang with him, but even Slowbolt couldn't tell him anything more of the lone human. It was as if she had disappeared from the face of the Deep.

Per's attention returned slowly from the vast Deep where he had been questing, listening. Like one of Typhon's children falling from the sky edge to settle at last into the eternal night of the Abyss, his mind descended back into the darkened place where Kitkit had been grieving for hundreds of years, alone.

"Show me the White Killers," Per said. "Let me learn about them. I want to help my people. I will try your way."

The memory opened before him immediately, as if Kitkit's mind had already been brooding on that place.

They were still in a dark room. Before them, Per saw what could only be a wall of glass. He guessed that behind it, there was a large tank of water, for a couple of technicians moved around behind the wall, evidently floating. They wore badges on their waist belts.

Per started. A voice had sounded in his ear. He put his hand up, and felt a smooth, shell-like object in his ear canal. As he touched it, it vibrated, and again he seemed to hear a voice. The technicians in the tank were reporting that conditions were normal.

They had electronic communications of a pretty sophisticated nature, he thought.

"Something is wrong?" said Kitkit, who had been watching him closely.

"It just puzzles me that you have these devices, but you don't have powered flight yet. On our world the sequence was a little different," Per said.

But Kitkit did not rise to the bait. He made the graceful hand-shrug of the Great People, to indicate that this concern was insignificant.

"Look," he said, pointing to the tank.

Per stepped closer. The tank was floored with grayish sand that had been scooped into a circular, nestlike depression. The nest was piled with globes a little smaller than Per's head. They glowed softly with a light that shifted through citron, amber, russet; the total effect was of an antique gold. The globes showed fugitive gleams within, pulses of jade, ruby, cinnabar.

"Those eggs look like the Kalko'uli eggs you showed me," he said.

"No. They are research," Kitkit said stiffly. "You will see for yourself. These eggs hatch White Killers. Watch—they grow in a controlled environment. They hatch."

Rapidly the scene shifted through time. Per felt a growing distress, and not only through his companion. The gold of the eggs shaded off toward a murky brown; their healthy pulsing dimmed. But they continued to grow; finally they began to rock and twist, and hatchlings emerged into the light.

The hatchlings had four legs and a tail; their bodies were moist and newtlike. Miniature spines crested their necks and their high-domed heads. Their eyes were large and bright; their tongues flickered, testing the liquid that surrounded them. They were moved to a different tank, one with access to the air, but still indoors. There was glass between Per and the hatchlings, but from their colors and their wheeking cries, he sensed their longing for freedom, much like his own.

The technicians fed them, but never enough. They struggled for the food, crying distressfully, striking each other with their baby claws. Their colors were not right. Per felt Kitkit suffering as he watched, but the Great Person made no move to set them free.

When the technicians entered the tank, they wore suits of rubber or some tough hide. The hatchlings scrambled piteously to reach the technicians and touch them, but contact was impossible.

"We denied them food; we denied them contact," Kitkit said, twisting his long fingers together in anguish. "Still they matured."

The hatchlings were large and their crests well defined, though they were lean and fierce. They began to dig and wallow restlessly in the sand at the bottom of the tank; at last they scooped out little nests and curled themselves tightly, until they looked almost as if they had returned to the egg. Their skins changed and stretched, as beneath the skin, the bones changed shape.

Kitkit shifted the time frame to speed up the waiting until the transformed hatchlings woke and tumbled out into the water again. They had changed from four legs to two. Their forms resembled Kitkit's, but not so tall, still somehow immature. Three of them were malformed, struggling just to stay afloat, not to sink to the bottom of the cavern. And the other four were pale as bone but strong, taloned and hungry.

They were born murderous, it seemed. Shreds of membranous skin still molted from them as they descended on their feeble brood mates and dispatched them. The malformed ones had only a moment to cry in protest before the pale ones had snatched their lives away with slashing claws. The water was cloudy with blood. Per sickened as he watched the pale ones tear the softest portions from their victims and turn toward others with shreds of flesh still caught in their teeth. When their crippled nest mates were dispatched, they turned on each other. They seemed to revel in killing.

The technicians unslung arm-length tubes from their backs, aimed at the pale ones, and fired. Per saw the trail of turbulence left by their projectiles. The projectiles clung to the pale ones' skin but barely slowed their activity.

"We tried calming motes, directly injected," Kitkit said. "We tried sleep motes. Nothing worked. Nothing stops them."

The hatchlings seemed to sense a threat and headed straight for the technicians. Suddenly, Per was no longer an observer. He was plunged into the midst of the pileup. Limbs thrashed and clung, pale hatchlings clawed and bit.

All he could hear and feel was Kitkit's command in water talk: *Kill them! Kill them!* Frantic to obey, to save himself, he caught at his personal weapon and struck back. He felt the claws slashing at him, and he struck in a frenzy. He killed the hatchlings. The tough suit protected him, but he was breathing their blood. It was on his skin and in his gills. He clawed the water to escape the green veil of blood that settled slowly into the depths.

Per struggled to escape the link with Kitkit. He had lost all objectivity. Kitkit was struggling, too. They snapped away from the memory and were back in the unrippled waters of Kitkit's pool.

Kitkit moaned.

"We tried to alter them," he said. "We tried to kill them. But the Paling enhances all their immune systems. The viruses we sent to change or kill were eliminated before they could have an effect."

"I don't understand," Per said. "If you, with all your knowledge, could not find a way to stop them, how can I do it now, all these years later, with no knowledge and no tools?"

"As we grow closer, I see your dreams more clearly," Kitkit whispered. "You come of a different world—a different world even from the others. On your world there are many disease weapons—vectors our kind has never encountered. I know that you were born among those who knew how to use such things. In your body are remnants of deadly motes. In the god is the power to change and nurture those motes. You will use your scholar's mind to find a weapon we can use to wipe the White Killers from the face of the Deep."

Per's shock and horror severed his connection to Kitkit's mind. He plunged far away from Typhon, into the Deep between worlds, the Deep of the past. But even there he found no refuge.

He twisted his consciousness, trying to return to the refuge of the miniature forest. He was short again; he was at eye level with the long, clever fingers that belonged to Rameau. But he was not in the garden of trees. He was facing a transparent wall. It was a tank, where Rameau adjusted the environment controls for the thing that slept within. Two men stood guard, one on either side. But they were not technicians. They were armed guards, in body armor and shields that obscured their faces.

Per let himself become aware of the tank's inhabitant. It had grown since he had last seen it. There was no longer room for its body to float freely in the tank. It had been forced to coil back and forth upon itself till it could barely move. A long clamp held its wide mouth closed and forced in the nutrients it required. Its mad red eyes could not shutter themselves against the light, for they were lidless. Most of the time they were rolled upward into its flat, reptilian head, flinching from the light, but ever and again they rotated to seek its surroundings and saw other living things nearby. Then the tail thrashed and the muscles of the wide jaw quivered as they struggled to break the bonds and kill. When the red eyes met his own glance, the boy Per quailed and tried to hide behind Rameau, but the man always forced him forward again.

"I don't care what Gunnarsson says," Rameau's precise, disdainful voice said above Per's head. "You tell him that *Rameau* says the release date must be moved up. If you hold this specimen in a confined space any longer, it may become deformed. We would have to destroy it and start over. If Gunnarsson wants those tunnels cleared within the next quarter, he can't afford the delay."

The pressure of Rameau's hand on Per's shoulder moved him forward along the wall, and he was devoutly grateful to leave the uneasily stirring coils of the sinue behind. The next tank held juveniles in a growth-retardant solution, waiting to be plucked forth and brought up to adult status when they were needed.

They weren't so bad. They looked like huge, leathery planarians. Their bodies were still truncated, their triangular jaws still immature. The growth retardant made them groggy, but sometimes one would flash awake for a moment and gape in rage against the unbiteable glass. Per flinched again when that happened, but the sinue soon drifted away again. At this early stage, it was still possible to see how they could have come from human genes. The fin claws still resembled tiny arms and legs.

"My children," Rameau said. The boy Per could not tell if he was joking or not.

Rameau turned from the glass; he had decided it was time to go. But the boy Per, who had been eager to leave before, now tugged at his hand.

"What do you want?" Rameau said.

"See Embla," the boy mumbled, glancing sideways at the guards as if they might try to stop him.

"Oh, very well," Rameau said. "Just for a minute."

For the first time, Per became aware of the boy's movements. His torso and arms swayed languidly in the air, the hands floating about chest-high, elbows bent. In contrast, his feet seemed unnaturally hard to budge. He had to use an elaborate, high-kneed gait, tugging each foot forcibly away from the floor and slamming it down again. Rameau walked in the same way, but he did it matter-of-factly and without strain.

"Release," Rameau said. The boy clicked something at his belt. Rameau's hand had also gone to his belt. Their feet lifted, as both of them pushed against the floor with a smooth movement, like ice skaters pushing off, and they soared along the corridor, horizontally, with surprising speed.

Per the adult realized, with an almost audible *click* in his mind, that there was no gravity in the corridor. The twin guards weren't really vertical. They stood at a slight angle to each other. Their boots stuck them to the wall somehow. They had aligned themselves almost identically by choice. They could equally well have pointed their heads in opposite directions.

While he was thinking this, they traveled a long way. Per's memory caught up with them near the outer ring of the ship. He could tell by the curve of the wall they followed that the next layer outward would be the hull itself.

They had to enter through an air lock set into a bulkhead as thick as the lock. Rameau had to bloodkey it. The boy Per knew, though the adult had forgotten, that "bloodkey" was an old word, from the days when the lock had actually drawn blood to read for identity. Now, the bloodkey was painless; you placed a finger in the hole and the eye of the lock scanned it, reading your blood with a beam of light. No need to pierce the skin.

Per thought at first that he was seeing more tanks. But they did not contain nutrient bath; they were just large rooms with transplex panels. The inhabitants floated together in a huddle on the far side, which was near the inner hull. The lighting inside was dim, and the boy couldn't really tell one from another at this distance.

He floated closer to the window. The first time he reached out too fast and hard and bounced himself away from the transparent wall. The second time he closed more gently and was able to stop his momentum inches from the wall. He planted one palm against it, then the other. If he was careful not to tense his muscles, his damp palms created a friction that would hold him there like a frog on a tree trunk.

Embla, he thought, praying she would see before Rameau grew impatient.

She did; a small, frail form parted from the huddle, growing gradually larger as she drifted toward the window. She came close enough to see Per distinctly, and she smiled. The smile was sweet to Per, though it did nothing to make her pointed, wide-eyed face less solemn. She raised one hand and pressed it to the transplex, matching Per's hand on the other side. Her flesh was fragile, almost translucent. It made Per's pale hand look dense and strong.

Slowly, he started to sweep his hand in a circle. She followed him as if an invisible thread linked them through the transparent wall. She placed her right hand against his left, and they moved both hands together in slow serpentines and figure eights. It took skill and care to move together without losing contact with the window.

He pushed too hard and broke contact; he spun slowly to bring himself back to face her, and saw her smile again as she spun in perfect synchronization. Their hands met again at the window. She swept her hand downward and let her body follow until the two of them were 180 degrees out of synch with everyone else. Their heads pointed in the opposite direction from the others.

This time she came off the wall first. Gamely, she fumbled her way back, but her hand struck the window several inches to the right of Per's, and she drifted away again. The smile faded. Shoulders slumped, she floated a foot from the wall.

Per pressed his palms to the window, his eyes pleading with her to continue the game, but he knew it was over for the day. Her eyelids drooped; a scattering of purple spots showed across her cheek and the corner of her lips. Her thinning hair lifted in the breeze from the vent, showing the patchy scalp underneath.

With infinite labor, she extended one tiny finger and tapped the glass where Per's hand still rested. Then she drifted very slowly backward until her features were hard to distinguish in the dimness of the big holding room.

"Had enough?" Rameau said briskly. Without waiting for an answer, he clipped Per's leash to his belt and pushed off, yanking the boy along with him.

The adult Per knew now that the boy had spent the trip back, as he often did, thinking over what he had been told by Rameau and the others about the toxicants—the "girl" and the other transforms in this tank. They looked more human than the sinue but were far more dangerous. Their bodies seethed with populations of mutant bacteria, viruses, or fungus spores. They weren't really meant to be humans at all; they were walking food supplies and transport systems for their lethal freight.

The human appearance had been kept only to enable them to pass among the target population more easily. Turned loose on human worlds, they would walk, and feed themselves so they could continue walking, and death would follow in their wake. Even if they took no nourishment at all, they would last for at least two weeks before collapsing. When they could no longer walk, they could still serve as substrate for the bioweapons until their bodies had been completely digested.

Unlike the juvenile sinue, they were not kept in growth stasis. But even their modified bodies could not support the unchecked growth of the infectious agents. The rapacious little organisms that colonized them stunted their growth and left them with little energy for themselves. The drugs they were given to keep the bioweapons in check dulled whatever consciousness they had. The girl could only play for a few minutes before confusion overcame her.

If she were a real girl, this would have been sad. But she wasn't a child. She was a bioweapon who looked like a child. Rameau had explained this to the boy. He could play with the girl if he wanted to, Rameau said, but it was like playing with a toy—not with a human companion.

Per recalled now that the boy had had much time, on many occasions, to ponder these thoughts. It was a long trip back to his quarters, near the center of the ship that held the steel garden, because the toxicants were kept next to the hull, so they could be vented out to space if anything went wrong.

For the first time, Per who had been a man thought maybe the Skandians had been right to deny him his memories. He wished he had never retrieved this one. For once it had come back to life, he did not know how to kill it again. It would long outlast the toy-girl, the weapon-child he had secretly named Embla. She must surely be dead now. The people the Skandians called shiptrolls had not vented the toxicants into space. Embla had still been sleeping in frost with the others when the gentle Skandians pushed the ship of death into the harsh furnace of their sun, to be purified beyond all retrieval.

Per who had been boy and man and now was neither had nowhere to go. Memory offered no refuge. The garden no longer seemed like a place of safety, nor did the quiet pool where Kitkit's unquiet history still stirred. Once Per no longer exercised control of his illusions, they faded. Again he hung in the eternal blue light of the cavern, where he could neither weep nor close his eyes.

꧁ 17 ꧂

Dilani had lured other newgens into the shallows, where they were evidently playing some game by moonlight. Soon there were sounds of splashing and laughter.

"Be quiet over there. You're keeping people awake," a voice called irritably.

"Can't sleep in the sand anymore. It's itchy."

More of the newgens joined her. The splashing continued.

Sofron decided she'd had enough of trying to sleep on-shore, and headed for the water, shaking off sand as she went.

The water was warm and silky, but finding a way to sleep there was difficult. Some of the newgens lay down on the bottom, but the waves gradually bumped them down the shore and deposited them back on the beach. Some were lucky enough to find a niche in the rocks, with their backs against stone so they couldn't be floated away. But those places were few.

Sofron waded to the beached raft and scavenged as much bark cord as she could find. Sushan and a couple of others were trying to sleep on the raft. They avoided the drying irritation of the sand, but the logs of the raft were too hard and rough for comfort. Sofron was sure the original Great People had never tried to sleep in the Dry.

"What are you doing?" Sushan said sleepily.

"I'm going to tie myself up."

"Huh?"

"In the water. Like a boat."

Sushan grasped the idea quickly. She helped to push the raft out into the water. The waves were gentle and the surf low; at anchor, the raft rolled gently but did not drag its rock anchor.

"But what about the guards?" Sushan said. "We don't want to be caught in the water by White Killers."

"Tell them to sit on the raft. They can fish one of us up when their watch is over."

Whitman gave up trying to sleep and sat up.

"I can't believe you're serious," he called irritably. "We could be attacked at any moment! Stay out of the water!"

"We could be attacked if we're in the water or not," Sofron said. "You have to stop thinking of the Deep as our enemy. Dry land is no longer our home. If the White Killers can chase us out of the water and keep us there, they will have won without a fight."

She could hear the argument continuing onshore as others took up one position or the other, but she ignored them.

She tied a line to the raft, looped the other end over her ankle in a circle loose enough to slide easily off her foot, and rolled into the water.

The method wasn't perfect; she had some trouble tying a cord to her ankle without galling the sensitive fin webs there. But once the loop was comfortably settled, she could stretch out at ease. The waves brought a constant flow of oxygenated water across her gills, a constant soothing of her parched skin. She bobbed up and down a little, but no more than a rocking of the cradle. To sleep in moving water seemed completely right and natural. She was so tired of cracked, itchy skin that she was willing to trade a small amount of additional danger for a comfortable rest.

She was awakened by the glitter of greatmoon on the surface just above her face. She sat up, coughed a couple of times to get the water out of her lungs, and looked around. A die-hard few of the old generation were sleeping inside the circle of firewood. The sentries were still at their posts, but their silhouettes were curled up and motionless; they had fallen asleep. So much the better. She had never intended to sleep all night. She meant to keep her own watch, a more dedicated vigil than theirs. She slipped the tether off her ankle and waded noiselessly toward the beach.

Some flicker of movement on the far side of the fire circle

made her freeze, crouching on the wet sand. Her gills fluttered as she sampled the damp air. There was a hint of old iron and mildew.

As she opened her mouth to shout the alarm, she saw the pale form, slipping in and out of shadows. There was only one. She swallowed her cry. It was hard to be sure—she *couldn't* be sure—but it looked like Wearra.

The movements were cautious and thoughtful, and the White One wasn't menacing the sleeping humans. Instead, his pale eyes focused on the thin silver poles glimmering in the moonlight. He crept toward them, looking around every few seconds to see if he was being followed. Sofron concluded that he wasn't part of a group. He had come alone.

One of the sentries stirred and muttered. Wearra crouched, tensely ready to spring away. But the sleeper relaxed again, and Wearra continued his slow, dogged creep. Clearly, the poles were precious to him. He wanted them.

And Sofron wanted him. She was afraid to move and frighten him away. She waited until he reached the poles, and she heard his low, almost inaudible hiss of satisfaction. As he turned his attention to the prize, she straightened up and showed herself.

He saw her and froze. His tongue darted out, trying to gather motes from the air. He looked at the poles, gauging the distance, obviously wondering if he could seize them before she raised an alarm. At last she had something he really wanted. She took another step toward him, signing "no."

He lowered his head.

"Make exchange," he signed, as he had when he visited them in their little shelter.

"Show me," she signed, holding out her hand for payment.

Wearra pointed to the two slender poles.

"Give me; then you follow," he signed. "See children—yes. Die—maybe."

She hesitated for an agonizing second, wondering if she should call out, wake someone. It might be good to have help. But they would probably try to stop her. They might even try to kill Wearra, if they could catch him. It was more likely he would escape again, and possibly never come back.

That decided her. She could not afford another instant of delay.

"Agreed," she signed. He seized the poles, split into two parts each, and used the sling harness to strap them to his back. This freed his arms for swimming. Sofron grabbed another set of poles from the ground and imitated his arrangement. Then she hurried after the White One.

As she passed the sleeping newgens, floating in a bunch like a catch of colorful fish, she felt a pang of regret at leaving them and Subtle. She had only begun to know them.

But then she was past them, heading for deep water.

Automatically, she followed the best channel through the broken reef. Traces of Wearra's motes told her that she was close behind him. But when they reached the open sea she panicked. The moving water was taking his motes away too fast for her to catch his direction. Was he trying to betray her, to escape her? He couldn't know what humans were like. He probably expected her to swim like a White One.

She spun, searching for him with her eyes. She caught only occasional pale flashes, and lost them again. They could have been glimpses of the fleeing White One, or passing fish, or moonslight. A faint whistle of distress escaped her.

The echo came back to her. It was like a flash of light revealing her surroundings for an instant. She sensed rocks nearby, small things moving, and somewhere an object about her own size. She reoriented herself and whistled again. The object was farther away now, but she sensed which way it was going. Her bones resonated to the true direction; her skin gave her sight. The next echo reflected like a spark from something bright. She was sure now that the moving object was Wearra with his smoothly polished poles that would reflect sound sharply. She swam after him, whistling to keep the ghostly landscape flickering along her skin.

She was elated to find out how the new soundsense worked. But she berated herself for not daring to enter the Deep before. She had been afraid of losing her way. If she had had more courage, she would have learned sooner how to find the way.

She knew that the sun came up eventually, because she

could feel the warmth of it filtering down to them. If only Wearra had gone up, she could have seen him. But he plunged deeper down, as if to escape the light. They left the rocking of the surface waves behind. She could feel the slow, ponderous currents of the Deep. It was bitterly cold, and the water pressed her down with monstrous weight. She was deeper than any human could have gone and lived. She could breathe where a human would have been extinguished, but she could feel the pressure against her gills. She felt dizzy. Her hands and feet were numb. She felt she could go no farther.

Her thoughts came very slowly against the tremendous weight.

I was wrong. He can't be looking for the children here. He must have something else in his mind. What he has for a mind. I've followed him—it—for nothing.

It was then that the shadows came. Her soundsense went as dark as her vision. Dark wings closed in around her, between her and her guide. It took a moment for her head to clear, for her to understand that the darkness was not in her numbed senses. The shapes were real, a flock of something unknown swimming near.

Her sight came back, as well. Glowing dots outlined the edges of the shadows, wavering as the dark winglike shapes moved in a slow glide. She was close enough to Wearra now to see an answering ghostly glow on his skin. He unslung the poles, took them in his hands, and raised them as if to stab the dark wings. The tip of each pole pierced a glowing spot between the wings. Sofron thought at first that he had stabbed it in the eyes. But there was no violent reaction. The White One vaulted to the winged creature's back and rode it. He began to move swiftly out of sight, leaving Sofron to fend for herself.

Treading water with her webbed feet, Sofron tried to match speed with the dark wings while struggling to manage the poles. If she dropped one, she would lose it forever. If she lost sight of Wearra now, he, too, would disappear forever into the liquid night around her. The dark shapes were circling closer to her, cutting off her echo vision. There! One banked beneath her, and turned, revealing two glowing spots. She stabbed with the poles and missed. The shape bucked, but she turned with it and thrust again.

There was a yielding sensation. The poles slid a little way, then seemed firmly fixed. The winged thing swerved, and she was lifted with it by her grasp on the poles. She braced her feet against its surface. It felt smooth, tough, yet springy. The skin had a rough texture that enabled her to keep her footing.

She clung to the poles, wondering how Wearra used them to guide his mount. She tried pushing on the left-hand pole. It tingled in her hand, as if electricity passed through it. She nearly let go of it. The surface beneath her curved and bucked, and she struggled to keep her footing.

Within the handgrip, her fingers felt smooth ridges. She pressed down on them as she tried to hang on. The winged creature banked and rolled. She was upside down, but now she knew how Wearra made the creature move. Rolling and swerving as Sofron tried all the possibilities, the winged creature finally turned and carried her in Wearra's wake. Sofron sensed the other dark wings around her occasionally, but she moved ever more surely and swiftly after her guide.

Now she understood why Wearra had taken such risks to recover the poles. They made it possible for him to move quickly at depths that would otherwise paralyze even a White Killer. And while he flew with this dark-winged flock, other creatures might hesitate to bother him.

Sofron wondered how the poles worked. She knew that some sea creatures generated their own electric currents and used them for sensing. Perhaps the rods transmitted a weak current, overriding the winged thing's own directional guidance.

They moved swiftly through the water for a long time. Then, ahead and below, she began to perceive a dim splotch of light. At first she thought it was an illusion, but when she blinked her multiple lids, it didn't go away. Wearra headed straight for it. Her echo vision brought her the impression of a nubbly, uneven surface, like a heap of smooth stones.

Then they were soaring out over it, and her eyesight joined with the echo sight as the two fields of perception merged into one. Below her, the dim glow resolved into a circle of gleaming spheres. It was hard for Sofron to guess their size, but she estimated they were a little bigger than a human torso. A continual shimmer of light passed over them—dark gold, umber, deep crimson. They looked like a bed of coals.

Confused by too much strangeness, Sofron tried to orient herself. The spheres nestled into the sediment of a flat area. But this couldn't be anywhere near the plain of the Abyss itself. They were a long way down, but not that far. It must be a plateau somewhere on the steep slopes that bordered the big island and its outliers. She whistled softly, and only emptiness came back to her. She took a chance and sent out a series of louder calls. The echo flashing back brought her a confused impression of ridges and grooves carved into the floor around the flat area. Looming somewhere beyond that were irregular walls crested with jagged spires. She wasn't good at judging distances yet, but the echo vision seemed blurry, as if the walls weren't very near.

Wearra was idling at the edges of the field. He seemed to be watching for something. Sofron let her hands relax. The muscular wings beneath her feet idled, too, flexing gently to stay balanced in the currents.

Something moved in the field, in the area Wearra was watching. The glow was brighter there, and one of the spheres seemed to be pulsing. Sofron sent out more whistle calls to get a clearer picture.

Just a few feet from her, the field of eggs roiled like a soup pot about to boil. One of the eggs bulged, rolling and scattering the others. Before her eyes, it stretched, making the glowing colors on its surface ripple like the shimmer on the surface of a bubble.

Then it burst open, splitting neatly along its center. An unfamiliar shape struggled out. It crumpled and compressed, then stretched itself and extended appendages that were placed like feet or flippers. Last came a head that thrust out on a long slender neck, then pulled back as if on springs.

Sofron pinged it with her soundsense to check on its shape. The echo came back with a slight delay, as if the surface it rebounded from was still soft and yielding, not a hardened shell. As if in response to her probing, she heard a high-pitched musical tone. It hummed through her, not unpleasantly. The hatchling turned its head toward her, and she felt a strange tingling sensation, like the electricity from the pole she held, passing through her body. They faced each other for a frightening moment, locked in each other's sensing.

I can feel it pinging me, she thought. *That means it can feel me, too.*

There was a sound like distant thunder.

She caught herself back. *What am I doing?* Wearra steered his mount over the eggs in a soaring loop. She started to follow him, but pulled up abruptly. Other White Killers on their dark mounts were soaring in toward the newly hatched egg. Something that appeared to her soundsense like a cloudy blur flew toward the hatchling. Was it a net? It stuck to the small creature and immobilized one of its flippers. The hatchling thrashed around in a circle, crying in melodious anguish.

I can't stop to think about this, Sofron realized. *I have to get to the children, and I'm running out of time.*

But it's alive; it's sentient, another part of her mind protested. *It's a child, too.*

Wearra was halfway across the field already. She goaded her mount to follow him. But more and more White Killers swarmed toward them. She felt the rush of a projectile swooping past her. The Killers glowed faintly in the Deep, so she could see where they were. But her soundsense brought her the knowledge of the shadowy beasts gathering in behind them. She was almost back-to-back with Wearra now.

She tried to force the thing she rode to flare its wings so they would come between her and the riderless attackers, but it would not obey her. She felt the water surging around her as the other dark wings plunged past the encircling White Killers to rush her and Wearra. Her mount bucked against her control. She squeezed the handgrips tighter; the winged thing shuddered and rolled. She was upside down again, and her weight dragged the poles from their sockets. She was falling free, and the dark wings reared high above her.

She tucked one of the poles under her arm and reached for

the tubelight on her belt. The greenish beam leaped out as she pressed the tube, and illuminated what she had been riding.

The topside had been smooth and inoffensive. Now she saw what was hidden under the winglike furl. Pointed teeth gleamed in a mean little underslung mouth. A cluster of long black arms dangled from the underside of the wings. They were thin and whiplike and ended in rows of barbed suckers and a final pair of talons. They scythed through the water toward her in a threatening sweep.

She had never thought to find herself fighting back-to-back with a White Killer. She let the tubelight drop to the end of its cord and stabbed at the dark beast with the pointed end of the riding pole. It gave ground; she dared a brief glance behind her to see how Wearra was defending himself. She hoped he knew more about how to combat these things than she did.

To her shock and dismay, Wearra was fleeing as fast as his mount would carry him. He had abandoned her, and there was no one to protect her back. All along her neck, the gill fringes burned with pain from the water pressure. She felt the full weight of the Deep wrenching at her joints when she tried to swim on her own. But she still had a chance.

The majority of the dark wings had not yet noticed her. The hatchling was their preferred prey. If the dark wings went after the hatchling first, she might still have a chance to get away.

And then the hatchling began to cry. The cry was music, a chorded piping of distress that pierced her ears and vibrated along her bones. The creature was nonverbal, but it was not mindless.

The dark wings sent out their own hunting cry—not the shrill whistle of the White Ones, but a whining and buzzing that crescendoed up and down the scale. But Sofron could still hear the hatchling's distress cry. A mind somehow like her own was calling for help.

Oh, damn it, she thought, but it came out as a sharp warble that echoed back to her, showing her the enemy close at hand. Worse yet, the hatchling was rapidly approaching, fleeing for its life, its distress cry coming upscale in her soundsense as it came nearer.

Her first thought was to shelter behind the hatchling; it was big enough to conceal her partially. She could even stab it herself. The White Killers and their dark allies might go into a feeding frenzy at the smell of blood, and forget about her for just long enough.

But she couldn't do it. The creature bobbed past her at surprising speed for such an ungainly shape. She hesitated for just long enough to realize that she was never going to execute her half-formed plan. And then the hatchling had dodged behind her, and it was too late.

Grasping the poles in each hand, she faced the enemy and charged. It was a slow and feeble charge; she fought against the impenetrable curtain of the Deep. But she jabbed with the poles until her senses darkened with the effort and the ember glow of the eggs blended with the dull red behind her eyes. The dark wings lifted away at her first onslaught, curling up to avoid the end of the poles.

But the dark wings recoiled only to gather again and descend on Sofron. The heavy wings beat down the poles. She had to keep turning, turning, as they banked to catch her from behind. The long tentacles whipped toward her, through her flickering perception. Weakly, she parried them, but twice the talons flicked her, leaving trails of fire across her shoulders and ribs.

Then the tentacles coiled around the poles and clung. Their strength was terrible; the weapons were wrenched from her hands. She grasped the tubelight and waved the green beam across the attackers' field of vision. They drew back for a moment while Sofron fumbled at her belt for Wearra's knife. She could still hear the frantic arpeggios of the hatchling's pleading above the deep, thunderous rumble that seemed to fill her ears and numb her senses.

Before she could unsheathe the knife, she felt the barbed tentacle wrap around her arm from behind. Something sharp slashed across her gill membranes. The pain paralyzed her as the taste of blood flooded into her throat.

I'm done for, she thought. But she was still struggling as a vast darkness swept across her.

18

"She's gone."

Subtle's head broke water. He was choking. Finally he got his breath and realized that someone had pulled him up into the air while he was still sleeping. His patience lost, he was about to snarl when he saw that the human who flinched from his ire was Bey.

"Be not waking this-I with chokings," he said. But he smoothed his skin into friendly colors for Bey.

"I'm sorry," Bey said. "But Sofron is gone."

Dilani pointed past the guards. "Gone," she signed.

"Yeah, we know," Bey said. Then he looked more closely in that direction. "Wait—you don't mean Sofron."

Subtle understood. The two silver poles that had been stuck into the ground, forming a narrow arch, had vanished.

They ran to the spot. The holes where the poles had been planted still showed. Next to them, the sections that presumably formed more poles were still piled.

"But not all," Subtle said. "There was being more."

He remembered the strange tale Sofron had told of the White One who visited her.

"She is saying the White One is trading-giving for made-things from the long-ago. Yesterday we-I is finding many bright metal madethings. Today the shining poles are gone. What is White One trading-giving for bright poles? Why is she going with White One?"

"He didn't give anything," Bey said. "There's nothing left behind . . . But he came alone and didn't hurt anyone. So it

188

probably was the same one. Maybe the payment he offered was to take her to the children."

"You-I thinking is this-I thinking, too," Subtle said. "She follows White One into great danger."

"But why didn't she wait for us?" Bey burst out. "We said we'd help her. She should have called us."

Subtle's torso undulated in his elaborate shrug.

"When Round Folk females is having eggs," he said, "is forgetting sleeping, eating. Guarding eggs is all of life, until life is fading away. Eggs is hatching; hatchlings is eating dead female."

"That's terrible," Bey said. "I mean, no offense. But it's not like that with humans."

"Is why this-I is hunting god," Subtle said. "Females' giving life for eggs is greatness, but is terrible, too. This-I is wanting new life without paying death for life. Is wanting friendship of females without causing mating death.

"Is being different with humans. Females is not dying for eggs. But after hatching, humans is knowing faces of hatchlings. Round Folk is not knowing hatchlings. They live; they die. We-I is not knowing any until they are grown. But humans is knowing hatchlings, and for hatchlings, they will die. Per is dying for hatchlings Bey and Dilani; Sofron is taking great risks for lost hatchlings. Hoping to live, but hoping more to save their lives. Humans will die for eggs not their own. This is greatness or craziness in you. This-I is not knowing which."

Bey wasn't paying much attention to Subtle's explanation. He kept his eyes on Subtle's skin, where the true feelings showed. Subtle's colors showed doubt and fear, but there was a faint hopeful tint.

"But can we find her now?" he said. "Will you help us?"

"The Deep is very wide," Subtle said. "Finding one small being is not easy. White Killers is finding we-I before we-I is finding her."

He thought of the depths where light faded, and the dangers that lurked where the buoyant water felt heavy and hard as stone.

"Is being only one way," he said. "We-I is speaking to god. If Per-god is not helping, we-I is never finding."

The sun had risen until it shone over the treetops, directly into the river and into the sandy circle where the wounded and the oldgens slept. It seemed that Whitman was already awake; he had climbed to the top of the rocky headland next to the river. Bey caught sight of his silhouette, and a delegation followed him up the steep slope. Whitman's eyes were crusty from sleeping in the sun, his skin peeling in patches from the dryness. He tried to scratch behind his shoulders, but could not reach the irritation.

They explained the situation. "A White One? Why didn't you wake me?" he demanded.

"We were asleep," Bey protested. "No one saw."

Whitman showed teeth in a grimace of frustration, and strode over to the guards.

"You're useless," he said to them, with a notable lack of his usual tact. "Why volunteer for a responsibility you can't fulfill?"

He peered down, but the riverbank was invisible from this viewpoint.

"Did you see them, Bey? Dilani? Who saw the White Ones?"

"We think there was just one," Bey said. "We think he took those poles. And we think Sofron woke up and saw him. But she followed him instead of giving the alarm. She's gone. Remember her story about the White One who came to warn her? Subtle thinks the same one came back, and that she followed him to look for the children. We have to go and look for her now. It's dangerous; she might need help."

Whitman's spines rose and clattered faintly together.

"I think not," he said loudly. "This mystery person shows up, demands that we follow her hell knows where, then disappears again, possibly in company with our worst enemies, and at a time when she knows we need every citizen. And she doesn't bother to wake any of us and warn us of our danger. I don't think we'll be following her anywhere."

"Whitman, for heaven's sake, this isn't a 'mystery person'

you're talking about, it's Sofron Nordby," Sushan said. "She's a member of our compact. A good friend! She's not an enemy."

Whitman cut her off.

"There's something a little more important to discuss here than the identity of a stranger," he said. "We already know that the White Ones can find us and seek us out here. We're lucky they didn't come back and kill us all last night. We already have wounded. If they come again, some of us may be killed. We can't protect ourselves with sticks and rocks."

He turned abruptly and pointed out toward the Deep.

"*That's* where we have to go."

It was low tide, and the line of rocks at the end of the island extended far out into the water. The last visible segment was a tall, dark mass that protruded from the water like the black snout of some leviathan about to rise from the Deep. All around the tip of the island, the paler colors of shallow water showed in circles and arcs.

"See that?" he said. "The island once had a wide shoreline area that's underwater now. If amphibians lived here before, as we suspect, that's where they're likely to have left traces. We've seen that there *is* technology available here. We just have to go and get it."

When they came down to the camp, breakfast was in progress. The newgens had caught most of the fish. They hooked them out of the river with their hands and made a communal pile on a layer of wet leaves. The oldgens made a fire and started to cook the fish on spits. The newgens munched as they fished, stripping the flesh from their still-flapping catch and discarding the bones and fins.

The food vanished quickly. They gathered in a rough circle, the tardy newgens sitting behind their elders, to discuss Whitman's proposal.

"A White Killer came into our camp and stole from right under our noses," Phun said. "You said we'd be safe here!" Her accusation was directed at Whitman. "We left the atoll because you said the big island would be safer, but it's ten times worse! We can't even go in the woods without being eaten by something, and they're still coming after us out of the Deep."

Her torn leg and pale, drawn face gave force to her accusations.

But Whitman didn't seem discouraged.

"That goes right to the heart of it, Phun. I did hope we'd be safer here. And it *is* safer than the atoll. If the White Killers had found us there—and we have to assume they would have, sooner or later—we would have been overrun. Here, we've been able to survive. So far.

"But the fact is, we won't be safe anywhere until we can reliably protect ourselves. That means we need weapons."

The forbidden word hung heavily in the air.

"We're Skandians," Askil said. "We don't use violence on others. We should just keep moving until we find a place without threat."

"There is no such place on this world," Whitman said. "We don't use violence; we only protect ourselves. These aren't humans we struggle with. They're only animals. It's all right to use tools against animals. But we have to *have* those tools. We found a few useful things here, but we have to get more. When we have the force necessary to protect ourselves, the White Killers will see it, and then they'll leave us alone. We aren't using forbidden violence. Only deterrent force against animals."

"This is pointless," Torker said. "You don't know where to find weapons anyway."

"We have a guide." Whitman pointed. "Him."

Subtle was taken aback as everyone looked at him.

"You have knowledge about the old places where sentients lived, don't you?"

Subtle searched his vocabulary to understand the human words.

"Is wanting cities of the Great People, yes?" Subtle croaked.

"Yes."

"You-I is being right in one thing," Subtle said reluctantly. "Long in the long-time, the places of the Great People is having different shape. Once there is city of towers, all stories tell. Now these towers is fallen deep down, under the Deep. Maybe metal things you-I is seeking lies there, under the dark water. Maybe."

"We have to go there," Whitman said. "They must have had weapons. Every advanced culture has tools that are indistinguishable from weapons. The weapons they had will protect us."

"Into the Deep?" Phun wailed. "But we can't! We'll be killed!"

"It's a calculated risk," Torker said. "We take a chance now, for safety later. If we retreat now, we could end up with our backs to the wall and not be able to break out later. He could be right."

"We take the rafts and sail along the chain of islands," Whitman said. "We'll be above water, where maybe the White Killers can't perceive us, and we'll sail faster than they can swim. If it takes more than one day to get there and back, we can pull out on one of the islands and fortify ourselves with fire."

Subtle could not perceive the leader's motes at such a distance, but Whitman's colors showed great stress. He did not wish to contradict the human leader, but he feared Whitman's desires were leading him to lethal optimism.

"White Killers is now seeking bright metal," he said. "Is knowing humans swimming in these waters. They is now waiting with sharp teeth for rafts of humans. We-I can't know how many is coming. This-I is not wishing to guide you-I to jaws of Killers."

"We can't just sit here waiting for them to come," Whitman hissed. His skin paled, and the scabbed lines of his unhealed wounds stood out grimly. "We can do this. We *must* do this. We can protect ourselves and finally create a safe environment on Typhon."

In his mind's eye, Subtle pictured Whitman with twelve limbs, dancing, shaping a pattern that would compel agreement from the confused humans. The Whitman in his mind danced vigorously; what the dance lacked in artistry, it made up in single-minded persistence. Swaying the motes of others was life's blood to this human, Subtle thought.

"What about Sofron?" Bey said. "We have to help her. This trip is no deal with the newgens unless we look for her first. We promised."

Whitman turned on him angrily, but before he could speak again, Subtle interrupted.

"This-I cannot guide where you-I is wanting. This-I has knowledge too small for fighting against White Killers. Before we-I is daring Deep for finding weapons, is needing to see Per-god. In long past, god is calling Round Folk to help against White Killers. God is helping we-I fighting Killers. And god is helping find Sofron if finding is possible."

"Yes! Find Per!" Dilani signed.

"Disquieting One is calling Bright Teeth," Subtle proposed. "If Bright Teeth is helping, we-I is finding god."

Whitman tried all his powers of persuasion to convince them that seeking weapons should be the first priority, but he could no longer mount such an operation without help from the newgens. Too many of the older humans were disabled by wounds or fear. When the newgens presented a united front, demanding that they seek out the god, Whitman gave back one step.

"If you can get the ketos to come, we'll try it," he said. "I'm giving you one day. We can't wait longer than that."

Clearly, he thought the ketos would not come, and that he would get his own way in the end.

Dilani swam out into deep water and swam slowly back and forth for most of the morning, playing her sound box. Subtle went with her to watch over her. He did not taste any Killer motes in the water on this day, but he did not want to take any chances. He put up with the noise; over a period of several hours, he actually became interested in the sounds. Occasionally Dilani succeeded in producing a sound that really did resemble the Bright Teeth language.

Nevertheless, he was shocked when Dilani turned to him triumphantly, taking her hands out of the box. "They're coming!" she signed. She had heard them even before he could find their traces in the water. But she was right. Soon he heard their racing chatter and tasted their motes. Then they were visible, thrusting fins high out of the water in greeting.

Dilani stiffened her body like a spear and dove at them, bumping heads joyously. They butted the box on her chest curiously, and they seemed to be conferring with each other about it. She wasn't sure what they concluded, but it seemed to be a positive decision, since they didn't try to tear the box off her.

Subtle was jaunting quietly back and forth in the water while all this was going on, trying to pick up some meaning from their speech. When Dilani had calmed down a little, he interpreted for her.

"This-I is thinking, Bright Teeth saying, 'Where you-I is going? We-I is waiting for you to be coming into Deep. Waiting long time!' True, though, that long time for Teeth is maybe not being long time by counting of humans. But they is saying for sure long days, more than one. Is saying, 'Why humans not coming to swim with us?'

"Also they is saying they is having surprise for you-I. They is saying you must learn Bright Teeth language. But this-I is not knowing how they mean. Then boss of pod is saying, 'Later, later.' They is laughing."

"Thanks," Dilani signed with a flip of her hand. She couldn't wait longer to swim off to play. Subtle watched her enviously. The Teeth would allow him to swim with them, but they never treated him with the same teasing affection. He was not one of them. And perhaps it was partly his own fault. He could never forget that the Bright Teeth often had teased Round Folk without affection—sometimes to their deaths. He had lost his friend Redheart to their teasing, long ago. They had not killed her directly, but she had died because of them, all the same.

He should simply turn his back on them and swim away, he mused. Yet he couldn't do that, either. Their speed and single-minded, fierce enjoyment of life fascinated him. Far from hating them, he wished he could be like them. But he was a scholar, one who had once looked in twelve directions at once. And though he had changed his shape, he had not changed his thinking. He still thought twelve ways at once, and the Teeth did not fancy his twelve-minded motes. They preferred Dilani, the Disturber, who was sudden and direct. Like them.

He swam back to shore and reported to Whitman that the Bright Teeth had come. He also reported his own impression that they had been there for some time. He wondered if it had been their presence that prevented the White Ones from coming again. It was puzzling that they had not announced their presence to the humans until now, but the Teeth were always unaccountable.

Though Whitman had declared they could not wait more than a day, it took them longer than that to get ready. They had decided to reconfigure one of the large rafts into two smaller ones for greater speed and seaworthiness. They chopped the big raft apart and assembled the smaller ones with painstaking care. Each of them was made up of two shaped logs joined by a light platform and topped by an improved, larger sail woven from the abundant supply of giling leaves available along this shore. It was hard, heavy labor with the few tools they had left, and with so many of the adults injured. By the end of the day, the work still was not finished.

Again, they set guards and built their fires, but they slept with far greater security, knowing that the ketos were present. There was no attack in the night.

Dilani spent the night in the water with her friends, but even in the Deep, she did not sleep well. She thought of Per and Sofron, gone, and wondered if they would all vanish one by one. She dreamed of pale ghost children in the water, and woke up with her heart pounding to find that the ghosts were only moonlight.

When morning came, she was tired and cross, but the bright sun made it impossible to sleep late. She ate breakfast with her friends and was getting ready to swim out to look for ketos again before Whitman could catch her and try to make her work on his boat. She considered the whole idea of rafts a very stupid one. The Bright Teeth could swim faster anyway.

She was ready to take off when she noticed a commotion on-shore. Everyone was watching Engku Lim and Miko Narayan, who stared at the brightening sky with expressions of horror frozen on their faces.

"I can't see," Engku wailed. "I'm blind!"

"I've gone blind," Miko echoed. "My eyes . . ." He moved his hands toward his face as if to claw at it. Melicar grabbed his hands.

"Take it easy," she said. She was trying to reassure them, but her voice came out as a shaky whisper. "Let me look."

But they were too agitated to stand still.

"Subtle, please," Melicar called. "Come here and help me."

Dilani stuck close by Subtle's side as he reluctantly approached the weeping adults. She drew her breath in with a hiss as she caught a drift of motes from them. They stank of White Killer.

Subtle twined his tentacles around their wrists. They tried to escape him, but he patiently followed them, sliding and refastening his grasp until they finally gave up and let him keep the contact.

Calm, calm. She felt him soothing them. She gritted her teeth and tried to quell her own reaction, to match her skin to his.

Calm, she thought. *I can be calm, too!* She wasn't sure this was true, but she was determined to make it so.

Miko and Engku sank to their knees under Subtle's influence and held still long enough for Melicar to examine them.

Knowing they could not see her, Dilani crept closer to watch them. Overnight their eyes had gone blank and pale, the pupils closed to slits. Their faces were ghastly. Bleached patches had begun to spread across their skins like a disease. They were white at the gills and the lips, and white streaks spread across their necks. Their fingers were pale.

"You're not blind," Melicar said. "There have been changes to the pigment in your eyes, and it's reduced your tolerance for bright light, that's all."

This reassurance did not help them.

"We're going to die, aren't we?" Engku said.

"We're all going to end up like those white things," Miko said.

"Try to calm down," Melicar said. "Your agitation might be speeding up the process."

"It's this damned planet," Miko said. "This disease or whatever it is that changed our bodies—we thought it was done with us. But it hasn't ended!"

He turned around and around, seeking Bey, but couldn't see him.

"You newgens," he yelled. "You and your monster friends! You got us into this. These changes were supposed to help us. We'd be able to live here now, you said. But there's no end to the changes until we're all dead."

"This isn't the same thing," Bey said. But Dilani could see that he wasn't sure.

"Well, you don't really know *what* it is, do you?" Miko shouted.

"Leave him alone," Melicar said. "None of us knows what this is. How is he supposed to figure it out?"

The adults gathered into a circle, as they did whenever an argument became public. The newgens watched, from the fringes of a wider circle. The water dogs pressed against their legs.

"It's contagious, isn't it?" Nila Kismati asked shakily. "It's something that came from the White Killers when we had to . . . touch them."

She scrubbed her hands in the sand as she spoke.

"We don't know what it is," Miko repeated, more quietly now. "Could be a disease we have and the Killers have, too. Could be a vitamin deficiency. We don't *know*." His voice began to rise again.

Whitman swept the circle with his eyes, trying to pull them back together.

"Who *does* know?" he said. "That's the information we need—not all this speculation and whining. Subtle! What about you? Can you tell us anything about this?"

Subtle let his tentacles slide away from Miko and Engku and rose to his full height, taller than a human.

"God is knowing," he said. "Per-god is knowing everything. We must be going to him."

There was no longer any argument.

They took the best weapons that would work underwater—their few, treasured harpoon guns, two crossbows with darts, and a couple of gaffs refitted with long handles. The strongest carried these; the others had only utility cutters that hung from their belts. Dilani wore the sound box around her neck. Though it often got in her way, she could not be parted from it.

They began to select the members of the party. Whitman had to take Dilani, and he had to take Subtle. Though Subtle did not know the exact location of the god, he knew the lay of the seabed and its currents better than any human. Without argument, Bey showed up, too, and ignored all attempts to send him back. Dilani was ready to refuse to help unless Bey could come, but in the end, Whitman backed down.

Dilani was a little surprised when Torker not only helped with the heavy work, but jumped aboard afterward. She made a questioning gesture to Bey, behind Torker's back.

"Don't know," he signed. "Once, he was Per's friend. Then, his enemy. Maybe he's curious to see what happened to him."

Bader clasped hands with them but did not offer to come.

"I have to keep an eye on them," he said, nodding toward the injured newgens. "And look out for the others." He strode away, followed by the two water dogs who had appropriated him.

Sushan remained for similar reasons. Henner and Uli, probably the best friends she had left, stayed to back her up.

"If you find Per," she said, "give him my greetings. Tell him he's our last hope—as usual."

They ran one of the new rafts out into the surf and were soon in deep water.

Subtle remained preoccupied and silent until they reached the margins of the Deep. As Torker guided the raft through the last tricky waves into open water, he spoke.

"Maybe Bright Teeth is not taking that-I to the god," he said, with a dismissive flick of the tentacle toward Whitman.

"What do you mean?" Whitman said, turning on him. All

Whitman's movements were quicker, more irritable than they had been.

"You-I has cuts from White Killers," Subtle said. "You-I is full of many angry motes. Bright Teeth is protecting-god. Why they is taking sick angry human there?"

To Dilani's surprise, there was no measured response from Whitman. He made an angry noise that sounded like "yaaaah!" and flashed spread talons at Subtle as though to slice his words to shreds.

Then his face paled around the mouth and eyes, like a blush of whiteness.

"You will make them take me," he said. The words were meant to be an order, Dilani thought, but his feeble colors and weak motes made it more like a plea.

"First have to find them," Dilani said, and slid into the water. She turned in a complete circle, bobbing gently to wash plenty of water through her gills, testing it for any tell-tale enemy motes. It tasted clean, sunlit, with no smell of dark things from down below.

The Bright Teeth liked to hang around just outside the reef. She played the few phrases she knew on her sound box—teasing, taunting, making tempting mistakes the Teeth would have a hard time to resist correcting. She played her friends' names, the way a pod sang their own—as a call signal, a location marker, and a challenge. "Tastes Like You (Not), Calm at Dawn, Long Thin Round One, Big Fishcatcher, Crazy Leader—we are here."

Calm at Dawn was the Bright Teeth name for Bey. Whitman's name in the song-speech was self-contradictory, like her own. To the Bright Teeth, "crazy" did not mean "lacking in logic," but something closer to "without a directional signal." So Dilani's name for him could have been translated "Mapless Navigator" or "Blind Guide." But "Crazy Leader" fit better in her own mind.

She felt the faint tingle of a response coming through the water before she could really hear it. They were coming, and she recognized them as Slowbolt and his cronies. It wasn't

the full pod, but the group of young males Slowbolt traveled
with and dominated.

Dilani thrust her head above water. She did not wait to
clear her throat, just signed with arms above her head.
"They're coming!"

Then she was surrounded by something like an underwater
tornado. On the previous day, the ketos had given her per-
functory greetings, but now she was getting the full-dress
treatment—perhaps because they wanted to impress her
human friends. The ketos circled her, spinning her in their
powerful wake. Each one nose-bumped her as it passed by. It
felt like being rammed at full speed, though she knew these
were only love taps compared to the full-force blows that
could be delivered by their blunt snouts.

They sang all the while—friendly insults that showed they
knew her. But she had to drop the sound box to pummel them
with her fists, since she couldn't nose-bump. She punched
them in the flanks to release the bitter, oily pod scent from
their glands. It clung to her gills and entered her bloodstream,
and she felt happy, fierce, accepted. She stuck her fingers
back into the sound box and squawked joyful curses back at
them in language that would have shocked the adult humans.

* * * * *

*Dump your smelly friends in water/To delightful dive
invite the delicate*
*So we can be disgusted by them/That we may mingle
exquisite aromas*

* * * * *

They sang sarcastically.

Dilani could not understand the witty weaving of over-
tones and side comments, but she got the most basic elements
of the speech.

With a powerful kick, she shot herself back above the surface and grabbed the raft.

"They say, come in the water and greet them," she said.

"We can't. We might lose the boat," Whitman said automatically.

"Then take turns," Dilani said.

"I can't go in the water with them," Torker said. "I shot that big one with the silver streaks, remember? Back on the old island, I was about to make steak out of him. He'll eat me for breakfast."

"Come in and meet," Dilani shouted impatiently. She could have explained it to him in the song language, but Skandian hardly ever made room for more than one meaning at once.

"They're Dilani's friends," Bey said. "I don't *think* she'll let them hurt you."

Dilani heard him; she hoped it was true, but she wasn't completely sure either. It made her admire the big fish boss a little bit more when he braced himself, and without any further fuss, jumped into the water.

The other ketos seemed to move out of the way to make room for Slowbolt. And he came like a comet, with ballistic thunder. He hit Torker at ramming speed and threw him straight up, out of the water. Torker screamed in a brief arc, from when he left the water to when he struck it again and the cry was cut off. Below the surface, the other ketos lashed back and forth in agitation, chanting grimly.

> ****Look out/he's mad/he's looking mad/he's out/****
> ****get out/or get mad/he's mad/look out****

Then Slowbolt screamed.

> ****Where is this big fish big boss thinks he's so big/**
>   I think him tiny, a tiny little fish can't see him where******
>   ***BITE ME I BITE YOU BITE ME I BITE YOU***

As he surfed past Torker, he turned in full threat mode, mouth wide open. Dilani saw the paler mark on one sleek side where Torker's harpoon had once pierced him. She glimpsed Torker's face between two rushes of bubbles. Torker's mouth was squared open, teeth showing, as if in a miniature mimicry of the keto. But he didn't look as terrified as he must feel. He just looked extremely concentrated, as if waiting for the last piece of some monstrous puzzle.

Dilani thought she had killed him. She had called him into the water to be killed. She wanted to kill the ketos. This wasn't fair. Torker was different now. He wouldn't kill for fun now. She couldn't think how to force these sounds from the box. Her fingers fumbled and made some squawks that went unheard.

She felt the vibrations of Torker's grunt of pain as the keto hit him again. There was blood in the water. A dark line smoked down Torker's chest, as if the keto had disemboweled him with one slash. Dilani screamed like a human, but it made only a foolish little sound under so much water. Then she remembered that she had a cutter at her belt. She was about to get it and use it, to defend Torker. Slowbolt's pale belly was exposed. She could cut him—

But then she realized what he was doing. The keto's great jaw had retracted into a normal position. He was moving slowly and delicately, for such an enormous being. He was rubbing belly slime across Torker's cut, to make the blood stop. And then he turned, exposing the glands on his flanks. The guarding flipper that could knock a human unconscious was held aside.

Torker hung curled in the water, in shock. Dilani no longer believed him to be seriously hurt, but he was too stunned to recognize the keto's peace gesture.

"Drink the fish milk," she signed to Torker, and when that evoked no response, she mimed, "Bite it! bite it!" His eyes focused on her and registered only complete confusion.

She was going to have to do for him what Per had done for her. She grasped him by the back of the neck and pushed his face against the keto's harsh-textured hide on the next pass Slowbolt made. She felt Torker gulp and then convulse. He had revived enough to throw her off and paddle back furiously, rubbing his mouth at the bitter taste, just as she had done.

Little tooth wounded great warrior then/now great tooth wounds tiny fish

Red drink//white drink
Makes us one

Slowbolt sang in a burst of elegant satisfaction.

Badtooth killer human//Good killer Bright Tooth
Becomes
Eats-us human enemy//human eats-enemies of us
Becomes
THEY BITE US WE BITE THEM THEY BITE US WE BITE THEM

The other ketos chorused cheerfully, as if that settled it.

Dilani swam over and grasped Torker's shoulder gently. He looked as if he was about to hit her, fearing that she would make him drink again from the keto's scent gland. "Wait a minute. Calm down," she signed. Carefully, she rubbed the healing slime over his cut, making sure every inch of it was sealed so no telltale taste of blood could escape into the water. As she had guessed, the cut had parted only millimeters of skin, though a razor-sharp tooth had done it.

As she tended Torker, Slowbolt swam by and bunted the back of her head in passing.

Scaredy scaredy scaredy/squeak squeak squeak

He mocked her, imitating the frightened noises she had made and laughing hilariously.

Now that the ketos were through with them, Dilani let herself and Torker rise to break the surface.

"What . . . ? What in hell's kitchen was that all about?" Torker demanded. He had trouble getting his mouth working.

Dilani understood it perfectly but couldn't explain it in human talk.

"You hurt him, but he changed his mind so he won't kill you, but—" She weighed one hand against the other. "It has to match, see? Both sides the same. You bite us, we bite you. See?"

Torker wasn't getting it.

"Symbolic restitution," Whitman said. He was the only one on the raft who was adept with human language, and even he was having trouble dredging abstractions from his mind, which was so much occupied with immediate concerns.

"Oh *duh*, is that what you call it," Torker said sourly.

"I get it," Bey said. "Slowbolt has to have vengeance to make things right, but he doesn't really want to kill him anymore, so he takes a pretended vengeance that leaves Torker alive. Then he bonds him into the keto pod so they can get him to fight on their side."

"What I meant," Dilani said. "Per made me drink the bitter milk. Why they call me 'Tastes Like Us.' They can smell you now."

Torker started to rub his chest, but he stopped when he felt the sticky slime that was keeping his cut closed.

"It's good we don't have any pants, that's all I can say," he said. "And that underwater it's already wet. I thought I was done for."

The ketos were still cruising around the raft, rocking it ominously as if to remind the humans that some of them were still shirking on board.

"They want you all in the water," Dilani called. The others jumped in; only Whitman clung to the raft.

"Come on, Papan. It can't be worse," Bey said.

Whitman was untouched by the lightening of mood, the relief the others felt when they learned the ketos weren't going to harm Torker. He wasn't smiling either; his eyes concentrated on something invisible. He balanced at the edge of the raft, one hand on the boom to steady himself, and stared down into the water.

"Make them take me," he muttered. It sounded like a prayer to the god in the water that he didn't believe in.

He let himself slip over the edge.

There was an explosion in the water, not unlike the consternation of water dogs. All five ketos surged backward, zigzagging on powerful tail tips, most of their bodies in the air and waggling powerfully in side-to-side motions of denial.

> **Ugh! No! The stinky madman! Badness beyond belief!**

Their outcries of rejection were not even shaped to melody. Dilani tried to reason with them, but she could hardly be heard in the uproar.

> **We're not listening. We're not listening. Na na na na na, brrpt brrrrptt!**

They screamed.

Whitman's head broke the surface, looking back and forth, totally bewildered. Bey looked pleadingly toward Dilani, though he said nothing. He looked really sorry for his father, and frightened.

"Don't worry," she signed. She jumped in with Whitman.

"Don't fuss. You're scaring him. We need your help," she hummed with the sound box. They were simple human statements, not crafted to win the ketos' interest. But the great creatures settled back into the water and stopped shouting anyway.

They were sculling, holding as still in the water as they ever did, and looking intently toward something that was approaching out of the Deep. Dilani was alert immediately, but the ketos did not seem frightened. They were very quiet. Then Dilani saw what was coming—points of blue light bobbing, dancing, drifting toward them. She recognized the lights.

Godbits were coming.

The ketos raised their heads and sounded one phrase in unison.

NOW IT BEGINS

They held the phrase, and held it and held it as the godbits thickened around the humans like snowflakes on a winter's night on Skandia.

Dilani was frightened by the cool kiss of the bubbles. The last time this had happened, the bubbles had carried her into a long nightmare of pain and changing. She had already changed. She did not want to change again.

But this time there was no sting in their touch. She did not even realize that they had haloed her head and joined her hands to Whitman and Bey on either side of her until she tried to reach up and rub the tickle against her forehead and found that she could not.

Then she did feel contact—a cool tingling at the back of her neck, as if a cool liquid were flowing into her mind, sending a million trickling fingers into her brain. When the contact was complete, she no longer used words or sign to describe the experience to herself, for it seemed that the place where words had been was entirely occupied by something else. There were no more words, and so the experience remained indescribable.

She knew that the ketos were circling them with swift grace, not in their usual playful mode, but as if they were following a plan with diligence and purpose. As they circled, they sang. The song was simple and clear compared to their usual glancing mockery, but it was still beautiful.

And the godbit membranes caught the song as her own ears could never do, and tuned it directly into her mind. This was the gift the ketos had been talking about. She never could remember how long that luminous blue and quicksilver time had been. Toward the end of it, she thought she was beginning to hear a song that went beyond the ketos' music. There was a deep, vast cycle of harmonies going on in a globe that encircled her and all of the Deep. It was this song that was giving birth to the ketos' swift, ephemeral chatter. All the sounds of the Deep, including her own clumsy efforts, were absorbed into that great structure.

When the godbits slowly slipped away and let the words

come flooding back in, she remembered one of Subtle's words that she had never fully understood. He had spoken of the Deepsong, and Dilani thought that now she had heard it. And it was not entirely strange. She had felt it for the first time when she was a deaf child. Then, she couldn't actually hear it; she could only feel it in her bones, calling to her. Now at last she knew what that call had been.

It was a big relief; the oldgens had thought her crazy when she signed to them about the Deep talking to her, and she had learned to keep it to herself. Now she, Dilani, knew for sure that she wasn't crazy—just smarter than them.

Ha, she thought, and the ketos broke from their sober circle and jumped, startled. She had sent out a sound to them at perfect pitch, and they had sensed her meaning exactly. They sang cheerfully, like children glad to be out of school.

*Now we go to the god**
human/keto
one pod
learn our language
learn new word
slow slow/human human
same thing!

They surged about, laughing at their own feeble joke. Then they got down to business and began to swim powerfully, out-pacing the raft. Dilani swam hooked to Slowbolt's fin. In that position she found it hard to make sounds. *Someday I'll figure out what to do about that,* she thought. But she could listen with unfailing pleasure. She could not catch the full spectrum of their voices, but she could distinguish the main theme well enough to follow the conversation.

She admitted to herself, though she decided she would never tell anyone else, that hearing was all right after all. There wasn't much point in hearing human conversations, but to hear ketos—that was worth it!

❮❮❮19❯❯❯❯❯

As the ketos reached their normal cruising speed, the sea floor flowed through Dilani's mind in one long line of song. She couldn't see it; she could only hear it as the ketos sang it to themselves. Despite her earlier optimism, she was jealous of them because sound was more real to them, a rich tactile dimension that she could never feel as completely as they did. It took them only two or three hours to swim the distance from the Big Dry to the submerged mountain where the god lived, but in that time, Dilani experienced an endless landscape through their song.

When she felt them climbing, she knew where she was. They were coasting up the smoothly curved slope of the old volcano where she and Bey had last seen Per. When they crested the crater lip, they were still twenty meters below the surface. The last time Dilani had been here, the water had been thick with predators and prey—all drawn to the god's summoning.

This time the summons was for them alone. The water was clear and empty as air. The ketos yodeled as they surfed over the lip of the crater on their own bow waves and flipped over, to slide down the long descent below.

Dilani remembered how the pellucid blue had deepened as they sank. It should have been dark below, but as they approached the bottom of the crater, a crystalline blue-green light, the color of the sparks in the godbits, began to glow. She had a brief flash of memory of how sick she had been when she had first seen that glow. It churned her stomach.

Per appeared in her memory. He had been patched with red

salt burn and the white of his sickness. He had been worse off than they were, but had fought for them to the last. To the last . . . when the god had taken him. And he had signed to her. Her free arm crossed her chest, with the fist clenched for emphasis. Per had signed one-handed, too. The other arm hadn't been functional at the time.

Slowbolt let her know by a quiver of his skin that it was time to let go of his fin and slide away, to leave him alone with his awe. Even the ketos were quiet in the presence of the god.

As they entered the cavern, Dilani didn't want to look at this thing that had eaten Per.

It hung there like a huge translucent moon in a misty sky. It was a globe big enough to hold a man with arms outflung, without allowing his fingers to touch the sides. *No,* she thought. *It's bigger than that.* It was hard to guess the scale, because it was hard to tell exactly how far away it was, how big the cavern was where it floated. Sometimes the globe seemed to loom over her, making her feel like a speck, as small as the godbits. Then her perception shifted, and she suddenly thought it was a delicate, toy-sized organism that she could pick up in her palm. She stretched out her hand, almost believing it, and suddenly was Dilani-sized again.

It catches me, fools my mind, she thought. She had been staring at it for a long time, but she could not tell how long, any more than she could tell how large the sphere really was. The perfect, gleaming roundness drew the eye into its depths, where lines and patterns of glowing particles stirred and faded along invisible channels.

But nowhere among all those patterns was there anything like a trace of Per. And the god sphere was clear—or almost clear, all through, between the interknit weavings of its life processes. There was nowhere it could have hidden him.

Without thinking, Dilani made Per's name-sign. She had kept his image in her mind, believing she would find it again, here, if she came back. Now she knew that that body was gone. If Per still lived, he lived in some way she couldn't see.

"Per, Per," she signed. For the first time she thought that Per might really be dead—completely gone from the only world she could live in. A fish spear or a cutter might be able to pierce the body of the god where her talons had failed. Maybe she could kill the god that had taken him. She could destroy whatever gave *it* form—see the tiny glowing cells spilled like a chain of broken beads into the darkness of the Abyss. She was sorry they had stopped the White Killers from doing it when they had a chance. This "god" had destroyed Per Langstaff, and it deserved to die.

But all the while, she had been staring into its lucent depths, and had not moved to harm it. She realized that she had been breathing the god motes for a long time. The sphere stared back into her mind like the blue eye of the Deep. If she had held the harpoon gun in her hands at this moment, she would not have been able to fire.

It had dominated even Whitman. In the blue light shining on his face, his colors showed only as dark shadows. His hands were in front of him—warding off the god? Or were they raised in amazement? She didn't know. Once again, godbits were approaching him.

Whitman stared at the approaching sparks as if he had been entranced. From the god's body, a twine of clear filaments, almost invisible, curved out, curled around his head and neck, tightly bonded to his skin. Crystal droplets of god substance flowed through transparent channels. Whitman went taut for an instant, an expression of anguish on his face. Then his arms and legs drifted slowly into a fetal half curl. His face relaxed completely. Whitman stared at the god, its blue gaze mirrored in his eyes. Only his hands moved, shaping whispers of sign.

Dilani had never seen him so helpless. He wasn't persuading, scolding, exhorting, or trying to control anything. The godbits had touched him, and he had given up. It frightened her a little. She wanted Whitman to wake up and be his bossy, obnoxious self again.

Bey nudged her.

It talks to his mind, Bey signed. *It's shaping him.*

Startled, Dilani turned toward the god. Could Per be speaking in the form of the god? But then, why wouldn't he talk to them? Why would he speak first to Whitman, who had always been his adversary?

"We're here. Talk to us!" Dilani signed. She made her hands bright with passionate appeal. She made the gestures big, so they could be seen in the dim light. She was willing even to let the god seize her as it had Whitman, if it meant communication from Per.

But there was no response.

Bey elbowed her to get her attention back.

"He can't sign; he has no hands," Bey signed. "We have to think of a different way."

Dilani slipped her hands into the sound box and played Per's name. The god had no ears, but she wondered if its watery substance might vibrate to the sound. She knew it heard keto speech, for the ketos spoke of talking with the god. She played the sound again, slowly. But still there was no answer.

Per had been called back from his trance of despair by the sound of ketos arguing. The Deep had rung with the sound of their reckless, casual duels before, but he had never heard them disagree about a matter of principle. It was a serious disagreement, enough to rouse a grieving god. Speakers for two factions contended. They were screaming.

****
*We follow the god/clear water/follows god
*To disobey/breathe putrid flavors/of the disobedient
*   (dead flesh rotting)
****

Per recognized the singer. It was Slowbolt. The keto's normal humorous defiance had turned to a deadly serious argument, counseling obedience for a change. It was strange to hear Slowbolt in this role. Per wondered what was at stake, what he had missed while his consciousness turned inward. The second speaker taunted Slowbolt.

***

Stinky you/swim nose to tail of smelly death/you stinker
Two-headed god/swims nose to its own tail/god of two bad
smells

> (your dead obedience stinks)

***

Slowbolt responded with a brief outburst at full volume.

***

Obey the life-preserving god
Help humans live/we live
***

The other's scorn was relentless, but Per thought he heard a
note of underlying fear.

***

Obey death-minded god?
Humans swim with death/we die
***

Slowbolt abandoned speech at this point. Per could no
longer hear coherent phrases—only a war chant declaring
Slowbolt's fierceness and singing his own praises, accompanied by rhythmic wave fronts that Per's senses translated as
mighty leaps above the surface. He could picture Slowbolt's
powerful tail propelling the keto into flight.

No more argument came from the adversary.

***

Tail wins/what head lost
***

He sneered, but his tones were muted. He was cowed, if not
convinced, and he swam a straight, humble course, without
more displays to provoke the victor.

Once the commotion of their dispute subsided, Per could

hear the more subtle sounds that revealed what they had been arguing about. He heard the slap of waves against wood, faint voices, and a distorted, mechanical imitation of keto speech. Humans were in the water with the ketos, and they had acquired some means of speaking with the ketos.

Now Per understood. Kitkit had commanded the ketos to bring the humans to himself, just as he had promised. In that, at least, he had not lied. Slowbolt had prevailed, and the humans would receive safe conduct, at least for now.

But there was still some dispute going on—this time not between ketos but between Slowbolt and the god. Slowbolt was trying to say something more, but Kitkit sent out a powerful vibration designed to jam the communication. Kitkit was trying to silence the keto. Per got a blurred image from the keto's song. The directional track was the clearest, as if Slowbolt knew that was the most important and broadcast it most insistently.

The image was like the transformed humans in shape, but it seemed to swim with a pale shadow, a thing with two legs and two arms, but bearing an inhuman aura of death and decay.

***

Seen . . . in darkness/swimming . . . with death

***

The song was fuzzy.

***

    One kin comes not/swims far from kindred
Lonely/ally
Foolish/wise one
Childless/parent
Trash/treasure
Of the god/insane one
Find her/find eggs/find treasure/find death
***

The swift, riddling song slipped through the god's jamming. Then Slowbolt's communication was drowned out by sustained harmonies from the other ketos, unified in a way that Per had never heard. As he listened, he realized that the god was using them to help the humans understand keto song. Per guessed that Kitkit wanted some way to communicate short of direct contact.

He felt a surge of hope and terror at the image of a lone human, swimming with what he had to assume was a White Killer. Slowbolt had spoken before of a lone human accompanied by a White Killer, and Kitkit had denied the possibility. But this time Per felt sure that Slowbolt had sent a message to him alone. Slowbolt understood Sofron's importance, understood that she was Per's pod mate.

Per gathered himself to send out an urgent call to Slowbolt and to the humans who could now hear him. Finally he could ask for information and urge them to search for her.

No sound emerged. He was voiceless. He could see, and he could listen, but somehow Kitkit had blocked him from contact with his own kin. He struggled as he felt the humans coming swiftly nearer, but he could not access Kitkit's consciousness nor call up the old god's form.

When the humans actually entered the crater, and he could sense them directly, he was still speechless. He might not have been able to speak, even if Kitkit had allowed it.

He saw his old friends, and was stunned by his own yearning to be among them again, to be human. At the same time, he saw—for the first time—the transformation he had caused. They were alive, and they were beautiful. But they were not human. No face was as he remembered it, not even the one whose motes and demeanor marked her unmistakably as Dilani. Now he knew how much he had attached to their human appearance, how he had dreamed of seeing them again.

That possibility no longer existed, and he was the one who had destroyed it. He had never understood why other Skandians considered him arrogant. Now he knew. And yet, what choice had he had?

Now Kitkit had prevented all communication with the Skandians. It seemed that all he could do was to stare at his kin from his transparent prison.

A familiar, insistent sound pierced through his frustration. He focused on the source. It came from the device Dilani wore around her neck, the one she had been using to imitate keto speech. But this was not keto speech. She was imitating a human voice this time, and the sound was his name.

Per abandoned his own effort to create sound, and tried to produce a godbit tap like the one Kitkit had sent out to Whitman. He understood the process, but he found himself unable to trigger it.

Per remembered what Kitkit had told him about the *bekkila*, the image spun out of god substance to communicate with other beings. It would be only a shifting of his own body, involving no direct contact between himself and other beings.

He extended his substance a little, and found that there was no apparent barrier to that movement. He attempted to shape hands and a face. Slowly a blister formed on the god's surface. The blister pinched itself into shape, like a blob of dough, and formed a torso with a head and two arms. The surface of this shape firmed and took on color. The head remained featureless, but the hands were disproportionately large, so that the fingers could be seen.

Kitkit, still absorbed in contact with Whitman, didn't notice his activity. But Per was afraid that if he used a language Kitkit knew, he might somehow catch the old god's attention. The sign language he had used with Dilani was possibly even older than that of the Great People. The *bekkila* moved its deft, minuscule hands, signing "Pinkman"—the name the young Dilani had once given him.

He waited, and hoped, not daring to do anything to call more attention to himself. It was the former cephalopod, the twelve-armed thing that was now a biped with extra tentacles, who responded first. Per saw him seize Bey and Dilani with his extra limbs, and repeat Per's sign.

"Per, is it you?" they both signed simultaneously. They suppressed their excitement, as Per had to suppress his own joy. At last, at last he was recognized by a fellow human being. But he had no time to express regret, his sorrow, or his joy. The need for action still drove him on.

"You're alive! I'm so glad!" Dilani signed. "I told them you were alive. Bey, too. But you know how they are. They never believe us."

She amended that. "Melicar believes. And Torker. And the newgens. But I don't know about the others. Whitman says you're impossible. But I won't talk about Whitman. Per— make a new body! Please! Come back. We need you."

"I'm trying," Per signed. "But the old god still lives in here. He's the one who is talking to Whitman now. He won't let me speak to you—would stop me if he knew I was signing now. Hurry and tell me, have you seen Sofron?"

They told him, as fast as possible, all they remembered about Sofron.

"And now she has gone into the Deep alone," Dilani concluded. "We think she followed the White Killer, to look for the lost children, the ones who were with her when the godbits came to change her. She needs our help. She wouldn't wait for us."

"Afraid you'd get hurt," Per signed.

"Maybe," Dilani signed. "I wanted her to stay. Everyone goes. She says she has to take care of the children because they are too small, and that now we're grown up. But I want her to come back."

"Me, too," Per signed. "I need you to find Sofron and tell her to come here to me. I think the god is sending Whitman to the old towers at the end of the island. From what the keto said, I think Sofron has gone that way, too. The god will send ketos with Whitman. Stay near them. There is great danger in that place. The god wants Whitman to fight White Killers. Avoid that. Find Sofron if you can, but try to avoid White Killers. They are very dangerous. They have a kind of sickness that may be catching. I'm trying to find a way to cure it. Meanwhile stay away from them."

"We've already fought them twice," Dilani signed. "Look at Whitman," she added laconically.

Per turned his attention to the colony leader, who still floated with mouth half opened, eyes half shut, in the grip of the godbit tap. There was always a problem with Whitman, Per thought. What could be new about that?

But even as he tried to brush it off, he felt a chill of foreboding. Something *was* wrong with the colony leader. Kitkit hadn't interfered with Per's share of the pheromone receptors. He could perceive clearly that the motes drifting from Whitman's skin had a strange and dark flavor. And Whitman's colors, if they could even be called that, showed like the last remnants of a fading bruise on livid skin.

The god mind yielded images of Great People in the first stages of the Paling. The resemblance was too close to be denied.

"I understand." The *bekkila* couldn't come close to expressing the horror he felt. "How many others are like this?" he asked Dilani.

"At least six, now. Maybe all, soon. Does it come from touching and fighting White Killers? Does it come from their motes or their blood? We don't know."

Per was certain that they, too, felt horror that could not be communicated through this stoic medium. He wanted to reassure them, but he had neither face nor voice. The only way he could comfort them was to solve the problem.

"I'm sorry," he signed. "I don't know yet, either. But I will find out and fix it. Just like before. Right?"

"Before, you made us like the old people, the wall carvers. And now we have one of their problems," Dilani signed. "You made us too much alike."

No mercy, Per thought.

"The other half of the god mind is from the old people. I'm trying to learn from him," Per signed. "But sometimes he lies."

"Don't trust him," Dilani signed. "Why does he talk to Whitman and not let you talk? Can't be a good reason."

Damn right, Per thought.

"Can you get the Bright Teeth to send me messages if you need to talk to me?" Per signed. "I don't think the other god can stop me from hearing them unless he wants to go deaf, too."

"Better," Dilani signed. She held up the device strung around her neck.

"This is the old people's song box, for talking to the Teeth. I can use it myself now."

"That's great," Per signed. "Only watch what you say with it, because the old god can hear."

He nervously kept a part of his focus on Whitman.

"When he's through with Whitman, you'll have to go," he signed. "Please find Sofron if you can. I need her help, her thoughts. But don't risk your lives. If it's too dangerous, just come back here. And watch Whitman. The god can lie to him, too."

Whitman stirred and looked around.

"I know what to do now," Whitman signed briskly to the other Skandians. "This isn't a god; it's more like a library. I learned a lot. And by the way, I saw no trace of Per. I don't know how he's supposed to be here—as a ghost or what—but I didn't see him.

"We have to remove the source of infection—the White Killers. We can't do that without better weapons. I have seen maps of the archaeological areas where we can get better weapons. We're going to go and retrieve them, and then we're going to destroy the problem at its source."

The Bright Teeth sculled away from the god to a polite distance; then, with a lashing of tails, they carried the humans away.

"What did you tell him, damn it?" Per demanded of Kitkit's image. "What did you tell him to do?" The waters of the pool rocked with his agitation.

Kitkit spread his crest low, trying to soothe Per.

"I learned from him that they have found some of the tools of the Great People, from abandoned stores I didn't know about," the Kalko'ul revealed. "Your people are ingenious. Moreover, your ally Sofron found the new hatching ground, and the Bright Teeth have told me of following her traces and seeing it.

"I have learned from your people what I suspected, but did not know: that the Killers have returned closer to the shore, closer to where we are living. They have found the old towers of my ruined city, and they are living and multiplying inside, where my Bright Teeth cannot reach them to slay them.

"If they continue to multiply like this, we are doomed. We must strike now! Your clan members will go to the towers and get the weapons they need. They will go to the hatching ground where the White Ones spawn, and destroy all the eggs. There will be no more White Killers, and no more fear."

"Well, I'll tell you what *I* learned," Per shouted. "I learned that you lied to me! You told me we were one, yet you cut me off from speech and hearing! But even without speech and hearing, I learned by looking at them that they have been infected by the White Killers. Your plan is making my kin sick!"

His spines were in full threat mode.

"Why in hell's name did you not let me know this?" Per said. "You said we would be partners. What are you going to do about my people who are already sick? How can that be? How can they be infected when they are a completely different species? And why didn't you warn them that they could be infected by contact with the White Killers?"

He did his best to pump motes of rage and disgust into their shared environment, since it was the best way he could express his anger.

"I can answer that question myself," Per said bitterly. "You would not warn them, because then they might seek to avoid the Killers instead of confronting them. That wouldn't have served your purposes.

"Well, you can think about *this*: I'm not going to go one step further with the weapon you want for killing White Ones—not until I've found a way to cure whatever it is that's infecting my kin."

He expected this to cause agitation for Kitkit, but he wasn't prepared for the shuddering of the waters around him, the surge wave of furious darkness.

"There is no cure!" Kitkit howled. "Have you understood nothing? There is no cure, except to kill them all. The White Ones must die!"

"How can I understand when you don't show me everything?" Per said. "You have not told me the truth."

There was a long pause. "The truth," Kitkit said. "There are no words for the truth.

"The Paling is a ghost from our past. It haunts us. You have that image, you Clan of Skandia? The dead shape that will not sink, that rises into the light and would speak, but utters only a cold breath from the Abyss?"

Per felt a cold shiver. "Yes. We, too, have those shapes in our minds," he said. "We, too, have ghosts that rise from the Abyss of a long and bloody history."

And I may be one of them, a voice in his head said. But Kitkit didn't seem to hear that voice.

"The Paling is such a ghost," Kitkit said. "The Pale Ones were a ghost from before we were civilized. When we lived in the Deep and times were too hard, sometimes a hatchling would go Pale—hungry, fierce, mindless. It would eat its own kin to survive."

"I've seen this in other species I have studied," Per interrupted, his anger somewhat allayed by the fact that Kitkit was giving him real information. "It's an alternate developmental path triggered by stress. The increased fierceness, the voracity, give the killer morphs an edge, ensure that at least some of them will live to breed again."

"But when we learned to change ourselves, to make tools and build, there was no need for the Paling!" Kitkit said. "Oh, sometimes it happened, sometimes something would go wrong with a hatchling, and when it changed, it would come back Pale. But there was no problem. The Pale One would flee to the Deep of its own will, or we would drive it away.

"But in our time . . ."

"In your time adults began to Pale—like my kin out there. Isn't that what happened?"

"Yes! Yes!" Kitkit snarled. His pupils narrowed to slits, while the color of his irises roiled dangerously. "They began to come back from the Deep in their changeling form, like dead bodies that refuse to sink. They clawed at our gates and walked through our streets. They sought their old homes—mindlessly, only to stand silent before the doors and bring a curse on their clan mates who still lived there. We caught them with nets, we dragged them away, we cast them forth or locked them in isolation. And still they came! And all who touched them Paled and maddened, and fell to the same fate. It was a curse on us! A curse, a curse . . ."

His voice sank to a hoarse whisper and he stared into the pool with eyes that saw fire and madness there.

"So it was contagious," Per said. "Did you ever find out how? Did it come through the air, or through touch, or through blood?"

Kitkit hand-shrugged morosely.

"Whoever came close to the Pale Ones also became Pale. It happened faster to those who were slashed or bitten by the Pale Ones. That was certain death. But there were those who tried to keep loved ones at home after they began to Pale. They did not call for my officers. Instead they locked the Pale Ones away and tried to care for them. They, too, went mad. We sometimes found locked houses where all within were mad or dead, having killed each other in their madness. Then we would lock the doors again and burn all within."

A stab of sorrow and pain from somewhere far off in time made Per shiver. It was not Kitkit's world he mourned, but another.

"We attached auxiliary engines to the derelict and powered it off-orbit, into the sun," the Skandian stranger's voice said. "It burned up. Everyone inside was dead, anyway. Or better dead." There was no feeling in the voice. It wasn't their home they had burned. They didn't care.

"Except for *him*," the second voice said. "Was it really

wise to pull him out? He looks like a child, sure, but you have no idea what he really is."

"That's why we needed him," the first voice said. "This ship breached our space by accident, but that shows they could still do it. What if they come for us on purpose? This may be our only chance to learn what makes them go."

Per remembered them discussing him as if he had no ears to hear them, as if he were a piece of salvaged machinery, not a person.

Per looked down at his imagined hands. He no longer saw himself as one of the Great People. Instead, he saw himself with their eyes, as Kitkit might see him. His fingers were pale and unarmed. His body was naked, wormlike, lacking spines and colors. Like something larval. And his pale skin repelled the Great Ones as it did the Skandians. On both worlds, white was the color of death.

He took a deep breath—a part of him knew that, outside this illusion, fragile membranes wafted more water through the networks that carried the god's oxygen. He tried to focus.

"Was the Paling contagious in the beginning? When one hatchling went Pale, did it spread to the whole brood?" he asked.

"How could we know? We kept no records then," Kitkit said.

Per felt certain Kitkit was evading him. He pressed on with more questions.

"When it happened in the old days, you said that the hatchlings went Pale," he said. "And after you began to transform yourselves with the godbits, sometimes the newly changed went Pale. When did adults begin to change? How could that happen?"

"I don't know when it began," Kitkit said. "Maybe it always happened. But so rarely. Not like our time. Then it spread like plague."

"So you experimented to find out," Per said. "Those eggs you showed me—they weren't Killer eggs. They started as normal Kalko'uli eggs, didn't they?"

He felt the torment of shame in Kitkit driving him to denial, so he didn't wait for an answer.

"You took normal hatchlings and tormented them, deprived them, made sure they'd go Pale. Why did you do that if you already knew what would happen?"

"We knew what would happen, yes! But *how* it happened! How to make it unhappen! For that, yes, we tortured the hatchlings."

Per could feel his questions marching to their own inevitable conclusion.

"What about adults? Did you ever torture the adults? To make them Pale? See what would happen then?"

There was a sudden wail of rage and anguish. Per felt himself *pushed*, as if he had been caught again in a typhoon wind. Something slammed against his whole body, lifting and shoving him beyond the room, out into darkness—or was it the room that shredded around him, leaving him behind in the dark?

Kitkit was no longer there, only the echo of his cry.

"I take that as a 'yes,' " Per said to himself.

He shivered again. There was a bad taste of smoke and madness still in his imagined mouth. He was locked in with a creature who was no longer wholly sane.

The Bright Teeth returned the humans to their rafts but continued to accompany them, so Dilani had the whole trip back to shore to listen to what the Bright Teeth thought of Whitman Sayid. "Crazy Leader" was the least of the names they had for him.

"He wants us to kill eggs for humans, for stinky humans!" Stripped of its poetry and sarcasm, this was the import of their song. The Bright Teeth would happily slay any tasty being that swam, but they considered egg killing a taboo that no intelligent species would breach. Whitman's mission appeared to their keen minds as a major disgrace.

So Dilani was prepared when Whitman climbed out of the water, looking stronger and more assured. She felt reluctant to leave the water. Many dangers were there, but so were her friends, people she could talk to, powerful people who would help her. The shore was the domain of treachery.

The Teeth had evidently been told to guard the humans at all times, from now on. They complained bitterly about this, as well. Assuring them she would be back soon, Dilani went ashore to see what would happen next.

She could feel right away a pall of sadness that hung over the camp and those who had stayed behind. Even the water dogs were subdued. If they could not cringe behind an un-damaged human with good colors, they immersed themselves in the water, only their heads showing, and stayed there.

"What's wrong?" Whitman asked the doctor.

Without speaking, she pointed to the awning that shaded the sick and wounded. Even at a glance, it was clear that they were worse. Madan was shockingly pale, and the long slash that split his skin looked ugly. Even the wound was pale, not bloody. Under the scab of skin gel, it hadn't healed at all.

Engku and Miko crouched nearby; their eyes were squeezed tightly shut against the light, and thick, salty tears crusted the lids.

Whitman started to speak, but Melicar interrupted him before he could say anything.

"Allfather, what is that you've got on your neck?" She stepped back defensively as she spoke. The number of alien growths and strange parasites she had encountered lately was beginning to be too much even for a doctor.

Whitman rubbed at the narrow ridges of god substance that still clung to his skin.

"It's nothing," he said irritably. "Leftovers. We encountered an organism."

Having his flesh invaded by alien life would have horrified the Whitman Dilani knew. His casual attitude alarmed her. He had changed.

"Yes, we found this being that has been referred to as a 'god,'" Whitman said. The sick were forgotten. "It's not a god. And I saw no sign that Per has somehow survived as a part of it.

"Nonetheless, it's a remarkable organism—like a biologically encoded library. I gained access to the records of the extinct civilization that created the library. I now know where to look for weapons and tools that may still be usable. Remnants of their city are submerged at the end of the island. We can go there."

"Whitman, this is no time to go on an archaeological expedition," Melicar protested. "We're under siege, and we have sick people who need help. Why didn't you ask this compendium of all knowledge about *that*?"

"Those are precisely the questions I did ask," Whitman said. "That's how I know that the expedition is the only solution. 'The Paling'—that's what this process was called—is a problem left over from the previous civilization. It is spread by contact with the White Killers. They are a mindless infestation that has run wild since the previous inhabitants became extinct. The only way to eliminate the problem is to eliminate the White Killers."

Noises of disbelief sounded from several points around the circle.

"How likely is that?" was the most polite comment, from Nila Kusmati.

Whitman's eyes gleamed, and he leaned forward persuasively.

"It is now completely possible," he said. "Once we have weapons, we'll be able to protect ourselves from the Killers for all time. And I've also learned the location of the place where the Killers cache their eggs. After I get access to the weapons—after *we* get access—we will proceed to that location and neutralize the next generation of White Ones."

"This is crazy," Uli Haddad said slowly. "This goes against everything we've been taught as Skandians. Skandians don't rely on weapons to solve problems. Skandians don't set out to destroy an entire species. There must be some other way."

"We should first try to move away from the threat," Phun said. "All of us who aren't infected could go as far up the mountain as possible. We can stay away from the Killers there. Maybe this will pass."

Whitman's spines shot out in full array, and he hissed and spat as if he had tasted something bad. His whole face paled with rage.

"We've tried that before, you stupid, stupid citizen," he hissed. "Haven't we learned anything? We tried to hide from the Deep. But it's relentless. You can't hide on Typhon. We have to go get those weapons, or we will be destroyed. There is no other way."

He pointed to the wounded on their pallets of leaves.

"Look at them!" he said. "Do you think hiding is going to help?"

By this time, the sun was sinking, but greatmoon had not yet risen, and the shadows were single and dark. As Whitman spoke, all eyes turned to the shelter. Dilani had been staring at Madan through the whole conversation. As the others chattered, she thought they were really just waiting for the moment when the irregular movements of Madan's chest would cease.

But the pale shape that was Madan had not ceased to breathe. As the sun sank and cooling shadows fell across Madan's pale body, he sat up. He rose, clawing the air as if it could hold him up. He wailed, the wordless cry of a lost soul. The discussion was over. They stared, frozen.

Only Melicar ran to him, instinctively, to restrain or to support. He hurled her aside like a toy. He got to his feet and staggered in a blind circle, crying out, but in no language. Ketut, who had been his friend, caught up with him and tried to put an arm around him, but Madan slashed at him with a hiss of rage like a hot iron plunged in water.

Whitman thrust a dry stalk of giling into the smoldering campfire. As it flared up, he swept its flaming end toward Madan. Over Whitman's shoulder, Dilani saw the light reflect from Madan's eyes. They flashed blank silver. If there was still a mind behind that opaque sheen, it was no longer visible.

"Control him," Whitman ordered.

He held Madan's gaze with the torch while some of the others ran for a rope and crept up behind Madan. The sick man tried to turn when he felt the rope, but by that time it was too late. The combined strength of four or five of the biggest adults was enough to bind him and throw him to the ground. He shrieked and struggled without stopping. Even after they had bound him, he continued to thrash in the sand and utter the uncanny hunting whistle of the White Killers. He had become indistinguishable from the enemy.

The water dogs cringed behind the newgens until Madan lay bound. Once they were convinced that he could not move, they made a desperate break for the water and disappeared beneath the surface.

"I can't stand any more of this," Wayan cried, pressing his hands to his ears. He turned and ran for the river, to plunge in with the water dogs. Most of the newgens followed him.

The adults were so ashen with fear that they looked almost like a pod of Pale Ones hovering over one of their own. Dilani crouched between the shore and the clearing, observing them. Subtle was beside her, his hand on her shoulder, and she could still feel his calming motes. Nonetheless, there was a bad, dark taste in her mind. The adults were trouble, she thought. They couldn't take care of themselves. Wherever they went, eventually there was a lot of screaming and a bad feeling. It was safer to stay away from them. Most of them, anyway.

Madan never stopped struggling. Even after he had worn himself out with shrieking, he continued to writhe feebly and to emit broken, whistling cries. His oozing wounds became crusted with sand, and sand stuck to his gills.

Dilani stayed well away from him. She didn't want even a taste of his motes.

"We've got to untie him," Melicar said. "That was a mistake. We're killing him."

"He's killing himself," Whitman said. "If he'd just be quiet—"

"I don't think he has any choice left," Melicar said. "Something is forcing him to act this way. This is not a reasoned response. He'll keep going till he dies. We can't treat him; we could at least make sure we don't do him more harm."

"Just what do you suggest?" Whitman said. He was raising his voice, and it had gained a ragged edge. "If we untie him, he'll go for us again."

"Maybe not," Melicar said. "Maybe he felt threatened by us. If we all stand back, he may not attack. When you all had the changing sickness, you were driven toward the water. Maybe he needs to be in the water."

"But if he goes in the water, we'll lose him. Madan wouldn't want that. If he were in his right mind, he'd rather die than become this kind of mindless creature."

"You can't know that for sure," Melicar said. "All we know for sure is that he'll die if we don't untie him."

"He's quieter now," Whitman said. "Maybe he's stopping."

"He's stopping all right," Melicar said. "Permanently."

She brought a shell full of water and poured it carefully over Madan's gills, trying to wash away the crusted sand. The cool water triggered another frenzy of struggling. There was no hint of recognition reflected in Madan's face.

"Well, I'm not asking your permission," Melicar said to Whitman. "I'm the doctor, as you keep telling me."

Madan had pulled all the knots too tight to undo. Melicar bent over and cut the ropes. As the last coil fell away, Madan leapt to his feet, lashing out with his clawed hands. He swung in a blind circle, as if groping for the way. Then he staggered toward the water. Newgens and water dogs scattered, shrieking, as he plunged into the waves and vanished.

Melicar looked dourly at her own hand, where blood welled from four parallel slash marks.

"So much for the doctor," she said. "Whitman, you'd better not try to tie me up when I go Pale."

Whitman turned, still holding to the stick he had used as a torch. Its blackened end smoldered faintly, though the embers looked dark in the pale moonlight. Was it ash on his hands, Dilani wondered, or was it the skin itself turning ashen? He looked up, and she knew. It was a ghost Whitman looking at them. She saw how the color was fading from his lips and eyes.

Soon he would look like Madan.

She had never liked Whitman much, but the thought of a pale, crazed Whitman who had no words, who would shriek and claw like a creature of the Deep, made her feel lost and sick.

But Whitman wasn't yet at a loss for words. He was still in command of himself.

"This is a tragedy," he said. "This is not the time to discuss our plans for tomorrow. We're safe for tonight—the ketos are patrolling the shoreline. We need to rest. Consider what I've said; we'll decide tomorrow."

Dilani found herself wishing that what had happened to Madan would turn out to have been a dream, or maybe that he would come back in the morning, and he would be better. There could be cheerful talk, and splashing after fish . . . no more talk about dark places. But she knew this was a child's wish. She envied Sofron's children. They were the only children left on Typhon.

In the morning Madan had not come back, and the others looked worse than ever. Dilani thought of a new wish—that Whitman would hurry up and finish talking so she could get back into the water with the ketos and carry out Per's request.

But Whitman was still speaking. However, he spoke in a low voice, as if he didn't want the sick people to hear him. The water dogs had come back and were peering curiously at the scene from under the arms or behind the backs of their favorite colonists.

"We're going to have to make some hard choices if we want to survive here," he said. "We must seek out and destroy the White Killers. But even that will not be enough. We have to quarantine ourselves to stop the spread of this contagion. The sick must be isolated until we see if they will become like Madan. If they try to return to the colony or assault us in any way, then . . ."

He seemed to have trouble actually saying it.

"We'll have to keep them away. If that means using weapons . . . even shooting them . . . then yes, it has to be done. Showing compassion for those who are no longer in possession of their own minds anyway will doom all of us. I will appoint a committee of volunteers to enforce this policy."

The deceptive peacefulness of the morning came to an abrupt end.

"You mean, if Madan comes back, we'll shoot him?" Ketut said incredulously.

Melicar jumped to her feet.

"You'll shoot *me* first," she said. "Whitman, I don't know how often I'm going to go through this with you. First you wanted to get rid of dysfunctional newgens. Said they'd be a drag on us all. Look around you. That turned out to be a mistake. Now you want to shoot the sick. I'm not putting up with it. And I'm the only doctor you've got, as you keep pointing out.

"I'll appoint my own committee of safety to pop you over the head with a big stick first," she continued, "and tie you up and put *you* in the water, where you'll poison the motes for miles around, no doubt. But we won't shoot you, Whitman, no matter how bad you smell, because we feel for you sincerely, with the kinship feeling of the Skandian commonality."

These were brave words, Dilani thought, but the other adults did not gather to Melicar's support. They looked away from her with worried faces, and Dilani knew they wouldn't back her up. The doctor's water dog, and a brace of others, splashed along the shore, whimpering, scared by the raised voices and excited motes.

Whitman briefly put his hand to his neck, rubbing at the welts of god stuff. Ignoring the doctor's outburst, he continued.

"Secondly, those creatures have to go."

That got the attention of most of the newgens.

"What do you mean?" Melicar said.

Torker focused on Whitman, his teeth beginning to show in displeasure.

"They look harmless," Whitman said, "but they're the immature stage of the White Killers. When they mature, they'll be vicious killers, living here among us. We have to dispose of them first. After that, we go to the hatching grounds where they're spawned. Once the eggs have been eradicated, this madness will stop."

The newgens grouped in defiance, arms spread protectively in front of their water dogs. The effect was spoiled by the fact that the water dogs thought it was a game and jumped happily around their protectors.

"You can't be serious," Melicar said uncertainly. "They're just pets. They're harmless."

"I'm completely serious," Whitman said. "They carry infection. They're dangerous. We can't leave them behind us while we carry out our mission."

Everyone was staring at him. They still couldn't believe he was serious.

"Think about it!" he shouted, his spines suddenly flaring viciously. "You adults, think about the barneys on Skandia! Remember them? Sure, every child in a northern living group wanted a nice, furry barney cub! And a year later, when they were grown, those 'pets' who had become accustomed to being fed by humans were killing and eating work crews! This isn't a joke! Creatures don't become harmless because they have pretty colors!"

He was paling visibly. He looked around wildly, found the harpoon gun leaning against a tree, and seized it.

"Get out of my way!" he cried. One of Torker's water dogs was in the open, frisking toward its friend's side. Whitman turned on it and fired, almost at point-blank range.

There was a whistle of agony, much like the death cries of the White Killers. The water dog writhed briefly, blood and slime pouring from its torn belly, and lay still. Its colors rippled and died.

The other water dogs rushed toward it, whistling and crying.

"Stand back," Whitman said. "I'll take care of this myself." Loading the gun again, he raised it and took aim.

Then, with a small, pained sound, he crumpled to the ground. Dilani stood behind him, clutching a stout length of firewood.

"I hit Whitman Sayid," she said aloud—as loudly as she

could, in her still-discordant voice. "You punish me later. Now I go to my friends. Bright Teeth. We help Sofron like Per wanted. Water dogs come, too, and no one kills them."

She paused to collect the right words.

"I am take full responsibility. Now who comes with me?"

All the newgens joined her, silently.

"Stop them," Phun said. "She's obviously out of her mind. Someone disarm her! Dilani, nobody blames you. We're all suffering. Just put the stick down, and let's not have any more violence."

But Dilani held the stick out, warding them off.

"Sorry I hurt Whitman," she said, casting a pleading glance toward Bey. "But this my decision. I am Dilani, and I say no more killing things we don't understand. We go now."

Torker stood looking at the dead water dog. His spines were down, his face inscrutable.

Whitman stirred and groaned.

"Is he going to be all right?" Torker asked.

Melicar felt Whitman's head.

"I think so," she said.

Torker picked up a couple of the rope scraps that had been cut from Madan and began to tie Whitman up.

"What are you doing?" Melicar exclaimed.

"Well, Whitman is right about one thing," Torker said. "We're not going to survive without trying something. I want him to take us to this place he talks about. Maybe we will find something that will help us.

"But I want to make sure he doesn't do any more shooting before we get there."

He dumped Whitman, not too roughly, on one of the rafts.

"Get going, Dilani," Torker said. "We'll be along in a minute with the rafts. Per tried to help—I see that now. I'm going to give Sofron a hand if I can find her. Make things even. But we'll need you and the ketos to protect us. Go talk to them."

Dilani hit the water in a smooth dive, sounding the call for Slowbolt almost as she split the surface. The other newgens followed, preferring not to be around when Whitman woke up.

"We go to help the god-friend," Dilani sang to the Bright Teeth. "To the god-friend our help goes, not to the Stinky One. The god has two minds, eyes on two sides. One eye is blind. We see for the god; we save for the god. His mind will thank us when his eye is open."

A change was taking place among the Bright Teeth, though only Dilani realized it. The reversal of thought came as suddenly as the turning of peaks to sea bottom. It exploded in the swimmers' minds like fire bursting up through the Deep. They had never openly disobeyed the god. They had evaded and willfully misinterpreted the god's commands, but had never defied them.

They could be risking their lives. The god might take an unknown vengeance. For this very reason, Slowbolt sang joyously, they must experience this new daring. The god was divided within, and they could take sides in this new circumstance. By changing their allegiance, by refusing to help the egg slayer, the Bright Teeth might even change the god. Once imagined, the danger must be savored, or the Teeth would be revealed as toothless, unable to bite the new, only able to chew on the bones of the old.

They burst from the water in a star-shaped explosion of anticipation, chanting Dilani's name. Unknown to herself, she had achieved a permanent reputation. Even if the rebellion she had goaded them into ended in disaster, her name would forever be a shining memory, for she had caused something entirely new to enter the song of the Bright Teeth.

Torker hesitated, looking down at Melicar.

"What are you going to do?" he said.

"Stay with them, obviously," she said. "Do what I can for them. But if the ketos are going on the expedition, I don't think we'd better stay on the beach like this. You can leave the one big raft for us. I'll take the wounded and whoever else wants to stay, and we'll go up the river to the garden area Sofron told us about. It sounds a little safer than the beach. We'll wait there for you to come back."

She smiled ruefully.

"Trusting in the gods of Typhon hasn't worked out too

well for us so far. But maybe the place of hatching will be lucky for us."

The community sorted itself silently into two groups—one to stay, one to go. They looked at each other for a minute.

"Luck," Torker said.

"Same to you," Melicar said. "Go on, or you'll never catch up with the ketos."

⟪⟪20⟫⟫⟫⟫⟫

Sofron found herself dancing slowly and majestically to profound music whose strains moved her like massive, gentle hands. Gradually, it dawned on her that she had not been fully awake for some time—hours, certainly—perhaps even days. But she was waking up now.

She was still underwater. And she was still breathing. There was plenty of oxygen, but there was no air. She was in a closed, dark space and could not move, and she felt that this should have disturbed her much more than it did. The water around her felt fresh and warm and invigorating, like the air on a spring day. She felt relaxed, yet alert. She should have been panicking, but for some reason it seemed impossible to be worried or afraid.

It was dark. She could not see, and yet, she *was* seeing. She moved through a country of hills and plains where she could see clearly across vast distances. Far away she detected airy spires rising into a region of dazzling brilliance. She soared above this landscape to the sound of music that was still with her.

When I last checked, she thought, *I was sinking into the Abyss, and those fang-tentacle things were about to tear my guts out.*

I give up. Where am I?

As if in response to her question, she felt a vast curiosity bending its attention toward her. The music touched her and turned her, as if she were a pebble tumbling in a streambed.

Oh, where have you been so long, you little ones? the great voice sang to her. *So long, so long, you have been absent from our music. Now you come again, weak, small, all alone. We taste you bleeding for our hatchling. We came to retrieve only her, but find you woven into her song. Too late to leave you— now you must always be part of our music. So long it was since we found such a surprise! This is great happiness. The song could not end darkly with sad cries sinking into silence. So we lifted you and carried you away in the hatchling pouch, like the little ones of the long-ago. So long you were gone. Where did you go? How did you come again?*

The musings drifted away, into regions where she could not go, became huge and incomprehensible.

Hey! I'm here! Come back! she cried. She couldn't really twist her body to recall the attention of the big voice, but she sent out the nerve impulses that would have called for vigorous writhing if they had not been blocked somehow.

Your taste is not of patience, little one, the big voice said, and there was a taste of amusement in the waters Sofron breathed; it made her feel as if bubbles tickled her. *We carry you in the hatchling pouch, as long ago we carried the little ones with their clever little hands. We give you soundsight, we feed you, as in the time when we made your mothers' mothers wise, so they could build their god and go. Why did you go?*

Sofron had no answer to that.

You've mistaken me for someone else, she thought helplessly. Then, to herself: *How in hell's kitchen am I hearing these questions? I haven't gone crazy; I still feel like me. But why do I have voices in my head?*

She felt the music vibrate through her, palpably, as if sound were a sense of touch.

We touch the speaking part in your mind, the voice said then. *As we touched the Little Hands long ago. You have a small mind part, for the small speaking of small ones. You are small but bold. You interest us.*

Again she tasted a vast amusement, and felt very small.

We touch your mind part, as we touch our own hatchlings, and make you wise. What is your tiny thought for look-look, touch-touch, ping-ping?

She heard the sound of probes bouncing back from a solid object.

Scan? she thought tentatively. *Are you scanning my brain?*

We thank you, said the voice. *Indeed, we scan. Make pictures. Ping small mind.*

Tell me what happened. Tell me who you are, Sofron demanded. *Please—I'm in a hurry. I have hatchlings, too.*

Something passed over her, like a hand that soothed; she guessed it was partly extra oxygen, because she suddenly felt stronger and more awake. But a good scent and a warmth came with it, and she could not identify those chemicals.

We saw you on our last pass through here; we saw you near the small ones' god, the voice said. *We thought you a new kind of small Pale thing, the bad ones who help the bad dark things, the ones who love to bite our hatchlings, those who are discords in our music. So we swam away.*

Then we saw you, fighting the dark things, hearing the hatchling's song. You have saved a long-cherished movement in this music; without you, its structure would have failed. We approached and tasted you. Your taste was strong, for your blood hurried out into the water. We saved you to taste again and think.

We decide. Your flavor is part of us. It shall not be lost. We will offer you if-then. You saved our hatchling; help us again, and we will help you to save yours. Do you understand if-then? This means wise mind, even in one so small. You understand?

I think so, Sofron answered cautiously.

We have made you strong now, the voice said. *We will carry you to the dark walls, the small places where we cannot go. Other hatchlings we have; some have been taken there, like yours. Help them if you can. Beware the bad Pale things, inside dark walls too small for us. That is if.*

After you save your hatchlings, you will come back to us. You will share our song again. You will be our Hands again, after so long. That is then. You understand?

Sofron thought hard, trying to pin down exactly what the voice was offering.

You healed what those dark wings did to me? she said.

Again came the comfortable feeling.

So now you're saying that if you take me to the place where I will find my children, and let me go, then I must promise to come back and let you—talk—or whatever this is, again?

You understand, the voice affirmed.

I promise, Sofron said instantly. *But, how long has all this taken? How long have I been unconscious? And where are we?*

The voice paused briefly.

Three blinks of the Eye, it said.

For a minute, Sofron interpreted that statement in human idiom, and was confused. Then she saw a bright image of the sun glittering on the surface. The voice meant that the sun had come and gone three times. It seemed to her the voice found this negligible.

Where we are you do not know, the voice said. *Small ones have small names, names lost now. We have a name that fits not in your small mind.*

What name do you have for yourselves? Sofron asked.

The laughter was enormous and multifarious.

The Name is big, your mind so small, the voice said. Behind and along with it the thunderous, laughing song went on. *The small Hands called us "Big," called us "They Protect." We live a life of many parts. First as eggs, then as hatchlings. Then we are gathered up and become hatchlings-inside, like you. Then we grow wise, grow strong, until we can swim alone outside, still fast, still small.*

In your short language, you might call us "iuvens" then. We grow and learn until we are ready to create an egg, and we seek for the hatchling when the egg is grown. We swim as egg makers, hatchling protectors for a long time; you might call us "maternes" then.

After the hatchlings grow, we live for the Song. We watch over all hatchlings of our own kind. Long ago, when our hatchlings had grown away, we sometimes would take up one of the small Hands and teach it part of the Song. You could call the old ones "veter"; a veter carries you now.

My part of the Name—to make it so very short for you— maybe you could call me Changing Light. Come, sing one tiny Name part before you go.

Sofron felt herself moving through space, picking up speed. The image of peaks and valleys spun around her.

How am I seeing this? she said. *It's dark in here.*

We give you soundsight, the voice said.

How do you do that?

A finger touches your brain, the voice said.

Sofron felt involuntary disgust.

Or a tongue is touching your brain and tasting you; do you like that better? Still she shuddered. Amusement sparkled over her again.

We will show you later.

Sofron felt a dive begin. They gathered speed. She felt the rich, dark muscles pumping, bathed in densely oxygenated blood. Abruptly the effort stopped; blood rushed back toward the center, and her mind tingled with the rush. They were flying. They soared downward and leveled out. The sea floor rushed past them—no, not the floor; the plunging black steep that led to the Abyss itself sang distantly, seductively, in Sofron's bones. This was a terrace clinging to the gateway of the Abyss.

The terrace was grooved and ribbed with carved markings. As they soared over them, their sightsong rebounded from the grooves and broke up into a reverberating fugue of echoes that thundered against Sofron's bones. Each groove had meaning, but the sightsong strummed across the grooves too fast for Sofron to comprehend. Their significances overlapped with increasing speed, leaving only tantalizing fragments in her grasp.

Their speed increased until the reflected sounds merged in one triumphant thunder, unceasingly shouting out the Name. Sofron's bones thrummed to the same harmonic. Her body reverberated with the same chord, joining in the song, but her mind could not absorb it. She lost consciousness.

When she woke up—again—the music was muted and

lulling. It seemed dark, the seascape around them dull and bland.

We are so sorry, the voice said. She thought there was a trace of anxiety in its flavor. *We forget your brain is so so small. We tried to sing one tiny Name part, but the Name is so big.*

Sofron had a pounding headache, though it receded rapidly as soon as she took notice of it.

Yeah, my brain is so so small, she said. *No kidding.*

Sorry, the voice said again. *We are fixing your head.*

What was that? Sofron asked, adding quickly, *If you can tell me without giving me another headache.*

We write the story of the Name on stone, on clay, the voice said. *We write it in shed shells, we write in weeds. All ways. Long ago the Hands used to help us.*

But why? Sofron asked. *What's it for?*

It is for beauty, the voice said. *For writing down the truth of all that happens. For making the Deep sing.*

The voice now seemed wistful, curious.

Do you have no way for remembering great names, you little ones? it said. *What will you call us, now that you have heard us name our Name?*

Sofron thought of something, and laughed.

We have a name that means some creature that is very big and swims in the sea—it's an old name, too.

"He makes the depths seethe like a cauldron,
He makes the sea fume like a scent burner.
Behind him he leaves a glittering wake—
a white fleece seems to float on the deeps.
He has no equal on earth,
being created without fear."

Leviathan—that's what you are.

The response was a cluster of notes that expanded like a flower in surprise and pleasure. Sofron shared in its delight, like a physical sensation.

We like your songs, the big voice said. *When you rejoin us, we will learn more of them. But now we have come to the place you seek. We can go no farther. We are too big.*

Something alien was growing in Sofron's perception. Four straight lines, vertical and smooth, marked the fluid Deep. They grew in soundsight as the veter approached them.

The Hands built this, the voice said. *They built away from the Deep, into cloud space, breath space, into great emptiness. They sang for the Eye of Fire. Then the Heart of Fire, the fire that lives below the Deep, took back their towers. Deep they sank, and high rose the Deep, and there was fire in the Deep and darkness in the clouds. Then the Hands went away, and did not come back. The Pale things live here now.*

This was the Hands' hatchling door in the old time. Now the Pale things seek hatchlings once again—yours and mine. If you go to seek them, you seek great danger.

The towers were dark, impenetrable to sound. The veter sent out the soundsight and showed Sofron where the ruined gates lay open.

You really think they're in there? she asked. The gate looked very dark.

We saw them go there; they have not come back. The voices crooned a sad chord for the hatchlings who had vanished through the door.

This was a city of many lights. This was a city where the towers had eyes—clear like shallow water, hard like stone. Light shone like many moons from a tower of cloud. Now the city is dark and the Pale things live here, far from the light. Many many Pale things, many many teeth. The Pale things dance in the greatlife; the Pale things sing, too.

The voices explored a minor dissonance.

But when the Pale things and their dark allies kill and eat our hatchlings, too too many times, they take the voices from our song. There is too much darkness. We lose our harmony.

The music modulated back toward a bright major key.

Help us find our hatchlings, and we will help you save yours. When we knit ourselves together, we will compose a fascinating architecture. It will be long remembered, through many cycles of our lives.

Sofron got the impression that the voice was offering her what it considered to be the ultimate glory. But her immediate problems were going to be practical ones.

Wait, she said. *You say there are a lot of White Ones in there?*

We see them swim in, the voice said. *But we can't see into their dark within. The city is a skin of rock to them. Sometimes we see inside the fragile skin of living things, but into the solid skin of stone we never see.*

I will need help in there, Sofron said. *I need the god to know that I'm in there. I need my friends to come with more sharp sticks and bring the Bright Teeth. Can you tell the god about me?*

The song broke into humorous ripples.

They copied their little god from us long long ago, the voice laughed. *We can sing to their god until the god spins dizzy.*

They got the god from you? Sofron was torn between the need to know and the need for immediate action. She would never get another chance like this to learn from the oldest beings they had yet encountered.

Shall we tell you what this is, that they call "god"? The voice was laughing again. Sofron couldn't stay worried when she was surrounded by that mirth.

Inside the hatchling pouch, where you are, we keep a special nest for hatchlings. We have all kinds of cells that keep and carry many different kinds of motes, for caring for the hatchlings and for communicating.

Our kind of animals, where we come from, we have an organ kind of like that, Sofron said. *Called the placenta. It connects the—uh—hatchling inside to the mother.*

Then you understand us! the voice said. *The little Hands borrowed some of those cells and cherished and fed them, because of the good motes they gave. When they were wiser, they taught their little god new things. They grew it into the god of changes who made them able to walk in the Dry.*

Sofron felt a kind of awe creeping over her.

So you are the true gods of Typhon, she said.

The laughter that surrounded her then was like a thunderstorm that danced. From the other leviathans, outside the veter that carried her, came a burst of soundsight that revealed the leviathans as they saw themselves—tiny cells hanging in the womb of the mother Deep, always seeking, always growing toward some unknown, greater form.

We are not gods, the voice said. *We have not yet been born.*

While she was with them, it was impossible for her to feel other than as they did. She could not be afraid or anxious. But somewhere in the back of her mind, a clock was always ticking.

One like me has been gathered into the god now, she said. *Tell him these things. Tell him you have seen me; tell him my hatchlings are in this place and I need help; tell him the nature of the god.*

We will tell him, the voice said. *We can't know if he will hear us. Not all that is sung is heard.* Echoes of laughter at the amusing folly of small beings died away slowly.

Good. Thank you. Then I'm ready. Sofron sent the message resolutely, before she could lose her nerve.

We are sorry we have lost your stick, the voice said. Sofron had to think hard for a minute to remember. It must mean the metal pole she had been wielding against the dark wings.

You still have your tooth on a string, the voice said helpfully. Sofron thought again, and remembered Wearra's knife. That was better than nothing, anyway.

We have no sharp sticks to give you, but while you were sleeping we gave you something that will help you. We have put in your mind all of the Deepsong that would fit. You can't sing like the Bright Teeth, because your body is not made that way, but now you will hear at least part of their rude music. And we have given you the dancing language that the Round Folk and the Hands used to use. Maybe even the Pale Ones will recognize this.

Now we must leave you, the voice said. *We will wait for you to open the eye of the dark tower. When you call us, we will come to you.*

Wait! Sofron said. *How can I call you?*

You will find the way, the voice said. *You know the songs now. Use what you find. We will hear.*

Sofron felt something happening in her head—severings, rearrangements, connections shutting down. For a moment she was coffined in a small dark space and fully aware of it. Then, just as she tensed for panicked resistance, she was expelled.

Per wished that he had Rameau with him in the true present. Since Kitkit now believed that Per's fear for the other humans had inspired him to search for bioweapons, the Kalko'ul allowed him to learn the god's basic processes. He learned how godbits of all different kinds were produced, and he learned to insert motes of all kinds, to be delivered to ketos or humans. The creation of godbits was a simple thing when viewed from the right perspective, a mere packaging of cells and chemicals the god's body was constantly producing anyway.

With each increment of knowledge, Per could feel his own mind knitting itself more completely into the god's nervous system. He was creating circuits of awareness and control that extended throughout the god's mind, just as the god had once sent filaments through his human flesh to assimilate him.

He now controlled the locus where templates of useful organisms were stored. He bypassed countless fascinating natives of Typhon to go directly to the Kalko'uli themselves. Again he had to exercise self-control to avoid getting lost in the intricacies of the first great transformation. He focused instead on the hormonal systems that controlled the change from hatchling to the adult form.

Kitkit's description had been accurate as far as it went. The Killer metamorphosis, an early and primitive mechanism to ensure survival in hard times, still remained, but the genes that induced it were not normally expressed. Under extreme, life-threatening stress, the genetic pathways could be activated. Then the maturing hatchlings would emerge as predators—vicious, violent, ever hungry, in a constant state of high arousal, with all higher brain functions subordinated to the sheer need to survive.

It was an elegant mechanism. As a biologist, Per admired it. It was a perfect solution for the violent world that was Typhon. No matter what happened to the civilization of the Great People, their genetic material would be preserved for another try.

But the Paling happened to adults. They were beyond the stage when that metabolic pathway should have been open to them. Under stress, chemicals analogous to human steroid hormones were released, producing a whole series of enhanced functions—increased strength and alertness, increased metabolic rate, lowered sensitivity to pain. In the Kalko'uli, suppression of the skin colors and secretions seemed also to be a function of stress. But, just as in humans, once the threat ended, enzymes should have neutralized the Paling hormones.

The Paling was like a stress attack that never ended. *The White Ones must be like soldiers on a lifetime dose of battle drugs,* Per thought. And probably the side effects were the same. They would be insanely irritable, paranoid, unable to focus on anything beyond the moment. Their lives would be violent and short, as the increased metabolic rate destroyed their internal organs.

Per thought the White Ones must have suffered some mutation that had destroyed their ability to produce the substances that would return them to a normal state. But there were other aspects of the problem that he didn't understand. In humans, there would be no pathway for such a mutation to leap from person to person. The Paling behaved like a contagious disease, but what could the vector be?

Per couldn't do field research. He couldn't observe live beings interacting. He couldn't use his senses. This was a crippling disability. He thought again of Sofron. If only he could talk to her . . . *exchange motes,* he thought.

And yet, he was afraid to see her, afraid to search for her. He had already taken her outward humanity away from her. He did not like to imagine what else she might be suffering now that he had plunged the humans into an ancient nightmare from the history of a dead race.

He found himself thinking about the *Langstaff*'s bioweapons again. He knew that that was where Kitkit wanted him to go. Kitkit wanted him to retrieve some memory that would help the god to devise similar terrors to use on the White Killers. Even in the absence of his body, Per felt horror at the thought that Sofron might already be experiencing the effects of what had driven the White Killers mad. The ketos had seen a lone swimmer following a White One. Why would she have gone that way unless she was already tainted? He thought again of the poisoned girl he had called Embla, drifting in her prison.

"Focus," he ordered himself.

Somewhere there must be a useful memory, some hint of how to repair the damage, not make it worse.

He was standing next to the toxicants' window again. Today Embla was not responding to his overtures. She drifted in the tank as if dreaming, but Per did not know if she dreamed. Perhaps her mind was simply empty at such times. But Per thought even that might be better than being awake and aware of herself, knowing she was a vessel for others' poisons.

"You're wallowing in it," Rameau said scornfully. "Stop it."

The boy Per shot his mentor a glance of pure hatred. But he said nothing.

"What? You think I'm heartless? You think I should be agreeing with you? I should be full of misery and sorrow over her sad fate; I should have tears blubbering down my cheeks?"

Per's expression answered for him.

"Someone should grieve for her," Per hissed. "Why not you? *You* made her. You made her to serve the pirates and suffer."

Rameau's hand flicked out and smacked the boy's face, hard enough to sting. The grown Per, watching, could feel the heat of the tears that surged out and choked the back of his nose.

"That was not for what you said but for the way that you said it. We are *guests* here. Our hosts on board ship are the

Original Man—a proud title and one they insist on. Do not use that other word again, or you may suffer worse pain. Later we will discuss where you learned it."

"I was reading in the files," Per said defiantly. "You said I could."

"Reading about how evil we are?" Rameau sounded amused. "Reading of how the only way the local arm can be made safe for mankind is through the extirpation of mankind's most egregious branch? Remember that that branch also holds the fragile flower that is your little playmate there. Those who would exterminate us would not spare her. To them, she's a monster worse than we are, because we at least share their appearance."

"I don't understand the words you use," Per muttered. "I just know it isn't fair."

He was hoping to goad Rameau to further explanations, to distract him. Secretly, even while Rameau scolded him, he had been tapping gently, almost imperceptibly, on the transplex that separated him from the toxicants. Even if Rameau had been watching, he might have thought the tapping was random, a mere tic.

Earlier, while Rameau had been talking to the guards, Per had drawn faint lines of glowpaint on the window, making letters from the alphabet. The toxicants were taught to read certain simple words so they could follow written directions. Per was tapping next to these representations. He wanted Embla to learn that taps and letters were the same, so he could talk to her through the transplex. She must know some words, if they had taught her to read commands.

Rameau flicked at his head again, but missed him this time.

"Pay attention," Rameau said. "I'm still speaking to you."

Reluctantly, Per stilled his fingers and kept his eyes riveted on Rameau's face. He must at all costs keep Rameau from noticing his game.

"Feeling sorry and weeping doesn't help them," Rameau said. "Forget feeling sorry and think instead of working to improve the situation."

"Improve the situation," Per said. "How can I improve the situation? *You* could. You could cleanse the bioweapons out of their bodies and let them be regular humans again. Then they could come out from behind the wall."

Rameau's face brightened, as if Per had presented him with an enjoyable challenge, for once.

"That's no solution," he said. "In fact, it would kill them immediately. They are made to live with their burden of microscopic life. If we removed it, they would die. There is no way to make the toxicants like us—if that is what you mean by 'regular.' Come with me; we'll view the design specifications together, and I will explain them to you."

Per's feeling toward Rameau became truly murderous then. The boy's heart was harrowed with sorrow for the sufferings of the creature he thought of as a friend; Rameau spoke of her as if she were merely an interesting technical problem.

But Rameau had him by the wrist and was already dragging him away from the tank and from the watchful eyes of the guards. At the last moment he glanced back.

"Look at that, you careless boy. You've left glowgoo fingerprints all over the window. Come, wash your hands immediately."

As he turned, Rameau brushed the window with his sleeve, smearing the glowpaint letters into a blur. He had known all the time what Per was doing, but had not betrayed or prevented him.

As they jaunted back through the long corridors to Rameau's work space, with its readers and holos, the boy Per abandoned—for the dozenth time—his half-formed plan to poison Rameau. Per was confused, and he wondered if he would ever see the sharp-eyed scientist clearly. Rameau's kindness so often had a sting in it, yet his hateful words concealed kindness. He was impossible to understand.

In his work space, Rameau had holoviews that could symbolically represent structures and processes too small to be conveniently seen. The boy Per liked to slip the stylus over his fingertip like a magic wand, wave it, and watch proteins form and curl around themselves like little nests of serpents. He liked to set antibodies loose in a pack of viruses and watch the body cohorts lock onto and destroy the intruders.

But he still didn't really enjoy entering this room, because most of the time it meant that Rameau was going to subject him to another grueling tutorial during which he would be expected to memorize and reason about all kinds of facts of no interest whatsoever.

This time, however, he watched with admiration as Rameau expertly delineated a moving three-dimensional diagram representing the toxicants' immune system.

"This is greatly simplified, of course," Rameau said, "because I've only included one infectious agent. But you see how the virus has infiltrated the cells of the subject's body, instructing those cells to produce more virus."

"Yes, I see," Per said grudgingly. "But so what? You could still attack the virus and kill it, and then the body would be normal."

"Ah, but then we do *this*." Rameau's stylus marked a change in the coded notches on the virus's surface. Then he called up, in a separate window, the body's chromosomes.

"And we make a pregestational alteration to the subject, here. Now what does that do?"

"It means that the body can't make this protein anymore . . . but I forget which protein that is."

Rameau rapped him on the top of the head, but lightly. "Never mind; we'll review that later. You get the main point. This body can no longer produce all the proteins needed to conduct its life processes. But, as long as it continues to produce the virus, the virus will provide the missing commands, and the protein will continue to be produced.

"So *now* what happens if we clear the virus from the subject's system?"

"They die, I guess," Per admitted reluctantly.

"Exactly. The toxicant and the virus have become symbiotic. One keeps the other alive. With a less-aggressive virus, it could go on forever. But in this case, the virus has been designed to be highly toxic. So it has to be held in check until the weapon is put in play. Then the demands of the virus eventually exhaust its host. But meanwhile, we have plugged viruses, bacteria, and fungi into so many nodes of the subject's life systems that it could no more exist without them than you could live without your mitochondria."

"But what if . . ." Per had been thinking hard, because for once it mattered to him. "What if you took the virus out . . . then replaced it with one that was harmless, but still produced the protein?"

Rameau gave him one of his unreadable looks; then he smiled.

"Good; that is a theoretical possibility. Except that these are very highly engineered toxicants. They have many lines of defense against any form of revision that would neutralize them as bioweapons."

"It's evil to make a being that is born sick and can't be cured," the boy said suddenly. His pale skin flushed until his ears were red. "It's wrong to make people just to be tools for others."

He braced himself as if to withstand punishment. The grown Per, watching, was surprised. His few memories of childhood had not included making judgments of any kind.

But Rameau did not move to punish him, even with a slap to his head.

"Oh, my my," he said mildly. "Evil, is it? Where did you acquire this weighty vocabulary? The history files, I suppose."

For the moment, he seemed not to be playing a part. He actually looked sad.

"I don't dispute your conclusion, little Per. But I must remind you that you are Original Man, even though you are without a cohort. You would not exist at all, if someone had not thought you would make a useful tool. In fact, on this whole ship there is only one of what used to be called 'normal humans,' one created freely and at random, for an unknown destiny."

"Who is it?" the boy said. His voice was alive with excitement.

Rameau smiled.

"That would be me," he said. "And I am the servant of all—the caretaker of mankind's broken toys."

21

Again Sofron found herself in a dark space—a vast dark space this time. She flung out arms and legs in a monkey reflex, fear of falling, from the human remnants of her brain. The water pumping through her gills was cold, heavy, astringent, compared with the sweet fluid she had been breathing.

She felt as if she had gone blind. The senses that had poured into her through the leviathans had been cut off. She was lost in the mighty shadow of the Deep. The dark towers with their ruined gate had vanished. She whistled into the shadows.

Thin and feeble the echo sounded; but it brought back a flicker of soundsight that showed the towers still standing, and very near. Above her a great nobbled curve of something slid away, taking the last vibrations of leviathan music with it.

The pressure of the water told Sofron that she was in pretty deep. She fluttered her neck spines but could not raise them fully against the water's weight. She forged her way stroke by stroke through the heavy fathoms and entered the dark gate. She felt wisps of cold sediment stirred by her passage, swirling up from the broad steps to circle her legs.

Cautiously she pinged the archway as she passed through, and measured its generous proportions. She spared a moment to run her fingers across the wall inside. Under a slick, puffy coating, she could feel the ridges and curves of Great People glyphs. She imagined briefly how the place must have looked when it lived in the light and air—sunlight sparkling on the great pool that formed the entrance to the city of the Great People. The walls had probably been thickly carved with their

252

boasting, with bas-reliefs showing them magnified in glory. Now all their histories lay buried in darkness. The Great People were gone. Sofron wondered if their carved faces still looked down on her struggle to keep humans from vanishing into the same abyss.

She left the gate behind and began feeling her way through the chamber beyond. It was so big that she wanted to keep one hand on the wall rather than cut straight across it. It was so dark that she could see nothing at all, not even the hueless shadows of the Deep. But it wasn't empty. Sensed by echo, everything was tilted, crumbled. On every course she chose, she found things in her way: blocks of stone; strange shapes of something that felt smooth, like metal; and thick, tangling veils of she knew not what. Only the soundsense kept her from running straight into them and hurting herself. In skirting the obstacles, she fought vertigo, and sometimes forgot which way was up.

How can I find the kids in here? she thought. *How would I know if they were ever here? I don't even remember the way out . . . And isn't this a fine time to think of that.*

At that moment, she tasted Killer motes. The scent was so strong she almost gagged. It flowed toward her from the far side of the great chamber. Fighting the urge to flee, she pulled herself up that current as if it were a rope. It led her through the broken wall and into the darkness beyond.

She sent out a sound probe, and it died as if smothered in velvet. There was a faint, muffled echo that revealed nothing of what lay beyond.

If I'd had these senses all my life, maybe I'd know what that is, she thought. *I'm like a baby here. I see things, I hear things, but I don't have the experience to tell me what they are.*

She stopped in the darkness, surrounded by the motes of her enemies: breathing them, tasting them, choked by the cold alien smell. She was fearful that if she moved ahead, she might touch Killers at any moment. The leviathans had healed her wounds, apparently; but her memory was still imprinted with the feel of ripping claws.

Despair began to gnaw at her. Here she was in the darkness, on a hopeless quest, and if she failed, her bones would be scattered in the ruins of a place that had already been destroyed and forgotten. Just minutes ago, she'd been soaring with the leviathans, happy and secure—laughing, even. Now she was fathoms deep in night.

Just remember, the leviathans chose you! she said to herself. *And not just for your survival value or your scientific knowledge, either. They picked you for your music—now there's something to live for. And they promised they'd be waiting for us.*

Already the leviathans seemed like a dream, but the memory of their laughter gave her courage.

Gripping the hilt of Wearra's knife, she forced herself to move on.

The substance that absorbed her echo turned out to be some kind of thick, fleshy growth lining the walls. She brushed against it and experienced an instant of panic. It felt cold and slick-firm, just like the wings of the black-tentacled creatures. Sofron lashed out wildly, kicking and slashing with the knife. If there had been air, she would have screamed; in the Deep, she whistled shrilly. The plaintive cry, probing for help and information, vanished into the darkness, and the darkness still enfolded her.

She nearly lost the knife when it caught on something she jabbed it into. That brought her to her senses again. Nothing was striking back. There were no hunting whistles proclaiming the arrival of the White Ones. She was the only thing moving.

Gripping the knife hilt with both hands, she wiggled it loose, then used her belt cord to tie it to her wrist. She couldn't see the knots; she tugged them tight and tested them repeatedly before she could bring herself to trust them.

Meanwhile, she was drifting in whatever direction her frenzy had impelled her. She could feel her heart laboring, the gill membranes trembling as they struggled to suck in enough oxygen. Something was wrong with the water. It tasted even worse than before, and there was grit on her tongue, in her throat. She was choking—the same sensation she remembered feeling above the surface when she had breathed in too much smoke.

She let herself drift while she tried to figure out what had happened. She put out a hand to steady herself and found that the fleshy growths were gone, replaced by a layer of sediment. Her hand sank in it up to the wrist, releasing another burst of choking grit.

She stirred up the muck with her struggles. Now it surrounded her in an invisible cloud, clogging her gills. She couldn't cough, but her throat spasmed painfully, regurgitating the muddy water. It didn't help. She was still choking. She needed clear water, but she had no idea which way was out. And the more she turned and twisted, looking for escape, the more sediment swirled into the water. A desperate squeaking sound filled her ears, and it was coming from her own throat.

That's a great way to call something nasty, she thought. *Keep on transmitting "I'm here and I'm helpless."*

But soon it wouldn't matter what kind of sounds she made. She was suffocating. She plunged forward, seeking oxygen, and hit her head a stunning blow on something hard.

It stopped her cold. She stopped whistling, too; she no longer had the strength to send out any sounds.

But she still heard something, like an echo finally coming back to her. It was a chittering sound—high-pitched, but not like the White Ones' hunting cry. Before long it was all around her. Then something touched her. This time it was a live touch, not the fungoid feel of the growths on the wall.

She was about to lash out with the knife, but stopped herself just in time. Nothing bit or clawed at her. There was no threat. Instead of striking, she paddled feebly, following the sound.

Soon she and her unseen guides were in clear water again. It tasted like champagne to her now, even though it still held traces of the White Killers. It washed the choking grit from her throat and gills.

It was still too dark to see. As soon as her gills were clear, she began pinging insistently, trying to discover what she had been following. She could feel it—or them—pinging her in return, and the chittering noise returned. It came from all around her, and the source of the sounds shifted rapidly. The water around her became agitated, as if by more than one body moving rapidly.

Whatever was swimming with her began to assault her arms and legs with continual nudges and nips that were painless, in spite of the fear they caused her. The creature, or creatures, were in constant motion, and her soundsense was confused. She couldn't pull together a clear image.

Cautiously, she spread out her hands and felt around. She touched a muscular, flexing body that shied swiftly away from her exploration. But then it came back, nudging again at her hand. The nudge came from a muzzle about the size of a large dog's. Her other hand touched something ridgy and sharp. She was sure now that there were several creatures around her. The nudging, the chittering, reminded her of something. It seemed like something from a very long time ago.

The water dogs! Those creatures we saw in the cave, just before everything happened. Before we changed.

She tried to reproduce the chittering sound. She felt tails thrashing around her legs as her startled companions fled. But they came back, as if they couldn't leave her alone. The nudging began again—this time from behind, as if they wanted her to keep moving.

Well, it's not as if I've had a lot of other offers.

She swam with them. Her soundsense told her that they stayed inside; always walls enclosed them. They traveled long enough for her to begin to feel deadly tired as the shocks of the day caught up.

At first they stayed deep, but after a while she felt almost sure they were rising again. Then she started to see a faint light ahead. She knew it wasn't daylight, because it was a pale, grayish shimmer, without the warmth of the sun. But she hoped that it might be moonlight. She wasn't sure what time it was in the outside world.

The waters around her were still too dark for her to see her escort. They slowed down, calling anxiously to one another. Sofron wondered how she knew they were anxious, then realized that she was tight with fear herself. She could taste the fear in the water. It was almost as strong as the taste of fresh Killer motes.

These weren't old traces. The Killers were near. And Sofron's recently ripped skin cringed from the other taste that went with the Killer motes—the scent of the dark-winged beasts with their taloned tentacles. Sofron was about to ping the darkness in an effort to locate the enemy, but she stopped herself just in time. Her signal might help them identify her.

Her escort began signaling. They emitted a bewildering variety of pings and squeaks. They herded closer together, pressing against Sofron until she could hardly move to swim. They were half carrying her, wedged between their bodies.

Sofron didn't resist, for she needed the help. In the confusion of sound around her, she couldn't locate anything. She didn't know which way to go to escape the threatening presences. Besides the constant chittering, her escorts flooded the area with fear motes until Sofron's muscles cramped with involuntary terror. She knew she was only responding to the chemicals in the water, but the response seemed beyond her control.

The echoes of water dog noises assumed a different resonance. Sofron guessed that they had emerged into a wider space, and beyond the now-visible mob of water dogs, the faint light was shining. Sofron forced her way between the bodies of her escorts and swam eagerly forward, into the light.

She felt a great gulp of water surge through her gills—the underwater equivalent of a gasp. The water tasted so strongly of the White Ones that it made her dizzy. She was floating near the roof of a huge, flooded cavern. She and the water dogs had apparently been swimming along a passage that paralleled the cavern. Perhaps it had once been a gallery, with arches of shaped stone opening into the great vault. She had passed through one of those arches without realizing it, and now she hung defenseless in the center of the vault.

The cavern might once have been spacious and sunlit, but

now it held no light of moon or sun. Cold, pale rays streamed up from below. It was bioluminescence, but it did not come from live plants. It seemed to glow from cracks in the walls and floor, where incrustations of some kind of life had burrowed in. *Bacterial mats, or maybe algae,* she thought. The scholar's part of her brain informed her that there had to be nutrients in the water for bottom life to survive.

The next thing she knew was that she herself might soon become nutrients floating freely in the water.

The cavern below was full of White Killers. There were dozens of them, drifting in clumps of three or four, their pale skins for once camouflaging them against the light-colored limestone rock of the interior.

Sofron instantly wanted to flee. Equally, she wanted to remain perfectly still and call no attention to herself. So, for a frozen moment, she hung poised at the top of the vault.

Suddenly, three more White Killers darted into the cavern, passing so close below her that she could feel the movement of their wake. They must have emerged from the same passage she had taken, so swiftly that they hadn't noticed her presence just above them. Among them, they carried something that still writhed and sent out broken cries. She couldn't see it clearly, but she guessed it was a latecomer from the group of water dogs that had accompanied her. She shuddered to think the Killers had been so close behind them. If she had lagged a little, she might have been the one picked off.

As the three of them plunged downward through the chamber, they bent over the struggling prey. There was a swift, well-coordinated motion, and the prey came apart into three pieces. Blood and spare parts spilled out, showering a cloud of particles down to the cavern floor. So much for the nutrients. The three White Ones began to eat, and to quarrel over the meal, shrilling and striking at each other. Sofron began to scull very slowly backward, hoping to reach the exit while they were still preoccupied.

And then the wave of Killer motes, mixed with traces of blood, reached her. She shuddered, frozen and sick. She sucked in more water, trying to clear her head, but only inhaled more of the Killer scent.

Suddenly she didn't want to flee. She thought of the innocent, friendly water dog and how it had come apart in their hands, and she hated the White Ones with a fury that boiled coldly in her veins and made her pale with rage. She poised to attack, and she must have made some sudden movement that drew their attention. All at once, a dozen pairs of eyes, from varying distances, flashed silver toward her.

The three most recent arrivals dropped the remnants of their meal and soared up toward her. What was left of her mind screamed, and she saw with a glance that she would never make it back the way she had come in. Even if she could reach the opening, she would be pursued in the dark until they caught her as they had caught the doomed water dog.

She gripped Wearra's knife in her hand and showed her teeth at the approaching Killers. She had just enough wit left to flee across the dome of the cavern, eyes flicking across its unwelcoming underside for any hint of shelter.

She tasted the crack before she saw it; a different flavor of water was coming down through it. At first she couldn't see it, because it wasn't the line of shadow she expected, but a line of light. Her soundsense told her that there was truly a gap ahead of her.

But the Killers were too close behind. If she dove for the gap now, they could follow, and seize her while she was too confined to defend herself. She swam for the rock ceiling at desperate speed, but at the last minute she tucked her head in and somersaulted, slapping her feet against the rock to send herself hurtling back toward her attackers.

Her hand, gripping the knife, was stretched straight out ahead of her. Her momentum caught a White Killer by surprise. The blade ripped through its belly flesh, where there was no bony defense. Then Sofron was entangled in a thrashing knot of limbs. But she felt no pain. She kicked out, felt her heel crack painfully against a hard skull, and used the obstacle to send herself back toward the narrow crack that was her one chance of freedom.

She struck her own skull against rough rock as she shot into the opening. It was so much brighter inside that for a moment she could see nothing. Her eyes were dazzled with pain. The opening was so narrow and so crooked that she scrambled and squeezed through it, and at every instant she expected to feel a clawed hand dragging her back. But she came out into a wider space and whipped around to face the enemy. She could smell the blood still drifting from her knife blade into the water.

The battle smell made her foolhardy again. She sculled back the way she had come and cautiously looked out. There was no pursuit. The two Killers who were relatively unwounded had turned on their dying companion and were tearing him to pieces. Others were swarming up from below, disappointed that the juicier prey had disappeared, but determined to seize a share of whatever was available.

The cold clamp of rage eased from her mind and left her remembering that she was warm-blooded and easily killed. She could feel her colors coming back. She remembered the children with a sudden anguish that hurt as if she had been bitten. How could she have forgotten about them so completely and thought only of killing—as if she had turned Pale herself?

These are powerful and dangerous chemicals we're messing with, she thought. She understood now why Whitman and the others had appeared so distressed after the battle with the White Killers. If they had felt anything like what she had just experienced, they wouldn't have known what hit them. The fierce emotions triggered by the pheromones in the water were more intense than anything Skandians normally experienced.

But most of all she wished, with a longing as powerful as if spurred on by some Typhonese pheromone, that she could see Per and talk it all over with him.

Meanwhile, she turned her attention to pulling herself upward as fast as she could go. She didn't want to be around if the White Killers decided they were still hungry. The quality of the light gave her hope that this time she might be headed for an opening to the outside world. She hoped so; she was worried that the passage she was in would narrow or stop, and she would be forced to turn back.

Soon she was squeezing past rubble—chunks of crumbled stone that partially choked off her passage. If it was true that this place had once been above water, she guessed that her escape route had been created when the catastrophe that sank the city had shaken the towers on their foundations. This crack must have opened up then. It was accidental and not part of the original architecture.

At last she pushed past a final slab of smooth black rock, much more regular in shape than the rest of the rubble, and found herself in a funnel-shaped hole wide enough that she could stretch her arms out to their full extension before touching the sides. There was a diffuse light coming from somewhere, turning the cloudy water to the color of pale jade. That gray touched with green seemed like the most beautiful color Sofron had ever seen. The dark stone around her was cracked, but smooth; it looked as if a floor had collapsed inward, toward the fissure she had been ascending.

She tasted the water carefully before proceeding. She wasn't about to swim into another ambush. There was a confused flavor of various organic substances, perhaps a hint of water dogs, but nothing else she could distinguish. She worked up the courage to rise, and was rewarded by a glimpse of a glimmering surface above her head. She kicked upward, and her head broke through that surface, into air for the first time in days. She coughed the water from her lungs and took a deep breath. Though the air was dank and chilly, it held plenty of oxygen.

She pinged the space around her, and the echo assured her that she was still in an enclosed space. It was a large space—at least ten body lengths, she guessed. There was a glimmer of light somewhere up above. The light and air made her think there must be an opening to the outer world, above the surface, but she could not see any break in the dark walls around her. The pale light didn't directly touch the water. It glanced off the walls above her head.

She swam forward slowly and carefully, and bumped into a stone ledge that was only a few inches underwater. She pulled herself up onto it and rested. Heads popped out of the water in front of her. She nearly screamed. Then she recognized them as water dogs. They grinned and chittered at her. Half a dozen swarmed the ledge and curled around her, rubbing their chins against her wrists. She stroked them absentmindedly; contact with them made her feel warmer and brought a welcome relaxation.

"You little guys are everywhere," she said to them. "You nearly scared me to death."

The biologist in her woke up and wondered how the water dogs could possibly fit into the ecology of Typhon. They seemed happy on the riverbank, up in the Big Dry, yet here they were, apparently at home in deep salt water, in the dark. They were big and fancy, and apparently pretty smart, judging by their social communications and their domed skulls.

"But where did you come from?" she asked them.

Like Wearra, they seemed to draw some kind of stimulation from her skin secretions. Sofron knew, by this time, that the transformed Skandians communicated anger, fear, and other basic moods to each other through chemical secretions.

"But you guys and the White Killers are completely different species from each other and from us," she said. "Aren't you? So how can it be that we get the same messages from one another's skins?"

Even the leviathans, so vastly different from anything else she had encountered, seemed to be able to tap into her pheromones, or whatever they were. The sentient and semi-sentient species on Typhon seemed to be linked together in a tight web of communication made up of shared senses that normal, unchanged humans didn't have. Somewhere in that web was the clue to understanding Typhon.

She felt again the frustration of being pushed by events, rushed from one urgent decision to the next without having time to understand her choices.

"We're making a big mistake here," she said. "Leaving something out. I can feel it."

But she could not indulge in the luxury of sitting and speculating. She had to keep moving.

She wasn't sure if these were the same water dogs who had accompanied her earlier, but she knew they had not followed her route to this room. That meant there was another way in, and that was disturbing, since the White Killers also might have access to it.

She rose cautiously to her feet, keeping one hand on the wall next to her. She felt above her; if there was a ceiling, it was beyond her reach. She edged along the stone shelf, trying to avoid tripping over the frolicking water dogs as they plunged in and out of the water. She paused to run her fingers across the surface of the wall. In places it had crumbled, but where it was whole, she could feel grooves and bumps that were regular and familiar—more Great People glyphs.

"If only I had more light," she said. It was eerie; just as she spoke, her hand brushed against a springy velvet substance, and a green glow welled up. Startled, she turned to examine the source. It was her old friends, the bioluminescent fronds. They were growing in thick clusters along the wall, but only up to a certain point; she assumed that must be the high-water mark. She passed her hand over them to see if they were still wet. As she touched them, they all began to glow.

"That's interesting," she said. "They didn't do that back in the pool, before I got bubbled. Possibly they're keyed to substances that I'm now exuding. So I must resemble their original creators somehow."

She intended to light up as many of the fronds as she could reach, hoping that more light would make the area discouraging to any White Killers who could find their way in. It proved easier than she expected; once she had touched one swath, they seemed to set each other off, and soon the whole wall was glowing.

Again Sofron wished briefly that she had time to stop and study the fronds. She didn't even know if they were plant or animal, or something different from her knowledge of either.

But now that she had the light, she turned to examine the rest of the room. And she had to hurry. She didn't know how long the glow would last, or how many places she would have to search before locating the children.

The room was semicircular, its walls of worked stone except for big discs of something smooth and dark that had been placed at regular intervals around the outer wall. They reminded Sofron of something she had seen before, but she dismissed the thought. It didn't really matter what the walls were made of.

As she turned and took in the full sweep of the room, she gasped again, in wonder this time. Shadowy, brooding giants leaned out from the wall, carved in stone and ornamented with stones and shells that would have sparkled brilliantly in sunlight. Even now they gave off a dim coruscation, like dying coals. The statues were like the carved relief of the Great People that she had seen by the pool just before her transformation, only these were three-dimensional, and even larger.

They leaned on long staves—not the slender poles used to ride the dark wings, but tubes with cylindrical cases at one end and carved grips with control devices near the bearers' hands. Sofron wondered if these were representations of weapons. The figures wore no clothes, but their chests were crossed with belts carrying medallions. Each medallion bore a different symbol, and all were coated with a metallic substance that gleamed greenish yellow in the glow. Probably it would have been pure yellow in the sunshine, Sofron thought. She wondered if this substance was gold. She knew that pre-Scandian people had used gold for ostentation. She herself had only seen small amounts put to engineering and scientific purposes.

The faces were beautiful, and if she was any judge of alien features, they were intended to express pride and confidence. The crests were carried high and were covered with adornments.

Next to each figure, a leaping keto formed a graceful arc, and kneeling, looking up at the ketos, were two more humanoid statues. Each of these wore a device strapped to its chest, like a breastplate, and their hands were gracefully arranged above the device, like the hands of someone playing a musical instrument. Sofron recognized the breastplate devices as similar to the sound box Dilani insisted on wearing.

"Allfather, maybe she's right," Sofron muttered. "Maybe it really is for talking to the ketos."

Then she shook herself. She had been staring, fascinated, at the statues for several minutes. What really mattered was the half-submerged arch they framed. This semicircular chamber she was in held nothing of any importance, but she guessed it might be an anteroom leading to something bigger—something that would justify all this impressive adornment.

Plunging back into the water, she swam through the arch. The water dogs followed her, but reluctantly. It was dark again in the next room. She could hear her companions complaining pitifully.

The next room was much bigger. She could hear the echo of the water, disturbed by her entrance, lapping against the walls. She paused and felt for the wall, to see if the builders had left a light source behind. She touched the velvety softness of the fronds, and they began to glow, but their light was uncertain, paler, not such a triumphant green. And it was patchy; the fronds covered only a few spots on walls that were much larger.

There were no impressive statues on these walls. They seemed to be covered with an all-over nobbly tiling. The room was oval, sweeping down to a prowlike angle with one of the flat dark circles on either side of the corner.

Suddenly, Sofron's perspective shifted, and she saw what the room was intended to represent. The decorative tiling was textured like the surface of a leviathan. The viewer was supposed to imagine herself as *inside* the leviathan, and although Sofron had never seen the eyes of the leviathan from any angle, she supposed that the dark circles at the end of the long room were meant to represent its eyes.

The leviathans had said to her, "Open the eyes of the dark

tower." She had thought that they were speaking poetically. Now she thought the phrase might refer to a real place, and this could be it. And if that were true, the children might be very near.

She plunged forward, full of hope, eager to search farther. The water dogs tagged at her heels, whining and getting in her way.

"What's the matter with you?" she said.

Then she saw it. The room had other, smaller windows down its long side, and one of them was evidently cracked, for through the crack, thick, white, fibrous stems were pressing. They unfolded into a woven screen of waving white tendrils. Tangleweed! It was mostly immersed in the water, and she couldn't tell how far its deadly branches extended below the surface. No wonder the water dogs were crying. Sofron was afraid to move lest she call the tangleweed's lethal attention to herself.

She sank beneath the surface, silently, without a ripple, to see if the tangleweed had really invaded the entire room.

There *was* something in the pool. There were shapes, floating near the far side. They seemed to hold a pale, fragile light of their own, and they resembled greatmoon rising—or bubbles caught halfway in their ascension.

She dove without another thought of tangleweed.

∞22∞∞∞∞∞

It was them. It had to be. She counted them over and over. They were the right number. They seemed about the right sizes. But it was only her longing that enabled her to find anything familiar in their faces. Already they were changing. The one she thought was Ling had its fist pressed to its face in Ling's familiar sleeping position. But there was no thumb inserted between rosy human lips. Fragile silvery eyelids stretched tight over the bulge of larger-than-human eyeballs. Thinning lips drew back from teeth that were small, but already pointed and sharp—not the baby pearls they had been. And the fingers were webbed, the nails already curving into talon shapes.

Sofron remembered the pain she had suffered while she endured this transformation. She tried to touch the children, to reach them with her presence, to wake them or at least to soothe them. But her hands slid from the smooth membranes that surrounded them. Very cautiously, she tried a talon against the surface, but the membranes were tougher than they looked. The surface yielded to pressure, but she could not pierce it. Wearra's knife might work. But she didn't know what would happen if she freed the children prematurely.

She ran her hands longingly over their bubble-wrapped faces. They were gaunt and strange with the changes—but was that truly a look of pain they wore? She was no longer sure.

Ling's legs were bent against her chest, like those of a fetus in the womb, but surely they were longer now? Sofron measured them by eye against Ling's bent arms. Yes, the legs had grown. The proportions were those of a normal child.

Sofron somersaulted to look at Ven's face. The ragged cleft that had marred his mouth and nose was gone. The child's lips stretched pale and thin over sharp teeth, like Sofron's own, and his mouth was smooth and unscarred.

She moved to Chilsong. The bubbles rocked to and fro, jostled by her agitated movements. She grasped Chilsong's bubble with both arms to steady it and peered in. His twisted frame folded neatly now, the legs and arms long and straight and even. His face had always been drawn awry by the sheer effort it cost him to breathe. Now an eerie peace rested on his features. The embryonic gills at his neck fluttered with the motion of his pulse, so she knew it was not the peace of death, but of rebirth.

Allfather, it's changing them. Just as it changed Dilani and Bey, and the rest of them. And me.

As hard as it was to tear herself away from the children, she decided that she had better go all around the pool and check it out completely, to avoid any more surprises.

Nevertheless, she was surprised. Her children weren't the only creatures in the water. At first she thought there were more water dogs, but they seemed oddly quiescent. When she approached them to get a better look, she wasn't even sure that they were still alive. Each one was curled up into a tight ball. The skin had become somehow translucent and sticky looking, as if it were half melted. Their limbs, too, were changing form. Both forelegs and hindlegs were growing longer, but their shapes were diverging, so the two pairs of limbs seemed designed for different functions. The translucent skin made it possible for her to find veins at the neck, ones that were pulsing. So they, too, must be alive.

She tried to assimilate the idea that this might be something that was going to happen to *her* water dogs; she already felt proprietary about them. Then she saw the pale child.

It rested in the water with the others, rolled into a ball like them, but it no longer looked like a water dog. Instead, it resembled her own children—so closely that her heart almost stopped. The webbed and finned hands and feet; the flattened, bony face with its large goblin eyes; the stubby crest growing along neck and head—all were the same.

The children's skins had color, pale and muted, but still live and shifting, like the colors on the skin of a fully changed adult. This creature looked like a ghost. There were faint traces on its still-iridescent skin. But if not for those, and for its diminutive size, it could have been Wearra sleeping there.

Sofron stepped back reflexively, her mind full of confusion. Her assumptions about life on Typhon shifted radically, in a moment's time.

But that wasn't her last shock. Moving back, she bumped into something smooth and faintly warm. She tried to catch herself, tripped, and fell backward over the obstacle. Floundering in the water, she saw the object bobbing serenely above her head. In the dim and colorless room, the glow of amber and rich russet color drew her like an underwater sun. She had wondered where the missing leviathan hatchling was. Not hatched yet, clearly; this was the egg.

Sofron put her arms around it as far as they would go. The egg was nearly as large as she was. The smooth, elastic surface was warm and slightly irregular, as if the hatchling inside had already expanded until its contours pushed against the smooth envelope. She wondered how soon it would emerge.

She was deeply afraid now. She had come this far, but it would be useless if she couldn't get back out again. And she had to take them all with her. What if the nearby tangleweed reached its pale, voracious arms this far and snatched the children away from her before she could get them out of this place? What if they didn't hatch in time? How could she take them out, past the many dangers she had encountered, all by herself? The water dogs swirled around her, responding to her growing agitation.

Instinctively, she placed herself between the children and the deadly tangle, so she could keep her eye on it. In swimming around in that direction, she found that there was a stone ledge only a couple of inches underwater, encircling the place where the children floated. She thought this must once have been an enclosed pool, like the one where their transformation had begun, but much larger. The stone wall would be some help against the tangleweed, though nothing could keep it out forever, unless the Great People had installed biological protections that were still in place.

Shakily, Sofron scrambled up onto the ledge, to the safety of the solid perch her human mind still found most comforting.

The water dogs were trembling, their skins paled to grays, mauves, ivories, nearly indistinguishable from white in the corpse-light of the glowfronds. As she crouched on the ledge, they crowded around her, and she welcomed their touch. Gradually their skins darkened. Only sunlight would reveal the true shades, but dappled patterns emerged, echoing those on her own skin. At the same time, Sofron began to feel less frightened. Warmth crept back into her own cold extremities.

She felt a tiny lick of joy, like the first flame curling along a leaf's edge, up in the world of the Dry. She had succeeded, after all. *She had found them.* Only now could she admit to herself how ridiculously small her chances had been. She laughed out loud. The water dogs scattered, then sat and watched her and added their barking calls to her laughter, almost as if they were mimicking her.

Returning to her side, they pillowed her arms and back as she sat and thought.

How long would it take for the change to be complete? Would the children hatch out on their own, as she had done? Did anyone else know they were here? Who had brought them? She had no clues to any of those questions.

She wondered how the children were fed, inside the bubbles. Did they live on stored reserves while the change took place? They didn't have much extra fat. Perhaps that was why they looked so thin and gaunt. Their appearance disturbed her, but she was more disturbed by the thought that the White Killers might return to this place.

And she was hungry herself. It had become a demanding distraction.

Sofron knew there were plenty of succulent fish in the midregions, but she didn't want to leave the pool to hunt them in this dark labyrinth. She wondered if the water dogs were smart enough to be trained, and how she could make them understand "bring fish."

"I am *so* hungry," she said, "I could lick every pot in hell's kitchen."

She focused on her hunger, experiencing every pang in her empty stomach, imagining the delights of fresh fish in her mouth, running her tongue over her teeth, feeling the dizziness in her head.

Hunger hunger hunger, she thought.

The water dogs became unnaturally quiet. They crouched uneasily, staring at her, then began to back away. One of them plunged into the pool, and the rest followed in a cascade, as if a button had been pushed.

"Well, *something* spooked them," she said to herself. "This will be an interesting experiment. Maybe they'll come back and feed me. Or maybe they won't come back at all."

She sniffed and licked her own arm to see if she could detect any special kind of motes. She tasted only the salt water. Once it would have tasted salty to her—now it had a flavor that seemed appropriate and good. She was still distracted by the implications of this when the water dogs came back.

They came back as they left—in a mob, hurtling over the edge of the pool to cower behind her. They keened distressfully, and their spines jutted out at full extension. Some of them dropped whole fish on the wet stone to mouth their protests. Sofron reached to gather up the fish, and the water dogs lunged at her arms and legs to hold her back.

"Calm down," she said. "You brought my lunch, and now I'm going to eat it."

The fish were in various states—some whole and still flopping, some bitten nearly in half, others partly chewed. Sofron wondered if the water dogs had figured out from her hunger motes that they should give *her* fish, or if the motes had merely been contagious. As she wondered, she brushed off the least-chewed fish and gulped them down as fast as she could.

"This transformation has done nothing for my table manners," she said, through a mouthful of firm pink shillik fillet.

She paused without swallowing as another head broke the surface of the pool. The water dogs, who had begun to calm down, started screaming again. Sofron dropped her fish and grasped the knife.

The head was pale, and the powerful shoulders that followed gleamed like bone. The pale eyes reflected the greenish glow of the fronds in the pool.

They had been followed by one of the White Killers.

Sofron spread her arms protectively in front of the water dogs. She didn't think they would be a match for the White One, in spite of their numbers. They seemed too terrified to fight.

But the Killer did not attack. It sculled backward to the other side of the pool, never taking its eyes from Sofron. In one fluid motion it pulled itself from the pool, to stand on the ledge. Sofron raised her knife threateningly and showed her teeth, warning it to keep its distance.

The White One raised empty hands, not in a show of talons, but palm out. Sofron could not have distinguished its face from that of any other White Killer, but in that gesture, she recognized it.

"Wearra," she said.

"Wearra," the apparition confirmed.

But she was no longer sure that this sign of peace meant he had peaceful intentions. He had agreed to guide her; then he had deserted her. She wanted an explanation. But that wasn't the most important thing she needed to know.

She pointed to the children.

"Who brought them here? And why?" she signed.

Like me. He pointed to himself—his pale skin, his teeth, his eyes. "People like me took them. Your pool there, this pool, same-same. It's very old place—" The next word was hard for Sofron to pick up. A frightening place? A place of awe, maybe—or a holy place. "Holy place," Wearra repeated. "Old holy place for—" Again there was a hard word. Egg-with-legs? *Oh, of course, hatchling,* Sofron thought. So it's an old holy place for hatching.

She was pleased that she had grasped this idea; then she realized that she had been signing and understanding ideas that she could never have communicated before. Wearra's body language had been impenetrable to her before; now she was catching flickers of meaning from it. What had the leviathans said to her? *We gave you the dancing language . . . Maybe the Pale Ones will understand.* She hadn't known what they had meant, at the time. Yet somehow, while she had been unconscious, they'd communicated a language to her.

It had been a long time since Skandians had bothered to learn any new languages. They had only one of their own, after all. The multiple languages of their history were links to a past they wanted to forget. They had no contact with other worlds, and the few historians who *did* bother to study the ancient documents usually used some sort of learning technologies, like sleep-teaching.

Maybe the leviathans had an even better way of accessing the recesses of the mind.

Sofron shook off these thoughts; they were distracting her from the task at hand. However they had done it, the leviathans had given her tools she really needed. Wearra was still signing.

"The all-we lived in the Deep before. Hatchlings used to come to White Ones from out of the sea, after the big changing. Not very many. Few survive dangerous Deep. Life is so hard, they become white."

Sofron wasn't sure she had understood that correctly. It didn't seem to make much sense.

"We find this place of the big old people, start to live here. Many hatchlings come to the old place. First thing they see is us! And they become white! Now we make more and more White Killers. We can rule the Deep. We can go back on land and take back everything the old ones took away from us."

He lowered his head and looked furtively around him before finishing his statement. "Even, they say, we can kill the god."

"Why would you do that?" Sofron signed. She couldn't keep her colors from flaring with alarm at the thought of the White People doing something that might hurt Per. The new senses were useful, but they made it hard to conceal her feelings.

The White One regarded her with only a slight raising and lowering of his neck spines.

"They say the god made us white and drove us out. The god made us live in the dark and cold. The god took the light from us and gave it to the old people. The god gave the Dry to the old people. The god gave them everything and made us suffer. They say, if we kill god, we can take what the old people had."

"The old people? You mean the ones who made the walls with pictures? The ones who lived up there, on the island?"

"Yes. The big old people. They hated us and killed us. But the burning came, and the big old people went away. We don't know where. Now they say the old people have come back again and are walking in the Dry again and making the small burning again. We hate them. They say we can kill them now and kill their god, too. Because now we can be many. Now we can gather all the four-leggers and they can grow to be white if we don't eat them. Sometimes the hunger talks to us and we eat, even if the mind says not."

"Is that why you brought my hatchlings here? To make them white?"

But Wearra slashed his hand back and forth, vigorously denying.

"No. We brought them here, but we did not—" He uttered a hiss and stopped signing. Sofron thought he sounded frustrated.

"We did not—" Again he stopped. He struck his own chest, slapped his palms against his cheeks, and wrapped his arms tight around his long, skinny body. "We out there, we lots of White Ones, yes we bring them here. But this-we here, this one we, *not* bring them. This-we doesn't want hatchlings to turn white. This-we looked for you, to help your hatchlings.

"But you changed. It takes a long time for this-we to find your smell after you change."

"Why do you want to help me?" Sofron signed. She wondered why he had so much trouble identifying himself as a singular pronoun, but that wasn't immediately necessary to know. His intentions were.

Wearra watched her with that one-eye-at-a-time gaze she found so disconcerting. Planes of light, like layers of mica, shifted within his eyes as they moved.

"This-we looks for things from the old people," he signed. "This-we goes a long way looking. This-we gets lost. Alone. This-we alone so long, long . . . Thoughts alone is different from thoughts we have. Thoughts we have are thoughts of hunting and killing. What we see, we eat."

He gauged the distance between them and lifted his thin lip over long, needle-sharp teeth. An unvoiced "haaah" drifted from his open mouth. Sofron smelled the darkness on his breath. Her heart jumped with pure terror, remembering what it had been like to be hunted.

But the mouth shut again, and the teeth disappeared like a hidden trap. Wearra's lips twisted in a grimace, and his long hand waved those thoughts away. He no longer fixed his eyes on her, but on something far away, beyond the walls of the cave.

"They are good-tasting thoughts," he signed. "But when we is we, we tastes only those thoughts. We can't taste any more the writing walls of the old people. We can't taste the water where the big brightness shines, and makes the water burn with burning that hurts eye, not skin. This-we wants that taste. This-we can only taste that if this-we is always so long alone. This-we is always cold and hungry.

"This-we can never see the big we, all of we, and swim with all, because all this-we eats and swallows the mind alone. Someday this-we will be so long alone, this-we will taste so different that all-we will eat the different one. And this-we suffers. Suffers! In the mind is burning, not in the skin. In the mind is hunger, not in the mouth. In the mind is pain."

Sofron paused to absorb the White Thing's tale. She made the sign for respect, bowing to him, though she doubted he would understand. By his own account, the White One was a predatory member of a group mind, yet knowledge meant so much to him that he would leave Sofron and her juicy children uneaten.

"I think you have just outdone me in your devotion to science, Teacher Wearra," she murmured.

But that didn't make Wearra her friend. Knowledge was a sharp edge that could be turned in any direction.

"My question—" she reiterated. "Why do you help me? What do you want from me?"

"This-we does not want the hatchlings to be white," Wearra signed. "There are many white hatchlings." His hands dismissed them. "There is some we like us-we. Some few. Us-we can't be together much or we is losing minds just like others. We see each other and we talk like this, across water. We talk: want to see if your hatchlings grow like old people. Old people could see the god. Old people made god change them.

"The us-we bring your hatchlings up here to hide them from others. Us-we put your hatchlings with ours, put Big One egg with little eggs, try all ways to see if any can wake up like the old people.

"This-we wants you to take this-we to see god. This-we wants god to take away the pain in mind. Make this-we like old people—able to walk in the brightness and be one mind without pain. Wearra keeps hatchlings away from the we out there. You help Wearra."

Deal with the devil, Sofron thought. The Skandians had dumped this outmoded entity from their official belief system, though his image lurked at the edges of their histories. *If we live here, we may have to bring him back to life, as well.*

"You said before you would help me," she signed. "You said you would take me to the hatchlings. Then you ran away. Left me to die. Why did you do that? Why should I believe you now?"

"You believe me *now*," he signed slowly. He put great emphasis on the time frame. "Now Wearra is Wearra. Believe when Wearra tells you—when the all-we comes, Wearra becomes all-we, too. The mind is eaten. You understand? There is no Wearra. Wearra can't help you then. You can't help Wearra. You can only help you."

"You mean . . . you ran away to avoid becoming like the others?"

"Yes. If I stay, I might eat you."

Sofron took a minute to let this sink in. She had witnessed the kind of group rage that made the Skandians so unlike themselves. The White Ones apparently had an extreme form of that process at work in them. Some kind of chemicals produced in their bodies—akin to hormones?—made them insanely predatory, preventing any kind of intelligent action. They lived like sharks caught in a permanent feeding frenzy.

"I have to tell you something, too," she signed. "We—my kind of we—are not the old people. We came here from another place. Far away. We belonged to the Dry. We couldn't live in the Deep. We were dying till the god changed us. It made us *like* the old people, but I don't think we're exactly the same. Can this happen to us? This all-we thing? Can we turn white?"

Wearra waggled its hand back and forth to indicate uncertainty.

"The all-we of you is very afraid of whiteness. Whiteness is coming to some of them. Their mind is in pain from whiteness."

He crouched down at the edge of the pool.

"The hatchlings—maybe they have pain from whiteness."

Sofron climbed down into the pool again and took another good look at the bubbles. She was able to see some things she had not noticed before. The children weren't simply enclosed in the bubbles; they were actually incorporated into them. A delicate, nearly invisible webwork of transparent filaments actually joined their flesh to the bubbles. The filaments entered the skin everywhere, but were particularly numerous at the throat and the back of the neck, around the wrists and ankles, and in the abdomen and torso, where major organs were located.

"It's like an organic life-support system," Sofron said.

"Nutrients must be feeding in through the filaments. But where does the bubble get its life support?"

Many of the various jellies and siphonophores she was familiar with were filter feeders. They caught tiny fragments of food from the water as it flowed through them. Some preyed actively on still-smaller beings, catching them with envenomed cilia. Some of them absorbed chlorophyll-containing organisms into a symbiosis that let them use the energy produced from sunlight. Possibly the bubbles were filtering nutrients from the water, but Sofron couldn't see how they were getting enough to feed the children from the water in the pool. There was no sunlight, and she couldn't see any prey, however tiny.

"There's not enough food for them here," she signed. "We need to get them out of here. This place is no good for them. It is only good for whiteness. You help me take them back to the brightness, and we will go see the god together."

"I will help you," Wearra signed. "But have to wait until they hatch. You and I can't carry so many eggs alone."

"Well, how long is that going to be?" she demanded.

"See yourself," Wearra signed. "They are almost finished. When finished, they will hatch. Then we see if people-like-you hatchlings turn white."

Sofron felt her colors fading at the very thought.

"Is that possible?" she signed.

"This-we hatchlings always turn white," Wearra signed. "Sometimes come out of changing sleep with colors. But they are hungry and scared. They see us; they fight; they run away. They get eaten, or they turn white. Always."

As he signed "hungry," Sofron saw his eye light on the fish left over from her meal. It didn't seem to bother him that they had been dead for some time.

"Eat," he signed.

It wasn't exactly a request, but she signed, "Go ahead." He cleaned up the fish with startling rapidity. Bones didn't even slow him down.

"That other hatchling in there, the one that's almost finished but not mine," she signed. "Is that one like you mean? One of you?"

Wearra signed "yes" while still chewing. He stuffed the remaining half of his fish in his mouth and continued.

"Sometimes change in Deep, sometimes here, but always turn white. Always, always."

"The water dogs—" She remembered that was not his word, and started over. "The hatchlings, do they all change like that? The hatchlings become White Killers?"

For the first time, he stopped eating, as if startled by this question.

"Yes!" he signed, as if that should have been obvious. "Egg—hatchling—White One. Always."

The water dogs rubbed their neck frills against her arms and gossiped to each other. It didn't seem possible that they would shortly become implacable cannibal predators. She tried to think of other species that underwent so radical a transformation. Swine had been a favorite domestic animal of humans through many migrations. There were none on Skandia, but she had read of them. The immature swine could be pets. They lived with human young without posing any threat. But later they could turn into immense, smelly adults with sharp teeth, and there were well-attested accounts of swine eating their human masters.

Sofron had a gut-level feeling that this was different, that there was something wrong with the sequence Wearra described. She knew better than to put all her faith in a gut feeling, but such a feeling sometimes pointed her toward new data that she *would* be able to put faith in.

Wearra had finished eating and was staring at her. Finally he signed, "You touch me."

He crept around the ledge toward her. This made her nervous. But apparently he meant no more than the exact, literal meaning of the words. The water dogs fled, chittering, to shelter on Sofron's far side. Wearra pressed himself uncomfortably close to her and rubbed his wrist against hers. He uttered a soft hiss of satisfaction. He just sat there, his skin pressed to hers, his second eyelid sliding shut over his eyes.

Sofron got tired of sitting on the hard stone, but she didn't move. She was facing the tangleweed, with nothing to do but stare at it and think. Considered as a decorative pattern, it was complex and fascinating. But its constant squirming motion, testing for something to eat, made her flesh creep.

It had nearly covered one wall. But she knew that tangleweed couldn't live without light. It didn't grow any deeper than the top of the twilight layer, so she didn't think it could grow inside this dark tower. This must be a branch of some larger plant that grew outside. She looked carefully around its edges.

Indeed, there was a space between the smooth dark circle and the stone wall. The dark inset had either cracked or had been shaken loose from its setting. The tangleweed had pushed in through that gap. Strangely, this made her feel a little better. There was an opening to the outside world, however small. Perhaps it could be enlarged.

Around the base of the tangleweed there was the usual litter of indigestible leavings. Tangleweed consumed only the pulp, the soft innards of things. It left bones and spines and shells in a heap. Old tangle infestations could be spotted by these moraines, even when the tangle itself had withered away. Sofron wondered how there could be enough food here to keep the tangleweed growing so vigorously.

The moraine held quite a few large bones and spines of various kinds. Sofron eyed them covetously. If the children hatched—*when* the children hatched—they would need weapons. She couldn't hope to get them out of here without arming each of them against possible danger. She began scheming to seize a few of those useful bones without getting caught in the tangleweed. Surely there was some way . . .

In spite of the discomfort of her perch and the unrelenting stink of the White Killer next to her, she found herself dozing off. The light coming in from the top of the room had faded, and the room was lit only by the patchy glow of the fronds. Sofron did not know how long she had been clawing her way through the towers, but she knew she was tired. Both sets of eyelids closed.

A sudden injection of alarm motes from Wearra woke her even before he jumped up and away from her. He gave a series of stuttering whistles, then realized she could not understand his signals and switched to sign.

"Hatching! You look, you see!"

She could see, because the light was streaming in through the ceiling now at a much more direct angle. It had the unmistakable warmth of sunlight. *It must be day in the outside world.*

Before her eyes, the almost-finished Pale child was slowly stretching out its cramped arms and legs. They were perfectly formed now, with no trace of the quadruped limbs they had once been. The skin had firmed and lost its gelatinous quality. As the arms and legs unfolded, strips of skin that had become stuck together peeled away and floated off into the pool. The new creature raised its head from the water, wheezing as it forced the water from its lungs. The eyes were faintly marbled with lavender, the pupils like slits. The sharp teeth showed under drawn lips. But the cry that came from those lips was not ferocious, but plaintive and desperate. The water dogs, with one accord, plunged into the water and disappeared.

The hatchling staggered across the pool, still crying. Its head swung back and forth, seeking for something. It blundered into the floating children before Sofron thought about where it was going. It slashed at one envelope, but the bubble membrane didn't break. It hissed angrily and reached for the next sleeping body, to try again.

Sofron jumped up.

"Hey!" She tried to yell like a human, but her new vocal cords gave the yell a whistling overtone that rang out in the big room. The hatchling turned toward her. It stretched its hands out toward her and floundered in her direction.

"Wearra! What does it want?" she shouted. Then she remembered that he couldn't understand. She signed to him, while moving slowly backward along the ledge. She didn't want the hatchling to switch its attention back to the children. She dared a brief glance in the White Killer's direction to see if he was replying.

"Hungry," he signed laconically.

Sofron picked up the knife again. The hilt was beginning to feel comfortable in her hand. She didn't want to kill this thing. It would be like killing a child—or a confused newgen. She wished Wearra hadn't eaten all the fish. They would have had something to offer it.

It jumped up on the ledge, and she kept backing away, around the pool. It was crying, whistling—a sound of despair, ascending up the scale toward frenzy.

"Be calm. It's all right," she said. "We won't hurt you."

It cocked its head for a minute, but continued. The words meant nothing.

"I don't want to hurt it," she shouted to Wearra. But she couldn't put the knife down to sign. The White Killer didn't make any moves to help her. He simply watched.

The hatchling was getting frustrated. It crouched, and she was afraid that it would jump back into the pool. Then, so fast she had no time to prepare, it leapt on her. Its talons barely missed her throat. They fell together into the water, on the far side of the stone wall. She kicked out as they went down, in a desperate attempt to regain her balance, and knocked the hatchling far enough away that it fell beside her instead of on top of her. They thrashed wildly together in the water.

She saw the open mouth with its pointed fangs coming at her and jammed her arm against the teeth to keep them away from her face. At the taste of blood, the hatchling seemed to go crazy. She kicked it again and jolted it just enough that the scything talons missed on their first swing. The next time she would be dead. She had to use the knife.

She could taste her own blood. She wanted to use the knife. She wanted to tear the hatchling with her own teeth. She could feel rage choking her again, as it had when she'd encountered the Killers in the cavern. She knew it was stupid and wrong, but it didn't make a mote's worth of difference.

She had forgotten that her feet had talons, too. Her kick had sliced into the hatchling, and she could taste its blood twining with her own. It tried to back away from her, but now she would not let it. She sank and bumped the submerged floor, then used the leverage to push forward with another kick.

Suddenly the hatchling was no longer resisting her. It was receding from her rapidly. She was about to spring after it when perception penetrated into her inflamed mind, and she saw that the tangleweed had seized her opponent and was reeling it in to the center of the node. Already the hatchling had ceased to struggle.

Immediately she was backstroking as fast as she had come in. Her foot struck the pile of debris. There, inches away, was a whole ribbonfish spine, ribs and all, and the teeth lying together in another heap where the tangleweed had dropped the head when it was sucked dry. Still fearless from the chemicals coursing through her blood, Sofron let the knife dangle and swooped to pick up an armload of bones and teeth, all she could grasp before the tangleweed was ready to notice new prey.

She dragged herself back onto the ledge and sidled around the pool, keeping away from Wearra. Her rage was subsiding. She felt ashamed of herself and stupid, but she was back in control enough to remember that Wearra could be dangerous when exposed to blood smell.

He stayed away, but his spines rose and his teeth showed a little. With her increased sensitivity to his body language, she wondered for just a moment if he might be laughing at her. She didn't know if White Killers could laugh.

She felt exhausted and terribly sad. She couldn't look at the tangleweed wall, where the drained remains of the hatchling were displayed like a trophy. Her arm wasn't bleeding very much. The sticky skin secretion had already clotted and sealed the cuts. But she was very hungry again.

She put the bones down carefully. At least she had successfully performed that maneuver. Without the added stimulus of madness, she might not have been foolhardy enough to try it.

"What for?" Wearra signed. He didn't bother to inquire how she was, or to express any feelings about what he had just seen. She decided there was no point in commenting on this.

"Weapons," she signed. "But I need—" She couldn't come up with a word for "sticks," so she just mimed long thin pieces of something and then pretended to jab at an enemy. She didn't have much hope of finding any. There weren't any bones long enough to serve as spear shafts. The ribbonfish teeth had little knobs at the jaw end that might do for handles, but she shuddered at the thought of her kids trying to use them hand-to-hand against White Killers.

"Down there," he insisted. "Swim down."

He must mean the next level, she thought.

"You help me," she signed. "Show me where."

He didn't seem pleased, but he led her down the long shaft the water dogs had gone through. The room below was full of water from floor to ceiling, and completely dark. Even with her transformed eyes, she could barely concentrate enough light from the surroundings to make out the pale soles of Wearra's feet flapping in front of her as he swam. Nonetheless, he seemed to know where he was going.

When he stopped, they were next to a wall that had been shifted crookedly sideways. Wearra bent down, and Sofron heard a faint clanking. He turned to her with an armful of long, stavelike objects. She tucked as many as she could carry under her arm. He picked up a few more. They made their way back up the shaft.

In the light, Sofron examined the objects. They looked just like the staves held by the statues in the anteroom. They seemed to be made of metal and ceramic or some equally hard and smooth material. There were various studs and grooves; holding the staff carefully, so neither end pointed at anyone, Sofron tried pressing, twisting, and pushing. But nothing happened. She supposed that the power source or something must be missing after all these years. It was a disappointment.

"We sorry, too," Wearra signed. His eyes gleamed as he made the comment. Sofron thought that maybe she wasn't so sorry now.

The next problem was figuring out how to fasten teeth to the ends of the obsolete weapons. Even if she unraveled all of her belt cord, she wouldn't have enough material to make a secure binding. She tried to communicate what she needed to Wearra, but he wasn't in the mood to help anymore.

"We fish; eat," he signed, and vanished as abruptly as always.

Sofron did not like being left alone with the tangleweed and the corpse. It struck her as odd that she had come to consider a White Killer as a companion of sorts, but it was true.

"I've been underwater way too long," she muttered. "It's affecting my brain."

After he had gone, a few of the water dogs trailed back into the room. They were not communicative, but they were friendly, and their skin had a much better flavor than his. She let them serve as pillows while she thought about the weapons problem.

She woke up with a guilty start, as the water dogs scattered. Something in the room had changed while she slept, besides the light. It took a minute to figure it out. The water level had changed. Doubletide must have gone out. The pool where she floated was still full, but outside the encircling wall, the floor showed under a mere foot or so of water. The tangleweed had collapsed into its low-tide form and floated in a big circle that covered the remnants of its earlier meal.

Safely perched on top of the wall, Sofron poked the tangleweed with one of the long staves. She liked the heavy feel of the staff, even if it wasn't functional as a weapon. The tangleweed recoiled, then extended a tendril to probe the intruder. It coiled tightly around the end of the staff and tugged, exerting a surprising amount of force. The staff nearly slipped from Sofron's hand, but the tangleweed lost interest when no body fluids were forthcoming.

Sofron had an idea. She remembered the little spear she had made when they first went up the river, using a binding of tubemouth skin. She picked up her knife in one hand and a staff in the other, and waded cautiously toward the tangleweed. It was a little harder to approach it without the aid of the rage motes. But in the low water, its range was clearly apparent. She was able to approach its edge without too much danger.

She pounced, pinning the end of one tendril down with the end of the staff, then slicing off the tip with a slash of the knife. She jumped back quickly as the other tendrils thrashed about in reaction. Then she reached in with the staff, pulled the cut tendril out, and laid it safely on top of the stone ledge, in the Dry. She cut a dozen tendrils in this way.

Then she carried out the second part of the experiment. Within moments the cut ends had already dried out a little, though they were still twitching. She took the staff and beat them vigorously, doing her best to flatten them against the rock. Then she tested them by briefly touching a finger to them. They still moved a little, but they did not sting.

She used the knife to slice them into thin strips, then tied the first of the ribbonfish teeth to the end of a staff. By wrapping the lashing tightly and tucking the ends under, she was able to get a fairly secure binding. And, as she had hoped, the reflex action of the muscle fibers made the tendrils contract even more tightly around the shaft.

By the time she had finished several of them, her fingers were beginning to get numb from surface exposure to the tangleweed toxin. The toxin still numbed, even though the dead tendrils no longer possessed the power to extend their stingers and inject it.

During this time, Wearra returned, and he watched her without moving. He seemed interested, but not enough to help. The White Killers already had spears, she recalled; probably better ones than this. But it made her feel much better to know that she had something to place between the children and Wearra's kin.

The water slowly seeped back into the room while she worked, and it was growing lighter. Tiny shafts of light pierced the gloom. They seemed to be shining through chinks in the flat insets, as well as through the ceiling. This place seemed riddled with small cracks and holes, but she still couldn't see an opening big enough to let her escape. She longed to get out. She hadn't spent this much time inside a structure since she'd left Skandia.

She put down the spear she had been working on and flexed her tired fingers. She thought about taking a break, and turned to see what the water dogs were doing. There was a great chittering going on as they nudged each other back and forth at the end of the pool. Wearra was watching them alertly, from a distance.

The water dogs were climbing over the leviathan egg, taking turns bobbing around on it and sliding off into the water. The egg flexed and glowed. The water dogs took a final spill, and then backed off as the egg began to come apart in the middle. The covering thinned and tore, and a leviathan hatchling, like the one Sofron had seen in the Deep, uncurled and stretched itself. Without bothering to break the surface, it uttered a melodious chord, high-pitched but piercingly sweet. It paddled itself around the pool, seeming to grow stronger with every stroke, and made constant music.

Sofron was fascinated by the miniature leviathan. The music was a far-off echo of the great music she had heard before, and there was a sadness in the knowledge that she had once been part of it and understood it, but now could only remember it like something in a dream. Remnants of the golden egg casing were dissolving in the water, flavoring it with an elusive scent that reminded her of the feeling she had had when the leviathan was carrying her.

She was so absorbed in memory that it was only by accident that she turned to see what was happening at the other end of the pool.

The membranes that encased her children, moonlight-silver by comparison, were also thinning and parting. She had enough presence of mind to wonder if the leviathan egg, in hatching, had released some substance that speeded the release of the children. But before she had time to complete that thought, Ling had opened her eyes and was sitting up, staring around her like a child sitting up in bed after a bad dream.

The others stirred and thrashed in the water, opening their eyes, choking and spluttering as they tried to distinguish between water and air. With a glad cry, Sofron swooped down to embrace them. A thin, piercing shriek of utter horror burst from Ling's lips.

"Sofi! Sofi!" she wailed. She shrieked again and tried to scramble out of the pool, but her legs wouldn't obey her. Jaya was fully awake and had his limbs under control, but when he tried to claw his way over the wall, he came face-to-face with Wearra, and he, too, yelled in terror.

Sofron had a quick flash of the peaceful blue of Subtle's face as he repeated patiently, *Calming motes—make smooth.*

"Peaceful, peaceful," Sofron muttered to herself, trying to think only calm, encouraging thoughts and to push peaceful motes from every pore.

It seemed to be helping. At least, after the first shock, the children seemed to recognize each other—perhaps by scent, since they had been floating so close together. They gathered themselves into a tight knot, clinging to each other and hyperventilating, but at least they stopped shrieking.

"I am Sofron," she said very quietly. She held up a hand to still the protests that burst forth. "Ask me anything you like. I know all of you. Ling, you used to have short legs. Now you're going to run like everyone else. Jaya, remember how you caught a shilluk the day before the White One came? I remember everything. Only my shape has changed. Your shapes have changed, too, but that's not important right now.

"What's important is that we're all together again, and we're going to get out of here and find our way back to shore. All right? As soon as you calm down enough to listen, I'll tell you the whole story of what happened."

Jaya was the first to find comprehensible words.

"But the Bone Thing!" he said.

"He's friendly," Sofron said. "At least for right now, he is. He promised to help us get out of here. It's Wearra, the one we know."

"Are we dead?" Ling said.

"No, we're not dead! Remember the keto who was in the pool? When Ling fell in, and then we all jumped in? The keto was carrying bubbles that changed us."

Ling frowned. "I remember that," she said slowly.

"I remember, too," Ven said, and then he put his hand to his face with a look of complete surprise. "My face," he said. "I can talk!"

Sofron moved toward them, and this time they threw themselves into her arms. There were enough joyful motes in the water for all.

Wearra watched inscrutably. He had been signing for some time before Sofron detached herself enough to notice.

"Someone comes," he signed, and pointed to the dark passage that led to the tower below.

23

Whitman was in a cold fury when he woke up on board the raft.

"Whoever did this is going to be expelled from the commonality," he said tensely. "Who was it?"

"I wouldn't like to guess," Torker responded.

"And untie me!"

"It wasn't me," Torker said, bending down to undo the ropes. "Calm down and tell us if we're heading in the right direction."

They had already passed beyond the reef and were heading north along the coast, toward the narrow headland at the tip of the island. Their keto escort showed itself occasionally, leaping in and out of the waves. Many of the newgens were still swimming with the ketos, avoiding Whitman. The sun shone brightly, and there was no sign of the White Ones yet.

Whitman squinted at the sun, and then shaded his eyes to look ahead.

"This is right," he said. "We're headed for those dark rocks at the end of the island. That's where the old city was. Can't you go any faster? Based on the maps I have, we won't get there until midafternoon. I don't want to search the towers in the dark."

"Maps? What maps?" Torker said. "If you have more information, I want to see it."

"It's not that kind of a map," Whitman said irritably. "I made contact with that organism. I saw the plan of those structures. It's in my mind."

"Oh, really? And what else does it show you?"

Whitman ignored the sarcasm in Torker's voice.

"The former inhabitants—those who left their records behind in that organism—they built a cluster of towers. They were interconnected at several levels. Somewhere near the top, there were storage areas that may still contain things we could use. That's all we need to know."

"What kind of things?" Torker asked.

"Weapons. Things." Whitman rubbed at the excrescence still clinging to his neck. "I don't know exactly! This wasn't like downloading an inventory, you know. It's a lot more complex than that."

Dilani had returned to the raft to rest, with her elbows propped on its edge.

"The god told him," she said. "Careful. Per says god can lie."

Whitman turned on Dilani. "How many times do I have to tell you—that thing is not a god! And Per does not exist. I saw no sign of him."

"I saw him sign," Dilani said. "God talks you. Per talks me! Find Sofron, he says!"

She did a backward somersault and disappeared.

"In my opinion, you're both crazy," Torker growled.

"Dilani has a point." Uli Haddad spoke up quietly. His ribs were still sore, but he had insisted on coming with them.

"Whitman, has it occurred to you that this god might be lying to you? What if the information he gave you is false? Or what if it's true, but his purpose isn't to help us? Maybe he just wants us to fight the White Killers, for reasons of his own. Dilani said the ketos talked of how the White Ones wanted to 'kill god.' Maybe we are being used as defensive counters in someone else's game."

"Of course that's occurred to me," Whitman responded scornfully. "Do you think I'm stupid? But what does it matter? It's *us* they're trying to kill. We won't survive here without weapons. And the weapons are there. Now I know how to find them.

"But that's not all. Somewhere, in whatever technology is left in the ruins, we may find materials that we need to reestablish communications with Skandia. Don't you see? That's the real key to survival. We cannot live here without human culture, human technology. We have to summon help from home."

"I think you're wrong, Whitman," Uli said. "That's not home anymore. 'Human' is going to be what we make of it, here."

"Wrong!" Whitman said, slamming his hand down on the deck. "And that's the other reason we need this 'god.' When we've established a safety zone here, we will begin putting pressure on him to reverse this metamorphosis. Once we are recognizably human again, we can prevail on the Skandian authorities to reinstate us."

A glance passed between Uli and Torker that clearly said "He's gone round the bend this time."

"We were dumped here because we violated Skandian law and custom," Torker reminded them. "How many hundred laws do you think we've broken now? I don't think they're going to want us back."

"If we master Typhon, they will want us back," Whitman said. "Now let's concentrate on getting into this structure."

They threaded their way among rocks and reefs that told of sunken land nearby, resting under shallow water. Subtle watched as Torker, at the helm, let the raft come up into the wind and then lowered the sail. Henner Vik, in the other raft, followed suit. The rafts drifted gently. Subtle and the new-gens tumbled overboard to find the bottom. It was only ten meters down, and the calm water was clear. They could see in all directions.

The group divided itself up. Whitman tried to get someone to stay with the rafts, but no one wanted to be left. Subtle descended with the team formed by Bey, Dilani, Bader Puntherong, and Torker. Whitman organized the others.

They started off in wide sweeps back and forth, checking the depth. On their left, the bottom dropped off steeply into deep water. On the right side, it was shallow enough for the raft to anchor in.

The peaks that had once been the tops of ridges on land now served as platforms for corals that had built sunward until they came within a few meters of the surface. Tortured ridges of the same dark lava they had seen on land extended above the sediment, frozen in the writhing coils that had formed when the molten rock first struck the water.

"You are seeing a ghost," Subtle signed. "The ghost of an island, hiding here under a little shadow of water. We follow ghosts of the Great People. The fire river took their cities, and then the Deep swallowed fire and stone together. Now all sleeps here. We come to disturb their dreams."

Subtle felt a sense of emptiness as he swam above the pitted and ooze-coated rocks. Where were the great towers, the wonder he had seen in the old dances? Suddenly he comprehended: the towers were below him. He felt again the vertigo of his changed form. He was scratching on the rooftops of the ancient world.

On edge, Subtle was alive to every hint of danger. He expected the White Ones to find them sooner or later. Yet in spite of the fear, he felt the thrill of the quest, as he had felt it when he had first aspired to be a scholar and had gone in search of the lost metal of the Great People.

They dove, following the steepening slope of the underwater mountain, through sunlit waters where the colors were still clear and bright, into the deep zone where everything was saturated with dim blue light.

They sent out sound pulses ahead, but the echoes showed only irregular rock. Subtle turned westward, moving around the mountain. Dilani thrust her hands into the sound box around her neck and sent piercing sounds into the dusky waters ahead. She bent her head from side to side to catch the direction of the sounds as their fainter echoes returned. Subtle listened, too, and paid heed to the sensitive receptors beneath his skin. But Dilani's soundsense was the most acute. She picked up the echoes first. Something tall, smooth, and straight loomed in the shadows.

Subtle had underestimated the size of the towers. *How could I possibly have imagined this?* he thought. The humans hung like tiny hatchlings against a sheer black wall that receded beneath them into darkness. Subtle ran his fingers over the wall, and his limb-tips as well. The structure was still smooth; here and there a speckle of shell marked a spot where some creature had clung doggedly. But for the most part, the towers had repelled all invasion, just like the other works of the Great People. At last Subtle was able to distinguish hairline cracks in the wall, perhaps lines where smoothed blocks were pressed together. But though he could feel them, he still could not see them.

Down, he signaled. Somewhere far, far below must lie the original doors, which once had stood open in the air, in the sun. But the leader, Whitman, stopped him. Whitman seemed suddenly to have become disoriented. He thrashed about in the water, turning his head back and forth as if searching for something lost. His motes expressed anxiety, almost panic.

"Where? Where?" he signed.

"Down below," Subtle signed again. He wondered why Whitman was so confused. Then he realized that if the human followed memories from the Great People, he would expect to see the towers as they had been long ago. Since then, the Deep had risen. Stone and water had changed places. The gate now lay far down in the shadows, where the White Killers lived.

Whitman's thrashing slowed. He floated, with his gill slits flaring as he sucked water for the extra oxygen he needed after his panic. He rubbed at his neck and stared off into the twilight of the Deep. Subtle thought he looked as if he were listening to a distant summons. Subtle listened, too, but heard nothing.

Finally Whitman moved his head in the human gesture of negation.

"Not down," he signed. "Too dangerous. Now I see it. I know. There is another way."

He swam quickly around the curve of the tower, as certain now as he had been confused before. Subtle saw the other humans look at Whitman as if what he had done was not normal for humans. But they followed him.

Whitman led them in a search pattern, back and forth across the smooth curve of the tower. He played the narrow beam of his tubelight across the surface of the rock, but the light revealed nothing. Dilani followed, chirping and listening.

The ketos had long since retired to the surface. They had no wish to swim into a trap.

Then Dilani and Whitman pointed simultaneously. The others approached, echo-sounding the space. Irregular remnants of some exterior structure stuck out from the wall at regular intervals, spiraling along the curve. It had been some kind of ramp, Subtle thought. Parts of it were missing now, but it might still point the way to the opening they sought. They ascended again, slowly, following this crumbling path.

Dilani pointed again. Although the velvet black of the break in the wall could not be visually distinguished from the matte black of the wall itself, the soundsense said there was an opening. Perhaps it had once been a doorway. Now it was only a jagged crack where two blocks had slipped past each other, smashed to fragments by the force of their collision.

Whitman, normally so cautious, shot through first, as if the narrow opening were a clear path. The others followed him. The blue twilight turned to absolute darkness. They were cut off from the surface with its light.

Subtle reached for Dilani so she would not get lost, but he had forgotten that they carried lights. A greenish beam lanced out from Whitman's tubelight, revealing that they were inside a box of stone, enclosed on all sides.

They formed a ring and explored its edges. The inner wall held another opening, larger than the one they had come through. But it led only to a shaft that seemed to extend vertically in both directions. Near the entrance to the shaft there was a series of niches that could have been a stairway; they floated upward in that direction and found themselves in another stone box, full of water but barren of artifacts.

They struggled through box after box, passage after passage. Each new niche was barren, though Whitman slowed their progress by insisting that they run their hands over every new wall, searching for hidden storage areas.

They paused to catch their breath. There was no reason to think the water here was less oxygen rich than anywhere else, but the darkness and the closed spaces were inescapably oppressive. Subtle could hear his own heart beating.

Then Dilani raised her hand into the beam of Whitman's light.

"Hear something," she signed.

It was a high-pitched, repetitive noise, not like the whistling of the White Killers. Before any of them could figure out what the sound was, they found themselves enmeshed in thrashing limbs and tails. Whitman stabbed all around him with his spear. But Subtle recognized the scent.

"Stop, stop," he signed, but Whitman was not watching. Subtle immobilized the human with his tentacles. When it became apparent that the water dogs were not hurting anyone, the humans stopped struggling against them. The water dogs flashed past, apparently in a hurry to go somewhere.

Subtle plunged after them, beckoning Dilani to follow. All the humans caught at the same idea—to follow the water dogs, hoping they knew the way out. The water dogs corkscrewed through a crooked passage partially blocked by fallen slabs of stone.

At last they emerged into a chamber so wide they could sound the opposite wall but not see it. And the light, beaming upward, showed a dappled, unsteady screen rather than a sheet of rock—there was an interface between water and air. They surfaced; above the surface it was still dark.

Coughing the water from their throats, they all spoke at once.

"We're back at water level," Whitman said.

"This must have been high up in the air once," Adil said.

Subtle trained a light on their companions, confirming that they were, indeed, water dogs. They flinched from the light at first, but then came fawning back, frisking around the newgens, keening happily.

Whitman slapped his spear against the water.

"Go away!" he shouted. *"Yi yi yahhhh!"*

The water dogs ignored him.

"Vermin!" he said. He seemed to have forgotten that noise might attract attention.

The water dogs swam ahead with deceptive ease, to a point where the floor rose up to meet them. The humans found themselves up to their necks, an uncomfortable depth because it was hard to decide if they should wade or swim. The floor seemed to be multileveled, and they were constantly stubbing toes against a step up, or tripping over a sudden step down. Subtle submerged himself and pinged the area with his soundsense. The whole floor was patterned with circular basins arranged in spiraling patterns—comfortable resting places, perhaps, for creatures who preferred damp skins.

Dilani, wasting no time on speech, splashed ahead. They heard a thump, and an angry exclamation. They pushed forward in alarm. Subtle saw tiny sparks of light, apparently dancing in the air. The next instant, he struck his head against something. For a moment he thought someone had hit him. He flung his limb out protectively, and hit the same surface.

He had walked into a wall. But a wall like no other; it was completely smooth and slick, and invisible to the eye. Examining it carefully, he realized that the sparks of light were coming *through* the wall. It was daylight, penetrating through tiny gaps in some kind of coating that apparently covered the other side of the barrier. He was just beginning to revolve in his thoughts the strange notion that the wall might be transparent, when there was a chorus of exclamations from the older humans.

"It's transplex," Adil said. "Or as near as makes no difference."

Torker rapped on it with his knuckles, then with the butt of the harpoon gun, and listened again.

"I don't think so," he said. "It's glass."

"But why would anyone go to the trouble of casting a sheet of glass this big, when transplex is so much easier . . ." Adil's voice trailed off. "Oh . . . this is Pre-Flight technology," he finished.

"Well, we don't know that these people were Pre-Flight," Torker said. "But they were different."

"So we're at sea level again," Bey said. "But if it's transparent, why can't we see out?"

"My guess is that those are stickies, reefbuilders, and so forth on the outside of the glass," Adil said. He turned the tubelight back on and held it close to the wall. An undulation passed through the mottled surface beyond the glass. Close up, they could see that the mottled area was a mosaic of muscular suckers, tube feet, and bits of shell cemented to the glass. Countless organisms had attached themselves here, blocking out the light beyond.

"It's midtide," Adil said. "Probably at doubletide, the glass is completely underwater. Tidal organisms that like sunlight and warmth have found a perfect home. It's like government housing for them, with free solar and a food delivery every doubletide."

"So why couldn't we see this structure above water, from the outside?" Bey said.

"Well, the tide may rise high enough to cover it entirely, at some times of the day," Adil said. "If we had more light in here, we could see if there's a high-tide mark on the wall. The tip of the tower, the part we're in, probably does stand above the tide at least part of the time. I think we did see it, as we sailed in. But we didn't recognize it as an artificial structure because it's partially encrusted with lava and coral, and the glass has been colonized, too."

"You mean, we're inside those rocky humps we saw offshore?" Bey said.

"We dove down, then swam up, and we corkscrewed around so much that my sense of direction is off," Adil said. "But that's the only thing that makes sense to me."

Bey felt claustrophobic. He wanted a way out, now. He did not want to have to reenter the labyrinth of twisting passages to find the door where they had come in.

Once Dilani had discovered the glass wall, she had lost interest. She waded along the barrier, trailing one hand against its smooth surface, until she came to a corner of stone. Beyond the corner there was another big plate of glass—it must have been a glass room. She stumbled into deeper water again, and her feet kicked against something heavy and sharp. She rubbed her painful toes, then dove to locate the offending object.

The shape was like a shell of unusual weight and symmetry, but the feel was the same as the slick wall. She pulled a sample free, and heard a clattering; a pile of objects shifted under her touch.

"What have you got there, Dilani?" Bey asked.

She held it out to the light, and was surprised by the dazzle of refractions. It was a flattened hexagonal prism, hard and transparent, that caught the light.

"A jewel!" she said—then felt embarrassed. There had been stories when the newgens were little, stories from the old cold world, where there were things like solid water that possessed rainbow colors. All the newgens had played at having jewels and gold money, but they had never found anything better than smooth stones to pretend with.

But to her surprise, no one was laughing at her. They seemed to think that the object might really be a jewel, that it wasn't stupid to think so. Dilani was even more impressed with her find.

"No, I think this is glass, too." Torker turned it over in his big hand. There was a bubble in the center, and within the bubble, a smudge of grayish corroded material that might have been metal once. A tiny cylindrical hole went from the bubble to one facet. Torker turned it and shook it, but the hole was too narrow for any of the corroded material to shake out.

"More under," Dilani said. She ducked into the water and came up with jewels in both hands.

They all went down with the light and looked. A line of the glass prisms lay haphazardly along the bottom of the wall. When the humans touched them, a powdery sediment puffed up. Here and there were cylindrical fragments that might have been made by hands, but when they were touched, they crumbled. The wall itself was inlaid with a linear decoration that looked like glass and metal. At intervals, some of the prisms were still attached to it.

"It looks like a lighting system," Torker said, shaking himself as he emerged above the surface again. "Don't ask me how it worked. Salt water's ruined it now."

"Still no weapons, nothing we can use," Whitman said.

"You could use these for sling stones," Torker said. "They'd be deadly."

Whitman was not amused. Disgusted, he hurled the prism he held into a far corner. It splash-landed among the water dogs. They broke from their cluster in a burst of chitterings; then came a simultaneous smooth splash, and silence.

"Hey! You scared them," Bader said.

"Where have they gone?" Whitman said. He shone his own light around the echoing chamber. The narrow beam revealed nothing. Dilani dove and found a rectangular opening where the water dogs had fled.

When she surfaced, Whitman was turning around in place, frowning at his metal detector.

"I don't understand it," he said. "I know there should be something here. The detector registers. But I can't see it."

He squinted at the glass wall.

"There should be lights," he said vaguely. "There were lights everywhere. You could see across the water. Why is it so dark?"

He put his hand to his neck again, wearily.

"This is the place," he said, more briskly. "It has to be. We must search."

The metal detector gave encouraging readings, but when they tried to follow in the directions indicated, they found their way blocked by heaps of stone, as if a wall had crumbled and spilled out over the floor. They half crawled and half swam over the rubble. Eventually, they abandoned this unsuccessful search. They organized a line and began moving rocks. They had to work cautiously to avoid destabilizing the rubble. The new hands were a disadvantage. The soft, damp skin wouldn't callus, and was soon torn and abraded.

When one section of the wall finally was cleared down to

about waist level, Subtle explored the wall with the delicate tips of his tentacles. The rock was smooth, with small, regularly spaced raised areas that were probably the usual glyphs.

"Stand back," Torker signed. "I'll bash it with a rock and see if anything crumbles."

"Be having calm one more short segment," Subtle signed. He moved his tentacles back and forth over the cleared area, searching every inch for some hint of an opening. Perhaps the opening lay in the section not yet cleared. If so, they would have to return the next day, or go home in the dark. Perhaps there was no opening. The metals might be a fiction of the human machine, or they might be nonmade nodules inside the rock.

Then his searching encountered a vertical line too straight to be nonmade. It was far too thin to insert even a talon's width. It might not even be a crack, but just an incised line on the rock's surface. He felt on both sides of it. Above his head, nearly out of reach, he found small round holes with smooth sides. He tried to insert two fingers, but could not penetrate to the bottom of the holes because the webs between his fingers got in the way. He tried inserting tentacle tips. He felt a surface at the back of the hole. But if this was some kind of opening device, it would not yield to his pressure.

The humans crowded around him, signing "Let me try!" but he stuck to his place. He thought about it. What appendages had he not yet tried? What would a two-arms think was important?

His two thumbs, long and narrow like those of the Great People, placed back to back, slid neatly into the holes. When their strong talons hit the back of the hole, he pressed, and felt the talons' width slide into a notch there. It gave under the pressure. But nothing else moved. Nothing slid aside or opened, as the cache had opened at Sofron's pool. Subtle stood back, disappointed. Perhaps the mechanism had jammed under the forces that had crumbled the stones.

He ran his hands down the wall, following the hairline crack that marked where doors might be. Nothing seemed to be blocking it, now that the stones had been moved aside. As he reached the lower end of the line, he realized that the water had been sinking away. It was now only chest-deep. If the rectangle marked on the wall was a door, it ended at about waist level. There was still nearly a foot of water in front of the door.

"Why can't you get it open?" Whitman said. He tried to poke the point of his spear into the crack, to pry at the door, but could only scratch at the hard, smooth surface. The spear was too crude and blunt to slip into so fine a line.

Subtle pondered. He was sure he had touched the unlocking mechanism, but for some reason, it had not yielded. The Great People seemed always greatly aware of the Deep and its effects. Perhaps they had designed their storage areas just so, to refuse to open if water was too near.

"The tide is going out," he said. "Maybe if you-I is waiting till water is far down, the door is opening."

Whitman was impatient with this idea. He drove them on to clear more rubble away while they were waiting, hoping to find another storage area that would be accessible without delay.

They found another set of doors, but it was as stubborn as the first. After that, they all sat down with one accord to bathe their abraded hands and wait for the tide to sink below the edge of the hypothetical door.

When the line was clearly above water, Subtle stood and tried again. This time there was an audible click, then a hesitation, and a grating sound as a slab of rock tilted on some hidden pivot. Subtle pushed gingerly on the edge of the slab. It swung wider, moving more freely now. Whitman had his tubelight trained on the wall. Suddenly there was a bright gleam of reflected light.

A slab had been carefully cut from the wall, the rock behind it carved out to form a cabinet, and the original slab rehung on pivots so exactly that it fit almost as closely as if it had never been removed. Within it, rock niches had been carved and lined with a substance that gleamed like sunlight.

Subtle was awed. He had heard of a shining metal that did

not change in the Deep. He bent and licked it to glean motes. The flavor was familiar. It tasted of the nodules that scattered some areas of the Deep Plain, where some of the oldest hermits of the Round Folk lived. It was known to the Round Folk that these nodules contained nonmade metal, but without fire, the metal could not be taken. It was said that the Great People had made use of such nodules by taking them to the surface and hatching them out within the stinging brightness.

Subtle was filled with awe that with his own skin he tasted the metal of the Great People. In his own form, he would have floated slowly deeper in contemplation. As it was, his limbs felt weak, and he sank to his knees.

If the humans felt awe, they were keeping it to themselves as they rifled through the objects that lined the shelves. The most numerous were globes like eggs or fruit, a little bigger than two fists together. Unlike eggs or fruit, their surfaces were not smooth or simple, but seemed to be put together in several sections fitting tightly together. A heavy triangular ridge surrounded three recessed circles, as if to prevent them from being touched by accident. A deep niche held dozens of the spheres.

Racks held long shafts that looked like spears, but on examination, were studded with beads. Pressing on the beads produced no result, but Whitman made them gather up a load of the long staves anyway. He said they were "airguns," and could be made to work.

Bader Puntherong picked up one of the small globes and began tossing it idly. It didn't make a good ball; the irregular metal surface hurt the catcher's hand if it were thrown with any force. That same surface held three buttons, not unlike those on the sound boxes. Bader tapped them idly. No sounds issued. He pushed all three at once and held them down. The ball began to emit a high-pitched squeal that pierced the ear painfully.

Bader shook the ball, hit the buttons again, and smacked it with his other hand, but nothing stopped the sound. There were angry grimaces, and shouts of "Turn it off!" from the other humans.

Bader shrugged helplessly. "I can't," he said.

The sound changed from a steady tone to a warble, then to a stuttering beep. Subtle was still wondering why the sound was so disturbing when Torker rose up, snatched the ball out of Bader's hand, and threw it across the room, where it fell behind one of the piles of rubble.

Bader's protest was obliterated by a noise so all-shattering that Subtle didn't experience it as a noise; it was an assault, a blow, as if the walls had fallen on him. All of them hurled themselves flat on their bellies without conscious thought. They could feel the water surging from side to side, from one wall to the other. There was a minor, grinding rumble, and more chunks of the ceiling crumbled into the water on the other side of the room, where the sphere had landed.

"H-how did you know?" Bey said. He could hardly hear himself. His ears were ringing.

"I didn't know," Torker said. "I guessed. I watched construction teams using explosives, on Skandia. Those charges beeped before they blew up, too."

"We could have all been killed," Henner Vik said shakily.

But Whitman did not seem upset. In fact, he rolled another of the spheres between his palms, smiling.

"Finally," he said. "Something we can use. Pack up as many as you can carry. Hurry—the tide's rising. We'll pack the first load back to the rafts and come back for more."

Dilani rose up and stood in his way.

"Forgetting something?" she signed.

"Sofron," Bader explained.

"She's not here," Whitman said. He went back to gathering up more spheres.

Dilani signed rapidly. Bey watched and interpreted.

"She says you told Torker the towers were interconnected. We can go to the other towers and look for Sofron."

"No, we can't split up," Whitman said. "If you begin wandering around, you could alert the White Killers and put us all in danger."

"We could at least check out the passage where the water

dogs went," Bey said. "Water dogs wouldn't go where there were White Killers—I don't think."

"Don't stop to argue," Dilani signed. "We're going."

"We have to look for her," Bey agreed. "That was the deal."

Bey, Dilani, Subtle, and Bader swam together, as usual. Torker hesitated and then called to them to wait.

"Let me go first," he said. "I've got the harpoon."

As they left, they could hear the rest of the group still in confused discussion—Whitman demanding that they carry their loot to the rafts, Henner and Adil urging that the group stay together, Wayan and the other newgens trying to get away without enraging their elders.

Dilani was right, Subtle thought. If you stopped to let Whitman phrase his arguments, he was already winning.

The water was rising rapidly. They submerged to swim through the opening the water dogs had shown them. They could feel a strong current. Water seemed to be flowing in from above them. Again they were in a narrow, dark passage full of water, and they were going down. Subtle felt a little anxious; even Whitman's invisible guidance was better than nothing. They were on their own now.

To Subtle's relief, the passage soon leveled out. He swam faster. Then he tasted a confusion of scents, as if water from different currents swirled together. His soundsense told him there were other openings nearby—but most important, it showed the shaft they swam in turning upward again.

But as they strove upward, searching for light, he began to taste familiar motes in the water. He almost dared to hope that Sofron had passed this way. Certainly, he tasted water dogs. But then the faint hints of Sofron's trail were overlaid by the scent of the enemy. White Killers had been here, too.

Then he heard shrill whistles of alarm from behind them, where Whitman and the others still lingered with their artifacts. He hesitated, and Bey bumped into him from behind. Should they go back? There was little room for consultation. Subtle twined one tentacle around Dilani's ankle. From her motes, and the way she kicked, he guessed her opinion. With one accord, they began climbing faster. Whatever happened, they wanted to reach Sofron first.

Faced with the possibility of a new threat, Sofron began pushing the children back behind her. Carefully controlling her motes to keep them all calm, she passed out spears.

Once over the first shock, they accepted their strange situation matter-of-factly. The most important thing was that Sofron was there to organize them. Everything was going to be all right.

"Keep the spear between you and any danger," she said. "Poke them with it, but don't let them grab it. And whatever you do, don't get into the tangleweed."

Now she could hear the noises from the lower level, the sounds that had alerted Wearra. More than one something was crashing about down there, uttering cries of alarm; and then came the ominous trilling whistle that always made her crest stand on end.

Water roiled above the shaft that led to the lower level, and the first intruders came swarming out.

They were humans. She recognized Bey and Dilani immediately, then Bader and Torker Fensila. Subtle's face and form were unmistakable. She couldn't identify the others right away, but they looked familiar. Then they saw her and the children, and the walls with no opening to the outside world.

Torker took in the situation right away.

"Uh-oh," he said.

"It's me, Sofron," she shouted. "I found my kids. Grab a spear if you need one. And watch out for the tangleweed!"

❧24❧❧❧❧❧

Then the White Killers came up the shaft.

At first there were no more than a dozen. Their aim had not improved much since the last attack, but in these close quarters, their darts found some targets no matter how poor the aim. Sofron saw blood leap from friends' limbs, and heard their cries of pain, and felt her heart pound with sickening speed.

She clung to the need to guard the children, but what she truly wanted was to charge the Killers in blind fury. One of the White Ones rushed in too close, and she stabbed him in the belly. Her reason reeled under the onslaught of motes. She stepped forward, stabbing again and again.

Only the repeated high-pitched cries of the children brought her back to self-awareness, just in time to slash the neck of another White One who was stalking them. She pitched his body into the tangleweed and jumped up on the wall next to the children.

Once she was no longer in the bloody soup where the pool had been, the rage receded enough for her to take a quick check around. The other humans, with crossbow and harpoon gun, had taken down several more of the Killers. She recognized Adil, locked in hand-to-hand combat. His arms were slashed, and he was snarling horribly. His face was shockingly pale, even his gills bleached by fury. They thrashed through the pool together; when the White One came uppermost, someone clubbed the Killer on the back of the head and then stabbed him as he reared from the water in pain. Adil got up, but he was reeling.

The leviathan hatchling was shrieking in aleatory arpeggios of distress. Somehow, with its stubby limbs, it floundered out of the pool and across the stone wall. Sofron thrust with her staff to turn it away from the tangleweed, where it was headed in blind panic. It bumped against the other smooth inset, the uninfested one, still crying.

There were only two White Killers left—with the exception of Wearra, who crouched in a far corner with his hands over his head—and one of them was dragging a useless arm. It was almost over, Sofron thought. They had won, and they were still sane.

Then there were three Killers, then four, then five. More were still swarming up from below. Floating on the water's surface, the human defenders were backing away, toward the inevitable wall, toward the tangleweed, toward a hopeless corner. They were chest-deep in water now, only a couple of feet from the questing tangleweed on their right, trapped by a wall on their left, and facing an ever-growing ring of White Killers. For the moment, their spears formed a spiny defense, but it wouldn't last. As the smell of blood circulated through the tower, they might eventually attract every Killer in the ruins.

Torker turned from his guarding position for a moment to hammer on the smooth surface behind them with the butt of the harpoon gun. The wall boomed beneath the impact, but did not give.

"It's *glass*," Torker shouted to Sofron.

The White Killers had tried to edge in as soon as his turned head gave them a brief opening. He whipped around and fired at them, but there were so many that injuring one of them had no effect except to thicken the maddening stew of motes.

The Killers took up their eerie whistling, but this time it didn't work for them as it had in the past. Angry and scared, Ling gave a piercing shriek of rage, and the other children took up the cry in a shrill chorus, pitting their defiance against the White Killers.

Still gripping her spear with one hand, Dilani stuck the fingers of her other hand into the sound box on her chest and blasted the enemy with rude pidgin squawks of Bright Teeth language. The leviathan's own song ascended to the edge of human hearing and drilled painfully into the more acute ears of the White Killers. Their group war cry couldn't drive the White Killers away, but it briefly strengthened their own spirits.

The leviathans had promised to be waiting—but Sofron suspected the glass must be blocking their hearing. She tried to remember what she had read about *glass*, that Pre-Flight material that Skandians used mostly for decorative purposes.

"Dilani!" she shouted. "Get to the wall!"

It was good that Dilani could hear, even through this bedlam. Dilani shot her one doubting glance, but moved to obey, squirming backward as the front rank closed up behind her. She dove and surfaced among the children, next to Sofron.

"Push your noisemaker up against the flat wall, here, and blast it as loud as you can," Sofron said. "Use Teeth language—call for help. Loud as you can! Keep doing it—don't think of anything else. We have other spears. Need you for this."

Help me, the box cried, in keto speech, at top volume. *Come help me.*

Sofron touched the glass and felt it hum and rattle. The small leviathan crowded eagerly to Dilani's side and added its notes to her plea. But the glass stayed dark and smooth and solid.

The humans pressed tighter and tighter together as even more Killers swarmed into the room. The water dogs keened and squirmed underfoot. Sofron gripped her spear and knife, awaiting the last onslaught.

Then she began to hear something, above the whistling and screaming. It felt less like a sound than like an assault, some kind of beating that grew until it attacked from inside. The intensity rose until Sofron thought she would be turned inside out by this inescapable noise.

It hit a certain frequency and began to hum until it felt as if her bones would fly apart with the vibration. The fighting stopped. Everyone was screaming, with hands over their ears. But that didn't help.

Sofron felt hot lines of blood bursting from her ears and trickling over her cheeks and chin, and she tasted her own blood-borne motes as they spilled over her gills. Suddenly she knew what was happening.

"Duck!" she yelled to the humans. The children obeyed her automatically and submerged; some of the others heard, and others either couldn't hear or couldn't respond.

The smooth surface burst apart, and the fragments blew in all directions, opening a hole in the wall behind them. Water surged through it, and the wave sloshed back and forth inside the room that now was open to the Deep. The Killers who had been too close to the tangleweed lost their footing in the surge and were pushed backward into its deadly embrace.

"Go! Go! Go!" Sofron shouted, choking as the wave sloshed over her face. She grabbed Dilani's shoulders and pushed her out through the jagged opening, then stretched back to drag the children with her as she was carried out into the open sea.

The humans had caught on to what was happening and were plunging through the broken glass before the Killers had realized what hit them. Sofron's first glimpse through sun-dazzled eyes showed her the black-and-silver stripes of the Bright Teeth outside. They were turning to face the Killers with their teeth glinting for the attack.

That first rush of pure, oxygen-tingling water across her gills made Sofron feel reborn. Her mind suddenly felt cool and clear.

We're saved, she thought.

She saw Uli and Henner surface, then Whitman. More were coming. But White Killers were boiling through the broken window behind them, as if there were an endless supply of enemies. Sofron looked around for Dilani; she wanted Dilani to get a couple of ketos to carry her children out of harm's way. Dilani was already clinging to a keto's side and riding to the attack, waving a spear.

One face stood out in the confusion: Subtle's blue skin and

powerful torso showed above the waves. When he saw Sofron struggling to reach him, he extended a tentacle to support her.

"What's happening?" she said. "Where are we?"

"We-I is coming on raft," Subtle said. "Over there." He pointed. Sofron lunged out of water and spotted the raft. It was way too close to the carnage.

"Come on, kids," she said grimly. They started swimming.

The children followed in her wake. They swam gamely, though the spears got in their way. Chilsong and Piersall, who had had the least mobility before their transformations, could barely dog paddle. They were still trying to get their arms and legs to work together.

Fighting was still going on behind them, and rapidly moving in their direction. Subtle covered their retreat.

"I will stop them," he said. "No Killers will get to the raft."

"This is crazy," Sofron said. "We need to get away. We can't stay here and fight the White Killers."

"Humans is having great anger," Subtle said. "They-I is losing colors. You understand?"

"I understand, all right," Sofron said. "Listen; promise me to go back and protect the children. It's what Per would want. Don't go back and join in the human madness. Protect the hatchlings."

Subtle curled a tentacle around Sofron's arm, where the scabbed-over bites still showed. Around the bites a patch of bleached-out skin was spreading, down toward her wrist, which now felt numb.

"Yes, I know," she replied to his unspoken question. "I don't have much time. I have to get the leviathans to help me. So you'll have to guard the children."

"This-I is protecting hatchlings, is honoring god-friend," Subtle said solemnly.

He boosted Sofron onto the raft. With her pulling and Subtle pushing, they got the children out of the water. They were barely in time.

Something big and dark rose and sank next to the raft, rocking it. The children screamed again. The colonists were all swimming toward the raft at top speed, drawing the enemies their way.

Subtle turned and faced the battle, ready to defend Sofron's children. But he couldn't see the White Ones; only a disturbance in the shadows, a moving darkness. Suddenly the shadows burst upward toward him with a deafening screech. Dark wings came straight for his face, banking away and downward at the last minute, revealing a knot of barbed tentacles that slashed at him and were gone before he could use his spear.

He struck out and felt his spear encounter something yielding. Next instant, a powerful tug nearly tore the weapon from his hands. He coiled his own tentacle around the haft and managed to keep hold of it, though sheer terror weakened his grasp.

Them! The Terrible Ones are here, the Claws of Darkness, the Death from the Abyss! He couldn't even shape their names, in his present form, but his skin shivered and paled with fear. What fatal quality in the nature of humans drew forth every ancient shape of fear from the Deep to confront them?

The dark wings surged toward him again. He felt their touch and smelled the smell of old blood and darkness. This time the claws drew fresh blood from his flesh. Panic from the humans smoked like blood in the roiled water as they fought to thrust themselves into the air and away from the enemies.

The panic was infecting Subtle. It was hard to think, hard to do anything but flee and scream. He summoned the colors of rage, forced the red back into his skin and jetted fierce motes, battle motes, into the water, masking and transforming the scent of blood.

From behind him, harpoon bolts shot past his shoulder. They tore through the black wings and sent them spinning, flapping, back into the darkness. But there were always more crowding out from below. Subtle jabbed again, this time not at the wings but at the pale enemy guiding them. Bone crunched under the spear point. The Killer slid from his place on the winged one's back, and his steed soared away, riderless. Subtle wrenched his spear free and thrust again.

The humans were tiring. In the center of their circle, the wounded were kept from sinking only by their companions' desperate support. That left fewer hands free to fight. The Killers and their allies closed in on them, grappling hand to hand, making it impossible to use the harpoons and crossbows. Subtle felt the colors of his mind darken in the rush of raging motes from humans and White Ones alike.

To rend, to slash, was all that mattered. He scarcely felt his own wounds.

Again, his soundsense saved him, forcing him to think, calling him back from mindlessness. An insistent whine bored into his bones, dominating even the White Ones' whistling. It was something very dangerous, perhaps even more dangerous than the enemy. It changed to a high-pitched, intermittent note. He wanted to get away from it, but the Killers swam in his way. He shortened his grip on the spear and used it like an extension of his own claws, but he could not thrust the Killers out of his way.

Then that concussive blast of sound came again, smashing at him, jarring his bones and stabbing at tender membranes like a spear point. And again he did not know what it was, could not truly experience it until it was over and he wobbled, reeling, unable to tell up from down. Now his soundsense shuddered, his ears rang, and with the ringing came shrieks of protest and agony. It was worse this time because he was wholly submerged and experienced the full force of the blast.

Again! Another explosion. He could bear no more. Numbed, paralyzed, he started to sink. There were no more White Killers below him. He caught glimpses of white and black, tumbling slowly through a cloud of blood that fouled his gills.

What happened? What happened? Finally his mind brought him an answer.

These were the death eggs Whitman had brought to cherish; somehow they had hatched. The blast had struck down the Killers. It had almost killed Subtle, too. He knew he had to stir his limbs and rise, but he was too stunned to move. He sent desperate messages to the body he no longer possessed, trying to spread his mantle, to use his water jet to move upward. He couldn't remember how to move the strange, heavy limbs that now dragged him downward.

Pain stopped him. Someone gripped one of his remaining tentacles tightly—too tightly—dragging him toward the surface. The taste of the gripping hand finally filtered through his bruised skin. It was Dilani who tugged and twisted at him until his senses returned and he writhed upward.

The water was still heavy with death. The humans drooped like tubeflowers torn from their rocks. Whitman's weapon had damaged them, too. Their skins were cut and torn, mostly by the enemy. Uli and Torker, the biggest and strongest, held up the pale, fainting bodies of Engku and Adil. Blood welled unceasingly from their wounds, and there were no godbits in this sea to stop the flow.

Flee now! Flee swiftly! Subtle's limbs jerked as he tried frantically to dance this urgent message. But he only floundered. He bumped against another swimmer who smelled like Whitman underneath all the fear and blood. Subtle tried to sign *danger, get out of the water* in the human way, but Whitman wasn't paying attention. Subtle grabbed the human and boosted him above the surface. When Whitman was able to breathe again, Subtle shook him hard. Blood rage boiled through Subtle with his returning senses. This ugly human had nearly killed him.

He was not the only one who felt that way.

"You've killed Wayan," Bader said bitterly.

He was clutching Wayan's body, dragging it to the raft. Now he laid him carefully down and touched his throat and chest. In the dying light, there was no hint of movement or breath.

"He can't be. He was all right a minute ago," Adil babbled.

"Do something," Bader said fiercely. "Give him air. Make him breathe. Doctor Melicar could do it!"

He bent and tried to force his own breath between Wayan's lips, but the air sighed out again through the gill slits, and there was no response. He shook Wayan; he pushed on his chest; but nothing brought back a flicker of life. Wayan's skin was cold and very pale. All his colors were dead. A rill of blood-tinged water trickled from his body across the raft, but even the blood was pale.

Torker put his hand on Bader's arm.

"Don't," he said. "He died back there, in the water. He's gone."

"He can't be. *Can't!*" Adil said, staring wide eyed as Uli lashed a belt strap around him to stem the blood from his slashed arm.

"I think he bled to death," Torker said, pulling Bader gently away.

"You killed him," Henner Vik cried. "Whitman, you son of a bitch! Was it worth it to you? Your precious weapons! You don't even know how to use them. You picked up the death tech and now we're all going to die."

"Yes, it was worth it," Whitman hissed. "Because at least some of us will survive. And Wayan died because of the White Killers. They did it. Not me! Not me!"

"You brought weapons out here. You couldn't wait to try them."

"The Killer used them first! I only retaliated! It's not my fault someone got caught in the crossfire."

"Yes—the *Killers* used them—but not first!" Henner was beside herself. "Do you realize what you've done? You showed the Killers how to use those things. They didn't know before. And there are a lot more of them than there are of us."

The children were clinging to Sofron, trying to hide their faces against her so they wouldn't have to see the body.

"There is no other way to stay alive," Whitman said. "It's over now; we have the weapons, and we can carry out the next part of the plan. When their hatching ground is destroyed, they won't outnumber us for long. We can make it if we don't lose our resolve."

"And where do you think the Killers are going now?" Sofron said. "Why would they leave us alone?"

"Because now we're armed!" Whitman said.

"There's another reason why they left, too," Sofron said. "They're going to kill the god. It's what they always have wanted to do. And now, if Henner's right and they do have weapons, they're armed to succeed."

"We have to stop them, whatever it takes," Sofron said. "The god is our only hope. Per is there. If we can give him enough information, he may be able to get us out of this trap. Without him, we'll all be White Killers soon—or eaten by them."

"We'll stop them, if that's what we have to do," Torker said wearily. "But only if the ketos will take us. We'll never survive on rafts, with every Killer in the tower after us."

"Can do it," Dilani signed.

"Meet me there, then," Sofron said. "I have to go ahead of you. Only the leviathans are fast enough."

The children heard nothing but the words "I have to go." They seized her arms to keep her from moving.

"Sofi, you can't go! You have to stay with us!"

"I don't want to go anywhere," she said. "But there's something only I can do."

She looked around at the others on the raft.

"You can't all go to save the god. Someone has to go back with the wounded. Take the kids with you, and watch out for them."

"I'll go," Henner said reluctantly. "I've hurt my arm anyway. I wouldn't be much good with a spear."

"I'll go with you," Uli said. "Sorry, Torker; but they have to have someone who can still handle a spear."

"I can handle a spear!" Jaya shouted.

"Good; you go with these people and help them out," Sofron said to the boy. "They're taking you back to the cave we found, by the river. Remember that place? Wait for me there. And don't worry. I told you the others would come to get us, didn't I? And they did come. I'll be back soon."

The ketos were leaping out of the water, whistling so loudly that they interrupted the conversation.

"They say boogers are coming! The Enemies!" Dilani shouted. "They say swim away now, now, or they leave you!"

"Wait—where's Whitman?" Uli said.

The other raft was no longer anchored where they had left it. Its sail was up, and it was moving swiftly away from them. There was only one figure on board.

"He left us? Where's he going?" Henner said.

They shouted his name, but the figure on the raft did not turn toward them.

"We don't have time," Torker said. "Uli, take the raft slowly down the coast. There's enough blood smell on it; maybe you can lure the boogers your way. Once we're gone, raise sail and get out of here. Good luck."

The remaining humans leapt into the water. The others joined the ketos, but Sofron dove deeper, seeking the source of the faint music she could still hear in the depths. The leviathans held aloof from the slaughter at the surface, but she was sure they had not abandoned her.

As soon as she entered the water, she felt a buzzing vibration that seemed to be coming rapidly closer. She recognized it as the sound of a booger pack, and it filled her with dread. She had seen boogers before, when she lived on the old island with the other colonists. They were attracted to the smell of blood. They moved in packs, and with their mean, triangular mouths and the caustic slime of their skins, they could clean a wounded swimmer to the bones in minutes. Here in the open sea, she couldn't do anything to protect herself except to find the leviathans.

She pushed herself straight down, past the eddies of blood and rage scents that the currents carried toward her. She began to feel the painful pressure against her damaged ears, but she also started to hear or feel the leviathan song vibrating in her bones again. As she moved down into the twilight zone, she could distinguish more than one song, not harmonizing in the glorious complexity she had heard before, but crossing and weaving in a focused pattern. She didn't know how to call them, so she just pinged them in her normal echo voice. The sounds came back, revealing mountainous shapes below in swift motion.

The echoes also brought her a picture of the booger pack, much closer than she had imagined. Their buzzing grated on her, dulling her senses just when she needed them most. She pinged again, then realized she shouldn't have done anything to give away her position. The main body of the pack kept going, toward the blood traces left in the wake of the raft, but Sofron could sense the pack bulging, changing shape. A smaller group broke off and headed in her direction.

She forced her weary body to move faster. No longer worried about revealing her location, she sent out constant shameless distress calls. What if the leviathans had forgotten her? What if they didn't realize she was in danger? They were so different.

The sound-shadow of the boogers curled toward her. Their buzzing filled her ears. She could feel the vibration in the water, and their acid flavor burned in her gills.

The next thing she knew, she had been swept aside by a soft but tremendous blow, and something had wrapped around her, immobilizing her. She felt a cool tingling at the back of her neck, not the abrasive agony she had expected. Then the leviathan's senses were once again channeling into her mind.

You little one with no patience, you swim always into dangerous times, the vast, amused voice said to her.

Where did the boogers go? she asked. The leviathan motes were calming her terror, making her feel that everything was all right, but she was still afraid for the other humans.

Tasty, the leviathan sang. *They have no minds, so it does not dampen our song to swallow them sometimes. The life that was them continues to live in us, but in a gentler form.*

I worried about your hatchling, too, Sofron said. *I didn't see it after we escaped.*

All is well, the leviathan hummed serenely. *It has been gathered in—like you. Now it will be carried until it learns to join the Greatsong and is strong enough to swim alone. What will you do? Will you swim with us until you are strong again?*

I can't, Sofron said. *I know I promised, but I'm still in trouble. I have to go and see the god right now. I have to do this to protect my own hatchlings. I came to find you because I have to get there fast. Can you help me again?*

The leviathan paused, and Sofron sank deep into the four-part fugue that it was creating with its friends: the deep tones celebrated triumph with a hint of bitterness, a darkness sinking into the depths, and joined melodies rising back into the light, leaving regret behind.

Your danger is still with you, the leviathan said, returning its attention to Sofron. *We taste it. The Paling threatens all of you little ones. Maybe like the others, you will disappear from our singing. It is decided. We will help you.*

Then release me now, she said. *I need to take one other with me. A White One.*

A ripple of startled laughter went through the leviathan.

Always with you there are surprises, the big voice said, but it did not sound displeased. *Where is this helper you need?*

I don't know, she admitted. *He probably swam away from the fight. The Pale Ones swim together, but he would probably swim alone. He might be hurt. Call him like this—Wearra, Wearra! Maybe he can hear you.*

She was astonished to hear the leviathans crying in high voices, perfect replicas of her own pitch and accent, but with tremendous power.

She could feel them sweeping the Deep in crisscrossing patterns. Changing Light showed her every shape their song reflected. She was beginning to despair of finding him, even with their help. The leviathans had found and dismissed more than one pale shape already tumbling into the Abyss, already dead.

Then they showed her a shape that floated, still feebly struggling to swim. Changing Light sucked in motes from the surrounding water and let Sofron taste them, too.

It's him! We've found him!

Then you must ride the skin now, Changing Light said. *No Pale thing can be our hatchling! Hold tight; we swim to rapid measures now.*

As before, it cost her a pang to leave the warmth and safety of the leviathan's pouch. Most of all, she missed the constant flow of communication. Once she was released, she experienced at once the full darkness and isolation of the Deep. And she breathed in, as well, the familiar, ominous motes that signified Wearra. His motes were worse than ever, for he was battered and bruised. His skin was very cold, and his inner eyelids were closed. But he seemed still to like her touch; he stirred when she reached out to him, but did not try to escape.

Quickly, she clasped him in her arm and dragged him across the leviathan's mountainous hide, to cling to the mighty fin. The leviathans surged forward as soon as she settled there. She hoped she could hold on.

❦25❧

No hint of the turmoil had reached Per yet. He found it harder and harder to maintain a sense of time. He knew their situation was urgent, and that with every day that passed, all the humans on Typhon were rushing toward the Abyss. But he wandered through so many times and places that it was hard to know how much time had passed here, in the unchanging blue light. He needed his body, with its hunger and fear, to anchor him.

"I need my body back," Per said to Kitkit. He knew that Kitkit wouldn't pay any attention to this statement, but he had to say it to someone. The ketos would just laugh. He envied them.

There was danger in searching his memories. He told himself that he was looking for clues that might help, but too often he found himself lured down blind alleys. And often the god was absent. If Kitkit had assimilated him into the god for the sole purpose of enlisting him to make a weapon, why did the Kalko'ul seem so unconcerned with results?

He imagined himself pacing back and forth on the rock shelf next to his shack, as he had often done in the flesh when a problem puzzled him. In his imagination, he saw the garden of miniature trees he had planted and tended there. It was a shock. Now he understood—knew that he had been trying to re-create Rameau's steel garden.

What a fool I was, he thought. *Homesick for a prison. And trying to be like Rameau. Now why would I do that?*

Maybe because he gave you the only useful advice you ever got, he answered himself. *At least he explained things, taught me. What was it he said? That I would not exist unless someone had thought I would be a useful tool. So Kitkit was not the first to have that idea.*

And yet, they didn't train me with a cohort, like the other Original Man offspring. Would they have allowed a potential tool to exist without training? Not likely. So Rameau was training me; funny I never remembered that. I thought he was just amusing himself. Maybe that's what he wanted everyone to think—that I was a pet.

If Rameau was training me, what was it for? What could he possibly have found useful in me?

At first Per thought he was back in Rameau's work space, but then he realized it was a different small, cramped space full of record-keeping and holo devices. Rameau pressed the metal studs on one inexplicably blank wall, and the wall seemed to dissolve. Per had a confused idea he might see stars; he had been told this was an interstellar jumpship. But what he saw looked like nothing at all. There were things resembling sparks and lines, but they seemed to be manifesting inside his head, not in his eyes. When he looked away from them, he suddenly felt sick and narrowly avoided throwing up.

"That's not jump," Rameau said. "It's only a representation. The best we can have. The only one with a better look at Jump is the shipmind who pilots us. Not many people can handle that. The navigators approach it mathematically—much safer."

Per looked around to see if there was a pilot in the room, but there wasn't. There was a hood with a maze of connections leading to more monitoring tanks, but the life-support chair beneath it was empty.

"We have a three-pilot redundancy," Rameau said. "Plus certain reserves. But the reserves aren't activated until they are needed. You see, pilots aren't good for much else once they're plugged in. So it's better to keep them working at another job until they're needed.

"And there's another problem. This is a warship, though we've successfully lurked our way out of combat for some time now. And there are wars on board, too—contending factions, of which it is well for you to know nothing. I have eyes on all sides of my head, eyes enough for two.

"Each faction must maintain a spare pilot somewhere, in case of emergency. Control of the ship is everything. But, if the various sides knew the location of the spare pilots, they could gain advantage by neutralizing them."

Rameau touched the chair's armrest. It hummed and arranged itself.

"Sit here," he said. "I want to test some of your basic functions. It won't hurt."

Per had been through many tests, some of them with devices much like this one, so he sat down obediently. The hood closed over his head. He didn't quite like this, but it was smoothly padded inside and had a pleasant, clean smell. Cool fresh air flowed past his face. He could see into a vague but well-lit space, so he didn't feel claustrophobic.

Suddenly the lighted space was replaced by a sparkling darkness. Per gasped and clutched at air.

"It's all right," Rameau's voice said, out of the air. "I'm checking some visual-spatial reflexes. This is something like a puzzle. I'm going to show you a place now."

At first Per thought it was a trick. What he saw didn't resemble a place at all; it was a kind of pattern, made of sparks and lines like the ones he had seen. But these did not make him sick. The picture had depth and reality, and he felt at home in it.

"Now I'm going to put you back where we are," Rameau said.

The pattern changed completely. There was a sort of twist to it, Per thought. It was like pulling a sweater on over your head, and then pulling it off inside out.

"Now I want you to figure out how to rearrange this pattern to place yourself back in the first locus I showed you."

More points appeared to Per. But each one was not really a point, he realized. It was a representation of something like a string, something he could pull to go in different directions, or combinations of directions. At first it made him dizzy, but then it became fun. He tried various pathways, but some of them did not have a good feel. There was a smell of burning to one, an unpleasant softness in another. Suddenly he was afraid that Rameau would be waiting. He did the sweater trick, gathering the lines up into a single swirl like the neck of a sweater. There was a sort of click in his mind, and he knew for sure that the pattern before him was the first one Rameau had shown.

The sparkling darkness faded into the neutral light he had seen at first. Then the helmet opened silently and glided away from his head. If he hadn't known that nothing surprised Rameau, Per would have thought that Rameau looked surprised.

"Did I do all right?" he said anxiously.

"Quite well," Rameau said. Then he stopped, as if he had decided to tell more for once.

"I could have seen what you saw," he said. "I'm not sure if I could have manipulated it as you did. That makes me one in a million, and you one in ten million. Most people couldn't play that little game. Five seconds, and they'd have to be in sensedep for weeks to get over it. Ten seconds, and they'd be permanently mad. They simply haven't the connections for it.

"So if you ever wonder again why you don't get cohort training, that's one good reason. Your mind is an instrument—not something to be slammed around by the cohort's practice sticks."

He looked sharply at Per.

"You want to do it again, don't you?"

"Yes," Per said. He could feel his mind reaching for those points, the way his hands kept reaching for the controls after a long session of his favorite simgame. But without the instruments in the headset, he couldn't perceive the patterns. The world around him felt plain and flat, like a paper cutout.

"We'll play this again as soon as I can arrange it," Rameau said. "And, of course, you can tell anyone you like about it. Only, if you do, you'll probably never be allowed here again."

Per came back slowly to the rock shelf. It was warm with the sun, he noticed vaguely. It felt pleasant. There was a whorl of a lighter intrusion in the dark rock; almost a Fibonacci spiral, Per thought, and he lost himself for a moment in tracing it. But the pattern wasn't complex enough to occupy him for long. He had to face what he had seen.

So, I'm the very best kind of tool, he thought. *I'm the tool that controls the others. And Kitkit thought he could deny me access to the god's mind.*

He felt almost ashamed of himself for allowing it to happen.

It was the fear of losing myself, he thought an instant later. *It happens to pilots sometimes. They get lost in jump and don't come back. That's one of the reasons why there have to be pilot replacements. That's why Rameau would never leave me in as long as I wanted.*

But I have to go in now, he thought. *And stay as long as I have to.*

He drew a deep sigh for the sun-warmed rock, and for the comfortable body he didn't really have anymore.

Then he began, slowly and carefully, to reconstruct Rameau's work space in his mind. Constructing and folding proteins in three-dimensional simulation was less complicated than navigating in Jump space. If he could do one, he could certainly handle the other.

He knew what he was looking for now: not an invading microbe, but a deliberate subversion of normal function. He called up the complex hormonal/pheromonal systems of the Kalko'uli. Then he drew out the records of White Killer physiology. Kitkit did not question his actions; the old god seemed busy elsewhere. The two systems were very nearly identical. Within that "nearly" lay his answers.

At last Kitkit answered Per's repeated summons and let his appearance and attention manifest in the pool.

"Have you found a weapon to use on the White Killers?" Kitkit said.

"I have found a point mutation in one of the genes that controls the morphone glands," Per said. "That is the name I gave to that set of glands around the neck and gills—the ones that produce most of the motes. Your name for it was hard to pronounce, even in my own mind."

Kitkit appeared to wave his explanation aside.

"I could have told you that."

"The mutated gene produces a protein that looks like *this*, instead of the normal one, here."

He drew the simulations in lines and nodes of fire on the air above Kitkit's pool. He no longer needed to reproduce the artificial appearance of equipment. He had gained complete control of that part of the god's mind. He was determined to make Kitkit look, whether the Kalko'ul wanted to or not. He could taste a prickling anxiety in the water that told him Kitkit was disturbed by this, in spite of his show of indifference.

"This means the enzyme that is supposed to attach to the hormone to disassemble it can't get a lock."

Again, he demonstrated.

"I'd have to have a lab and some subjects to work with, to prove it, but I'm almost sure that's the problem."

"What difference does it make?" Now Kitkit was becoming agitated. "There's no way to fix it! Why do you waste your time with such things?"

"I have questions about this," Per said. "How does a mutation spread through the population in such a short time?"

"I told you," Kitkit said impatiently. "The Paling is contagious."

"Even if it is," Per said, "the time frame doesn't look right. I made a graph for you."

Again he traced the design in the air, and it hung there, glowing.

"You see? If there was one mutation, or even several at once, there would not have been time for it to spread as fast as it did. The only model that matches this one is that of an epidemic that breaks out from several sources at once."

The graphics he overlaid on each other were memories of things Rameau had shown him—what happened on a planet's surface when the toxicants touched down, for instance.

"What is the point of this?" Kitkit said.

"These are maps of the spread of diseases that, like the one

you want me to make for you, were deliberately induced.
Weapon diseases. And this is a map of the spread of the
Paling, from your memory. See how they match?"

"What are you saying?"

"I am saying that the Paling was not a misfortune. It was a
decision."

The memory leapt into Kitkit's consciousness as if he
brooded on it constantly. Immediately he tried to sever Per's
access to his thoughts, but Per was able to reroute his sensing
around the simple block that had once stopped him.

Again he stood in Kitkit's footprints. Kitkit had evidently
been gifted beyond most of his generation and had risen to a
higher rank than his brood mates. But the loyalty of kin was
still there. Kitkit's ruff stood out with pride as he watched his
brood mates in the clan form ranks to begin their mission.
Their medallions and weapons gleamed. They were tall and
well shaped, their skins bright with health and courage. Kitkit
felt great pride that so many of his own brood mates were included in the new program.

Privileged as an observer because of his rank, Kitkit clung
to the swaying airfin as it swooped over the battle taking place
on the border. Here he could no longer distinguish his brood
mates from any of the others, but the entire line performed
magnificently. Their ferocity was unparalleled. The hostile,
intruding clan was thrown back and overrun, chewed to
pieces and left lying in fragments. Kitkit made swift notes
with his stylus, recording the encounter as a victory and a de-
cisive success for the new process.

The call to regroup sounded. But instead of resuming its
well-disciplined pattern, the line raged onward at random. In
horror and disbelief, Kitkit watched as the tall, beautiful soldiers of the Clan of Fire turned the same ferocity on each other.
Even when reinforcements from the regular force reached
them and attempted to disarm them, they continued to rage
and tear.

A pitiful handful survived, shot down like animals with
sedative guns, to be hurried back to secret medical facilities.

Sorrow hung heavy over the city. Every clan wore mourning symbols. They had been told that a victory had been won, but that secret enemy weapons had caused unexpected casualties. This explained the loss of the finest flower of the young soldiers and the secrecy surrounding the wounded.

Because he had been involved in the project from the beginning, Kitkit was one of the few allowed into the infirmary. The survivors lay in shallow baths, receiving continuous sedative drips and synthetic motes. Kitkit stopped next to one of his favorite clan members, a youth of great promise. The young one's bright colors were hardly a shadow now. Across his chest—as on those of each of the wounded—lay a silk honor sash in the defiant crimson of the Clan of Fire, each with a gilded medallion threaded onto it. Kitkit reached to read the symbols on the decoration. It was a posthumous award.

At his touch, the warrior stirred. His eyes opened briefly, but without recognition. He showed his teeth at Kitkit. Then a grave, silent nurse hurried Kitkit away. That had been his last memory of his clan brother: skin drained of color, eyes glistening with madness. Kitkit was the one who had urged his promotion and had recommended him for inclusion in the special project.

Kitkit had gone to his quarters and had washed his hands with disinfectant until the skin bled. But others had received the treatment. Soon madness walked the streets.

"They were you," Per said to Kitkit. "The Killers are not a different species. They are your own flesh and blood. They are what you made of yourselves. You sent those monsters to stalk your future. Now you think you can use us to kill your past."

He felt Kitkit struggling to escape his scrutiny, but Per's vision was that of the god—unending and clear in all directions.

"You called me here," he said, pinning the Kalko'ul with ruthless attention. "If I were an ordinary human, I would have lost my mind. But you sampled me, didn't you? You knew there was something different about my mind, so you risked assimilating me. You wanted to use me. And you were right—I am a tool. But not *your* tool."

Now he knew why Rameau had nurtured him. He was Rameau's key. Rameau was in prison, as much as any of the creatures he monitored in their cells of glass. Per was his hope of someday reshaping the pattern. Per saw again the pattern of jump-light that he could turn in his mind like a crystal in his hand.

I could have taken him home. But he never had time to show me where home was.

"Why did you do it?" Per said to his fellow captive. "You were living in paradise, and you created your own demons. Why?"

Kitkit's narrow tongue flickered angrily in and out, in angry desperation.

"*You* designate this a paradise," he responded. "*We* had no such idea. We had to struggle to survive. In my time we were sorely pressed. Our share of the marshes grew ever narrower, encroached on by other clans."

"But you had all the Deep," Per protested.

"Yes—for food! But without the marshes there is no breeding! There could be no eggs! We had to fight for our nests! The scholars had traced the pathways that created Whiteness. The Pale Ones felt no pain, no weariness, no fear. The warrior clan put strong pressure on the clan of scholars to use this knowledge for our good. They thought we could induce a temporary, reversible state of Paling that would make our clan invincible."

"And they were wrong."

Kitkit bent his head.

"There is a feedback loop for the stress hormones," he said. "After a rise in those hormones comes a rise in the enzyme that disassembles them. A buildup of stress hormones mimics the Paling state. But only for a time, in an emergency. Then the hormones are destroyed and equilibrium is restored.

"We used the god to tailor a virus that would carry a replacement gene into the cells of what you call the morphone glands. The gene caused reproduction of a different version of the hormone, altered just so much that the enzymes no longer destroyed it—the point mutation you saw. We thought it would give our warriors a measure of added strength."

"What happened?"

"The virus was supposed to die out, eventually, and be cleansed from the cells. But something went wrong. The virus regained the ability to reproduce. It established itself throughout the glands. The buildup of the stress hormones triggered a cascade of irreversible changes. The adults mimicked the Paling that occurs in hatchlings.

"And what was worse, these motes eventually overbalanced the minds and bodies of all those who were close to them. They, too, entered the Paling state and produced the same motes, to poison all around them.

"We tried everything. Change agents in viral or bacterial vectors were useless. The enhanced immune system of a White One destroys the vector before the DNA it contains can have any effect. And as for calming motes, or sleep drugs, the Paled system is ferociously effective in excreting poisons. It enables them to eat everything, you see. All this enhancement shortens their life span and supplants alternative functions. They become raging predators with no time to do anything but kill and eat. But they survive. Oh, lords of the Deep, how they survive."

The words poured out from Kitkit as though he was relieved, in the end, to be forced to share what he had lived with alone for so long.

Per voiced no sympathy, but continued to press the Kalko'ul. He wanted the whole truth. In return for his life, he thought he deserved no less.

"There's still one fact that makes no sense. If the Paling was so all-powerful, if no one could fight it, then how did one clan member outlive his clan? The city was dying. All was lost. All but Kitkit. He survived."

Kitkit's spines flared.

"I would have died!" he said. "Gladly I would have died."

"Yet somehow you escaped," Per said. It was dangerous to

needle his mind-mate, but he needed to provoke the Kalko'ul to revelation.

"It was no escape," Kitkit said. His voice wasn't angry and defensive, as Per had expected, but dry and flat. "It was given as an order, by the high-most elder of my clan. Had this one commanded me to throw myself into the river of fire, more joyfully would I have obeyed. Instead, he commanded me to preserve myself, when all my kin were dying.

"Our scholars were sent on a last mission to the god, and I was sent as their protector. My order was not to die as long as one of them remained alive."

Kitkit fell silent, brooding, and the flavor of the water was dark and grim.

"Where are the scholars you were sent to protect?" Per said. "It seems you failed in your mission."

Kitkit turned on him, hissing, and Per felt a moment of fear. But if Kitkit could actually harm him, now was the time to find out.

"Yes, they died," Kitkit said. "But I could not prevent it. 'When wind and tide set to the west, the fool vows "I shall swim only east." ' "

"Lovely proverb," Per mocked. "And so convenient, for the only survivor."

Kitkit's hand appeared to descend toward Per as if to tear him apart. But instead, it tore a rent of darkness in the simulated calm before him. Per was thrust into the fire-torn night, tossed and shaken till he couldn't tell sky from water. His hands were planted on a smooth, wet surface, as they had been when he thought he was in Kitkit's pool, and he clung to that as his only safety until a sense of direction returned.

A hissing and roaring, as if the sky itself were being torn apart, confused his soundsense. The wind that flogged his skin was hot and full of ashes. No stars were visible. Great-moon showed as a lurid patch behind clouds of smoke, lit from below by a red glow that flared and faded.

Beings moved in the sky, so for a minute he thought he had reversed directions and was looking at swimmers in the Deep. Then he saw that they were Great People riding one-person flying craft. He had not time to see how the craft were built and powered. The hot wind tossed them aside. The frail wings crumpled, and the riders fell with a shriek into the sea.

Per realized that he was clinging to a small, swift craft with a narrow hull and gossamer sails. A dozen others rode with him. Most, like himself, crouched with lowered heads. The shores behind them were incandescent with fire, making the path ahead seem that much darker. From the burning shore came cries that were faint yet still terrible to hear. Like the others, Per would have covered his ears, but he needed both hands to cling to the tossing deck.

Now Kitkit had the advantage over him. This was fine vengeance for his taunts—to make him relive his own agony, watching the city burn as the colony of the Skandians had once burned in Per's own lifetime.

You escaped; you escaped, his own voice clamored in his ears.

"No," he moaned. "Stop it—please!"

His plea was lost among so many others. Kitkit was not going to spare him.

The hot wind came closer. Embers rattled down on them like winter hail on Skandia, but where this hail touched, it burned. Per's lungs were on fire. His skin crackled, the protective moisture sucked away. He wanted to throw himself into the sea, but his companions in this vision were still working.

The sails came down, and the mast folded into a groove in the hull. The narrow craft nosed down and plunged like a spear into the healing coolness of the Deep. The passengers clung to their handholds and dove with it.

But even the Deep was not safe. Invisible currents of boiling water poured through it from great tears in the seafloor where dark fire was rising. They detected the presence of the currents by a keen awareness of the density of the water. Per's Deep senses were less keen, and he clung to the craft in terror of being boiled like a shrimp, knowing only what he could learn from their colors and their brief signs to each other.

Per looked out from his perch and saw the outer reef passing by. The reef was much farther from the shore in his day, unless Kitkit's memory had shifted their journey in time. And this reef was thronged with ghosts. Countless shadowy shapes of bony Great Ones lined its fans and ridges. Their skeleton hands reached out in greeting. Their crests were raised, and though their faces were unfleshed, new eyes of gems and pearl still gazed outward, watchful against danger from the Deep.

The Reef of Bones. Kitkit had shown him this before. But in this time, no set of human bones had come to rest there yet. That was still far in the future.

A deep rumble shook the bones and made the little craft vibrate. The Great Ones whistled to each other and gestured, but Per could not understand them. A shock wave like an invisible wall rose and struck them. The craft tumbled and spun, shedding its riders, but Per still hung on. The rumble was pain in every bone, excruciating pain like knives driven into Per's ears. The floor of the Deep dropped away with a shuddering roar, and blasts of heat shot past them.

This was the moment when the reef had become farther from shore, as Per remembered it. The city was sinking beneath the waves, under shock after shock as the planet's crust shifted. They heard the grinding of the planet itself changing shape.

The Great People's craft went tumbling out of control. Per found that he had let go his hold and was spinning alongside Kitkit, who held on fiercely to a cargo net containing some heavy and bulky treasure. Per held the net, too—not because his imaginary hands had any force in Kitkit's memory of a long-settled past, but simply because Kitkit remembered hanging on to the net, and Per could experience only what Kitkit had seen.

At first Per thought that Kitkit had lost all his companions. Then a handful struggled back to rejoin him. Two more caught hold of the net and helped him carry it. The others spread out in formation, weapons ready, to protect the mission. Even in this extremity they performed their duty. Per found himself close to one of the Great People who tugged at the net. This one wore a cross-belt linked with many medallions, and the spikes of his crest were sheathed in flexible metal foil. Whenever another concussion shook the Deep, the others reflexively moved to shield him.

Per knew where they were going now. Even in the confusion of earthquake and eruption, he recognized the sea fields beneath him, on the slopes of the ancient mountain. The god slept in its crater. Perhaps they would find safety there.

But too many others had fled with the idea of seeking refuge in the crater. The Great Ones brought down the mindless predators, the ribbonfish and boogers, with darts from their weapons, and something that looked like concussion shells—small pods with the power to stun. Then they came face-to-face with a drift of White Ones—like a snowdrift, like an iceberg, like a row of grinning teeth.

Alone among all the species there, the White Ones seemed to be enjoying themselves, oblivious to the catastrophe. They caught everything that tried to move in their vicinity, ripped it apart, and gorged themselves. The water around them was laced with bits of flesh upon which the boogers fed with glee.

Every other creature seemed to feel the motes of prohibition that the god sent out, to keep all but the Great People from approaching too closely. But the White Ones were not inhibited. When they saw Kitkit's shrunken squadron, they attacked at once, and followed them into the very chamber of the god itself.

With his companions fighting all around him, the medallioned senior appeared to shake off Kitkit. There was a brief dispute; then Kitkit swam for his life, away from the god, toward the sides of the chamber, where the lava was riddled with holes and tubules. Kitkit dragged the precious net with him, single-handedly. Per could not help him, but was forced to follow in the wake of his memory.

One of the chambers held a bed of soft glowfronds, as if it had been prepared for this cargo. Kitkit dumped the contents of the net, fumbling in his haste, but still with agonized care. Even in the pale blue-green glow, the contents gleamed like jewels. They were dense ellipsoids the size of Per's head. The outer surface was firm and hard, but with the hardness of rubber rather than ceramic or metal. Within, the half-seen contents shone with the colors of the Great Ones—amber, crimson, indigo.

Per began to understand. This was a cache of eggs. Kitkit's mission had been an attempt to save a piece of the future. By storing eggs in the presumed safety of the god's cavern, they preserved hope that their kind might live again, even if the adults all died.

But there was more to understand, for Kitkit abandoned the eggs with one backward look, and fled for the main chamber where his kin were battling. A terrible sight met Per's eyes.

The sacred chamber reeked of blood. The last of the Great People were locked in death struggles with the White Ones, while the corpses of those already dead drifted slowly toward the depths. The elder, too, drifted alone, dark fronds of blood streaming from his wounds. His protectors had all sacrificed themselves in the vain attempt to save him. All were dead now save Kitkitdildil, the Flower of Rushes. He was the last, the very last.

Towing the bleeding body of his leader, in a final, desperate effort, Kitkit approached the god as it hung luminous and apparently impassive amid chaos. His hand touched the god. Triggered by the blood of the clan elder, the god's surface began to weep tears of pearl—godbits that rapidly enclosed the dead leader and engulfed Kitkit as he supported his elder's bleeding corpse.

Per felt the sting and then the numbness as the god's kiss penetrated his skin. He threw himself backward in a violent spasm of revulsion and hurled himself out of Kitkit's memory, back into the cool peace of the room.

"And so it was that I *survived*," Kitkit said. "That I *lived*. That I *escaped*. I survived by perishing. I lived by dying. I escaped by entering an eternal prison. For the sake of my kin and our children. I think you, of all beings, have little reason to mock my choice."

It took Per long moments to collect his thoughts. He expected to smell smoke, to see burn marks on his skin. But the marks, like the skin itself, existed only in his mind.

"I didn't intend to mock," he said. "I just wanted you to

explain. You did this to me, but you don't give me the information I need."

"Understanding comes gradually, as in life," Kitkit said. "I cannot hand it to you all in one piece, like a lump of rock. Your mind creates the network within which information exists. I tell, I show, but I do not control all."

The explanation made sense. Yet Per still felt that Kitkit was hiding something from him.

"The burden you carried here," he said. "It was eggs of the Great People? Do the eggs still exist? Within this place?"

"Some yet live," Kitkit said, and Per could taste his anxiety, his longing. "I send the god substance to preserve and nourish them. It was planned by our scholars, and I am not fully aware of how this happens. But I know the locus within the god where it does happen, and I nurture the process. The godbits nourish the eggs, but something is added to prevent the eggs from growing."

"They are maintained in stasis," Per said. He focused tightly on the words and only the words, walling out any pictures associated with them. He did not want Kitkit to see the transplex tanks where the sinue had bided their time.

"Those are the words," Kitkit said. "In the beginning, when the fire died, I tried to hatch them. It took me a long time to regain my mind after the god took me. It was supposed to be him—my elder, my prince of scholars, the noble mind. He would have been a true god, one all-knowing. He could have brought my people back from the Abyss. I died to save *him*. But it was I who imprinted with the god. It was too late for him. His understanding had already fled beyond reach of the god. Only mine was left. That was not enough. This is why I must have you with me. You are like the lost one. You can help me."

"The eggs," Per prodded him. Kitkit's intensity disturbed him.

"When I regained use of the mind," Kitkit continued, "the Deep seemed quiet. So I sent motes to awaken the eggs and make them grow. I am thankful I kept some back, did not use them all at once.

"The eggs hatched, and the hatchlings swam away. I do not

know where they went. Perhaps to the gate of the city where the hatchlings of my clan always entered, seeking the bond of their clan. They came not back. Never anymore. But the White Ones were seen, again, and still. They survived the fire. They live in the Abyss.

"I sent my servants, the Bright Teeth, to follow the hatchlings. As I thought, they swam to the river gardens and to the gates. Beyond the dark gates I could not see. But those in the temple of the gardens, the Teeth watched over. They rose in the shape of Great Ones, but the Bright Teeth followed them and saw their end. They were taken by the White Killers. Some were eaten, and some were changed. They Paled like my kin of old. They joined the hunt of the White Killers, and their madness, and they were lost to me. They could not hear my voice or receive my motes.

"I tried again and again, one precious egg at a time. Some I sent in pairs or threes, hoping kin would give them strength. But all were lost. Even the great burning could not cleanse the Deep. The evil lives and destroys us, after so many hundred years.

"And when I knew this, the colors of my mind grew dark, and I do not know how far I sank into the Abyss of the mind or how long I drifted in darkness.

"There was nothing I could choose. If I didn't wake the eggs, they would die. Even with all the sustaining of the god, they cannot live forever. Already some have gone dark in the nest. Soon the rest must follow. But if I chose to wake them into life, I would be sending them to the curse that is worse than never being born."

"And then we came," Per said slowly.

"Yes! You came! My servants began to bring me news of you. At first I thought you were a new evil, some new kind of White Killer. You lived in the Dry, yet you swam in the Deep. You were a mystery to me. I sent the Teeth to bring you here, but you resisted. They could not establish communication with you. You had not the Deepsong. You were too different.

"Then luck turned his face of fortunate colors toward me once again. I had long sent out a call for the Round Folk. But they are few and slow. They had drifted far away since the days of the Great People. At last one heard me. He brought you to me. There I learned that the change motes were already twisting you. To you they were a sickness. You offered yourself to the god so the god could understand you and complete the change. And so it happened. So we find ourselves here together.

"And together we will complete my mission. The last of the White Ones will die, so the Great People can be born again. Now you know the whole truth, and now you will give me the weapon I need."

Per paused only briefly, but in the consciousness of the god it was a long, blue moment.

"No, I will not," he said. "I lived with such weapons, and my own ghosts are as terrible as yours. I will not be the one who sets them free to stalk another world."

He did not know what he expected, but he thought that surely Kitkit would retaliate in some way. It might be a howling blast of rage, as before; it might be visions of tormenting fire, or true annihilation of his part in the god through poisonous chemicals or simply through starvation. Or it might be his worst fear: complete isolation until he went mad.

He was not prepared when Kitkit simply smiled.

"I hoped that you would help me. It would have been easier. But it doesn't really matter. The remnants of your flesh have already told me all I need to know."

"What is it? What is it that you think you've found?"

"When you wore a human body, you were injected with parts of many viruses. Some were even whole, with just one part altered so they could not reproduce. You were like a little god yourself, a storage facility for many different kinds of cells. The god is full of tools for repairing little organisms. It was not hard to bring one of them back to life."

Per was relieved.

"You already told me that the White Killers' immune systems are too strong to be infected," he said.

"That was true for the organisms we tried—but they had been known among the Great People for many years, and even without enhancement, our bodies were well adapted to defeating them," Kitkit replied. "The organism I found in you has never been seen in this world before. It is very potent. I do not think that even the White Killers can identify it before it has taken hold of them. When I set it loose among them, their flesh will dissolve and there will not even be any corpses to further foul my city."

Per's cry of anguish rocked the water in the cavern and caused the ketos to remark that something must have bitten the god.

"You don't know what you're doing!" he cried. "If you turn this loose in the Deep it may live forever! You're only creating another plague!"

"It is indeed a terrible thing," Kitkit agreed. "Your kin must have all been criminals, really bad people, to create such a thing without even the excuse of White Killers to make them desperate. But I do not fear for the future, because I can also grow the harmless, altered organism and use it as your people did, to protect the innocent from suffering.

"I will bring the Killers here. Your own people will lure them to me. I will impart death to the Killers, and then at last I will awaken the eggs in safety."

Per's motes must have been truly terrible, for Kitkit actually tried to soothe him.

"You will be happy when the Great People come back," he said hopefully. "You will see. They will be beautiful. The Deep will be bright again. It will not be lonely as it is now. And you will be honored, for I will tell them that it was all due to you."

Per was stunned. He had thought himself so clever, and all the time Kitkit had been outwitting him. Kitkit had only pretended to care about keeping secrets, inducing Per to spend his time trying to find out what happened, while Kitkit calmly took what he needed.

"Leave me," he croaked.

"For a time," Kitkit said, withdrawing.

«©26»»»»»»»

I could still stop him, Per thought. Kitkit did not know yet how completely Per had woven himself into the fabric of the god. If Per caught him by surprise, he could still deny Kitkit access to the storage sacs within the god that held the deadly viruses. Or he could destroy the supply before it could be used.

But could he go on fighting that battle over and over again? Kitkit had the knowledge now. He could create more deadly infections any time he wanted to. Per might not always be able to prevent him.

And if Kitkit brought the White Killers here, and Per destroyed his weapon, the White Killers would probably succeed in killing the god and anyone else who was present. Sofron. Dilani. Bey. Sushan.

Perhaps Kitkit was right! What right did Per Langstaff have to preserve the lives of one species—cruel, ugly, and mindless—and risk the lives of others who were far more deserving of life?

And yet he resolved to stop Kitkit, or die trying. To help Kitkit would be to justify the Skandians in their judgment that Per and his ugly companions hadn't been worthy of life, to justify those who created Embla and her sisters for a life of suffering. He couldn't do it.

He was grateful to Kitkit, in a way, that he had been able to remember Embla and the others, and that at last he would be able to do one thing in memory of them, though they would never know it.

He knew that to stop Kitkit, he would probably have to shut down a large portion of the god—perhaps enough to kill both of them, or severely damage their consciousness. It would be difficult. He would have to hurry.

He stretched his senses into all the dimensions of the Deep, to see how soon his doom was coming. He had learned to experience this sensing as a marvelous pleasure, to see/hear/taste the full extent of his surroundings. For that, too, he was thankful.

He could taste the traces of the White Killers, phosphorescent and cold like snail tracks, winding like spiderwebs all around the island. But where was Sofron? Images of her reflected face no longer came to him from small creatures scattered around the shore. She was still lost in the Deep.

Then Per heard a mighty, slow, and rhythmic pattern moving through the depths. Before he had expanded his presence in the god's mind, this song had been too big for him to grasp.

The Guardians, he thought in awe. Kitkit had said, "We do not rule them."

No, but now we hear them, Per thought to himself.

They were singing of a dark old city, now in ruins, a place inhabited by monsters, by broken toys abandoned by their masters. They were singing of a wall, a smooth darkness, of the tiny sparks of life encapsulated within. How long would these sparks endure? There was no hurry in their song, only the wonder of life's tenacity and the poignant suspense of its brief hovering over so deep an abyss. The song was great art, though not designed for human ears.

Per cared nothing for that, for he had found what he sought: the flavor of Sofron! Motes that would have been indistinguishable to the Skandians' most sensitive devices were embedded in the flavor of the Guardians' song, and finally Per could taste them.

He gathered every organ of speech and sent out a mighty call into the Deep. He felt it resounding all around, reflecting the sea floor and the lives of the startled beings that grazed there, and he felt it rebound from the Bright Teeth, changing their song.

Startled, they came to attention, so strong was the call.

*Night has two bright eyes/The day but one
*The god has opened his third and brightest eye.
*Now shines his hidden face/His hidden voice is singing
*As the Great Brightness reveals its face to the turning
    Deep/
*From the peaks of the Dry sings the wind
Showing/telling of the hidden lands where no Tooth
    swims.
The Brightness seeks its own face, hidden in the Deep/
Hidden in the midnight zone, its pod mate the god seeks.
Can you catch the light that dances on the water?/
Can you bite it with your hungry teeth?/
Can you find me the brightness of my pod mate?/
Bring me the light of her face/In the song of the god you
    will dance.

After a lag in which Per trembled with impatience, the response came back. The first answers had no word shapes;
they were wordless whistles of admiration. In hundreds of
years, the Teeth had not enjoyed such a surprising day. They
outdid themselves in the speed they employed to obey him.
And Per heard the funny squawkings of Dilani's sound box,
giving them directions.

Even the Guardians had been interested by his song. It was
now being incorporated as a motif while they waited to see
how the grand pattern of their own symphony would work itself out.

At last he heard the ketos squawking joyfully. They had
found her, and a group of them were gamely trying to obey
Per—but rather than bringing her with them, they were trying
to catch up with her. For once a human was traveling too fast
for the Bright Teeth.

Where? he called.

They thought it was a tremendous joke—so funny that they
had difficulty ordering their thoughts to report. She was
riding the leviathan—and she carried a White Killer with her!

Per sent out a leviathan-reaching call.

"Let me talk to my pod mate," he begged them. "Send me her words."

Per waited again in agonizing impatience. It took some time for the leviathans to come around to a point in their song cycle when they could insert a response to this minor interruption.

When they did respond, they expressed mild surprise, flavored with a hint that surprise was not entirely unwelcome. They crooned to him that it was not possible for the song of his beloved to be heard now, for she was not in contact with them, and surely any song she might sing, unamplified, from their back, would be too small to pierce the veil of the Deep.

But then their song took on a merrier note, as they found some consolation for him and sympathetically rejoiced in it. Per wanted to ask why they had not bothered to contact him before, but the little that he knew of leviathan lore was enough to tell him that this would be pointless. Leviathan time was on a wholly different scale, and his reproach would mean nothing to them.

They were pleased to share a few measures with him now. They sang in a cheerful round of the joy of sharing the Deepsong with a little one in the pouch, of the pleasures of contact with a nimble alien mind, though a small one, and finally, in a set of variations on a comic theme, they explained how the Little Hands, once upon a time, had borrowed placental cells from the leviathan, and had then forgotten their origins and revered the thing they made as a god.

Per gave them his thanks. He longed to hear Sofron's own voice, but even to receive some piece of information that she had thought would interest him was a great gift. He didn't have much time, but knowing that Sofron was coming, that she would arrive first, spurred him on.

Rameau thought you could handle the view of jump-space, he thought. *Surely you can hold in your mind the structure of this one little god.* He was ready to work, but he hesitated. He still needed to find a way to keep Kitkit from seeing what he did and preventing him from doing it. There must be a way to seal off different portions of the god, if only to create separate sectors where separate processes could take place.

Sofron's message nagged at him while he tried to concentrate on other things. There must be something in it that was important, or she wouldn't have sent it. He knew nothing much about the placenta, or placental analog, more likely, in a leviathan. A mammalian placenta supplied nutrients and immunities, and carried away wastes—much like the god. It was the interface between offspring and maternal body, and as such, it could either pass materials through or withhold them. And when the offspring was expelled into the world . . . then the placenta could be sealed off!

Feverishly, Per began searching through the catalogs of all the different tissues the god maintained within itself. Among the oldest and most basic was a type that fit the leviathan's description. It was quite different from the Kalko'uli-based areas, the microorganisms, and those based on marine life. This tissue provided the underlying structure of the entire god. Per scanned it and saw within it a metabolic process that would seal off any section, preserving what was within but allowing nothing out.

He was ready.

He began to search through Kitkit's records for lists of all the possible remedies for the Paling that the Kalko'uli had tried. It was an impressive list. He could see why Kitkit had said that they had tried everything. They *had* tried everything within their experience. They had tried every possible vector for introducing new genes to replace those they had willfully changed.

And the Killers' immune systems had indeed shot them all down—viral vectors of all shapes and sizes, liposomes and various other packages. No type of packaging had fooled the system for long.

He could see why they had found it necessary to package everything. Living in a liquid environment, it must have seemed vital to protect the genetic material from mixing with seawater and the other things that lived in the Deep.

But Per had learned from deft and more sophisticated hands.

Elsewhere within the god, Kitkit was becoming disturbed,

so much so that he was making it hard for Per to stay in control of the god's vocalizing. He had heard the ketos sing of Per's mate and that she was accompanied by a wounded White Killer streaming blood and vile motes that would invade the god's sacred refuge. After the painful memories Kitkit had just revisited, even the sight of the creature made him seem to tremble with rage.

"He's poisoning them! Can't you see it?" Kitkit screamed. "If you have any decency left, any concern at all for the fate of your kin, order them to kill that thing!"

Per knew that he could wall Kitkit off from communication, as Kitkit had done to him, but he did not want to. He was afraid Kitkit might fall into complete madness, isolation, and fear, accomplishing what the Killers themselves had failed to complete: the destruction of the god.

Experimentally, he tried to send Kitkit the same kind of calming motes the Kalko'ul had used on him. It seemed to help. Their joint environment felt lighter.

The leviathans were very close now. He could hear their melodious thunder and feel them passing over his submerged mountain like clouds trailing a rain of music. They almost never came within the crater; that space was too confined for them. But they cruised nearby, waiting to see how the story would come out.

And then at last he saw Sofron. She descended from the leviathans in a trail of silver bubbles. In one hand she held a long knife of white bone, and her other hand trailed behind her, pulling the skeletal frame of the wounded White One down toward the god. Her hands were ashen, but the colors of her face were bright like dawn, and her motes were joyful.

She was singing as she dove, combining motes and notes in Guardian style, simpler and yet more full of feeling than the edgy, tightly patterned language of the Teeth.

"Per—
I'm here.
We kept our promises,
Defied all fear.

I'm half frog, half lizard, far from shore,
But if I hear your voice I'll be transformed once more."

And the god sang to her. The water trembled, and the rim of
the cavern rang faintly like the rubbed rim of a wineglass.

She believed it was Per. No other human being, she
thought, would be able to make a jellyfish sing. She could see
translucent membranes stretching and contracting within the
god's body as the tones shifted.

"You've never been more beautiful," she sang joyfully.
"What a fascinating organism!"

A part of Per was filled with such joy that the water itself
seemed saturated with it. But the other part was wrestling
with Kitkit. As the White One descended into his sacred
space, the god was maddened by desire to kill. Kitkit tried to
send forth lethal godbits laden with the killer virus and
learned for the first time that Per had bound him tight in
his own body. Now he was screaming in terror and rage,
screaming that the White Ones were coming and all would be
lost if Per did not let him go.

They warred along the interface of cells, knitting and un-
knitting proteins, a constant stream of nutrients pumping into
the god's processors. Most of Per's thought flickered, folded,
and was absorbed with the changing molecules.

"What is it? What's wrong?"

Sofron switched from song to sign. To sing as a human,
even a transformed one, underwater, was a difficult process.

Per realized that to her it had been only moments since she
arrived, and he had not yet spoken to her. She had sensed his
turmoil.

He couldn't sing to her and keep his grasp on Kitkit at the
same time. He wanted to keep her at a distance, to speak to
her only through external means, because he was afraid of
what might happen if he let her come any closer. But he no
longer had a choice. He surrendered.

"Touch me," he sang.

She placed her palm against the god's surface. The substance parted and let her hand in, tasting the mote-rich mem-

branes, reading the speech of her skin. He was touching her, and he could have been perfectly happy for years.

Before he could stop himself, Per had sent out a tap like the one Kitkit had used on Whitman. And there Sofron was, next to him in the light of the god, just as he had imagined it. He perceived her thoughts as directly as he could perceive Kitkit's. A part of him was a human heart that broke with longing. But the rest of him was a cool blue mind that had no time to cherish the taste of her or feel terror at the power he wielded. And Kitkit within him still clashed his teeth and screamed. *The Killers are coming! All is lost, lost.*

The joy of touching her shifted Per's concentration, and Kitkit twisted free of him, enough to pour out a stream of godbits. Kitkit was sending them into the scooped-out caverns in the wall of the crater, where gently waving plants filtered the water and gave out their blue-glowing light.

Per's focus was wrenched toward this new source of danger. Quickly he sampled the bits and found that they were vaccine, not virus. Per remembered that in his vision, Kitkit had deposited the eggs of the Kalko'uli in the caverns, long ago. Kitkit must want the eggs to be protected, and Per did not want to stop him. He let the godbits go.

He thought this would improve the Kalko'ul's state of mind. But godbits drifted back from the caves to report. As the god received those motes, even the leviathans above recoiled, and Per knew that the god he was part of had screamed aloud along with Kitkit's internal cry.

Then he heard the strange sound of the Kalko'ul weeping.

Per had forgotten that Sofron would share his perceptions.

"Allfather," she said. "Who was that screaming? What is happening?"

"It wasn't me," he said, struggling even as he said it to keep his separation from Kitkit. "It was him—the other one who is in here with me, the old god. He's one of the old people, the Great People. He had eggs of his kindred in stasis there. He has not seen them in a long time. He sent the godbits to them, and now the godbits come back and say the eggs are dead."

"I'm going to go and look," she said instantly. He could

taste the curiosity roused by the thought of seeing the eggs of the Great People. But he could hardly bear to let her go. She was a danger for him; while she was with him, he struggled to focus.

"Wait!" he said. "This is important. Do you see those god-bits moving toward the crater wall?"

Belated bubbles, sparked with blue, were making their way toward the hidden cache of eggs.

"When you get there, you must touch them—put your hand in them," Per said. "Wait—not yet. Let me finish. I have a supply of those motes that I'm going to release into the water when the others get here. Make sure everyone gets some. You have to share motes with them if they don't get their own dose.

"Kitkit—the old god—has reconstituted one of the killer viruses that I was immunized against as a child. He has a whole bag of death stored up inside us, but I won't let him use it. He wanted to infect the White Ones and kill them that way. But he also made a vaccine. I'm not sure he meant to share it with us, but he just has."

Fearlessly, Sofron withdrew her hand from the god. Per watched her dart across the crater, growing smaller as she went. The crater was larger than it seemed from the fixed perspective of the god. She caught up with the chain of bubbles and then vanished with them into the pitted wall of the crater.

She returned more slowly. Her wrists were adorned with blue-sparked bracelets, but her motes were sad.

"I don't know what these eggs were supposed to look like," she said, "but I've seen live eggs in the hatching ground. They were beautiful, like gems in deep rich colors. There was a moving glow inside them; they shimmered, like coals. Those over there are dull and motionless, like stones. They felt cold and hard. Is that him screaming? I'm very sorry."

Kitkit howled and wept. *Egg killers! Murderers! They are dead, dead, and now you will let them kill us, too, and all will be lost! They're coming here to kill us!*

"He is right about that," Sofron said calmly. "The Killers are coming here. The other humans are swimming with the ketos, so they'll get here first. But the Killers were following fast, with blood in their eyes. And thanks to Whitman, they have weapons now."

"How did that happen?"

"The Killers found their way into the towers of the old city. Whitman and the others went there to find weapons. But when they did, the Killers followed them, so now they're armed, too. The Killers are saying, 'Kill god, kill god,' or so the leviathans tell me."

Per could now hear both keto and Killer whistles, coming closer.

"So if there's anything we can do to stop them, this would be the time," Sofron said. "Meanwhile—"

She withdrew from Per's contact again. Each time it was harder for him to resist immobilizing her, to prevent her going.

She swam to the White One, who was drifting forlornly, and towed him back to the god. As she clasped the pale hand in hers and drew it toward the god's surface, even Per felt some faint shadow of Kitkit's revulsion. In Kitkit's eyes, this was an abomination.

"Give him the vaccine," Sofron said. "And watch. You can analyze in there, can't you? I could feel you sampling me."

Per watched in horrified fascination as the White Killer's taloned hand sank through the god's skin. The vaccine passed directly through the Killer's sensing pores, without need for godbits to enter the bloodstream. Wearra was safe from Kitkit's weapon.

No, no! Kitkit moaned. *You can't do that. Now they will live forever. You are evil, and my eggs are dead. But I will have vengeance! In just a few minutes, their eggs will die. I will know at least that they are dead, before I can be killed.*

Per tried to shut out the mad god's ravings. All his attention was focused on the gift Sofron had brought him.

"Give him calming motes," she said. "I saw him get them from my skin. But you can flood his system."

Fascinated, Per watched with his god senses as the motes

traveled into the White One's pores. Immediately the Killer's skin began to flush with a faint color.

Per spun off godbits from his body, encircling and enveloping Wearra. Then they spread and grew until he wore a gleaming helm and gauntlets of transparent silver. His fierce face, beneath the mask, smoothed and relaxed.

"If you can help him, then you can fix the other humans who are starting to go Pale," Sofron said. "That's why I brought him here."

"But it won't work," Per said. "They tried this. His system will eventually eliminate the calming motes. You can't immobilize them forever, and as soon as they revive, they revert to their old selves. I've seen it.

"The only way to cure this is to correct the mutation. I found the faulty gene, and I have the corrected DNA ready to go—but I can't find a vector. When the Killers come, I'm going to inject as many of them as I can with the naked DNA and hope it takes. It's the one thing the Great People didn't try. But . . ."

Her mind had always worked as quickly as his own. He had no need to explain just how unlikely it was that this desperate try would succeed.

But her motes didn't reflect despair. Instead, he sensed a wild surge of hope. She knew their time was short, and she did not waste words, either.

"Direct contact," was all she said, and her attention was fixed on the sensing organs at Wearra's wrist and neck, the organs all of them shared. "I knew we were missing something, and that's it. If you'd been out here with me, you'd have seen it long before."

Per had sent the god's physical systems into overdrive almost before his mind finished processing the new idea.

"Not into the bloodstream, but directly into the sensing organs," he said. "The DNA can be taken straight to the morphone glands, where the mutation occurred. The Paled immune system will have no chance to destroy it. If I can tag it with a marker for morphone uptake—

"I can do this. We have a chance. Hold still."

Even as he spoke, he was setting the process in motion for Sofron and her Pale companion. He gathered himself for a final effort that would require the last drop of the god's resources.

But as he tried to focus his attention on that alone, the Bright Teeth burst into the cavern. As always, they were impossible to ignore. Far from hanging back in guilt, they tried to gloss over their moments of mutiny with sheer impudence.

* * * *

Oh, rare gifts we bring/bring us rewards most rare, oh
Bumping the nose, we find precious metals/Bumping the
    god's command, we find precious cargo
In the same net—god-loved/god-hated—in the same net
* * * *

Per was awash in familiar motes that tugged irresistibly at his emotions. Bey and Dilani slid from the ketos' backs, along with Bader and Nila and others of the newgens—and several unexpected, wriggling guests.

"We brought some water dogs with us," Dilani signed. "They were looking lost, and I was afraid they would get eaten."

Within the god, Kitkit was strobing through every color of the rainbow, as if he would burst in his agitation.

"They look healthy—perfect—" he moaned. In Per's distraction, Kitkit had seized enough control of the vocal organs to make himself heard to all. "Oh, where did they come from?"

Dilani stared.

"That's not me," Per sang hastily. "That's him—the old god."

Even as he spoke, he sent a filament of the god's substance snaking through the clear water to nip one of the water dogs.

Almost as soon as he could finish the sentence, he knew the results, as did Kitkit. The blood sample was digested, blended with reagents, separated into its constituents. Per perceived it as tiny glowing fragments twisting and dancing around each other.

"They're perfect," Kitkit sobbed. "There's no trace of the Paling in them. They're ready for the changing. They're perfectly healthy. Oh, where did they come from?"

"From the hatching ground, of course," Dilani signed.

Kitkit screamed again.

"I sent your kin to kill them! Oh, but they're doomed anyway. Why do you torture me? You know that if the White Killers live, these hatchlings will turn Pale and die before they can grow up."

"One problem at a time," Per said. "We can still stop Whitman from killing the eggs.

"Dilani, Bey, please make one more effort. Take the Bright Teeth and hurry after him. Swim as fast as you can. Speak to the Guardians as you go."

Dilani grabbed Bey's hand and whistled to the ketos. The Teeth had already heard the god's command. They had never had such a day. They vanished with tireless speed.

"They bonded with humans," Kitkit was still wailing to himself. "I did not foresee this! How could I foresee it? With humans!"

Within the god's mind, Kitkit's image vainly tried to catch hold of Per. His ravings had changed from cursing to pleading.

"If the hatchlings can bond with clan members," he cried, "if they exchange motes with the adults, they can transform to healthy adults. Without healthy adults, there is no next generation. If they are bonding with your young ones, they could live! I did not know this was possible. I did not know these hatchlings even existed."

He was panicking again.

"But they will all die; I know they will. When they become adult they will go Pale, like the rest."

"No," Per said. "There is a cure, now. But you must stop fighting me. It will take all our resources. Let me have control."

As he spoke, he was completing the final steps of the process he had set in motion. He had segmented the aspects of the god that had to be isolated for his plan to succeed. He let the impulses flow to Kitkit's portion of the mind, revealing to him what was about to happen.

It's impossible, the Kalko'ul gasped, within Per's hearing alone. In Per's inner sight, Kitkit's colors trembled and paled for the last time.

"What's the point of being a god if you can't work miracles?" Per said. "It's our only chance."

Per felt the Killers enter his envelope of water, but he no longer feared them. They seemed far away and small. The important thing was to complete the pattern and return to the perfect locus before it was too late.

As Kitkit screamed and the White Ones drew near, Per used what Rameau had taught him to search for and retrieve the codes he needed.

"Listen to me!" Per sang out to his human kin. "The Killers are descending even now. I believe this is the first direct order I've ever given, god or not, and it may be the last, so please obey me in this: do not attack them, no matter what you see. Defend yourselves if you have to, but wait until you're absolutely sure. Give me time to work. Sofron knows what I'm doing. I can cure the Paling. Just don't put blood in the water."

He could feel the accelerated production of godbits and freshly synthesized motes churning within the god's body as he spoke. He was using every ounce of energy for that purpose. His peripherals were sucking up even the last cells of Wearra's shed blood to power that production. He couldn't continue at this pace for long and maintain the god's other functions, he knew. Already some of his senses were beginning to shut down.

He could still perceive Kitkit, though. The Kalko'ul was bewildered by so many shocks, and was fighting with all his failing strength to remain in the globular body that had imprisoned him so long.

Do not do this. You leave us defenseless. We must fight them. We must . . .

At last Per felt true pity and a kind of fellowship for the Clan of Fire warrior.

We cannot fight them here. Blood, death, the Pale motes, spilling over our hatchlings and our kin—it would be their ending. You know it would overwhelm all their defenses. They would Pale, just as they Paled in the City of Fire. Then, truly, madness would rule. This way lies darkness and danger, but maybe, at last, our freedom. You called me here to free you. I cannot complete this mission alone. Help me, clan brother.

Kitkit's fading consciousness heard the appeal that once long ago had been so familiar, and he ceased to struggle.

"Sofron, I might not see you again very soon," Per sang, with the last of his exterior strength. "Don't give up. I have a plan."

Gently, he withdrew the tendrils that had briefly made them one in mind. He set her free. She would live her own life, not a virtual existence as the pawn of a god.

The touch of your hand has been my only key to freedom, my only taste of peace. Your hand on the other side of the glass.

He sang to her as darkness took his senses and he ceased to be a god. He did not know if she could hear any of it.

Sofron, I swear we'll touch with human hands. No glass between.

"To the elements be free . . ."

The whisper faded away.

The White Killers swarmed down into the place of the god, daring at last what they had never dared before. Their whistling filled the chamber, echoing from its round sides until nothing else could be heard, and the sound itself was almost enough to rob their prey of all reason. This time they didn't come by the handful or even by the dozen; they came by troops until no more could come. All who had nested in the old city and who had not been killed by Sofron and her friends had come to seek revenge.

They craved revenge for their latest defeat; and revenge for the lightless centuries, for the perpetual cold and dark, for lives reduced to a snap of teeth and a gulp of blood. They could not reason, but they could hate.

Hope left Sofron like a bright leaf tumbling down into the depths. What difference would it make if she fired on them or held fast? No weapons could hold out for long against such an army from the Abyss. But Per had said he had a plan . . .

She faced outward and gripped her weapon.

The ketos caught Whitman just as his raft was closing on the hatching ground. Dilani had had to warn the Teeth repeatedly of the dangers of metal eggs that exploded. The Teeth couldn't really visualize this and still thought of anything round, from a skull to a floating fruit, as something to play with. So Dilani had emphasized that if any playing was to be done, they must bat the balls once, and make sure they flew far away.

They saw Whitman dropping round metal things over the side as he saw them coming. Slowbolt put on a terrifying burst of speed and bunted the first egg out of the water. Dilani did not have time to leap from his back, and anyway, she would never have heard the last of it. She decided that it was better to risk being blown up than to be certain of lifelong mockery.

The other Bright Teeth followed Slowbolt's example, catching most of the eggs as they fell and hurling them aside, or tossing them out of the water to explode in midair. Finally one of them landed close enough to the raft to knock Whitman off, and give him a concussion. Bey went to his rescue as he floundered, choking and disoriented. That ended it.

But one of the eggs had fallen too far for the Teeth to retrieve it. Slowbolt had been trying, but Dilani frantically restrained him, using every plea and death threat she could squeak out in thirty seconds. Finally he was laughing so hard that he had to surface.

The death egg made it all the way to the bottom before it exploded on the edge of the hatching ground. Slowbolt sobered instantly when he saw the gray cloud of sediment mushrooming upward in solemn silence. When he cruised over and sounded the bottom, sensing the wreckage below, he turned back to butt Dilani in gratitude. Then he showed his tail to Whitman in a majestic leap of fury and defiance. "Egg slayer!" he screamed as he leapt. But Whitman did not accept the challenge.

One of the destroyed eggs had belonged to the Guardians. Their dirge for the lost egg had just begun when Dilani turned for home. The sound of that song lodged under her ribs somehow, like swallowing a fish bone. It was a song of long sorrow, for a life that could have outlasted the cities of men, but had ended like a wave sinking into the sand. The Guardians would sorrow for their child long after Dilani Ru had ceased to live.

That song did something to her. She could feel it working inside, like Subtle's famous calming motes. Only it was not very calming. Perhaps she would speak to Sofron later. Sofron understood the Deepsong better than the others.

Somehow, the song prepared Dilani for what she would see when she returned to the place of the god. She knew Per was not dead, but she knew that something sad and strange but marvelous had happened. The Guardians put all that into their song.

Sofron did not see at first what was happening. The luminous ribbons of silver streamed past her from behind, like banners in a silent wind. They seemed to weave a net between her and the Killers, until the White Ones wavered as if seen through old, uneven glass. The streamers glimmered as if they had been embroidered with tiny pearls and blue sparks of diamond, where countless minuscule organisms from within the god hurried to bestow their gifts. They glowed with a pure, sourceless light. It was the most beautiful thing she had ever seen. She stared and let the haunting, singular scent of those motes course through her gills, and her weapon hung unused in her hand.

The Killers seemed mesmerized as much as she. One after another, their weapons dropped as the silvery streamers passed about their faces and wound around their gills and swathed their taloned hands, rendering them harmless. They struggled briefly, but soon they were wrapped in sleep and had to give in. The whistling died to an equally eerie silence.

Only then did Sofron turn to see what the god had been doing.

The god was gone.

Her mind reeled.

She was still drifting among the White Killers in their silvery wrappings, and staring at the serene blue of the empty cavern, when Bey and Dilani came back with the raft.

"What happened?" Dilani signed even before she reached the swarm of silent, floating White Killers.

Sofron could only shake her head.

Bey touched her shoulder.

"You know," he signed.

I guess I do, she thought. But she wasn't sure how she would ever explain it to Dilani. The sweet taste of those last motes was replaced in her mouth by a surpassing bitterness. Her skin squeezed away all color until she was nearly as livid as the White Ones.

Yes, she knew what he had done. He had split the god apart, using every fragment of its strength to immobilize the White Ones, provide them with the corrective motes they needed, and give them the chance to return to a normal existence. Not for their sake alone, but because he knew that under such an onslaught, the humans would have lost everything. Even if they had fought back, they would have been infected and destroyed by the very thing they fought. He had made the judgment in the split seconds he had left. And he had been right.

But it was so unfair. So bitterly unfair. She had held out to the end, and Per had really come for her. She had been within arm's length of him, and then he had vanished in the most final way possible. Now he was truly gone, forever. And he hadn't even said good-bye.

Wait a minute. What did he say? He said he had a plan . . . Oh, damn him, he always had a plan.

Would he have given himself away like that without leaving

himself any out? Vanished without a trace? Not the Per
know. Not if the least chance remained.

But this time, it seemed there was truly nothing left.

Bey touched her shoulder again.

"I hate to bother you," he signed, "but can you help me
with my father?"

Whitman was far gone in the Paling. Some of the oldgens
looked more normal, but they were all distraught.

Sofron had forgotten all about Whitman and his mission.
For a minute she feared that in the absence of the god there
would be no cure for him or for those left on the shore, but the
godbits that encased the others in the cavern swept off a stream
great enough to band the wrists of the last of the humans.

I should have realized he would think of that, too.

"Share lots of good motes with them, too," she signed. "It
will help. Now we have to go share with Sushan and the rest
of those onshore. They probably think we're dead—again."

☾27☽☽☽☽☽☽☽☽

By the time those onshore had been inoculated and tended, the sun had gone down and the moons had risen. Most of the colony slept like stones in the shallow water, sleeping without fear for the first time in years.

But Sofron woke up as greatmoon was setting, trailing its silver shadow across the bay. She had been awakened by the sound of leviathans singing. She swam out into deep water and waited to be noticed. Changing Light, whose song signature she recognized, sounded gently. Sofron tried to speak to them with Dilani's box, but they laughed softly and told her that that was not necessary. They wished to enfold her.

"But we killed your egg," she sang with the box, sadly and without much grace.

Come, they reiterated. So she swam down to Changing Light and let herself be drawn into the hatchling pouch. She was conscious and calm this time, and felt a little nervous, but as before, when Changing Light linked with her, the anxiety faded into the exhilaration of motion and song.

We sing our egg, Changing Light crooned. *As long as we live, our sorrow will travel with us like an egg of sunset color. It has happened before that an egg has died before completing its journey. It is a sadness that adds its texture to the song. We sing, we sing, until the lost egg hatches into eternal music.*

Sofron told them about the battle, or nonbattle, of the cavern, and of the god's division and disappearance. Their song changed markedly at that. She felt they conferred within it, and were startled. It was tremendous and a little frightening to feel surprise on such a scale. But there was a deep and rich laughter in their voices at the end of that stanza.

Little human Hands are surprising, Changing Light sang. *When will you come to perform your if-then promise? When will you come to help us sing the world's beauty?*

"Not until these hatchlings change and grow," Sofron told her. "And I don't know when that will be, because I don't know how to take care of Great People hatchlings at all!"

They considered that carefully.

When the Eye turns around from the north and goes south, when the water troubles and then is calm again, then we will come back for the surprising tiny human pod sister, they sang. She sensed agreement in the whole pod. *Maybe then you will travel with us.*

Sofron stood on the shore. It was still early morning, and a breeze made music in the giling fronds behind the row of beach houses where most of the colony was still sleeping. Like the Great People, they now preferred to sleep in water, but as humans, they also liked a feeling of shelter, so they had built a canopy above a tidal pool that usually stayed pleasantly wet.

The newly changed, the hatchlings who had recently attained biped form and had come to join them, slept in a tumble at the edge of the surf, as they had when they were still water dogs. One of them shadowed Ling as she ran to and fro in the surf, trying to catch the cricket-sized arthropods that burrowed into the wet sand. Sofron watched Ling's strong little legs moving as tirelessly as the waves. Typhon had given the children back what it had originally stolen from them, and they were satisfied for now.

"Look, Sofi, I'm teaching him to talk," Ling shouted. "Go on, say it!"

"Ying," the young Kalko'ul repeated, laughing. He pointed to Wearra, who paced at Sofron's side, and said "Weala!" Then he added an aside to Ling in a flurry of sign.

"He says I am your shadow," Wearra said aloud. He was no longer white all over, but his colors when they appeared had assumed a sober palette of umber, ochre, and dull violet, giving him a dour, scholarly appearance. Wearra made a remarkably ugly Kalko'ul. He would always be too bony, his head too large and knobby. He found Skandian difficult to speak, as well, and preferred the familiarity of sign.

The third who usually joined in the early-morning walk was Subtle, taller by a head than the other two, and powerfully built even without the addition of the two tentacles he usually carried wrapped around his waist. "Prince of Darkness," Sofron sometimes called him. He, too, found Skandian difficult, so he and Wearra often conversed gravely in sign and color, knee-deep in the waves.

Wearra smiled cautiously, taking care not to show too many teeth. It was a gesture he was somewhat sensitive about.

"You have shadows of many colors," he signed. "You still make up a 'we' of so many different speakers."

Out by the reef, Dilani and Bey were occasionally visible when the Teeth tossed them high into the air. Sofron wondered if they patrolled the reef in the morning for the same reason she paced the shore.

"They is liking this life now," Subtle said, waving one tentacle tip behind him, toward the beach house. "Crazy Leader is losing self-respect, but is having what is always wanting—weapons, and secrets.

"New old people happy they is being alive, is not knowing difference otherwise. Past White Ones happy not being white. What else is matter? And old Skandians is being happy because they is not sick anymore, is fishing, sleeping, looking for old people's things. Is like females of Round Folk—not being studying and making brain wrinkle, just hunting-eating.

"Only we three, and little Disquiet maybe, is not being all happy now. We is waiting, is wanting see god. Just like always. All this-I life, this-I is waiting see god. Still waiting!"

"The god reassembled its body after everyone hatched out," Sofron said. "It's hanging there in the cavern, looking as complete as ever. Only I feel something is missing when I go there. It's eerie, like an empty house."

"God is having no mind now," Subtle said. "We is still waiting for Per-god with mind, and maybe old one, too. This-I is wanting asking many questions. This-I is scholar and is needing understanding, not just fat fish. Wearra, too, is needing ask questions, yes?"

The former White One bowed his head in serious agreement.

"And you-I is not ask questions, maybe," Subtle said, turning to Sofron. "Maybe just hitting head with big stick, like Disquiet." His colors flickered to show he meant to be humorous.

Sofron turned to look back at the shelter on the beach. On the rocks above the tidal pool, Dilani had carefully planted Per's miniature tree, which had survived so much journeying. Every day, she visited and tended it. She had chosen a spot where the tree could be seen from sea and land. Its narrow, silvery leaves seemed to thrive in the salt spray and wind.

"He will come back," Dilani had told her. "The tree lives. Per lives, too. When he comes back, he will see the tree is living. And me, too," she had added, signing her chest for emphasis. "Me, too."

Sofron shook her head.

"Do you think there's any chance he's still alive?"

"The Deep is very wide," Subtle said. "Per-god is very wise. Is possible. Is always being possible he sleeps somewhere, and will return out of Deep, like hatchlings rising from their changing, finding their way home."

Sofron fell silent, gazing out across the glittering plain of the Deep. Somewhere beneath that blue surface, the leviathans swam, threading their way through the underworld of storm and fire and reef. Perhaps Per was dreaming in the Deep somewhere, hearing their secrets as they sang. His kin would always be listening for him in the voices of the blue world that he had given back to them.

DEL REY® ONLINE!

The Del Rey Internet Newsletter...

A monthly electronic publication e-mailed to subscribers and posted on the rec.arts.sf.written Usenet newsgroup and on our Del Rey Books Web site (www.randomhouse.com/delrey/). It features hype-free descriptions of books that are new in the stores, a list of our upcoming books, special promotional programs and offers, announcements and news, a signing/reading/convention-attendance calendar for Del Rey authors and editors, "In Depth" essays in which professionals in the field (authors, artists, cover designers, salespeople, etc.) talk about their jobs in science fiction, a question-and-answer section, and more!

Subscribe to the DRIN: send a blank message to
join-drin-dist@list.randomhouse.com

The Del Rey Books Web Site!

We make a lot of information available on our Web site at
www.randomhouse.com/delrey/

- all back issues and the current issue of the Del Rey Internet Newsletter
- sample chapters of almost every new book
- detailed interactive features for some of our books
- special features on various authors and SF/F worlds
- reader reviews of some upcoming books
- news and announcements
- our Works in Progress report, detailing the doings of our most popular authors
- and more!

If You're Not on the Web...

You can subscribe to the DRIN via e-mail (send a blank message to join-drin-dist@list.randomhouse.com) or read it on the rec.arts.sf.written Usenet newsgroup the first few days of every month. We also have editors and other representatives who participate in America Online and CompuServe SF/F forums and rec.arts.sf.written, making contact and sharing information with SF/F readers.

Questions? E-mail us...

at delrey@randomhouse.com (though it sometimes takes us a little while to answer).